15 September 1989

Dear Steven,

This is the best fiction I've read in ages— hope you enjoy it, too!

I love you,

Margery

THE
MAMBO KINGS
PLAY SONGS
OF LOVE

ALSO BY OSCAR HIJUELOS

Our House in the Last World (1983)

THE
MAMBO KINGS
PLAY SONGS
OF LOVE

OSCAR HIJUELOS

FARRAR
· STRAUS ·
GIROUX
NEW YORK

Library of Congress Cataloging-in-Publication Data

Hijuelos, Oscar.
The mambo kings play songs of love: a novel/Oscar Hijuelos.
p. cm.
I. Title.
PS3558.I376M36 1989   813'.54—dc19   89-1248

The author gratefully thanks the National Endowment for the Arts, the New York Foundation for the Arts, the Ingram Merrill Foundation, the American Academy and Institute of Arts and Letters, the MacDowell Colony, and the Corporation of Yaddo, for fellowships awarded during the period in which this novel was written.

And heartfelt thanks to Angel Martínez, Renaldo Ferradas, Chico O'Farrill, and Harriet Wasserman.

. . . with a flick of your wrist on your phonograph switch, the fiction of the rolling sea and a dance date on a Havana patio or in a smart supper club will become reality. Certainly, if you cannot spare the time to go to Havana or want to revive the memories of a previous trip, this music will make it all possible . . .

FROM *The Mambo Kings Play Songs of Love*

TMP 1113

Orchestra Records
1210 Lenox Avenue
New York, New York

IT WAS A SATURDAY AFTERNOON on La Salle Street, years and years ago when I was a little kid, and around three o'clock Mrs. Shannon, the heavy Irish woman in her perpetually soup-stained dress, opened her back window and shouted out into the courtyard, "Hey, Cesar, yoo-hoo, I think you're on television, I swear it's you!" When I heard the opening strains of the *I Love Lucy* show I got excited because I knew she was referring to an item of eternity, that episode in which my dead father and my Uncle Cesar had appeared, playing Ricky Ricardo's singing cousins fresh off the farm in Oriente Province, Cuba, and north in New York for an engagement at Ricky's nightclub, the Tropicana.

This was close enough to the truth about their real lives —they were musicians and songwriters who had left Havana for New York in 1949, the year they formed the Mambo Kings, an orchestra that packed clubs, dance halls, and theaters around the East Coast—and, excitement of excitements, they even made a fabled journey in a flamingo-pink bus out to Sweet's Ballroom in San Francisco, playing on an all-star mambo night, a beautiful night of glory, beyond death, beyond pain, beyond all stillness.

Desi Arnaz had caught their act one night in a supper club on the West Side, and because they had perhaps already known each other from Havana or Oriente Province, where Arnaz, like the brothers, was born, it was natural that he ask them to sing on his show. He liked one of their songs in particular, a romantic bolero written by them, "Beautiful María of My Soul."

Some months later (I don't know how many, I wasn't five years old yet) they began to rehearse for the immortal appearance of my father on this show. For me, my father's gentle rapping on Ricky Ricardo's door has always been a call from the beyond, as in Dracula films, or films of the walking dead, in which spirits ooze out from behind tombstones and through the cracked windows and rotted floors of gloomy antique halls: Lucille Ball, the lovely redheaded actress and comedienne who played Ricky's wife, was housecleaning when she heard the rapping of my father's knuckles against that door.

"I'm commmmmming," in her singsong voice.

Standing in her entrance, two men in white silk suits and butterfly-looking lace bow ties, black instrument cases by their side and black-brimmed white hats in their hands—my father, Nestor Castillo, thin and broad-shouldered, and Uncle Cesar, thickset and immense.

My uncle: "Mrs. Ricardo? My name is Alfonso and this is my brother Manny . . ."

And her face lights up and she says, "Oh, yes, the fellows from Cuba. Ricky told me all about you."

Then, just like that, they're sitting on the couch when Ricky Ricardo walks in and says something like "Manny, Alfonso! Gee, it's really swell that you fellas could make it up here from Havana for the show."

That's when my father smiled. The first time I saw a rerun of this, I could remember other things about him—his lifting me up, his smell of cologne, his patting my head, his handing me a dime, his touching my face, his whistling, his taking me and my little sister, Leticia, for a walk in the park, and so many other moments happening in my thoughts simultaneously that it was like watching something momentous, say the Resurrection, as if Christ had stepped out of his sepulcher, flooding the world with light—what we were taught in the local church with the big red doors—because my father was now newly alive and could take off his hat and sit down on the couch in Ricky's living room, resting his black instrument case on his lap. He could play the trumpet, move his head, blink his eyes, nod, walk across the room, and say "Thank you" when offered a cup of coffee. For me, the room was suddenly bursting with a silvery radiance. And now I knew that we could see it again. Mrs. Shannon had called out into the courtyard alerting my uncle: I was already in his apartment.

With my heart racing, I turned on the big black-and-white television set in his living room and tried to wake him. My uncle had fallen asleep in the kitchen—having worked really late the night before, some job in a Bronx social club, singing and playing the horn with a pickup group of musicians. He was snoring, his shirt was open, a few buttons had popped out on his belly. Between the delicate-looking index and forefingers of his right hand, a Chesterfield cigarette burning down to the filter, that hand still holding a half glass of rye whiskey, which he used to drink like crazy because in recent years he had been suffering from bad dreams, saw apparitions, felt cursed, and, despite all the women he took to bed, found his life of bachelorhood solitary and wearisome. But I didn't know this at the time, I thought he was sleeping because he had worked so hard the night before, singing and playing the trumpet for seven or eight hours. I'm talking about a wedding party in a crowded, smoke-filled room (with bolted-shut fire doors), lasting from nine at night to four, five o'clock in the morning, the band playing one-, two-hour sets. I thought he just needed the rest. How could I have known that he would come home and, in the name of unwinding, throw back a glass of rye, then a second, and then a third, and so on, until he'd plant his elbow on the table and use it to steady his chin, as he couldn't hold his head up otherwise. But that day I ran into the kitchen to wake him up so that he could see the episode, too, shaking him gently and tugging at his elbow, which was a mistake, because it was as if I had pulled loose the support columns of a five-hundred-year-old church: he simply fell over and crashed to the floor.

A commercial was running on the television, and so, as I knew I wouldn't have much time, I began to slap his face, pull on his burning red-hot ears, tugging on them until he finally opened one eye. In the act of focusing he apparently did not recognize me, because he asked, "Nestor, what are you doing here?"

"It's me, Uncle, it's Eugenio."

I said this in a really earnest tone of voice, just like that kid who hangs out with Spencer Tracy in the movie of *The Old Man and the Sea*, really believing in my uncle and clinging on to his every word in life, his every touch like nourishment from a realm of great beauty, far beyond me, his heart. I tugged at him again, and he opened his eyes. This time he recognized me.

He said, "You?"

"Yes, Uncle, get up! Please get up! You're on television again. Come on."

One thing I have to say about my Uncle Cesar, there was

very little he wouldn't do for me in those days, and so he nodded, tried to push himself off the floor, got to his knees, had trouble balancing, and then fell backwards. His head must have hurt: his face was a wince of pain. Then he seemed to be sleeping again. From the living room came the voice of Ricky's wife, plotting as usual with her neighbor Ethel Mertz about how to get a part on Ricky's show at the Tropicana, and I knew that the brothers had already been to the apartment—that's when Mrs. Shannon had called out into the courtyard—that in about five more minutes my father and uncle would be standing on the stage of the Tropicana, ready to perform that song again. Ricky would take hold of the microphone and say, "Well, folks, and now I have a real treat for you. Ladies and gentlemen, Alfonso and Manny Reyes, let's hear it!" And soon my father and uncle would be standing side by side, living, breathing beings, for all the world to see, harmonizing in a duet of that *canción*.

As I shook my uncle, he opened his eyes and gave me his hand, hard and callused from his other job in those days, as superintendent, and he said, "Eugenio, help me. Help me."

I tugged with all my strength, but it was hopeless. Still he tried: with great effort he made it to one knee, and then, with his hand braced on the floor, he started to push himself up again. As I gave him another tug, he began miraculously to rise. Then he pushed my hand away and said, "I'll be okay, kid."

With one hand on the table and the other on the steam pipe, he pulled himself to his feet. For a moment he towered over me, wobbling as if powerful winds were rushing through the apartment. Happily I led him down the hallway and into the living room, but he fell over again by the door—not fell over, but rushed forward as if the floor had abruptly tilted, as if he had been shot out of a cannon, and, wham, he hit the bookcase in the hall. He kept piles of records there, among them a number of the black and brittle 78s he had recorded with my father and their group, the Mambo Kings. These came crashing down, the bookcase's glass doors jerking open, the records shooting out and spinning like flying saucers in the movies and splintering into pieces. Then the bookcase followed, slamming into the floor beside him: the songs *"Bésame Mucho," "Acércate Más," "Juventud," "Twilight in*

Havana," "Mambo Nine," "Mambo Number Eight," "Mambo for a Hot Night," and their fine version of "Beautiful María of My Soul"—all these were smashed up. This crash had a sobering effect on my uncle. Suddenly he got to one knee by himself, and then the other, stood, leaned against the wall, and shook his head.

"*Bueno,*" he said.

He followed me into the living room, and plopped down on the couch behind me. I sat on a big stuffed chair that we'd hauled up out of the basement. He squinted at the screen, watching himself and his younger brother, whom, despite their troubles, he loved very much. He seemed to be dreaming.

"Well, folks," Ricky Ricardo said, "and now I have a real treat for you . . ."

The two musicians in white silk suits and big butterfly-looking lace bow ties, marching toward the microphone, my uncle holding a guitar, my father a trumpet.

"Thank you, thank you. And now a little number that we composed . . ." And as Cesar started to strum the guitar and my father lifted his trumpet to his lips, playing the opening of "Beautiful María of My Soul," a lovely, soaring melody line filling the room.

They were singing the song as it had been written—in Spanish. With the Ricky Ricardo Orchestra behind them, they came into a turnaround and began harmonizing a line that translates roughly into English as: "What delicious pain love has brought to me in the form of a woman."

My father . . . He looked so alive!

"Uncle!"

Uncle Cesar had lit a cigarette and fallen asleep. His cigarette had slid out of his fingers and was now burning into the starched cuff of his white shirt. I put the cigarette out, and then my uncle, opening his eyes again, smiled. "Eugenio, do me a favor. Get me a drink."

"But, Uncle, don't you want to watch the show?"

He tried really hard to pay attention, to focus on it.

"Look, it's you and Poppy."

"*Coño, sí . . .*"

My father's face with his horsey grin, arching eyebrows, big fleshy ears—a family trait—that slight look of pain, his quivering vocal cords, how beautiful it all seemed to me then . . .

And so I rushed into the kitchen and came back with a glass of rye whiskey, charging as fast as I could without spilling it. Ricky had joined the brothers onstage. He was definitely pleased with their performance and showed it because as the last note sounded he whipped up his hand and shouted *"Olé!,"* a big lock of his thick black hair falling over his brows. Then they bowed and the audience applauded.

The show continued on its course. A few gags followed: a costumed bull with flowers wrapped around its horns came out dancing an Irish jig, its horn poking into Ricky's bottom and so exasperating him that his eyes bugged out, he slapped his forehead and started speaking a-thousand-words-a-second Spanish. But at that point it made no difference to me, the miracle had passed, the resurrection of a man, Our Lord's promise which I then believed, with its release from pain, release from the troubles of this world.

SIDE A

In the Hotel Splendour
1980

NEARLY TWENTY-FIVE YEARS after he and his brother had appeared on the *I Love Lucy* show, Cesar Castillo suffered in the terrible heat of a summer's night and poured himself another drink. He was in a room in the Hotel Splendour on 125th Street and Lenox Avenue, not far from the narrow stairway that led up to the recording studios of Orchestra Records, where his group, the Mambo Kings, made their fifteen black brittle 78s. In fact, it could have been the very room in which he had once bedded down a luscious and long-legged party girl by the name of Vanna Vane, Miss Mambo for the month of June 1954. Everything was different then: 125th Street was jumping with clubs, there was less violence, there were fewer beggars, more mutual respect between people; he could take a late-night stroll from the apartment on La Salle Street, head down Broadway, cut east on 110th Street to Central Park, and then walk along its twisting paths and across the little bridges over streams and rocks, enjoying the scent of the woods and nature's beauty without a worry. He'd make his way to the Park Palace Ballroom on East 110th Street to hear Machito or Tito Puente, find musician friends at the bar, chase women, dance. Back then, you could walk through that park wearing your best clothes and a nice expensive watch without someone coming up behind you and pressing a knife against your neck. Man, those days were gone forever.

He laughed: he would have given anything to have the physical virtuosity now that he did when he was thirty-six and first brought Miss Mambo up those stairs and into the room. He used to live for that moment when he could strip a woman down on a bed: Miss Vanna Vane of Brooklyn, New York, had a mole just below the nipple of her right breast, and, boom, his big thing used to stick out just like that, just by touching a woman's breast or standing close to her and sensing the heat between her legs. Women wore nicer clothes back then, more elaborate delicate things, and it was more fun to watch them undress. Yes, perhaps that was the room where he'd take Vanna Vane on those glorious unending nights of love so long ago.

He sat in the flickering street-lit window, his languorous heavy-jowled hound's face glowing like white stone. He'd brought up a little phonograph, used to belong to his nephew Eugenio, and a package of old records made by his group, the Mambo Kings, in the early 1950s. A case of whiskey, a carton of cigarettes—filtered Chesterfields ("Folks, smoke Chesterfields, the preferred tobacco, the Mambo King's favorite!") that had wrecked his nice baritone voice over the years; and a few other items: paper, envelopes, a few BiC pens, his tattered address book, stomach pills, a dirty magazine—something called *El Mundo Sexual*—a few faded photographs, a change of clothes, all packed in a beaten-up cane suitcase. He was planning to stay in the Hotel Splendour for as long as it would take him to drink that whiskey (or until the veins on his legs burst), figuring he'd eat, if he had to, at the Chinese place on the corner with its sign saying, "Takee Out Only."

As he leaned forward, placing on the buzzing phonograph a record called "The Mambo Kings Play Songs of Love," he could hear footsteps on the stairway, a man's and a young woman's voice, the man saying, "Here we are, baby," and then the sound of the door opening and closing, and the moving about of chairs, as if they were going to sit in front of a fan together to drink and kiss. Black man's voice, Cesar figured before clicking on the record player.

A sea of scratches and a trumpet line, a habanera bass, a piano playing sentimental, sad minor chords, his brother Nestor Castillo in some faraway place in a world without light, raising the trumpet to his lips, eyes closed, face rippled by dreamy concentration . . . the melody of Ernesto Lecuona's *"Juventud."*

Sipping whiskey, his memory scrambled like eggs. He was sixty-two. Time was becoming a joke. One day, young man; next day, old man. Now, as the music played, he half expected to open his eyes and find Miss Vanna Vane seated on that chair across the room, slipping her long legs into a pair of nylons, the cheery white light of 125th Street on a Sunday morning burning through the half-open window shade.

On one of those nights when he could not sit still in their apartment on La Salle Street back in 1954, he was in the Palm Nightclub listening to the fabulous Tito Rodríguez and his orchestra and watching the cigarette girl: she was wearing a too tight leopard-skin leotard and her blond hair was long, curled, and swept to one side, so that it fell pouty over half her face, like Veronica Lake's. Every time this blonde walked by, Cesar Castillo bought a package of cigarettes from her, and when she would set her cigarette box down on the table he'd hold her by the wrist and look deep into her eyes. Then he'd give her a quarter tip and smile. In a sheeny black top, her breasts were splendid and large. He'd once overheard a drunken sailor saying to a pal in a bar, "Look at the torpedoes on that broad, mamma mia!" Loving American expressions, he thought of torpedoes with their pointed tips, and was enchanted by the line of sweat congealing across her diaphragm.

After he'd bought his eighth package of cigarettes from her, he invited her to have a drink. Because it was very late, she decided to sit with them, these two handsome brothers.

"My name is Cesar Castillo, and this is my brother Nestor."

"Vanna Vane. Nice to meet you."

A little later he was out on the dance floor with Miss Vane, putting on a hell of a show for the crowd, when the orchestra broke into a furious jam: a conga player, a bongo player, and a drummer with an American kit, pounding out a fast, swirling, circular rhythm. Their playing was so conducive to spinning that the Mambo King unfurled his breast-pocket handkerchief and in a variation of the scarf dance slipped one end of it between his teeth and urged Vanna to do the same with the other. Joined by a pink-and-light-blue handkerchief clenched between their teeth, Cesar and Vanna started to spin quickly like two whirling acrobats in a circus act. As they spun, the crowd applauded, and a number of couples imitated them on the dance floor. Then they dizzily zigzagged back to their table.

"So you're a Cuban fellow like that guy Desi Arnaz?"

"That's right, baby."

Later, at three in the morning, he and Nestor walked her to the subway.

"Vanna, there's something I want you to do for me. I have this orchestra and we've just made a new record. We're thinking of calling it something like 'Mambos for the Manhattan Night,' that's my idea, and we need someone, a pretty girl like you —how old are you?"

"Twenty-two."

"—a pretty girl to pose with us for the cover of this record. I mean to say"—and then he seemed flustered and bashful —"that you would be good for this. It pays fifty dollars."

"Fifty."

Decked out in white silk suits on a Saturday afternoon, the brothers met Vanna in Times Square and walked over to the photographer's studio at 548 West 48th Street, the Olympus Studio, where their photographer had outfitted a back room with fake palm trees. Turning up with their instruments, a trumpet, a guitar, and a drum, they looked quite slick, their thick heads of hair conked high into shining pompadours. Miss Vane wore a ruffle-skirted, pleat-waisted party dress with a tight bodice, gleamy black seamed nylons, and five-inch-high heels that lifted her rump into the air and showed off her nice long legs. (And behind this memory, he didn't know what they called that muscle up at the high end inside a woman's thigh, that muscle which intersected the clitoris and got all twisted, quivering ever so slightly when he'd kiss a woman there.) They tried a hundred poses, but the one that made the album cover was this: Cesar Castillo with wolfish grin, a conga drum strapped around his neck, his hand raised and coming down on the drum, his mouth open in a laugh, and his whole body bending toward Miss Vane. Her hands were clasped together by her face, her mouth forming an "Ooooh" of excitement, her legs bent for dancing, part of her garter showing; while to her left, Nestor, eyes closed and head tilted back, was blowing his trumpet. Later the artist who did the mechanics for Orchestra Records would add a Manhattan skyline and a trail of one- and two-flagged notes spewing out of Nestor's trumpet around them.

Because Orchestra Records worked on the cheap, most of their recordings were 78s, though they also managed to put out a few party-size 33s, with four songs per side. In those days, most record players still had three speeds. Pressed in the Bronx, these 78s were made of a heavy but brittle plastic, never sold more than a few thousand copies each, and were to be found in *botánicas* — religious knickknack shops—alongside statues of Jesus Christ and his tormented disciples, and magic candles and curative herbs, and in record stores like the Almacén Hernández on 113th Street and Lexington Avenue in Harlem, and in bins in the street market and on tables manned by friends at dances. The Mambo Kings would put out fifteen of these 78s, selling for 69 cents each, between 1949 and 1956, and three long-playing 33s (in 1954 and 1956).

The A and B sides of these 78s were titled "Solitude of My Heart," "A Woman's Tears," "Twilight in Havana," "The Havana Mambo," "Conga Cats and Conga Dolls," "The Sadness of Love," "Welcome to Mamboland," "Jingle Bells Mambo!" ("Who's that fat jolly guy with the white beard dancing up a storm with that chick? . . . Santa Claus, Santa Claus dancing the 'Jingle Bells Mambo!' "), "Mambo Nocturne," "The Subway Mambo," "My Cuban Mambo," "The Lovers' Mambo," "*El Campesino,*" "Alcohol," "Traffic Mambo," "The Happy Mambo!," "The New York Cha-cha-cha," "Cuban Cha-cha," "Too Many Women (and Not Enough Time!)," "Mambo Inferno!," "*Noche Caliente,*" "Malagueña" (as cha-cha-cha), "*Juventud,*" "Solitude," "Lovers' Cha-cha-cha," "How Delicious the Mambo!," "Mambo Fiesta!," "The Kissing Mambo!" (And the 33s: "Mambo Dance Party" and "Manhattan Mambo"—1954 —and their full-length 33, *The Mambo Kings Play Songs of Love,* June 1956.) Not only did the Mambo Kings feature winsome and beautiful Miss Mambo pinup girls on each of these records, but sometimes a dance instruction box was included. (By the mid-seventies, most of these records had vanished from the face of the earth. Whenever Cesar would go by a secondhand store or a "classic" record rack, he would search carefully for new copies to replace the ones that had gotten smashed or lent out or given away or just worn out and scratchy from so much use. Sometimes he found them for 15 cents or 25 cents and he would walk happily home, his bundle under his arm.)

Now the narrow entranceway of Orchestra, where those records were made, was blocked off with boards, its windows filled with the remnants of what had become a dress shop; a few manikins were leaning backwards against the glass. But back then he and the Mambo Kings used to carry their instruments up the narrow stairway, their enormous string bass always banging against the walls. Beyond a red door marked STUDIO was a small waiting room with an office desk and a row of black metal chairs. On the wall, a corkboard filled with photographs of the record company's other musicians: a singer named Bobby Soxer Otero; a pianist, Cole Higgins; and beside him, the majestic Ornette Brothers. Then a photograph of the Mambo Kings all dressed in white silk suits and posed atop a seashell art-deco bandstand, the photograph crisscrossed with looping scrawls.

The studio was about the size of a large bathroom and had thickly carpeted floors with corkboard- and drape-covered walls, and a large window looking out on 125th Street. It was hot and airless on warm days, without air-conditioning or ventilation when they were recording, save for the rusty-bladed fan that sat atop the studio piano, which they'd turn on between numbers.

Three big RCA ball microphones in the center of the room for vocals, another three for the instruments. While making their records, the musicians would remove their shoes and walk quietly about, careful not to stomp their feet during the recording session, as this would get picked up as "thumps" on the microphones. No laughing, no breathing, no whispering. The horn players would stand to the side, the rhythm section—drummers and string bass and pianist—on another.

Cesar and his brother Nestor side by side, the Mambo King playing the claves (the wooden instruments making the 1-2-3/1-2 clicking sound) or shaking maracas, strumming a guitar. Sometimes Cesar played trumpet melodies with Nestor, but usually he stepped back and allowed his brother to take his solos in peace. Even so, Nestor always waited for his older brother's signal, a nod, to begin. Only then, would Nestor step forward, his mournful solos flying like black angels through the group's lavish orchestrations. With that, Cesar returned to the microphone or the pianist took his own solo or the chorus sang. Sometimes these sessions lasted until the early morning, with some songs coming easily, and others played again and again until throats grew hoarse and the streets seemed to blur in a phantasm of lights.

Like his music, the Mambo King was very direct in those days. He and Vanna had just been out to dinner at the Club Babalú and Cesar said to her, as she chewed on a piece of plantain fritter, "Vanna, I'm in love with you, and I want the chance to show you what it's like to be loved by a man like me." And because they'd been throwing down pitchers of the Club Babalú's special sangria, and because he had taken her to a nice movie —Humphrey Bogart and Ava Gardner in *The Barefoot Contessa* — and because he had gotten her a fifty-dollar modeling fee and an expensive ballroom dress with pleated skirt so she could appear between himself and his younger brother on the cover of "Manhattan Mambos '54"; and perhaps because he was a reasonably handsome man who seemed earnest and knew, as wolves know, exactly what he wanted from her—she could see it in his eyes —she was flattered enough that when he said, "Why don't we go uptown?" she said, "Yes."

Maybe it was on that chair that she had first set down her fine ass while going about the delicate business of hoisting up her skirt and unsnapping her garters. Coyly smiling as she rolled down her nylons, which she afterwards draped across the chair. He lay down across the bed. He'd taken off his jacket, his silk shirt, his flamingo-pink tie, stripped off his sleeveless T-shirt, so that his top was bare—save for a tarnished crucifix, a First Communion gift from his mother in Cuba, hanging from a thin gold chain around his neck. Off with the lights, off with her wire-reinforced Maidenform 36C brassiere, off with her Lady of Paris underwear with the flowery embroidered crotch. He told her exactly what to do. She undid his trousers and gripped his big thing with her long slender hand, and soon she was unrolling a heavy rubber prophylactic over it. She liked him, liked it, liked his manliness and his arrogance and the way he threw her around on the bed, turning her on her stomach and onto her back, hung her off the side of the bed, pumping her so wildly she felt as if she was being attacked by a beast of the forest. He licked the mole on her breast that she thought ugly with the tip of his tongue and called it beautiful. Then he pumped her so much he tore up the rubber and kept going even when he knew the rubber was torn; he kept going because it felt so good and she screamed, and felt as if she was breaking into pieces, and, boom, he had his orgasm and went floating through a wall-less room filled with flitting black nightingales.

"Tell me that phrase again in Spanish. I like to hear it."

"*Te quiero.*"

"Oh, it's so beautiful, say it again."

"*Te quiero,* baby, baby."

"And I '*te quiero,*' too."

Smugly, he showed her his *pinga,* as it was indelicately called in his youth. He was sitting on the bed in the Hotel Splendour and leaning back in the shadows, while she was standing by the bathroom door. And just looking at her fine naked body, damp with sweat and happiness, made his big thing all hard again. That thing burning in the light of the window was thick and dark as a tree branch. In those days, it sprouted like a vine from between his legs, carried aloft by a powerful vein that precisely divided his body, and flourished upwards like the spreading top branches of a tree, or, he once thought while looking at a map of the United States, like the course of the Mississippi River and its tributaries.

"Come over here," he told her.

On that night, as on many other nights, he pulled up the tangled sheets so that she could join him on the bed again. And soon Vanna Vane was grinding her damp bottom against his chest, belly, and mouth and strands of her dyed blond hair came slipping down between their lips as they kissed. Then she mounted him and rocked back and forth until things got all twisted and hot inside and both their hearts burst (pounding like conga drums) and they fell back exhausted, resting until they were ready for more, their lovemaking going around and around in the Mambo King's head, like the melody of a song of love.

Thinking about Vanna threw open the door to that time. The Mambo King found himself walking arm in arm with her —or a woman like her—into the Park Palace Ballroom, a huge dance joint on 110th Street and Fifth Avenue. That was his favorite place to hang out on his nights off, when he wanted to have fun. It would feel good to make an entrance with a pretty woman on his arm, a tall blonde with a big heart-shaped ass. Vanna Vane, with big hips and big breasts, in a bursting black sequin-disk-covered number that blinked and wobbled clamorously when she'd walk across a room. He'd strut in beside her, wearing a light blue pinstriped suit, white silk shirt, light sky-blue tie, his hair slick and his body scented with Old Spice, the mariner's cologne.

That was the thing in those days: to be seen with a woman like Vanna was prestigious as a passport, a high-school diploma, a full-time job, a record contract, a 1951 DeSoto. Dark-skinned men like Nat King Cole and Miguelito Valdez would turn up at the dance halls with blond girlfriends. And Cesar liked to do the same, even though he was a white Cuban like Desi Arnaz. (Why, he knew of this fellow, hung around in the clubs, who made his brunette girlfriend dye her pubic hair blond. He knew it because he'd taken her to bed once, when she was still a brunette, and then later, on the sly, he'd talked her into going somewhere with him, maybe the Hotel Splendour, where he planted a kiss on her navel and slid her panties off, slipping his tongue into the sweetness of her new, improved golden Clairol hair.) Moving through the ballroom crowd, he liked to watch the heads turning in admiration as he and his girl would make their way to the jammed bar. There he'd play the sport and buy his friends drinks—in the 1950s, rum and Cokes were the rage—joking and telling stories until the orchestra broke into something like the "Hong Kong Mambo" or the "Mambo de Paree" and he would take his girl back out onto the floor and dance.

Later he might go into the cavernous Park Palace rest rooms to get his fancy two-toned shoes shined, or to place a bet with one of the bookies who worked out of a long stall where magazines and newspapers, condoms, flowers, and reefers were sold. A dollar tip for the shoeshine boys, a piss in the urinal, a comb through his wavy hair, and then back out, his metal-heeled shoes tap, tap, tapping down the tiled halls, like shoes in the arcades of Cuba, toward the beautiful music. Then he'd dance again or rejoin his quiet brother at their table, sipping drinks and gratefully observing the juicy babes around him. (Yeah, and even if he's in the

Hotel Splendour, it's as if he's back in that dance hall again, checking things out and noticing that there's a nice brunette looking over at him. And who should come by when his date gets up to use the ladies' room but that brunette, and even if she's not a blonde, she looks seriously fly in a tight pink dress and bops toward him with a drink in her hand, and *Dios mío,* but she looks hot from dancing, with beads of sweat rolling off her chin and onto her breasts, her stomach damp and transparent through the clingy material of her dress. And what does she say but, "Aren't you Cesar Castillo, the singer?" And he nods and takes hold of her wrist and says, "My, but you smell nice," and he gets her name, cracks her up with a joke, and then, before his date returns, he says, "Why don't you come back here tomorrow night and we can talk some more and have a little fun," and he jumps ahead, feeling her nipple stiffen in his mouth, and then he's back in the Park Palace, watching her walking off—he can just barely make out the outline of her panties through her dress, and she's in bed tormenting him with the ball of her thumb, a rolling motion over his opening that makes the head of his penis the size of a Cortland apple, and then his girl comes back and they have some more drinks, he remembered that.)*

---

*Then, behind that another recollection about the way the ladies dressed back when: they wore skull-hugging turbans, low-riding cloches, banded berets, and feathered pillbox caps. Heavy drop earrings made with fake rubies, crystals, and pearls; white creamy pearl necklaces hanging down into low-riding necklines, breasts plumped up and sweet underneath; sequined dresses with slit skirts and pleated midriffs, tied up by black sable belts. Frilly slips, step-ins, girdles and garters, brassieres, lacy-fringed and transparent at the nipples. Good for kisses on the belly, roll of the damp tongue on the navel, nose roving over a line of black pubic hairs below. Flower-crotched flame panties, black-seamed white panties, panties with felt-covered buttons, fluffy ball panties, panties whose waistbands snapped tight and left faint pink lines along the ridges of tender female skin; hips warm against his face; black sable panties, fake leopard-skin panties, butterfly-wing panties. (And if these ladies didn't wear the right kinds of little things

The Mambo King flourished in that ballroom with its friendly crowds, good food, booze, companionship, and music. And when he wasn't out to dance or to play jobs with his orchestra, he was visiting the friends he had made in the Park Palace and other dance halls, fellow Cubans or Puerto Ricans who would invite him over to their apartments to eat dinner, play cards, listen to records, and become a swaying ring of arms in the kitchen, singing and always having fun.

It was at the Park Palace that the Mambo King and his brother found many of their musicians. When he and his brother had first turned up in New York in early 1949, the beginning of the mambo boom, they had gotten jobs through their fat cousin Pablo, with whom they had at first lived, working in a meat-packing plant on 125th Street by day so that they could have enough money to party and set things up at night. They met a lot of people then, a lot of musicians like themselves, good players. There was Pito Pérez, who played the timbales; Benny Domingo on the congas; Ray Alcázar on the piano; Manny Domínguez, who played the guitar and the *cencerro;* Xavier from Puerto Rico, the trombone; Willie Carmen, the flute; Ramón *"El Jamón"* Ortiz, the bass saxophone; José Otero, violin; Rafael Guillón, the rattle gourd; Benny Chacón, accordion; Johnny Bing, saxophone; Johnny Cruz, horn; Francisco Martínez, vibraphone; Johnny Reyes, the *tres* and the eight-stringed *quatro.* And, among them, the brothers themselves: Cesar, who sang, played the trumpet, guitar, accordion, and piano; and Nestor, flute, trumpet, guitar, and vocals.

Like the brothers, many of the musicians were workers by

---

underneath, he would head into the lingerie department of stores like Macy's and Gimbels, flirting with the salesgirls and happily looking over these little things in the display cases. Like a student preparing for an exam, he would squint and arch his handsome brow, checking out the names on the labels: Tropical Rhapsody, Bronze Twilight, Tigress, Nights of Desire.

"Ohh la la," he would say to the salesgirl, shaking his right hand as if his fingertips were on fire. "Which one would you wear, miss?")

day, and when they played jobs and were on a stage, or went out
dancing, they were Stars for a Night. Stars of buying drinks, stars
of friendly introductions, stars of female conquest. Some of them
were already famous like the Mambo King wanted to be. They
met the drummer Mongo Santamaría, who had an act back then
called the Black Cuban Diamonds; Pérez Prado,* the emperor of
the Mambo; the singer Graciela; the pianist Chico O'Farrill; and
that black fellow who liked Cubans so much, Dizzy Gillespie.
And they met the great Machito, a dignified and dapper-looking
mulatto, who would hang out at the bar of the Park Palace, his
diminutive wife by his side, receiving his fans and their gifts of
jewelry, which he would calmly tuck into his jacket pocket. Later
the jewelry would end up in a teakwood Chinese box that Machito kept in his living room. Visiting with Machito at his apartment in the West Eighties, the brothers would see this box, thick
with engraved watches, bracelets, and rings, its lid decorated with
Chinese swirls and inlaid with the image of a mother-of-pearl
dragon devouring a flower. And Cesar would say, "Don't you
worry, brother, that's going to be happening to us one day."

---

*Puff of smoke, a swallow of whiskey, the sensation that some-
thing was pinching the small of his back, something with razor-
like claws, making its way along the mysterious passages of his
kidneys and liver . . . *Pérez Prado*. When the Mambo King,
ensconced in his room in the Hotel Splendour, thought about
Pérez, he recalled the first time he saw the man on a stage, off in
another world and bending his body in a hundred shapes, as if he
was made of rubber: prowling like a hound, on his haunches like
a cat, spreading out like a tree, soaring like a biplane, rushing like
a train, vibrating like a tumbling washing machine, rolling like
dice, bounding like a kangaroo, bouncing like a spring, skipping
like a stone . . . and his face a mask of concentration, conviction,
and pure pleasure, a being from another world, his stage another
world. Thin Pérez giving the Mambo King some of his jazzier
stage moves, the loquacious and cheerful Pérez out by the bar,
telling everyone around him, "Fellas, you must come and visit me
in Mexico! We'll have the time of our lives, tell you what, my
friends. We'll go to the races and the bullfights, we'll eat like
princes and drink like the Pope!"

Cesar had a picture from one of those nights, tucked in the soft cloth pocket of his suitcase in the Hotel Splendour: the two brothers decked out in white suits and seated at a round table, the mirrored walls and columns behind them reflecting the distant lights, dancers, and the brass of an orchestra. Cesar, a little drunk and pleased to death with himself, a champagne glass in one hand and, in the other, the soft, curvaceous shoulder of an unidentified girl—Paulita? Roxanne? Xiomara?—looking a lot like Rita Hayworth, with her nice breasts pushed up into the top of her dress and a funny smile because Cesar had just leaned over and kissed her, licking her ear with his tongue, and Nestor beside them, a little detached and to the side, staring off, his brows raised slightly in bewilderment.

Those were the days when they'd formed the Mambo Kings. It started with jam sessions that used to drive their landlady, Mrs. Shannon, and their other neighbors, mostly Irish and German people, crazy. Musicians they knew from the dance halls would come over to the apartment with their instruments and set up in the living room, which was often noisy with wacky saxophones, violins, drums, and basses that screeched, floated, banged, and bounced out into the courtyard and street, so that the neighbors slammed down their windows and threatened the Cubans with hammers. The casual jam sessions became regular sessions, certain musicians always showed up, and so one day Cesar simply said, "Let's make a little orchestra, huh?"

His best find, though, was a certain Miguel Montoya, a pianist and good professional who knew the secrets of arranging. He was also Cuban and had been kicking around in different orchestras in New York City since the early 1930s and he was well connected, having played with Antonio Arcana and with Noro Morales. They'd see Montoya over at the Park Palace. Dressed in white from head to toe, he wore large, glittering sapphire rings, and sported an ivory crystal-tipped cane. Rumor had it that although he'd show up in the dance halls with a woman he was effeminate in character. One night they went to Montoya's apartment on Riverside Drive and 155th Street for dinner. Everything in his home was white and fleecy—from the goatskins and plumes that hung on the walls to the statues of Santa Barbara and the Holy Mother that he'd draped in silk, to the furry love seats, sofas, and chairs. In the corner his white baby grand piano, a Steinway, on which he'd placed a thin-necked vase filled with tulips. They dined on delicate slices of veal which Miguel had cooked with lemon, butter, garlic, salt, and olive oil; scalloped potatoes; and a grand salad, which they washed down with one bottle of wine after the other. Later, as the Hudson gleamed silver in the moonlight and New Jersey blinked in the distance, they laughed, turned on the record player, and passed half the night dancing rumbas, mambos, and tangos. Cultivating Miguel through flirtation, Cesar treated him with real affection like a beloved uncle, constantly patting and hugging him. Later in the evening he asked Montoya if he could spare the time to sit in with their orchestra, and that night Montoya gave in and said he would.

They formed a mambo band; that is, a traditional Latin dance band given balls by saxophones and horns. This orchestra consisted of a flute, violin, piano, sax, two trumpets, two drum-mers, one playing an American kit and the other a battery of congas. Cesar had thought up the Mambo Kings while looking through the advertising pages of the Brooklyn *Herald,* where half the orchestras had names like the Mambo Devils, Romero and the Hot Rumba Orchestra, Mambo Pete and His Caribbean Crooners. There was a certain Eddie Reyes King of the Bronx Mambo, Juan Valentino and His Mad Mambo Rompers, Vic Caruso and His Little Italy Mambonairs, and groups like the Havana Casino Orchestra, the Havana Melody Band, the Havana Dance Orchestra. Those same pages advertising DANC-ING LESSONS NOW! LEARN THE MAMBO, THE FOX-TROT, THE RUMBA. DANCE YOUR WAY INTO A GIRL'S HEART! Why not Cesar Castillo and the Mambo Kings?

Although Cesar considered himself a singer, he was also quite talented as an instrumentalist and adept at percussion. He was blessed with tremendous energy, a surge of power from too many slaps in the face from his foul-tempered father, Pedro Cas-tillo, and a love of melody because of his mother and the affec-tionate maid who had helped bring him into the world, Genebria. (Here he listens to a distant trumpeting on a Mambo King recording, "Twilight in Havana," and sighs; it's as if he's a kid again running through the center of Las Piñas at carnival and the porches of the houses are lit with huge lanterns and the balconies garlanded with ribbons and tapers and flowers, and where he runs past so many musicians, musicians everywhere on the street corners, on the church steps, on the porches of the houses, and continuing on toward the plaza, where the big orchestra is set up; that's the trumpet he hears echoing in the arcades of his town as he passes the columns and the shadows of couples hidden behind them and charges down steps past a garden, through the crowds and the dancers, to the bandstand, where that trumpet player, obese in a white suit, head tilted back, blows music up into the sky, and this carries and bounces off the walls of another arcade in Havana, and he's blowing the trumpet now at three in the morning, reeling around in circles and laughing after a night out at the clubs and brothels with friends and his brother, laughing with the notes that whip into the empty dark spaces and bounce back, swirling inside him like youth.)

He and his brother actually preferred the slower ballads and boleros, but they set out with Montoya to build a sound dance band, because that's what the people wanted. It was Montoya who did all the arrangements of pieces like *"Tu Felicidad," "Cachita," "No Te Importe Saber,"* pieces made popular by the likes of René Touzet, Noro Morales, Israel Fajardo. He knew how to read music, which the brothers had never really learned— though they could struggle their way through a chart, they presented their songs with simple chords and with the melodies worked out on instruments or in their heads. This sometimes annoyed the other musicians, but Cesar used to tell them, "What I'm interested in is a man who can really feel the music, instead of someone who can only play the charts." And then he talked about the immortal *conguero* Chano Pozo, who was shot to death in 1948 over a drug deal* and whose ghost was already turning

---

*From Manuel Flanagan, a trumpet player who knew Chano: "I remember when Chano died. I was down on 52nd when I heard the whole thing. Chano was up on 116th Street at the Caribbean Bar and Grill, looking for this man who'd sold him stuff. That

up in Havana mambos, and of musicians like the great Mongo Santamaría. "Just look at Mongo," Cesar would say to Nestor. "He doesn't read. And did Chano? No, *hombre,* he had the spirit, and that's what we want, too."

They'd rehearse in the living room of their cousin Pablo's apartment, on days when the walls were subject to wild fits of clanking boiler pipes and when the floors rumbled because of the subways, as if in an earthquake. They'd rehearse on days when the boiler had shut down and it was so cold steam oozed out of their cuticles and the musicians would roll their eyes, saying, "Who needs this shit?" But they continued because Cesar Castillo treated them well: they'd show up dead-tired from their day jobs and play their hearts out, knowing that at the end of the rehearsal they would crowd into the little kitchen: Pablo's wife would cook up big platters of steak and pork chops—smuggled out of the meat-packing plant under shirts and long coats—rice and beans, and whatever else they wanted. Having consumed great quantities of food and beer, they'd laugh and head back into the chilly universe feeling as if Cesar Castillo and his brother had really looked out for them.

Hands moving around in circles (after taking a sip of beer, drag of a Chesterfield), he'd explain his ideas about a song: "For this ballad, we should come in quietly like cats. Miguel, first you on the piano, the minor chords and all that business on the high notes, then, Manny, you come in with the bass, but *suavecito,* *suavecito,* and then, Nestor, you come in with the horn,

---

was in the morning. He'd injected it, gotten sick, and then later went out on the street looking for him. He found him in that bar, pulled a knife on him, and demanded his money back. Now, the man wasn't afraid of Chano and Chano wasn't afraid of the man; Chano had already been shot up and stabbed in Havana and had survived it, you know, so that Chano took his knife out and lunged at the man, even though he'd pulled out a gun: Chano kept coming at him because he thought the spirits were protecting him, but these spirits, Yoruba spirits, couldn't stop the bullets from tearing him up and that was that."

talatalatalata, then the congas and the other brass. We go through one verse and then we come into the turnaround and I'll sing the verse."

"We'll play," Manny the bassist was saying. "And you sing with that priestly expression on your face."

When they finally had the songs worked out, lyrics and simple chords, the melody lines memorized, he used to take them to his arranger, the elegant Miguel Montoya. Sitting down beside him, he'd whistle the melody or pick it out directly on the piano, so that it could be written down as music. Many a night, passersby on Broadway and Tiemann Place would hear these melodies being worked out by the Mambo King and his brother. People would look up and see their silhouettes in the window, heads arched back. Or sometimes they went up to the rooftop with a few bottles of beer and steak sandwiches on Italian bread, smothered in onions and salt, and set out a blanket, feasted and drank, passing the night improvising songs as if for the red-yellow-blue-and-white-lit buildings of the city.

Jobs were hard to find at first, with so many good dance bands already out there. On his days off, Cesar did a lot of the footwork, going from club to club on Eighth, Ninth, and Tenth Avenues, and to the Bronx and Brooklyn and uptown, Harlem. He was always trying to set up auditions with jaded, tan-suited Puerto Rican gangsters who owned half of the mambo singers in New York. But they did get some jobs: parish dances, grammar-school parties, weddings. Many hours of rehearsal, few dollars of pay. It would help a lot that Cesar Castillo was a white Cuban bolero singer like Desi Arnaz, what they called in those days a Latin-lover type, dark-haired and dark-featured, his skin being what was then called "swarthy." Swarthy to Americans, but light-skinned when compared to many of his friends. Pito, a wiry Cuban from Cienfuegos, was as dark as the mahogany legs of the easy chair in their living room on La Salle. A lot of the fellows who turned up at the apartment with their squealing, guitar-shaped wives and girlfriends were dark, bony-limbed men.

A flier from May 15, 1950:

The Friendship Club on 79th Street and Broadway presents for your dancing pleasure a double bill of top Mambo Entertainment. Tonight and tomorrow night (Fri. and Sat.) we are proud to present the Glorious Gloria Parker and Her All-Girl Rumba Orchestra! And, sharing this bill, the Fabulous Cesar Castillo and His Mambo Kings of Cuba! Admission $1.04. Doors open at 9 P.M. No zoot suits and no jitterbugs, please.

They started playing jobs all over the city. The Café Society on 58th Street, the Havana Madrid on Broadway and 51st, the Biltmore Ballroom on Church and Flatbush, the Club 78, the Stardust on Boston Road in the Bronx, the Pan-American Club and the Gayheart Ballroom on Nostrand Avenue, the Hotel Manhattan Towers on 76th Street and at the City Center Casino.

He'd get up on the stage, dancing before the microphone while his musicians took the music forward. The glory of being on a stage with his brother Nestor, playing for crowds of café-society people who jumped, bounced, and wriggled across the dance floor. While Nestor soloed, Cesar's heavy eyelids fluttered like butterfly wings lilting on a rose; for drum solos his hips shook, his arms whipped into the air: he'd take backwards dance steps, gripping his belt with one hand and a crease of trouser with the other, hiking them up, as if to accentuate the valiant masculinity therein: outline of big prick through white silk *pantalones.* Piano taking a ninth chord voicing behind a solo, he'd stare up into the pink and red spotlights, giving the audience a horse's grin. Woman in a strapless dress dancing a slow, grinding rumba, staring at Cesar Castillo. Old woman with hair coiffed upward into a heavenly spiral, staring at Cesar. Teenage girl, Miss Roosevelt High School Class of 1950, thin-legged and thinking about the mystery of boys and love, staring at Cesar Castillo. Old ladies' skin heating up, hips moving like young girls' hips, eyes wide open with admiration and delight.

Audiences everywhere seemed to like them, but if there was one place they "owned," it was the Imperial Ballroom on East 18th Street and Utica Avenue, Brooklyn. Here they were the house band—hired at first because of Miguel Montoya, but kept on because of Cesar and Nestor's popularity. They were constantly playing contests which awarded $25 prizes for the Best Peg Pants, Loudest Shirts, Best-Looking Woman, Best Dancer Holding an Umbrella, Shapeliest Legs, Weirdest Shoes, Most Outrageous Hat, and, on one Saturday night, the Best Baldhead contest, for which a huge crowd turned out. Their greatest moment of glory at the Imperial came on that memorable night when they engaged in a battle in the war between Cuba and Puerto Rico. Under the sterling hip-swinging, pelvis-grinding admiralship of their singer, Cesar Castillo, the orchestra pulled a victory out of, to quote the *Herald*'s entertainment column, "the ravages of da-feet."

And, on another night, Cesar met one of his best and lifelong friends, Frankie Pérez. This was in 1950 and the orchestra was playing one of Cesar and Nestor's original compositions, "Twilight in Havana." Frankie was a hammy dancer, knew every rumba, mambo, and cu-bop* step on earth. He was a *suavecito*

---

*"Cu-bop" being the term used to describe the fusion of Afro-Cuban music and hot be-bop Harlem jazz. Its greatest practitioner was the bandleader Machito, who with Maurio Bauza and Chano Pozo hooked up with Dizzy Gillespie and Charlie Parker in the late 1940s. The American jazz players picked up the Cuban rhythms, and the Cubans picked up jazzier rhythms and chord progressions. Machito's orchestra, with Chico O'Farrill as arranger, became famous for dazzling solos played over extended vamps called *montunos*. During these furious breaks, when drummers like Chano Pozo and players like Charlie Parker went nuts, dancers like Frankie Pérez took to the center of the ballroom floor, improvising turns, dips, splits, leaps around the basic mambo steps, in the same way that the musicians improvised during their solos. (Yeah, and there was that other sneaky move he'd picked up from Cesar Castillo. While dancing with a pretty woman he would touch his forehead with his index finger and make a sizzling sound as if he was burning up and then he would fan himself, to cool out from love's mighty heat, sizzle some more, hop around as if on hot coals, fan himself again, and blow a kiss, all the time feeling cu-bop crazy, man.)

who had been a natural wizard on his toes since he was a kid in Havana, and could make any partner look good dancing with him. At that time, he'd make the rounds of the major ballrooms of the city three or four nights a week: the Park Palace, the Palladium, the Savoy, the Imperial. That night he was dressed in a green zoot suit with a pink oversized purple-brimmed hat, cream-colored Cuban-heeled shoes, and green argyle socks. Dancing happily near the stage, he was oblivious to the troubles of the world, when he heard pop, pop coming out of the manager's office. Then the crashing of glass and screaming. Someone shouted, "Get down!" and people scattered across the dance floor and hid behind the mirrored columns and under the tables. Two more pops and the orchestra stopped playing, the musicians ducking behind their music stands and jumping down off the stage and hitting the floor.

Two men came running out of the manager's office onto the dance floor and they spun around firing off shots as they made their way out toward the door. One of them was thin and eagle-beaked and carried a satchel of money. The other man was heavier and seemed to have trouble running, as if he had a lame leg or had been hit by the gunshots fired from the office. They looked as if they were going to make it, but once they got outside they ran into a barrage of gunfire; some cops had been driving by when they heard the commotion. One of the robbers was hit in the back of the head, the other surrendered. Later, when everyone was huddling by the bar and throwing down drinks, Cesar and Nestor struck up a conversation with Frankie. When they finished with their drinks, they made their way out into the street, where a crowd had gathered. The dead man was still lying face-down in the gutter. He was broad-shouldered and dressed in a pinstriped jacket. Nestor had no stomach for this, but Cesar and Frankie made their way over to the corpse to get a better look. Leaning up against a brick wall, their solemn faces peering out into the world from the shadows, they sadly and confoundedly contemplated the dead man's fate. As he watched, Cesar had one foot lifted behind him, the bottom of his sporty cordovan shoe pressed to the wall, and was lighting a cigarette and listening to all the sirens when a white camera flash went off. Foof. Aside from becoming friends that night, he and Frankie ended up on page 3 of the next morning's *Daily News,* part of the photograph whose caption read: BALLROOM ROBBER DIES IN POOL OF BLOOD.

A spectacular evening among so many spectacular evenings. How the rum flowed then, Jesus, how the bottles of booze multiplied along with the thick latex prophylactics and quivering female thighs like the miracle of fish and bread.

VISAS IN HAND AND SPONSORED by their cousin Pablo, they had turned up in New York as part of the wave of musicians who had been pouring out of Havana since the 1920s, when the tango and rumba crazes swept the United States and Europe. That boom had started because so many musicians lost their jobs in pit orchestras when talkies came in and silent movies went out. It was stay in Cuba and starve to death or head north to find a place in a rumba band. Even in Havana, with so many hotels, dance halls, and nightclubs, the scene was overcrowded. When Cesar had gone there in 1945, with the naïve idea of making it big, he became just one of a thousand bolero singers struggling to earn a living. Havana was jammed with first-rate underpaid singers and musicians like himself and Nestor, island musicians who played arrangements that sounded quaintly archaic next to the big brass American jazz bands like those of Artie Shaw, Fletcher Henderson, and Benny Goodman, who were much in vogue at the time. A musician's life in Havana was poor, sociable. Pretty-boy singers, trumpet players, and *congueros* gathered everywhere—in the arcades, plazas, and bars. With the Paul Whiteman Orchestra playing in the casino, the more authentic Cuban music was relegated to the alleys. Even musicians who were in the popular tropical orchestras of Enric Madriguera and René Touzet used to complain how badly they were being treated by the mobsters who ran the casinos and paid the Cuban musicians shit. Ten dollars a night, with cleaning charges for uniforms, black skins and mulattoes in one door, white musicians in another, no drinks on the house, no overtime,

and Christmas bonuses of watered-down resealed bottles of whiskey. This at clubs like the Tropicana and the Sans Souci.

The best—Olga Chorens, Alberto Beltrán, Nelson Piñedo,
Manny Jiménez—worked in clubs with names like the Night and
Day, the New Capri, Lucky Seven. The fabulous Ernesto
Lecuona at the Montmartre, Beny More at the Sierra.

The brothers had mainly worked in Havana as strolling
troubadours and in a cheap social band called the Havana Melody
Boys. They'd played in the lounge of a gambling casino, entertaining audiences of soaked-with-alcohol gamblers and spinster
tourists from the American Midwest; shaking cocktail mixers
filled with shot, strumming guitars and blowing horns. They
wore frilly-sleeved mambo shirts and orange toreador pants so
tight their paterfamilias gnarled up like big tree knots. (Another
version of the Havana Melody Boys picture tucked inside the soft
cloth pocket in the Mambo King's cane suitcase that he'd brought
with him into the Hotel Splendour, in a clump of old photographs, letters, and song ideas: a row of frilly-sleeved mambo
musicians in white-striped blue *pantalones,* seated on a bamboo
stage that is made up to look like a hut. There are nine musicians.
A window opens behind them to a fake view of Havana Harbor,
the sky thick with stars and a half-moon.) They had even made
a record back then featuring the Fabulous Cesar Castillo, something called *"El Campesino"* (he'd make a later version of this
with the Mambo Kings in 1952). Printing about a thousand copies
of this 78 as a demonstration record, they sent them around to
local radio stations, even got a few into the jukeboxes of Havana
Amusement Park and up at La Playa de Maríanao. It was not a
hit and got lost in the sea of boleros and ballads coming out of
Havana at that time. A thousand crooners and female torch singers, and for each one a black plastic disc, a record for each foam-
curled wave in the rippling mambo sea.

Tired of singing with the Havana Melody Boys, Cesar Castillo wanted to put together an orchestra of his own. Coming
from a small town in Oriente, he had been inspired by the stories
he'd heard about Cubans who'd left for the States. A woman from
Holguín had become an actress and gone to Hollywood, where
she had gotten rich making films with George Raft and Cesar

Romero. (Raft appeared as an Argentine gaucho in a jingle-bell-rimmed gaucho's hat, performing the tango with this woman in a film called *Passion on the Pampas.*) She made enough money to live in a radiant pink mansion in a place called Beverly Hills; and there was another fellow, a rumba dancer named Ernesto Precioso, whom Cesar had known from the dance halls of Santiago de Cuba and who had been discovered by Xavier Cugat, for whom he'd starred as a featured dancer in a Hollywood short with Cugat called *The Lady in Red* and with the pianist Noro Morales in *The Latin from Staten Island.*

Others who'd done well? Alberto Socarrás playing in a nightclub called the Kubanacan in Harlem, Miguelito Valdez (the Magnificent) crooning away for Xavier Cugat at the McAlpin Hotel, Machito with his widespread New York popularity and his European tours. Tito Rodríguez at the Palm Nightclub, and the Pozo Brothers.

But the most famous success story would be that of a fellow crooner whom the brothers knew from Santiago de Cuba, where they sometimes performed in dance halls and in the *placitas*, sitting out under the moonlight, strumming guitars. Desi Arnaz. He had turned up in the States in the thirties and established himself in the clubs and dance halls of New York as a nice, decent fellow and had parlayed his conga drum, singing voice, and quaint Cuban accent into fame. And there were others: Cesar Romero and Gilbert Roland, Cuban chaps who'd made it in the movies playing nightclub gigolos and gun-toting, sombrero-pated, spur-booted *vaqueros*. Cesar was impressed by Arnaz's success and sometimes daydreamed of achieving that fame (he laughs now). That Cesar was white like Arnaz (though to some Americans he would be "a Spic") and had a good quivering baritone and blunt pretty-boy looks all seemed destined to work to his advantage.

In any case, the scene might be better in New York. Musician friends from Havana traveled north and found work in the orchestras of people like Cugat, Machito, Morales, and Arnaz. Cesar heard rumors and received letters about money, dance halls, recording contracts, good weekly salaries, women, and friendly Cubans everywhere. He figured that if he went up there he could stay with Cousin Pablito, hook up with an orchestra, get away from trouble, make some money. And who could say what else might happen for them.

The day the brothers arrived in New York, fresh from Havana, in January of 1949, the city was covered in two feet of snow. Flying out of Havana on a Pan Am Clipper to Miami for $39.18, they then took the Florida Special north. In Baltimore they began to encounter snow, and while passing through a station in northern Maryland, they came across a water tower that had burst and blossomed into an orchid-shaped, many-petaled cascade of ice. Pablo met them at Pennsylvania Station, and, *hombre,* the brothers in their thin-soled shoes and cheap Sears, Roebuck overcoats were chilled to the bone. On the streets, people and cars seemed to disappear in the snowy winds like shredding phantoms. (They dissolved in a snow that wasn't anything like the snow they'd seen in the movies in Havana, nothing like Bing Crosby's angelic "I'm Dreaming of a White Christmas" snow, or the snow they'd imagined in dreams, lukewarm like the fake frost on a movie house *Air-Conditioned* sign.) Their thin-soled Cuban shoes soaked through, and when they stomped their feet in Pablo's lobby, they could smell the fumes of gas and electric heaters in the halls.

Pablo and his family lived at 500 La Salle, west of 124th Street and Broadway, in uptown Manhattan. It was a six-story tenement, constructed around the turn of the century to house the servant class, and it had a simple stoop with black curlicue railings, a narrow doorway framed in a crenellated brick archway. Above this rose six floors of black wrought-iron fire escapes and lamplit Venetian-blinded windows. It was two minutes from the 125th Street El, an overnight train ride and forty-five-minute flight from Havana, and five minutes from Harlem, the heartland of syncopating rhythm, as they used to say in those days. From its roof you could see the Hudson River and the domed and pillared mausoleum that was Grant's Tomb toward the northern edge of Riverside Park at 122nd Street and all the way over to the docks, and the lines of commuters and cars waiting to board the ferryboats for New Jersey.

That same night, Pablo's wife cooked them a great feast, and because it had been snowing and their feet were cold, she washed their numb toes in a pan of hot water. She was a practical and kindhearted woman from Oriente, for whom marriage and child-bearing were the great events in her life. She lived to take care of the men in that house, slaved washing their clothes, cleaning the house, cooking, and attending to the children. Those first cold days, the future Mambo King spent most of his time in the kitchen drinking beer and watching her prepare big pots of stew and rice and beans and fried *plátanos*. Frying up steaks and pork chops and long strings of sausages that Pablito would bring home from his foreman's job at the meat plant. The smoke would escape out the windows, and neighbors, like their landlady, Mrs. Shannon, would shake their heads. Pablo's wife would cook breakfast, fried *chorizos* and eggs, and then iron their clothes. She sighed a lot, but immediately after sighing, she smiled, a statement of fortitude; her plump, dimpled face highlighted by long, long eyelashes whose shadows were like the hands of a clock. That was what she was like, a clock, marking her day with her chores, her sighs punctuating the hours.

"A family and love," he heard again. "That's what makes a man happy, not just playing the mambo."

And in those days Pablo would drive them around in his Oldsmobile to see the sights, or the brothers would ride the subway all over the four boroughs, faces pressed against the windows, as if counting the pillars and flashing lights for fun. Cesar favored amusement parks, circuses, movie houses, burlesques, and baseball games, while Nestor, a more quiet, docile, and tormented man, enjoyed nature and liked going to the places that Pablo's children loved the most. He liked to take the children to the Museum of Natural History, where he would revel in walking among the remains of so many reptiles, mammals, birds, fish, insects which had once vibrated, shimmered, crawled, flown, swum through the world and which were now preserved in row after row of glass cases. On one of those days, he, Cesar, Pablo, and the kids posed proudly for a photograph before the looming skeleton of Tyrannosaurus Rex. Afterwards they walked over to Central Park, the brothers strolling together as they used to down in Havana. Back then it was tranquil and clean. Old ladies sunned themselves everywhere and young men snuggled in the grass with their girls. Picnicking on the green, they ate thick steak heroes and drank Coca-Colas, enjoying the sunshine as they watched boats float across the lake. Best was the Bronx Zoo in springtime, with its lions prowling in their dens, the buffalo with their great horns and downy fur foaming like whitewater beneath their chins, long-necked giraffes whose heads curiously peeked high into the skirts of trees. Beautiful days, beyond all pain, all suffering.

At this time in New York there was a bit of malevolent prejudice in the air, postwar xenophobia, and budding juvenile delinquency on the streets. (And now? Years later? A few of the Irish old-timers stubbornly hanging on can't believe what happened on their street, the sidewalks jammed now with dominoes, shell games, card players, and radios and fruit-ice wagons, those old fellows wandering about furtively like ghosts.) Cesar would remember being shushed on the street for speaking to Nestor in Spanish, having eggs thrown at him from a rooftop as he marched up the hill to Pablito's in a flamingo-pink suit. They learned which streets to avoid, and not to go walking along the docks at night. And while they found this part of life in New York depressing at first, they took solace in the warmth of Pablo's household: the music of Pablo's record player, the aroma of cooking plantains, the affection and kisses from Pablo's wife and his three children made them happier.

That was the way it happened with most Cubans coming to the States then, when every Cuban knew every Cuban. Apartments filled with travelers or cousins or friends from Cuba —just the way it always happened on the *I Love Lucy* show when Cubans came to visit Ricky in New York, *de visita,* turning up at the door, hat in hand, heads bowed demurely, with expressions of gratitude and friendliness. Cubans who played the castanets, shook the maracas, danced the flamenco, juggled bones, who trained animals and sang, the men of moderate height with wide-open expressions, the women buxom and small, so quiet, so grateful for the hospitality.

Sleeping on cots in the living room, the brothers were chilled on some nights by the Hudson River wind seeping in through the loose windowpanes, alarmed by the clang, clang of the fire trucks down the street, startled (at first) when the ground shook and the building rattled with the arrivals and departures of the 125th Street El trains. In the winter they shivered, but in the spring they were serenaded by a band of strolling Italian minstrels —mandolin, violin, guitar, and singer. On Sunday afternoons, they searched the radio dials for nice music and listened to Machito's "Live from the El Flamingo Nightclub" broadcasts on WHN, the brothers happy whenever the percussionist bandleader would say a few words of Spanish between numbers: "And this is a little number for my *compadres* out there . . ." Leaning out the window, they watched the scissors man in his heavy black coat, bent back and grizzled face, limping up the street with a grindstone slung over his shoulders and ringing a bell. They bought buckets of ice for their drinks from the ice man, who drove a small black truck. They watched the junk man in his horse-drawn wagon. They were warmed by the coal that came rushing down a chute into the basement, barked at by wild herds of street hounds, and blessed by the priest of the red-doored Catholic church.

When they weren't out sightseeing or visiting friends, the two brothers wore sleeveless T-shirts and sat in the kitchen studying to improve their English. They read something called *A Better English Grammar for Foreign Speakers,* Captain Marvel and Tiger Boy comics, the *Daily News,* the Brooklyn *Herald,* the racetrack "blue" sheets, and the golden-spined storybooks about enchanted swans and whorl-eyed trees in the Black Forest that Pablo's kids would bring home from the parochial school. Even though the brothers already knew how to speak a polite if rudimentary English that they'd learned while working as busboys and waiters in the Havana chapter of the Explorers' Club on old Neptuno Street ("Yes sir, no sir. Please don't call me Pancho, sir"), the twisted hard consonants and terse vowels of the English language never fell on their ears like music. At dinner, the table piled high with platters of steaks and chops, *plátanos* and *yuca,* Cesar would talk about walking on the street and hearing a constant *ruido*—a noise—the whirling, garbled English language, spoken in Jewish, Irish, German, Polish, Italian, Spanish accents, complicated and unmelodic to his ear. He had a thick accent, rolled his rrrrrrs, said "jo-jo" instead of "yo-yo" and "tink," not "think"—just like Ricky Ricardo—but got along well enough to charm the American women he met here and there, and to sit out on the fire escape in the good weather, strumming a guitar, crooning out in English "In the Still of the Night." And he could walk down the street to the liquor store and say, "One Bacardi's dark, please . . ." And then, after a time, with bravado, saying to the proprietor, "How the hell are you, my friend?"

He was proud of himself, as in those days it was a mark of sophistication among the Cubans of New York to speak English. At the parties they attended, given by Cubans all over the city, the better one's English, the higher his status. Conversing rapidly in Spanish, Cesar would offer proof of his linguistic facility by throwing in a phrase like "hep cats at a jam session." Now and then he fell in with a Greenwich Village crowd—American girls with bohemian spirits who would turn up at the Palladium or the Palm Nightclub; wild va-va-voom types who did not wear brassieres underneath their zebra-patterned party dresses. Meeting them on the dance floor, the Mambo King impressed them with his moves and Latin-lover mystique, and retired with them to their Village pads (with bathtubs in the kitchen) where they smoked reefers (he would feel a sugarcane field sprouting in his head), listened to bebop, and made out on dog-haired carpets and atop spring-worn couches. He picked up the words "jive" and "crazy!" (as in "Crazy, man, give me some skin!"), and with avuncular sexist tenderness lent them money and took them out to eat. In the period when he briefly went to work at the Tidy Print lithography plant on Chambers Street, to earn some extra money to buy a car, he would spend his lunch hours with this Jewish kid from Brooklyn, Bernardito Mandelbaum, teaching him Spanish. In the course of this he learned a few Yiddishisms. They'd trade words: *schlep* (dope), *schmuck* (fool), *schnook* (ignoramus), *schlemiel* (wastrel, fool), for *bobo* (dope), *vago* (lazy lout), *maricón* (fairy), and *pendejo* (ball-busting predatory louse). At some of these parties, where only English was spoken, he was famous for impressing even the driest Cuban professors with the exuberant variety of his speech. And he was a good listener, too, passing entire evenings with his hand on his chin, nodding and repeating, "Ah, yes?" and later, on his way home with Nestor, reciting the new words he had learned like a poem.

In the cane suitcases they'd brought with them from Cuba were bundles of paper on which they'd written down many of their ideas for songs. These mostly had to do with little bits out of their lives. Finding romance and country-bumpkin living funny, Cesar wrote unrestrained lyrics that tended toward obscenities, the change of a word for a laugh *("Bésame Mucho"* to *"Bésame Culo")*. Hangovers often inspired him: in the days when he and Nestor slept on cots in Pablo's living room, he would wake up after an epic night out in dance halls and supper clubs, with his skin and hair smelling of tobacco, perfume, and booze, inspiration would strike him, and the Mambo King would drag himself out of bed, take hold of his orangewood Brazilian guitar, strum chords, and with one slippered foot atop the radiator, and head pounding with ironies and pain, write a song.

He wrote the 1950 ballad "Alcohol" on a morning after he woke up on the living-room couch with a balled-up pair of nylons in his jacket pocket and a bitten-up lip, feeling as if he had a large heavy-winged blackbird inside his head. Inspired, he picked up the guitar, whistled a melody, made up some lyrics, putting together a rudimentary version of the song that the Mambo Kings would record in 1952, the lyric asking, *"Alcohol, why have you wrested away my soul?"*

Other compositions came to him in the same effortless manner, songs written to take the listeners back to the plazas of small towns in Cuba, to Havana, to past moments of courtship and love, passion, and a way of life that was fading from existence.

His (and Nestor's) songs were more or less typical of the songwriting of that day: ballads, boleros, and an infinite variety of fast dance numbers *(son montunos, guarachas, merengues, guaracha mambos, son pregones)*. The compositions capturing moments of youthful cockiness ("A thousand women have I continually satisfied, because I am an amorous man!"). Songs about flirtation, magic, blushing brides, cheating husbands, cuckolds and the cuckolded, flirtatious beauties, humiliation. Happy, sad, fast, and slow.

And there were songs about torment beyond all sorrow.

That was Nestor's specialty. While Cesar knocked his songs out, Nestor worked and reworked the same compositions over and over again. Loving the torture of composition, he would spend hours hunched over a notebook with a guitar or his trumpet, trying to compose a ballad, one beautiful song. Rafael Hernández had done it with *"El Lamento,"* Moisés Simón with "The Peanut Vendor," Eliseo Grenet with *"La Última Rumba."* And in those days, his heart filled with an unbearable pain, he was writing the song they would perform on television, that mournful tune that would bring them closest to fame, *"Bella María de Mi Alma,"* "Beautiful María of My Soul," a song which in its early stages consisted of only a few pitiful utterances: "María . . . my love . . . María . . . my soul"—words contained in a thorny cage built around three chords, A minor, D minor, and E7th, a song that he would strum so often and sing with such a melancholic tone in his voice that even the bemused Cesar Castillo would say, incredulously, "What a horror! If I hear about María one more time, I'm going to throw your guitar out the window."

Then: "Why don't you forget about the song and come out with me? Come on, bro', I'm nearly ten years older than you . . . and I don't want to stay home . . ."

"No, leave without me."

Slick and godlike, Cesar Castillo would shake his head and go out the door, disappear up the kiosked stairway with the pagoda roof and smoked-glass windows, to catch the subway downtown. Late on those nights, when he had no diversions, Nestor would think about the past from which there was no escape. His insides twisted into shit, the weight of his skull crushing the pillow, sheets entangled around him, a thick blue wormy vein boring across the brow of his melancholic head. Some nights he heard every sound in the alley: the cats skulking around in the dark basement doorways, the wind dashing television antenna wires against the walls, coffee cups, plates, and utensils being washed, low voices murmuring in the kitchen, bed noises, someone belching, the Jack Benny show on the neighbors' television, and, mocking him, the frantic breathing of a neighbor across the way, the immense, floppy-breasted, freckle-bottomed Irish girl,

Fiona, whom he'd often see through her window, making love and screaming at the top of her lungs in ecstasy.

On those nights, Nestor went to bed hoping for beautiful dreams about gardens and the early-morning sunlight which he associated with love, but walked instead down a long dark hallway of misfortune into a room of tortures where Beautiful María of His Soul, naked and desirable, placed him on a rack and turned a great wheel whose ropes began to tear out his limbs and debone his member. He would wake with his heart beating as if it would burst and with shadows swirling against the walls. Worked up in this way, he would sit by the side of the bed, his body sweaty, and light a cigarette, wishing he had gone out with his older brother.

And what would happen then?

The phone would ring and he'd answer it, hearing something like this:

"Hey, brother, know we have to go to work tomorrow, but why don't you get dressed and come down here right away. I'm down at the El Morocco and my friend Eddie here is going to be throwing a little party soon, with lots of nice little girls" —and in the background the delighted squeals of women and the music of a twenty-piece orchestra tearing up the joint.

Nestor answered in his quiet manner, "Yes, give me an hour," and, despite his practical and introspective nature, got dressed and went to the club.

Always the more somber and silent of the brothers, he was the big-eared fellow who would have to throw down five drinks before loosening up and showing the world a toothy grin. A woman pressing against him, in a crowd of happy partyers around a champagne-glass-covered table, her breast soft through the silk of her dress, didn't have a chance with him. It didn't matter if she was sweet, affectionate, sexually voracious, and pretty; he always seemed somewhere else. A few drinks would fill his face with shadows; in the men's-room mirror, those shadows would ebb and flow over his features like caressing female hands. When he had first arrived in the States, every woman he looked at had seemed as lifeless as a doll. He could not look at another woman, and the only way he overcame this unbearable pain was by daydreaming about María: Would she suddenly write him the most adoring letter? Would she turn up on the next airplane, a little bag packed with her frilly underthings? Would she weep unabashedly over the telephone, begging his forgiveness?

Cesar, despite his shortcomings, always thought this: Don't be an idiot, forget about her! But Nestor couldn't. He relived their life over again so often that he sometimes had the sensation of being buried by the past, as if the details of this shattered love (and the other sadnesses of his life) had been turned into stone, weeds, and dirt and thrown over him.

He even took his dreams about María to the meat factory where Pablo had gotten him a job, working over a vat in which the bones and viscera of certain animals were crushed and ground up for making hot dogs and sausage fillers. The blades churned and he would pass the time staring at the whipping entrails —intestines, stomachs, backbones, brains—as if at a sunny garden. The crush of bones, the whirring of machines, memories, music, and his dreams of María. The plant was in a long, flat warehouse alongside the river, with huge metal doors that opened for deliveries and pickups by freezer trucks. He'd work there from seven in the morning until four in the afternoon, spending those hours at the vat whistling to himself and trying to improvise a song about María. What did he seek to accomplish? To write a song communicating such pure love and desire that María, far away, would magically reinstate him into the center of her heart. He thought that she would "hear" these melodies in her dreams and that something would possess her: she would sit down and write him a letter begging his forgiveness, a letter admitting to confusion and foolishness, that one day she would leave her husband—if he was her husband—and he would hear a knocking at the door, make his way down the hall, the panting hound behind him, and find María of his soul standing there, this woman who had somehow become the lost key to happiness.

But as many letters as he wrote her, she never answered him. As many gifts as he sent her, he never received as much as a thank-you. For more than two years, not a day went by that he did not think about flying down to Havana to see her. It was hopeless, he felt his heart drawing in, constricting. He didn't talk about María of Havana, but he passed most of his days thinking about her.

He'd carry around a little photograph of her in a cinch-waisted bathing suit, his María rising out of the foamy tides of a Havana sea, take it out, speak to the picture as if she would hear him. After work he'd go on a solitary walk up to Grant's Tomb to check out the dead President and his wife, then head down a path into Riverside Park, where he would lean up against a stone wall and watch the sparkling ice floes on the river, imagining himself inside. Constriction in his dreams. Under the ground, in tunnels, in blocks of ice. He went over his feelings about María so often they became as mashed up as the innards in the crushing machines at the plant. The more he thought about her, the more mythic she became. Every ounce of love he'd received in his short life was captured and swallowed up by the image of María. (*Mamá,* I wanted María the way I wanted you when I was a baby feeling helpless in that bed, with welts covering my chest, and lungs stuffed with thick cotton. I couldn't breathe, *Mamá,* remember how I used to call you?)

That was Nestor the young man in the sleeveless T-shirt whose body was like a letter K in the window of the apartment on La Salle Street, one leg bent at the knee on the sill, arm up against the windowframe, smoking a cigarette like a languishing movie star waiting for a call from a studio, and humming a melody line. That was Nestor on the living-room couch, strumming a chord on the guitar, looking up, and writing in a notebook. That was Nestor's voice heard on the street at night, on La Salle, on Tiemann Place, on 124th Street and Broadway. That was Nestor down on his knees playing with the children, pushing a toy truck into a city of alphabet blocks, the children climbing on his back and riding him like a horse, while in his head there bloomed a thousand images of María: María naked, María in a sun hat, María's brown nipple filling his mouth, María with a cigarette, María commenting on the beauty of the moon, María dancing long-legged, her body wobbling in perfect rhythm in a chorus of women in feathered turbans, María counting the doves in a plaza, María sucking a pineapple *batida* through a straw, María writhing, lips damp and face red from kisses, in ecstasy, María growling like a cat, María dabbing her mouth with lipstick, María pulling up a flower . . .

That was Nestor, eyebrows arched with the scholarly concentration of a physics student, reading science-fiction comic books at the kitchen table. That was Nestor up on the rooftop stretched out on a blanket and sipping whiskey, waking up screaming at night, decked out in a white silk suit, blowing a trumpet on the stage of some dance hall, quietly attending to the drinks, filling a punch bowl during a party in the apartment, dreaming about some of those nights spent with María in Havana, her presence so strong in his memory that around three o'clock in the morning the door to the apartment would open and María would walk like a spirit into the living room and pull off her slip, sliding one knee onto the cot and then another, lowering herself so that the first thing Nestor felt moving slowly upward over his shinbone and then his knee was María's vagina. And then she would take hold of his thing and say, *"Hombre!"*

He was the man plagued with memory, the way his brother Cesar Castillo would be twenty-five years later, the man with the delusion that the composition of a song about María would bring her back. He was the man who wrote twenty-two different versions of *"Bella María de Mi Alma,"* first as "The Sadness of Love," then "María of My Life," before arriving, with the help of his older brother, Cesar, upon the version they would be singing one night in 1955 in the Mambo Nine Club, "Beautiful María of My Soul," a song of love, that night when they drew the attention and interest of their fellow Cuban Desi Arnaz.

S PENDING LATE NIGHTS OUT, they'd find themselves climbing the stairs to their cousin Pablo's fourth-floor apartment on La Salle Street at five in the morning. Rooftops burning red, and black birds circling the water towers. Cesar was thirty-one years old then and out to have a good time, preferring to look forward and never back into his past: he'd left a kid, a daughter, behind in Cuba. Sometimes he had pangs for his daughter, sometimes felt bad that things didn't work out with his former wife, but he remained determined to have a good time, chase women, drink, eat, and make friends. He wasn't cold-hearted: he had moments of tenderness that surprised him toward the women he went out with, as if he wanted truly to fall in love, and even tender thoughts about his former wife. He had other moments when he didn't care. Marriage? Never again, he'd tell himself, even though he'd lie through his teeth about wanting to get married to women he was trying to seduce. Marriage? What for?

He heard a lot about "a family and love" from Pablo's plump little wife. "That's what makes a man happy, not just playing the mambo," she'd say.

He had moments when he thought about his wife, a hole of sadness through his heart, but it was nothing that a drink, a woman, a cha-cha-cha wouldn't fix. He had hooked up with her a long time ago because of Julián García, a well-known bandleader in Oriente Province. He was just a young upstart from Las Piñas then, a singer and trumpet player with a wandering troupe of *guajiro* musicians who would play in the small-town plazas and dance halls of Camagüey and Oriente Provinces. Sixteen years old, he fled to the dance halls, had a good time meeting and entertaining the people of small towns and bedding down poor country girls where he could find them. He was a handsome and exuberant singer, with an unpolished style and a tendency toward operatic flourishes that would take him off-key.

These musicians never made any money, but one day when they were playing at a dance in a small town called Jiguaní, his youthful exuberance and looks had impressed someone in the crowd who passed his name to Julián García. At the time he was looking for a new crooner and wrote a letter simply addressed "Cesar Castillo, Las Piñas, Oriente." Cesar was nineteen then, and not yet jaded. He took the invitation to heart and made the journey down to Santiago the week after he'd received it.

He'd always remember the steep hills of Santiago de Cuba, a city reminiscent in its hilliness, he would think years later, of San Francisco, California. Julián lived in an apartment over a dance hall which he owned. The sun radiating against the cobblestone streets and cool doorways from which one could smell the afternoon lunches and hear the comforting sounds of families dining at their tables. Brooms sweeping out a hallway, salamanders skulking along the arabesque tiles. García's dance hall was a refuge of shady arcades and a long, cool inner hallway. The place was deserted except for García, who sat in the middle of a colonnaded dance floor tinkling at the piano, stout, sweaty, and with a head damp with running hair dye.

"I'm Cesar Castillo, and you told me to come and sing for you one day."

"Yes, yes."

For his audition he opened with Ernesto Lecuona's *"María la O."*

Nervous about performing for Julián García, Cesar sang his heart out in a flamboyant style, using extended high notes and long, slow phrasing, arms flailing dramatically. When he'd finished, Julián nodded encouragingly and kept him there, singing, until ten o'clock that night.

"You come back here tomorrow. The other musicians will be here, okay?"

And in a friendly, paternal manner, his hand on Cesar's shoulder, Julián led him out of the hall.

Cesar had a few dollars in his pocket. He was planning to wander around the harbor and have some fun, fall asleep on one of the piers by the ocean, as he had so many times before, arms thrown over his face, in fields in the countryside, in the plazas, on church steps. He was so used to looking out for himself that it surprised him to hear García ask, "And do you have a place to sleep tonight?"

"No." And he shrugged.

"Bueno, you can stay with me upstairs. Huh? I should have told you that in the letter."

Remaining that night, the future Mambo King basked in Julián's kindness. High on that hill and overlooking the harbor, that apartment was a pleasant change for him. He had his own room, which opened up to a balcony, and all the food he could eat. That was the order of the household: all of García's family, his wife and four sons, lived for their evening meals. His sons, who performed with him, were immense, overfed, with cheerful, angelic dispositions. That was because Julián was so loving, an affectionate man who even challenged Cesar's macho resolve to need or want no one.

He began to sing with Julián's outfit, a twenty-piece orchestra, in 1937. They had a pleasant "tropical" sound, depending heavily on violins and sonorous flutes, and their rhythm section dragged as in the style of fox-trotters of the twenties, and Julián, who conducted and played the piano, had a penchant for dream-like orchestrations, clouds of music that seemed to float upward on waves of tremolo-choked piano. The Mambo King would have one photograph of that orchestra—and this sat in that envelope in the Hotel Splendour—of himself in a formal black suit, wearing white gloves, sitting in a row with the others. Behind them, a backdrop of Havana Harbor and El Morro Castle, flanked by pedestals on which Julián had placed small statues of antique themes—a wingèd victory and a bust of Julius Caesar, and large ostrich-plume-filled vases. What was that look on Cesar's face? With his black hair combed back and parted in the middle, he was pleasantly smiling, in commemoration of that happy time in his life.

Julián's orchestra packed dance halls all over Oriente and Camagüey. He had conservative tastes, never playing original compositions but relying on the songs of the popular Cuban composers of the day: Eduardo Sánchez de Fuentes, Manuel Luna, Moisés Simón, Miguel Matamoros, Eliseo Grenet, Lecuona. He was the warmest human being Cesar Castillo would ever meet in his life. That portly orchestra leader exuded pure love for his fellowman—"A family and love, that's what makes a man happy"—and showed this affection to his musicians. That was a time when the Mambo King was close to becoming a different kind of human being.

Cesar never let go of his liking for women. He maintained his king-cock strut and manly arrogance, but around Julián and his family, he felt so peaceful that he calmed down. And it showed in his singing. He gained more control, became more lilting, and developed an affectionate tone in his songs, which people liked and responded to. He had not yet found a way of transforming that into the world-weariness of his records in the mid-fifties. (And if you heard the wrecked voice of Cesar in 1978 and compared it to the golden-toned voice of the 1930s and 1940s, you would have a hard time believing they came from the same singer.) They played all over the provinces in towns with names like Bayamo, Jobabo, Minas, Morón, Miranda, Yara, El Cobre, and in the larger cities of Camagüey, Holguín, and Santiago. They traveled in three trucks and they would make their way down dirt roads, struggling through the brush and forests of the countryside, and into the mountains. They played for *campesinos,* soldiers, bureaucrats, businessmen. They played for people who lived in houses with palm-thatch roofs, for those who lived in grand-style Spanish villas, and in the plantations and sugar mills, and in beautiful citrus groves, for the Americans who had constructed New England frame clapboard houses, with little back gardens and front porches. They played in towns without modern plumbing or electricity where people hardly knew the name of Hitler, in countryside so dark that the stars were a veil of light and where the thready luminescence of spirits moved through the streets and over walls at night and where the arrival of Julián's orchestra was greeted like the Second Coming of Christ, with children and dogs and crowds of teenagers following behind it, clapping and whistling wherever they went. They played weddings, baptisms, and confirmation parties, *fiestas de quince,* and *fiestas blancas,* where the participants dressed in white from head to toe. They'd perform waltzes and *danzones* for the old people, and floor-sliding tangos and steamy rumbas for the young.

Julián was a good orchestra leader and a good man. Cesar would have thought of Julián as a "second father" if the word "father" did not make him want to punch a wall. In that time, he learned much about putting together an orchestra and singing from Julián, and enjoyed the glory of performance. He used to throw himself completely into his songs and lived for the moment when the entire ballroom would be on its feet either dancing or applauding.

"Just make them feel that you care for them. You don't have to overdo it, because they know that, but let them know all the same."

While singing with Julián's orchestra the Mambo King became well known. He could walk down the street of many a small town and there would always be someone to come up to him and

say, "Aren't you Cesar Castillo the singer?" He started to acquire
a lordly bearing, though one that fell apart when it came to
chasing women. Returning to the farm in Las Piñas for his
monthly visits, he would feel as if he had come home to a haunted
house, the site of many of his fights with his father and the sadness
of his mother's weeping that filled the halls. He would return
with presents and advice and with a desire for peace that always
erupted, after a day or so, into another fight with his father, Don
Pedro, who considered musicians effeminate, doomed men. He'd
return and give Nestor music lessons, take Nestor to town. Always impressed with his brother's musicianship, he had plans to
take Nestor into Julián's orchestra when he was of age and the
family would let him leave the house.

Now he remembers and sighs: the long approach to the farm
along the riverbank and forest, the dirt road past the houses and
over the water, the sun bursting through the treetops. The
Mambo King riding on a borrowed mule, a guitar slung over his
shoulders . . .

He had been in the orchestra for four years when he attended
a weekend party at Julián's apartment in Santiago and there made
the acquaintance of his niece, Luisa García. He was the handsome
young crooner at the end of the table, reveling in the friendship
of this older man, guzzling Spanish brandy all night and feeling
light-headed enough to easily fall in love. And there she was,
Luisa. Sitting across from her during the meal, he smiled and kept
staring into her eyes, but she would turn away. Shy and thin, with
a plain face, Luisa had a large beaked nose, pretty eyes, and a
kindly expression. She liked to wear simple dresses. Although her
body was not spectacular, her skin gave off a nice scent of oils and
perfume, and when he stood beside her, filling a glass from a
punch bowl, he knew she would turn out to be a passionate lover.

She was a schoolteacher and, at twenty-six, three years older
than the Mambo King. No one in her family held out much hope
that she would get married, but that night the way Cesar kept
looking at her became a subject of family gossip. Julián could not
have been more delighted. He would call them together and
speak to them jointly. "I wanted to show you both the view from
this window. Isn't that something there, the sun's rays spreading
everywhere. *¿Qué bueno, eh?*"

Who knew what she felt? She had the downcast look of a woman who was in the habit of taking nervous sidelong glances into mirrors, a woman who was used to taking care of herself. But Cesar? Sitting at that happy table in the company of the first man who had ever really looked out for him, he felt that he wanted to be a part of that family. So he began the most dogged courtship. She'd seen the way he had looked at her cousin Vívian, his eyes looping around the curvaceousness of her rear end, and she had told herself, "No, no, no, no matter what he says to me." But she gave in to Cesar and started to take walks with him along the streets of Santiago. Always gentlemanly, he held doors open for her, and never cursed in his conversation. Around her, he would make flamboyant gestures with his hands and always dressed neatly, usually in a white linen jacket and clean trousers, and his cane hat, the brim pinched in, pulled low over his brow.

They had their picture taken in front of a movie poster advertising the Betty Grable film *Moon Over Miami.*

Sometimes he'd get her alone, the two of them sitting in a little deserted park among the flowers. Her iron resistance amused the Mambo King. She'd allow him a few kisses and embraces and one evening he unbuttoned the four left-sided pearly buttons of her blouse and got his hands inside, touching her tender breasts, but she never let him go any further, and he'd laugh out, telling her, "Don't you know, it'll happen sooner or later—even if I have to marry you!" There was something funny about this man who'd bedded down many women being foiled by this girl who used to blow air into his mouth and who'd lock her legs tight whenever his long musician's fingers prowled under her skirt, searching out her most precious "treasure." How this courtship turned into marriage, no one would be able to explain.

For a time he trusted Luisa in a way he had never trusted anyone. She was an unlikely partner for the Mambo King, especially when put next to the cheap floozies he usually preferred, but Cesar, who had been seeking peace since the days of his childhood, wanted to marry her.

Privately, in her company, shut away from the rest of the world, he was content. But as soon as he stepped out into the street he became a different man. When other women walked by, he would look, his penis would get stiff in his trousers, and Luisa would know it. Quickening her pace, she would march off and leave him behind. His macho temperament never knew how to deal with this, and it would be days before loneliness and his affection for the family brought them back together again.

When he asked her to marry him, Luisa had her doubts, but fearing old-maidhood, and because Julián had sworn by Cesar, she said yes. This was in 1943 and they went to live in a small apartment in Santiago (another beautiful memory: their little home on a cobblestone street, sunny from morning until night and busy with merchants and children). When he brought her home to the family in Las Piñas, his mother, María, liked her very much, and so did Nestor: everyone, including the irascible Pedro, treated her civilly.

What happened? He did as he pleased. It took about a year for the elation of joining García's family to wear off. The Mambo King found himself sitting at these meals in García's house, day-dreaming about some of the women he had seen on the streets. He even behaved in an annoyed fashion at García's, because García had placed at his feet a woman who seemed to weep if you offended her! Because she knew well her uncle's schedule in advance, it became difficult for Cesar to disappear for two or three days at a time, and this bothered him. So he developed the excuse of returning home to Las Piñas, where he would hole up with some country girl, resentful and angry over his situation. He would return from these sojourns maintaining a silence for a week at a time. He would walk through rooms muttering phrases like "Why have I allowed myself to become a captive," and "What am I doing with my youth," in clear earshot of Luisa. For a long time she did what she could to make him feel better . . . She would beg him to come around, and he would leave the house, her question "Why are you so cruel to me?" circling his head like a summer mosquito.

One day in 1944, Luisa happily told Cesar that she was pregnant, as if the birth of a child later that year would shore up their crumbling marriage. They would turn up at Julián's house for weekly meals, and as a family they seemed content. But then one night Julián, who was not made of sawdust and had heard about and seen the way this crooner was treating his niece, called

Cesar out onto his balcony and as he looked into the distance over Santiago Bay said, "I feel very close to you, my boy, but no matter what, I expect you to treat my family with respect. And I'll tell you now, if you don't like what I'm saying, *señor,* you can walk out the door."

His sternness depressed Cesar. The man had been sick for a time with poor breathing and edema of the limbs and he was no longer playing much piano with the orchestra and preferred to conduct, halfheartedly waving a baton, from a chair. The man could hardly walk across a room (as the Mambo King could not now). It was as if Julián's huge weight had crushed his lungs, his breathing was labored and he had trouble moving. And so the future Mambo King blamed Julián's ill health for his temper.

"What you hear isn't true, Julián. I love Luisa with all my heart, I would never want things to go badly for her."

Julián rapped him on the shoulder and hugged him in his friendly way and his anger seemed to subside. This brush with him turned the Mambo King into a better husband for a time and he and Luisa passed through a period of happiness that revolved around a picture of future domestic bliss, with Cesar as dutiful bandleader-crooner-husband, and his wife and child(ren) waiting happily and lovingly at home for him. Yet, when he conceived of this tranquil scene, he saw himself pushing open the door of that house with a hard kick, the way his Papi used to; he saw himself shouting and angry and slapping his child's face as he had been slapped, saw himself pacing in circles and cursing everyone around him, as did his father. He had thought that marrying into Julián's family would inspire a mundane, normal happiness in him, but now he found himself regretting the whole business again. Not because he didn't love Luisa, but because he felt that abuse and discontent boiled in his blood and he did not want to hurt her . . .

And the pregnancy which made the act of love a too-delicate operation also troubled him. (Here he remembers the first time he made love to her. Her skin was white and her hips bony and her triangle of pubic hair wet at its center because of all their kisses. He was not a heavy man then, but he was twice as thick as she and he undid her virginity in one spurting thrust which led, through the succession of days, to many other thrusts: they did it so much her hipbones and buttocks were covered with black-and-blue marks and his thing, which never failed to rise, finally fainted dead away at three o'clock one Sunday afternoon, due to heat and exhaustion. But when he was in love with her, he loved the Luisa who was the key to her Uncle Julián García, the thin, pensive Luisa who was there for his pleasure and who never expected anything from him.) He found himself restless, spending many nights with the whores of those small towns. Luisa knew, she could smell these women on his skin, in his hair, she could tell by the sated sleepiness and the blueness that ringed his eyes.

"Why are you so cruel to me?" she'd ask him again and again.

(And this cruelty, I didn't want things to be that way, I was just being a man and doing as I saw fit, Luisa, but you didn't know, didn't know my restlessness and my disbelief in such simple things as a tranquil married life, you couldn't see how it all struck me as a final trick, that enslavement and humiliation perhaps awaited me. The situation was already turning your Uncle Julián away from me, he'd used to look at me with pure love. So I was led around by my penis, so what? What did a few laughs, a few fucks with women I'd never see again, have to do with anything, especially our love? Why did you have to take it so badly? Why did you have to weep and then shout at me?)

That was when he really started to drink. One night he drank enough rum at Julián's to feel as if he were floating down a river. When he stumbled out of the house, two of his fellow musicians were sent out to help him down the stairs. Of course, he pushed them away, repeating, "I don't need anybody," and slipped down two flights, conking his head.

He woke to an idea: going to Havana.

Away, away, away from all this was how Cesar saw it. He had many reasons for moving to Havana: that was the place to be in Cuba if you were a musician. But he also believed that he could resolve things with Luisa in Havana, and at the same time, away from her family, he could do as he pleased. Besides, he was twenty-seven years old and wanted to work in an orchestra where he might perform some original songs. He and Nestor had been writing boleros and ballads for a long time and had never performed them with Julián García. In Havana, they might be able to put something together. What else could he do, remain with Julián and play the same dance halls for the rest of his life?

In any case, things with Julián's orchestra had changed. Julián was so ill that he spent most of his days in bed. One of his sons, Rudolfo, took over as orchestra leader and wanted to teach Cesar a lesson in humility for treating his cousin so badly, relegating him to the trumpet section, alongside his brother Nestor, who had recently joined the band. This lesson just intensified his resolve to leave the orchestra, and in 1945 he took his wife and baby to Havana.

They had been in Havana for two months, living in a *solar* in the inexpensive section of La Marina, when word came that García had died. With Julián gone, the Mambo King felt like a prince who had abruptly come out from under a spell. By the time they returned with their baby from Oriente after the funeral, he had no stomach left for the matrimonial bond. (Now you must see him at a party in Manhattan circa 1949 with his right hand slung across his heart, the other held up high as if doing the Pledge of Allegiance to the flag, sweat pouring off his forehead, hips shaking, a drink in hand, happy, happy.)

Though they lived in a cheerful and noisy *solar*, their cramped two-room apartment was a somber place. He'd gotten work for a time as a pit musician in a big movie house, backing up the singers and comedians who would entertain the audiences between films; loaded crates in the market; and then, through a new acquaintance, got himself—and his brother Nestor, who had come out to join him—jobs as busboy and waiter over at the Havana chapter of the Explorers' Club. With people on the streets, and friends in the cafés and bars and dance halls, he was a cheerful man, but when it came to his wife he'd spend hours without saying a word to her, and when she crossed a room, he didn't notice. She had become this invisibility who sometimes shared his bed and who'd carry his daughter in her arms across the room, to sit in a square of sunlight.

In those months he completely gave in to a family affliction: every other woman walking the streets of Havana seemed infinitely, painfully more beautiful and desirable than his own wife. He'd come home at night, get dressed up, and head out to the dance halls, a dandy in a black-brimmed cane hat. He pretended not to hear her calling out, "Please, why don't you stay home with me?" Pretended not to hear her "Please don't go."

He found himself whistling at the girls walking on the promenade of the Prado; he was the slick macho with hat tilted low over his brow, out on the sidewalk in front of the El Dandy clothing shore, giving the up-and-down to women; he was the crooning guitarist, eyebrows cocked high, serenading the pretty tourists on their way into the Hotel Nacional, the T-shirted man in plaid bathing trunks, skulking along the balconies of the hotel and heading clandestinely for a stairway the fuck out of there, the fellow writhing on a sun-baked bed on a Tuesday afternoon in a room facing the sea.

After a while, he simply pretended that he had never been married: he kept his thin wedding band tucked away in a cane suitcase among the sheets of paper on which he'd written down his ideas for songs with names like "Ingratitude," "Deceitful Heart," "A Tropical Romance." Occasionally he grew nostalgic for that time of happiness when he had gotten close to Julián and his family, when he had fallen in love with Luisa, and then he would settle down again and they would be happy for weeks. But things went in cycles with him. The baby made it really difficult. He would storm around saying, "If it wasn't for the kid, I'd be a free man." He horrified his wife, who kept trying to make him happy. This went on for six months, then he finally pushed her too far.

He was in a fruit market down the street from where he lived, a market crowded with wagons and stands, ice sellers and coffee vendors, fish and poultry sellers, wandering among the tubers and thick plantains, when he noticed a woman, no prettier than most women, but exuding, in his opinion, a rampant sensuality. She wore a wedding ring. She looked bored. Perhaps her husband no longer made love to her at night, or perhaps he was an effeminate man who could hardly get it up, or perhaps he liked to abuse her at night, squeezing her breasts until they turned black and blue. Circling around the arcade, Cesar followed this woman, who avoided him coyly, as if they were playing a game, disappearing among the columns.

He would turn up at her *solar* in the afternoons when her

husband was working. He couldn't remember her name, but in the Hotel Splendour the Mambo King remembered how she would get all violent during the act of love and had the bad habit of yanking hard on his quivering testicles at the moment of his climax, so hard he would have pain for days. The sordidness of all this turned his stomach years later, but back then he took this woman for granted, in the same way that he took his wife and all women for granted. One day it caught up with him. When he'd gotten tired of this woman and moved on, she turned up at the *solar* one afternoon and told Luisa about her affair with Cesar. (And did she describe the tattoo of an angel over the nipple on the right side of his chest, did she describe the burn scar on his right arm, the birthmark in the shape of a horn on his back, or his thing that used to creep up a hand's width above his belly button?) By the time he came home that night, Luisa had left the apartment.

He found a letter saying that his abuse had driven her away. The family was waiting for her, she would manage better by herself with his child than with a man who did not appreciate the truly good things in his life, who spent his life chasing after tramps.

Hearing the word "cruel, cruel, cruel" in his sleep, he had a dream in which he was walking up that hill and meeting Julián García again for the first time. Then he started all over again with Luisa and for a time his pain and sorrow went away. He wrote her a letter begging her forgiveness, and she wrote back saying that she might forgive him if he returned to Oriente to talk things over with her. He felt relieved that she still cared for him but in the end declared in his macho manner, "No woman runs my life." He believed that since she had left him, it was her duty to return. He spent a few months waiting, thinking that the door to the *solar* would open and that she would walk in. It never happened. He couldn't understand her problems with him. Couldn't she see that he was handsome and she was plain? Couldn't she see that he was still a young man and wanted to have his way with other women? And how did she have the right to deprive his baby of her father? Hadn't she watched him with Mariela? Seen how the baby cooed and fell happily asleep in his arms . . . Hadn't he told her about the rough circumstances of his upbringing?

(You didn't believe me, that for me as a kid it was a slap in the face and a kick in the *fondillo* in the name of my father, who did as he pleased and shoved it up my ass.)

At first he spent many a night missing her, a humiliating pain gnawed inside him, a pain that said life was sad. If only she had known what it was to be a handsome *caballero* with a nice singing voice and a bestial thing between his legs and youth burning in his veins, wouldn't she have known better?

"If she turns up at my door, then we'll see."

But living in Havana without her got him into a really bad way—many a night found him charging madly and drunkenly down the streets of La Marina.

"My little daughter, my precious little daughter, Mariela."

Sip of whiskey.

"Mariela . . ."

Then he softened and backed down from his stubborn stance, given the distance of time and nostalgia. He had speeches all prepared. He would go back to Oriente and sweet-talk her. "I have no excuses . . . I don't know what it is. I've always been alone. You know my father, he was *un bruto* with my mother, I never learned any other way."

He decided to return to Oriente to reclaim his daughter, and showed up at the house of Luisa's parents, where she had been staying, pounding the door with a shoe and demanding that he be shown the proper respect.

"Only if you behave in a civil manner," he was told.

He expected to find her in bad shape, pale and gaunt. But she seemed happier, and that bothered him, made him angry. "She couldn't have loved me very much" is what he came to think. They sat facing each other in the parlor of the house, the family skulking in nearby rooms. The formality of the situation startled him. They spoke like old, passing acquaintances rather than a husband and wife of nearly three years. He had searched his mind for the right words that would break her down, force her to accept his actions. He refused to admit to any wrongdoing, refused to concede that he had treated her badly. He said that his letters had already confessed to his sins. Why should he be humiliated again? Despite the fact that he was the budding composer of beautiful romantic boleros that exposed the sweetest sentiments, he felt at a loss for the proper words. It was the one time in his life, he would tell himself years later, when he had truly lost his composure and suffered dearly for it. After demanding that she return to him, he had been told by his wife, Luisa, in a calm and delicately toned voice, "Only if you behave like a decent gentleman, then I'll accompany you."

For two months they lived under the same roof in Havana. But, in that city with its exciting night life, he grew restless, and this restlessness took him back to the women he had here and there. He loved his daughter, never went out without bringing her a little gift, a doll, a bag of candies, a little hand mirror, anything he'd happen to see in the marketplace that she might like. He'd cover her face with kisses and rock her on his lap by the window overlooking the street. These moments of real tenderness sometimes inspired reconciliations, but as soon as Cesar spent any time with his wife, their struggles began again. By the end of those two months she was looking worn and exhausted, and he was impatient for solutions.

He moved out of their *solar,* and stayed with Nestor, who had gotten his own little place, seeing his wife only once a week, when he would faithfully give her half his pay from the Explorers' Club and the band in which they played. It wasn't that he didn't care: when he saw her, he was polite and almost conciliatory. It was she who told him, "Never again." He would bounce his daughter on his knees, carry her around the room, planting kisses on her face. For a time, he would meet other women and speak sadly of the loss of his little daughter. They divorced, through her family's connections, and she ended up marrying someone else, from Havana.

Now as he sat in the Hotel Splendour his life with Luisa fluttered like a black moth through his heart. He felt a great sadness, recalling how in his youth he had never believed that love really existed—for him. But back then, while living in Havana and later strumming a guitar in Pablo's living room in New York, he just told himself, "That's life," dismissing his sadness and bringing down a macho wall between himself and his feelings.

Snap of the fingers, just like that.

Toward the end, she had told him, "For someone who sings so many songs of love, you are cruel."

"My little daughter, my precious loving daughter . . . Mariela."

Sip of whiskey.

"Mariela . . . Luisa . . ."

At least he got a song out of it, he thought now—"Solitude of My Heart," a bolero from 1949.

ONE DAY IN 1950, A YOUNG, pretty Latin woman was standing by a bus stop on 62nd Street and Madison Avenue. She was about twenty-one and wearing a raincoat and white tennis shoes. By her side, a shopping bag filled with soap, rags, a work dress, scarf, and duster. She was carefully reading a book, her lips barely moving, but moving just the same. She had been waiting for about fifteen minutes when she looked over and noticed the young, well-dressed man with a black instrument case by his side. He was watching the street for a bus and whistling to himself. He had quite a pensive manner, and even though he looked at her, and nodded politely, he seemed to be concentrating on the whistling of the tune, his brows creasing in creative fervor. She liked that, and even though she knew where the bus went, she said to him in Spanish, "Excuse me, does this bus go up to 125th Street?"

"Yes, this is the stop for that bus. It goes all the way up."

They stood for a few minutes in silence, and then he asked her, "Are you Cuban? *¿Tú eres cubana?*"

"Oh, yes, I am."

"I knew it." He looked her over, gave her a nice up-and-down.

"What do you do? Working?"

"Yes, I clean house for a rich man. He's so rich he's unhappy. You?"

"I'm a musician."

"Ahhhh, I can tell just by looking at you that you're a good musician. Have you had much luck?"

"Well, I have a little *conjunto* with my brother, my older brother. He's the real singer in the family, but sometimes I do a few songs myself. We're trying to get along, but it's difficult. I mean, I have to work days in a warehouse."

"I can tell that you'll succeed at whatever you want."

"Everybody says that, but who knows. What's your name?"

"Delores Fuentes. And yours?"

"Nestor Castillo."

She was so used to being around men who were happy and aggressive, and here was this musician, quiet, polite, and a little gloomy.

They rode up Madison Avenue together, sitting next to each other. He was jotting down the lyrics of a song on a piece of paper, and from time to time he'd whistle part of a melody, look out the window at the gray buildings, whistle again.

"Is that something you're making up?"

"Yes, a bolero."

"A love song, yes?"

"Something like that. Been working on it for a long time."

"What are you going to call it?"

" 'Beautiful María of My Soul.' Something like that."

"And this María?"

He was somewhere else, though he looked her straight in the eyes.

"Just a name. Maybe I'll write it using your name."

They both got off at 125th Street. He was going to walk west toward Broadway and up the hill to La Salle Street, where, he'd explained, he lived with his brother. And she was going to catch the number 29 bus for the Bronx. Before he left her, he'd said, "Do you like to dance?"

"Oh, yes."

"*Bueno,* we're playing this coming Friday night in Brooklyn. At a place called the Imperial Ballroom, have you heard of it? That's on East 18th Street, off Utica Avenue, Brooklyn, one of the last stops on the number 4 line. I'll write it down for you, okay?"

"Okay."

It took her another hour to get home. When she made the long trips to and from the Bronx, she preferred buses over subways. She didn't mind the long trip because she always carried a few books to read. That day she was halfway through a James M. Cain novel, *The Postman Always Rings Twice,* and she was also reading something called *A Simpler English Grammar* by a Hubert Orville which she studied diligently for her night-school English classes. She liked to read because it took her mind off her loneliness, gave her feelings of both solitude and companionship. She'd gone to work cleaning houses because she'd gotten tired of her job at the five-and-ten, a Woolworth's up on Fordham Road, mainly because the manager was giving her a hard time with pinches and casual caresses. But that was her story with just about every man on the street. It seemed they were always trying to pick her up. She had an elegant face with large, pretty, and intelligent eyes, black hair that fell over her shoulders, and a curious and introspective expression which men read as lonely. Men chased her everywhere, tried to get hold of her. GIs, businessmen, young kids, college students, professorial types who would come into that Woolworth's to buy pencils. Men trying to look down her cleavage whenever she bent over, men looking at her out of the corner of their eye while examining the quality of a fountain pen, looking into the slit of her blouse where the meat of her breasts met with the white cloth of her brassiere. Some men said, "Maybe we can go out tonight," meaning, "Maybe I can fuck you tonight."

She lived with her older sister, Ana María, who had come up from Cuba to keep her company after their father, with whom Delores lived, had died. Ana María was a live wire. She liked to go out dancing and on dates and was always trying to get Delores to go with her.

"Come on, let's go dancing, have some fun!"

But she preferred to stay home and read. One of the nice things about her job cleaning houses for the rich people was that they always gave her books. The rich man who lived on 61st Street and Park always gave her some time off during the day to do as she pleased, saying that she could help herself to any of his books, and he had hundreds in massive shelves that rose up to his Florentine molded ceilings. She would sit happily by a window overlooking Park Avenue, eating rare-roast-beef sandwiches and salad for lunch, with a book open on her lap. She didn't particularly care what she read, as long as the language was not too difficult, and she prided herself on reading at least two books a week. Not bad for the daughter of a barely literate man. And in English, too! Besides, the books took her mind off the terrors of the world and the sadnesses that ran madly through her heart. It was funny, she felt that same kind of sadness from the musician at the bus stop.

She read so much that Ana María, who liked to go to the dance halls, said to her one night, "You're going to be an old woman all alone in a house without children or grandchildren, without a husband or love, you'll have nothing but books coming out your ears unless you get serious about finding yourself a man."

So, at her sister's urging, she'd go out on dates. Some of them were Americans and some of them were Romeos just up from Cuba or Puerto Rico, friendly, garrulous fellows who seemed more like children than like men. She liked a few of the American boys, but would have nothing to do with them romantically. She always had the feeling that she was "saving" herself, for what or for whom she did not know. She'd sometimes feel saddened by her increasing indifference to romance but would tell herself, "I'll know a good man when I see him."

She went out, petted, necked a little, allowed these men the chance to feel her body. But she didn't take it too seriously, finding the whole business of love and courtship disorienting. A man would take her to see *Pecos Bill Meets the Apaches,* and while she would sit absorbed in the excitement of stampeding horses and whooping Indians, the man would whisper, "You're just so beautiful . . . Please, *querida,* a kiss." And sometimes she'd kiss the man for the sake of being left alone. She'd double-date with Ana María but disliked it when the evenings lasted until three or four in the morning. She went out because she didn't want to be a wallflower, but she was always happy to get home to the privacy of her room, where she could turn on the radio and read her books. She read books in Spanish and studiously read books in English. Having completed only two years of high school, she went to night classes twice a week.

When she came into the apartment, Ana María was ironing clothes in the kitchen, listening to some happy music on the radio and humming along. As usual, Delores got undressed and ready for a bath. It was always "Should I cook up some dinner tonight?" from Ana María, and "Maybe we should go to a movie? Huh?" But that night, as Delores made her way down the hall to the bathroom, it was Delores who said, "Why don't we go dancing this weekend?"

"What made you think of that? My God, did someone ask you out?"

"A musician."

"Oh, musicians are exciting!"

"This one's like me, a quiet type of person."

"Well, if you want to go, then I'll go."

That evening she took a nice long, leisurely bath. She sometimes took books with her, reading ten or twelve pages at a time, the book held out of the water, her breasts and thick pubic hair floating on the surface. She read a few pages, the scene where the man and woman kill the Greek in the Cain novel, and then she just decided to float and enjoy the water and the flight of her thoughts, speculation about that nice *simpático* young musician in whom she saw certain similarities to her father.

In the same way that the Mambo King's mind kept circling certain events as he sat in the summer's heat in the room in the Hotel Splendour years later, just as others in the family daydreamed about that past, Delores Fuentes heard her own kind of music and closed her eyes.

It was 1942 when Delores Fuentes, thirteen years old, and her father, Daniel, arrived in the Bronx from Havana. Her older sister, Ana María, had stayed behind in Cuba with their mother, who had refused to join him. He had come from the countryside and had found nothing but bad luck in the city, misfortunes that Delores was too young to understand. Why would his luck change in New York, her mother used to argue, where things were more difficult? She had refused to be thrown to the wolves and told him to go alone. Reluctantly, he got a visa and left Havana, taking his daughter with him.

Daniel was forty and did not speak English, and that made finding a job difficult, manpower shortage or not. Each evening she waited for him by the window, listened for his footsteps in the hall. For three months he looked for work without success. No English, no work, until he finally found a delivery job with a seltzer company, carrying heavy wooden boxes of metal-topped seltzer bottles up and down the stairs of one building after the next. His shift began at six-thirty in the morning and lasted until six at night. Their one bit of luck was finding an apartment through a friendly Cuban he'd met on the street. He'd come home to their walk-through apartment on 169th Street and Third Avenue with his back bent and muscles aching so much he'd just barely have the strength to eat his dinner in silence. Then he'd take a bath and retire to his big empty bed, undraping his bath towel and lying in the summer heat naked.

In imitation of her mother in Havana, Delores would cook for her father, making do with what she could find at the market in those days of war rationing. One night she wanted to surprise him. After he had taken to his bed, she made some caramel-glazed *flan*, cooked up a pot of good coffee, and happily made her way down the narrow hallway with a tray of the quivering *flan*. Pushing open the door, she found her father asleep, naked, and in a state of extreme sexual arousal. Terrified and unable to move, she pretended that he was a statue, though his chest heaved and his lips stirred, as if conversing in a dream . . . He with his suffering face, it, his penis, enormous . . . The funny thing was that, despite her fear, Delores wanted to pick up his thing and pull it like a lever; she wanted to lie down beside him and put her hand down there, releasing him from pain. She wanted him to wake up; she didn't want him to wake up. In that moment, which she would always remember, she felt her soul blacken as if she had just committed a terrible sin and condemned herself to the darkest room in hell. She expected to turn around and find the devil himself standing beside her, a smile on his sooty face, saying, "Welcome to America."

Around that time, she started to gush thick black pubic hair, which curled like flames and weaved out from her body; a single strand that she plucked out of curiosity was nearly a foot long, and there were so many she had to trim this shock of hair back with scissors. Her breasts ached with their weight, and she started to wake up bleeding on those sheets which she'd always kept meticulously clean. Then other things started to happen: boys on the street began to invite her to play games of tag and hide-and-seek down in the basement and tried to touch her breasts and get their fingers down under the rim of her brassiere. She would look in the full-length mirror tacked to the door in her room, asking herself, "Do I want this?" Did she want men giving her these looks on the street? She tried to dress like a boy, in trousers, but in the end her feminine vanity brought her back to the few dresses she owned, items that were getting tighter and more alluring each day.

One night, around Christmas, a year after their arrival, her father came home drunk with some of his friends from the seltzer plant: a couple of Italians, a Jewish fellow, a Puerto Rican, men feeling good after a Christmas party and happy to be free for a few days' holiday. They came to the apartment with big boxes of pizza and cheese *calzone.* Her father never used to drink, but that night she saw him and the others drinking a lot of whiskey. Faces twisted, they were clapping hands to the dulcet strains of the Guy Lombardo Orchestra on the radio. Delores sat quietly, hands folded on her lap, watching them. Her father kept asking her, "What's wrong, darling? What is it, tell your *papá*, huh?"

What could she tell him? That she felt a strange, nearly unbearable desire to release him from his pain by lying naked beside him on his bed? That she would never do it in a million years, but felt that she should? That she felt like an exile in her own apartment?

As the Italian turned up the music, her father said, "Come on, Delorita, have some fun with us, it's Christmas."

And the Italian joined in, "Yes, yes, sugar, don't be a stiff!"

Then her father took her by the hand and swung her around in circles, bouncing on her, then off her, he was so drunk. Then, sweaty, panting, he leaned up against the wall, patting his forehead dry with a kerchief. He stared at her and saw that she looked like her mother; certainly he was surprised that she was so pretty a woman. And he made her nervous, and she shut her eyes.

Perhaps her father had misread her expression, but what he said would buzz through her bones for years afterwards. "Don't be ashamed of your father or be worried that I embarrass you, *niña,* because one day you'll be free of me for good."

Here her desire to remember faltered. What had he meant by that? Had she somehow added to his woes? Was it something about the way she was treating him? She only knew that, with time, her father's unhappiness seemed to increase, and she passed these first years in the States trying to take care of him. She went to a Catholic school and, to help pay the bills, managed to find a job in the Woolworth's on Fordham Road. That was one occasion when her good looks were of help to her. The manager hired her because he liked pretty girls. She was grateful to get the job, worked there part-time and then came home to take care of her father. She cooked his meals, made his bed, washed his clothes, packed his lunches, and in the evenings listened to him talking about the solitude of his days.

"A man is nothing without his family, Delorita. Absolutely nothing. Nothing without family, nothing without love."

He would come home from the seltzer plant now with bottles of cheap, homemade Italian wine for which he'd paid ten cents apiece. He'd sit in the living room drinking until the pains in his back and in his heart left and his lips started to turn blue.

Usually the evenings found him at home, but one night, when she was sixteen, the wine so heightened his spirits that he got all dressed up and said to Delores, "I'm too young to stay in all the time. I'm going out."

He had been looking through the newspapers and came up with the addresses of a few dance halls that his friends had told him about.

"Don't worry about me. I'll be back in a few hours," he said, touching her face with his warm hands. She studied an English grammar book until one in the morning, lingering by the living-room windows and watching the street. Hours later, she was asleep and dreaming about playing with her older sister, Ana María, in Havana, the sun shining and the day radiant with hope for the future, when she heard her father in the hallway. She found him there, leaning against the wall, drunk and exhausted. It took him a while to focus on her, but when he finally did, he said, "I've just been having myself a good time. And you?"

She helped him to his bed, took off his shoes. When she looked over at the table clock, the time was 4:45 and the poor man would have to get up in exactly forty-five minutes for work. She remained with him, sitting by the bed and watching her *papá* snore away, his breathing troubled, head turning from side to side. She watched his powerful body, virile and frightening, and felt confused by her tender feelings toward him. Occasionally, he would say a few words, and her memory of those words, "Please, *Dios,* release me," would come back to her years later when she would have her own family and her own troubles. "Release me," when the alarm went off and she watched the man open his eyes. Like a corpse coming back to life, he popped up, yawned, stretched his arms, and then made his way down the hall to the bathroom, where he washed and put on his gray seltzer-plant deliveryman uniform.

The following week, the same thing happened. Then, after a while, it became his habit to go out two or three nights a week, just as he used to down in Havana.

"A man's got to do as he likes, or else he's not a man," he'd tell her. And: "You know it's not easy for me to be alone all the time."

And what about me? she used to ask herself. She passed those nights worrying about him and fighting feelings of loneliness. Her main refuge? Listening to the radio and studying her books. Sometimes she would visit with neighbors, with whom she would talk. Between her job at Woolworth's, her high-school classes, and her friendships in the building, she became quite good at speaking English. But what good was her English when she was so alone? She liked people, but always felt so bashful. She was beautiful and her body used to make men stare hungrily at her. But even so, she thought herself unattractive, that some kind of mistake was constantly being made about her looks. If only she was not so lonely on those nights when her father went out, if she didn't feel as if some part of her might burst.

And her father, why was he always going out when he looked so exhausted?

"*Papi,*" she asked him one night, "*adónde vas?*"

"I'm going dancing."

"By yourself?"

"With a friend."

Her father was going out in New York in the same way he used to back in Havana. Suddenly Delores found herself feeling what her mother must have felt. All those nights of shouting in the house hadn't turned into air. She had the shouts inside her, and when she saw her father slicked up to see his woman, Delores found herself saying, "*Papá,* I don't think you should go, you'll be tired."

"Don't worry about me."

And he'd give her a kiss and make his way down the stairs. He was usually drunk by the time he'd leave the apartment. She'd follow him out into the stairwell, watching him fading into the shadows. At first thinking, Don't fall. Then: Fall and don't get up.

He's going to a dance hall with a tramp is what she would think, watching him head down the steep hill of 169th Street toward the El, from their window. She'd imagine the woman: wearing a hat crowned with flowers, a too-tight dress, the top bursting. And she'd have thick lipstick-gummy lips, and thick-thick hips.

Alone in that apartment in the Bronx at night, she'd try to calm herself. She loved her father, who worked to take care of them. Wasn't it fair that he go out? Yes, poor Papi, and she would sit by the window listening to a neighbor's radio in the courtyard, or try, as usual, with a dictionary in hand, to read a newspaper or one of the books that her neighbor, a schoolteacher who was touched by her efforts to improve her reading, would leave for her by the door.

Some nights she'd write her mother sympathetic letters, saying things like "*Mamá,* as I get older I understand more about how *Papá* must have hurt you."

Because her mother had refused to accompany him to the

States, Delores had judged her harshly. Thought her cruel. There were things you don't understand about us, she used to tell Delorita—but now she was starting to understand. Hadn't he spent many nights away from their home, back when?

Weeks would go by in which she would await an answer, never receiving one. She'd think that her mother was right in hating her for siding with her father. On those nights alone, Delores would ask herself, "And now what do I have? Neither my mother nor my father."

She'd remember how her mother would sit, her arms crossed tight over her lap, the posture of anger that her mother adopted in the days when her *papá* used to do as he pleased. Delores would also sit with her arms crossed tight over her lap, waiting to hear her father's footsteps in the hall, and wanting to shout at him.

But she always softened and took care of him instead.

In her own way, Delores became something of a stoic. Life would have its limited pleasures. There was sunlight, there were boys and men to give her the up-and-down on the street; there were funny letters from her older sister, Ana María, in Cuba; there were the Hollywood films at the big movie house on Fordham Road; there were romantic novels; there were little boxes of bonbons; there were diaper-dragging two-year-olds toddling on the sidewalk outside her building; there were flowers in the park and pretty dresses in store windows. But there was nothing to overcome her feeling that the world was veiled by a melancholia which emanated from her poor father's sadness. She was stoic enough that few things bothered her, and although she was at an age when young girls fall in love, she never dreamed about it, until one night, when she decided to follow her father to a dance hall.

That night, while her father was out, Delores went searching the apartment for some paper and found a flier for the Dumont Ballroom on East Kingsbridge Road. She felt an overwhelming desire to see him. Dressed up, she walked down that steep hill, caught a Jerome Avenue subway north, and arrived at the ballroom. There she found herself in a zoot-suit haven of slick young men. Many of them were tough, lean veterans of the war who whistled at her and called out to her. Lines like "Enchantment, where are you going?"

"Enchantment" found her father at the bar drinking, his shirt covered in sweat. He was talking to a woman who looked just the way Delores had imagined her. She was in her late thirties, quite plump, a little overripe in a cheap dress. She has the face of a whore, Delores had first thought, but when her father, acting as if nothing was out of the ordinary, introduced Delores to this woman, the woman's face brightened with friendliness.

"My, but you're pretty," the woman said to Delores.

Delores blushed at the compliment. What could she be angry about? Her father had his arm wrapped around the woman's fleshy hips. He was smiling in a way that she hadn't often seen before, happily. And exhaustion had left his expression. What could she be angry about, at these two lonely people trying to comfort one another at a bar in a dance hall? Onstage, the orchestra was playing *"Frenesí."* Her father leaned close to Delores and asked, "Delorita, what is it that you want?"

"Papi, I want you to come home."

He didn't even answer that, just made a looping motion with his cigarette and said to the woman, "Now, can you see that? My own daughter's giving me orders. Me, the man."

Then he smiled.

"Come on, don't be like your mother."

Then the orchestra started to play a tango and the three of them stepped out into the crowd of shadows. Right then and there she saw that her father was a fabulous and graceful dancer, and that this dancing seemed to offer him release from his pain. He took hold of her by the hand and began showing her the three-strided slides of the tango. With her cheek pressed against his warm face, with the lights swirling about, and the perfume-scented shadows swarming around them, she had a daydream about dancing with him in that same way forever . . . Then the song ended and the woman came out to join them. Delores moved off to the side and watched as her father went back out onto the dance floor. Delores watched them spinning in circles. He was a good dancer. He did the lindy hop and the rumba and he jitterbugged with the best of them. Up on the bandstand, an outfit called the Art Shanky Orchestra, a troupe of pinstripe-suited musicians, were playing their hearts out. Their golden trumpets seemed magical because of the way they rejuvenated her father. He danced right into a spotlight and threw a silhouette that crept up the curtained walls of the dance hall a hundred feet high. A crooner got up and started to sing "Moonlight Becomes You." That's when her father and this woman went back to the bar. Exhausted by the fast dances, her father then said to his daughter, "This place isn't so bad, now, is it?"

He leaned with his back against the bar, and as the woman wiped off his forehead with a handkerchief and dabbed sweat from his lips, it seemed as if she was wiping years of strain and unhappiness off his face. For one moment, a moment when he seemed spellbound by the spotlight and the music, he lifted out of himself, floating upwards to a place of eternal relief and comfort. He lit a cigarette and said, "Delorita, over there, that American fellow's looking at you."

At the end of the bar was a tall man, looked Irish or German, with a head of wavy blond hair. He was dressed in a sports jacket and bow tie and seemed quite clean. He was in his mid-twenties. Delores was now seventeen.

The man smiled. A little later, he came over and respectfully asked Delores to dance. She'd already turned down a number of other requests, and she turned him down, too.

"I just wanted to talk to you anyway. My name's— And I know this seems a little unlikely, but you have to believe me . . . See, I work for the Pepsodent toothpaste company and we're holding a beauty contest down in Coney Island in a couple of weeks, and so, I just thought that you might like to enter. I mean, if you give me your name and all that, I can take care of everything . . . There's a first prize of one hundred dollars." Then, looking away, he added, "And you're certainly pretty enough to win . . ."

"What do I have to do?"

"You just put on a bathing suit—do you have a bathing suit? —and you get up in front of the people. It's on a Saturday morning . . . Why don't you give me ya address, huh? It would be a nice thing for you."

He put up his hands as if to say, "I'm not armed . . ."

She blushed, looking away. "You can find me at the Woolworth's on Fordham Road. I work there part-time." And she wrote down her name, Delores Fuentes.

He looked over the piece of paper and said: "You have really beautiful handwriting."

"I can write down poems for you. I write my own, and I learn poems in English."

"Yeah?"

"You want me to write one down?"

"Sure."

She turned to the bar and meticulously wrote out the poem "Annabel Lee," by Edgar Allan Poe.

"You're kidding me?" And he scratched his head, put the poem in his pocket, and said, "You're really classy, you know that?"

Later, around three o'clock, when the dance was winding down, Delores no longer felt angry or anxious about her father. As a matter of fact, she now seemed happy about the dance hall. And her father didn't even seem drunk. As they left the dance hall together, he walked with his back straight and his head held high. It made her happy to think about coming back here. People paid you compliments, and said you were pretty enough to enter a beauty contest! She and her father were heading to the bus stop, and as they crossed the street to catch a downtown bus, the American fellow dazzled Delores, pulling up alongside them in a 1946 Oldsmobile. It was a convertible and the canvas-top roof had been pulled down.

"Let me drive you folks home."

And so they climbed into his car, feeling like wealthy people. Her father plopped down into the plump leather upholstery of the back seat. He put his arm around Delores, eventually falling asleep and snoring, as the car drove away.

The fellow she'd met in the dance hall was a nice man. He would show up at the Woolworth's to make sure that she'd enter the contest, brought her a box of chocolates, a bouquet of flowers, a little cuddly teddy bear. On the day of the contest he drove over to the Bronx from his apartment on Dyckman Street and then took her down to the boardwalk of Coney Island in his open convertible. He was a sporty-looking fellow. That day he wore a light blue summer suit, with a light pink shirt and a red bandana around his neck. As they drove along, his golden hair whipped like a sea flag in the wind. He was *muy guapo*—handsome —and seemed prosperous. That day the beach's sand warmed the bottoms of more than a million people, and while looking at them from the stage, she experienced vertigo. Being seen by so many people in that endless crowd was like flying through the air, especially when she stepped out of her robe and marched her winsome body out to where the people could see her. Greeted with a deafening volley of whistles and hoots, she took third place in the beauty contest and won twenty-five dollars. Then the nice man took her to the amusement park, paid for all the rides and treats she wanted. Then it was getting late and he said, "Now for the surprise." And they drove beyond Coney Island and off to an Italian seafood restaurant by Avenue X.

He kept saying, "Well, this is our special little meal."

Toasting her, he said, "I can't believe that you didn't win first place, but it was probably rigged, ya know? But there's always next year."

Then he ran out of that subject and said, "Pepsodent has this contest every year. Wouldn't it just be swell if we could come back here next year?"

"Yes, it would."

"And it's good to get out of that hot sun. Trouble with New York in August, it just gets too darn hot."

The waiter brought them a big platter of linguini with clam sauce, and this was followed by a large steamed silver-finned fish. And he said, "Gosh, we're having a feast, aren't we?"

He was enthusiastic and happy about just everything, and she couldn't imagine that she'd stayed home so much, without dating any of the American fellows who looked at her on the street.

"You're from Cuba-way, huh? My uncle goes down there like clockwork every winter. Down to Havana. Says it's a nice place."

"Yes, I haven't been back for a long time. But I'll go back one of these days."

Then she talked about herself and the books she liked to read, romance and detective stories; told him that she wouldn't mind studying one day to be a schoolteacher. He nodded intently and smiled a lot, and when he sat back she could see that his ears had turned a livid red from the wine. It was a noisy, cheerful restaurant. The Italian waiter was delighted with her, everyone was so nice to her.

"I guess it's time we got back," the nice man said, looking at his watch. "It's almost eleven o'clock." Then, as they were getting some little mints out of a bowl by the cash register, he stopped and said, "I grew up around here, can I interest you in looking at the house where I lived?"

"Okay."

In the car she sat demurely beside him, not sure what she should do. She was worried about alienating him. A lady in her building who had lots of experience with men had told her, "If he's nice to you, give him a kiss and let him fool around a little bit, but don't let him do anything under your skirt."

They drove beyond the restaurant, along the boardwalk, where the beaches started to hook out more into the sea, and where there were fewer houses.

"Keep going in this direction and you end up in southern Long Island," he said. She noticed that there weren't as many residential streets now, only occasional streetlights in the distance. The sea was gray and churning with a yellow moonlit foam.

"Are we almost there?" she asked.

"Yeah, we are."

She thought he would turn left, but he turned right. By then they were on a street somewhere far beyond the Rockaways and Coney Island, where the subway line veered inland and disappeared. Abruptly he turned the car to one side and drove it out under a deserted boardwalk and through a forest of sea-rotted piers before finally stopping.

"Know what," he said, letting out a deep breath in concern. "My car's overheated, just feel the dashboard."

She put her hand on the dashboard and it was hot.

"What say we sit here for a bit and enjoy the night air?"

They sat for a time watching the sea and he talked about how his mother would take him there in the afternoons and he would sit out by the shoreline with a toy bucket and shovel, making castles—his house wasn't far away. And she just sat waiting for the moment when he would turn to her so that she could give him a kiss, and then it happened, just like that: he took a swig of some whiskey from a little flask, took her by the wrists, and said, "Delores, I've been wanting to kiss your pretty face all day."

She felt him pressing close to her, and she said, under her breath, "Me, too."

Then they started to kiss: he planted kisses on her cheeks and around her nose, and then he gave her real kisses, and his hands were touching her everywhere. She allowed him to fondle her breasts; then he tried to get his hands inside her bathing suit and slid them to between her legs, which she clenched shut like a vise. And, just like that, the fellow got a quite disbelieving look on his face, which was now a little twisted, and he said, "What's that supposed to mean?"

"I'm sorry."

"Now relax, will ya? I'm not going to eat you." But all the same he was still trying to hitch up her skirt and get his fingers inside the bottom part of her bathing suit, and then she pushed him away.

And just like that he seemed more disdainful and tore at the top of her bathing suit, shredding the straps and pulling down on the front of the suit so that he could get his mouth on her breasts; she squirmed under him, under his kisses and thick tongue.

"If you knew, Delores, how I feel right now," he kept repeating. She tried to push him away, but he was a strong man and, at one point, annoyed with her resistance, slapped her face and said, "I'm not fooling with you, come on now, Delores. What the hell's wrong with you, anyway?"

Then it hit her all at once that she was about to lose her virginity in the worst way imaginable. With this *pendejo!* Oh, Papi! There was nothing she could do to avoid it. Where could she go? Run off under this boardwalk out into those streets where there wasn't a soul? It was so desolate she wished she was a mermaid so she could swim out into the beautiful sea. And she went through the possibilities of resistance and of compliance and felt herself in a world of pure gloom. How could she have been so trusting, so stupid? What could she do but sit back in the seat, feeling pity and shame in her heart and almost a fondness for his ardor. All these thoughts turned into a feeling of overwhelming sadness about being a woman. And where was this man's kindness now? She rested back in the seat and he stood up, pulling off his shoes and then his socks. Then with the same manic devotion with which he had torn at her bathing suit he tugged at the erection inside his trousers, grabbed it proudly . . .

By the time he had undone his zipper she had gotten to the point where she wanted to get it all over with. He pushed open the door of the car and was standing over her when down to his knees went his trousers and his polka-dotted boxer shorts. And there it was, his member, slightly bent and wavering in the air. She thought, It's like a child's.

Something between a look of pity, mirth, and pure contempt crossed her face as she told him, "Go to hell, *hombre.*"

And as she turned herself around in that seat and drifted away like the wood and foam and debris that floated at the water's edge, he kept trying to jam his thing into her bottom, he was so angry, and while this was going on, she had the impression of being in that room with her father the day she saw him naked; that she was now on the bed beside him and looking at his member, huge and powerful, an entity beyond the bodily weaknesses that would one day kill him.

Her poor father would die in 1949, collapsing on a stairway while making a seltzer delivery, boom, down two flights of stairs, dumbfounded, his last sight twenty bottles of seltzer bouncing off the steps, spraying everywhere and shattering to bits. Years later, she would say to herself, "Whatever anyone says about you, Papi, you were a worker, a protector, and a man, a sweet and gentle man, Papi, not like that bastard who abused me."

That night, as she was assaulted on the beach, the word "virile" floated through her thoughts, brushed like a silk scarf against the edge of sexual speculation about her father. She was not on the beach but sitting on the edge of the bed, rubbing oil into her father's aching back, and running her hands up and over his shoulders, hearing him say, *"Ay, qué bueno!—*How good it feels!" and happy at his sighs of pleasure, even if he was a spirit in her thoughts. But in those few moments, while the Pepsodent man tried to enter her womb, now dry as a bone, she heard the man crying out in frustration: "Bring me off!" And then, "God-dammit!" When she opened her eyes, he was masturbating himself to help along the ejaculation that had started against his will, during the moment of his failure . . . With a certain amusement she watched the temper and passion drain from his face, watched him hitch back his trousers and all the rest, his back to her. He said to her: "I should drown you in the water. Now get out of my sight!"

That night he left her on the beach among the gnats and the fleas and the crabs that moved in clusters across the sand, feeding slowly, and she had to wander the streets searching for someone to help her. By morning she was sitting on a curb some seven blocks inland where there were houses. A milk truck pulled up and the man, dressed in white, leaned out and said, "Rough night, huh, lady?"

Then he drove her to a subway fifteen minutes away.

The night of the dance, Delores was thinking about what her sister Ana María had told her: "Love is the sunlight of the soul, water for the flowers of the heart, and the sweet-scented wind of the morning of life"—sentiments taken from corny boleros on the radio, but maybe they were true, no matter how cruel and stupid men can be. Perhaps there'll be a man who'll be different and good to me.

And so Delores put on a red dress with a pleated midsection and slit skirt, dark nylons and black high heels, a fake pearl necklace, got her hair done up like Claudette Colbert's, dabbed some Chanel No. 5 behind her ear and between her breasts, and poured a few drops over the talcum-powdered crotch of her panties, so that the woman who would walk into the ballroom only remotely resembled the cleaning woman Nestor had met at the bus stop.

What Delores and Ana María saw posted outside the brass doors of the ballroom was:

!!! CONTEST!!!!!CONTEST!!!

★ ★ ★ ★ ★ ★ ★ ★

AT THE IMPERIAL BALLROOM
for the
BEST
and
MOST OUTRAGEOUS
BALDHEADED COUPLES!

★

$50 first prize! & CASE OF CHAMPAGNE &
A SET of YOUR VERY FAVORITE RECORDINGS
!!!!!!!MUCH MUCH MORE!!!!!!!

★ ★ ★ ★ ★ ★ ★ ★

featuring
THE FABULOUS MAMBO KINGS!!

★

Adm. $1.06. Doors open 9 pm

Checking their hats and coats, Delores and Ana María, their asses pinched by naughty hands, made their way through the bald and full-haired crowd gathered at the Imperial Ballroom. She was now in the world of courtship for which Delorita thought she had no use. But, just the night before, she'd dreamed about the musician she'd met at the bus stop. She was lying naked in a bed, pressed against him, and they were kissing, kissing; so tightly were they pressed together that her hair had wrapped around him like a coiling rope and their skin burned and, at the same time, she had the sensation that all the pores in her body had opened and that from each pore dripped a warm sweet liquid like honey. That dream soon blossomed into a funnel of sensations through which her body floated like a cloud: she awakened in the middle of the night, imagining the musician's long, sensitive finger touching the juiciest valve in her body. As she moved toward the stage to point Nestor out to her sister, she blushed, thinking about that dream.

The Mambo Kings were up on the stage, looking much as they did in photographs of them from that time, in white silk suits and set up in two rows across, the elegant Miguel Montoya seated behind a grand piano, a percussionist standing before a battery of congas, bongos, and *timbales*, a drummer before an American kit, then Manny with his stand-up bass, and then the trombonist and two of the horn players. And in front of them the saxophonist and flutist, their two violinists, and then the brothers, standing side by side before the microphone. The spotlight was on the handsome Cesar Castillo, and at first Ana María, liking his looks, asked, "Is that him?"

"No, the shy one standing off to the side."

And there he was, waiting for the turnaround of a habanera, and then, given the nod by Cesar, he stepped before the microphone, tilted his head back, and began to play his solo. Like his older brother, who had slipped back, he was decked out in a white silk suit, flamingo-pink shirt, and sky-blue tie. He was playing the solo to his brother's composition "Solitude."

"Isn't he beautiful?" Delores asked.

And then, when the song had turned around again and Cesar sang the last verse, she stood under the stage where the trumpet player was standing, and smiled at him. He had been lost in a stony-faced concentration, but he was happy to see her. Then they went into a fast number, a mambo. Sly smile on his face, Cesar Castillo gave a nod to the percussionist, whose hands were taped up like a boxer's, and he started to bop, bop, bop on a *quinto* drum, and in came the piano with its Latin vamp, then the alternating bass. Another nod from Cesar and the others came in, and Cesar started dancing before the big ball microphone, his white leather, golden-buckled shoes darting in and out like agitated compass needles. And Nestor, standing in with the brass, blew his trumpet so hard in his exhilaration over seeing Delores, whose presence seemed to soothe his inner pain, his face turned red and his pensive head seemed ready to burst. And the crowds on the dance floor wriggled and bounced, and the musicians enjoyed Nestor's solo and were shaking their heads, and he played happily, just hoping to impress Delores.

Then another slow song, a bolero.

Nestor whispered to Cesar, who said, "This little number is an original composition entitled 'Twilight in Havana,' and my brother here wants to dedicate it to a pretty girl named Delores."

Head back, he stood beside the microphone, a backlight throwing his shadow down over the floor and rising up along the insides of her shapely legs, lingering on the dampness between them and giving her a lick.

That evening, Delorita and her sister Ana María were a couple of killer-dillers and would spend the night dancing with one man after the other. Ana María with pure joy, and Delorita with a sweet wistfulness, her chin on the shoulder of her dance partner, her eyes on the stage and that spotlight on the microphone and the pained, soulful countenance of Nestor Castillo. Though she could have ended up with one of the handsome men there that night, Delores waited for Nestor. When he came down off the stage during the band's break, when the other orchestra played, he seemed happy and enchanted, his somberness broken, after two years of suffering over Beautiful María, by the prospect of a new love. He attended to Delores as if there was nothing in the world that he wouldn't do for her. He bought Delores and her sister drinks from the bar, wiped a bead of sweat from her brow with his lilac-scented handkerchief, and when she said, "I like to dance, but my feet get so sore," he offered to rub her warm, nyloned soles.

When she asked, "Why are you so nice to me?" he told her: "Because, Delores, it feels like my destiny."

He remained at her side as if he had always known her, and when, for no apparent reason, he dropped his head melancholically, she touched the back of his neck with her hands gently, thinking, "My poor Papi was that way," and because she seemed to understand his pain and because he did not have to make jokes around her and hatch romantic schemes to trap her, the way his brother did with women, he felt that there was a chance for a strong connection between them. Like a forlorn bird in a bolero, he felt his wings being singed by the flame of tender love.

When the musicians returned to the stage, they were joined by the squat, mustachioed MC for the evening, who wore a black tuxedo and a thick red silk cummerbund around his immense belly, like a foreign diplomat. He stood before the microphone, announcing the event for that evening:

"And now, ladies and gents, it's the moment you've all been waiting for: our best baldheads dance contest! Our judges for tonight are none other than the famed rumba dancer Palito Pérez, and his wife, Conchita." And they bowed from the stage. "The ever-fabulous Mr. Dance himself, 'Killer' Joe Piro, and last, that crooning marvel with the Mambo Kings orchestra, the ever-fabulous Cesar Castillo! Before beginning, I would like to remind you that this event has been jointly sponsored by the Sons of Italy Organization and the Nostrand Avenue Rheingold brewery. Maestro, you may begin."

When the contest had been announced, mainly through pamphlets and posters and a few radio spots, there had been a rush to the barbershops of downtown Brooklyn, the Bronx, and central Harlem. A huge crowd had turned out, among them several hundred couples who had shaved off all their hair: purple and green eggheads, baldies in white tuxedos and evening gowns, baldies in giant baby diapers (the woman's diaper discreetly pinned and joined at the back of her neck), Mr. and Mrs. Moon, baldies as oranges, baldies as people from the planet Mars, baldies as hydrogen bombs, baldies posing as baby chicks, and who knew what else. There were clowns and harlequins and couples draped with ball-bearing-sewn robes, couples with feathers and bells. The costumed entrants to this contest not only had to look weird but also had to demonstrate virtuoso and light-footed dancing, expertise in the arts of the mambo, rumba, tango, and cha-cha-cha.

Standing amid the ring of tipsy onlookers, Delores rooted for a couple who were the prettiest pair of baldheads. The woman looked like Queen Nefertiti and wore glittering necklaces and bracelets, all reflecting light into the world, and a butterfly-sleeved red dress whose skirt curled upwards like the roof of a pagoda. Her partner had peacock feathers for a collar and wore huge loop earrings and oversized purple silk pants and resembled a genie; but the main thing about them was that they seemed so much in love, smiling and kissing with every turn, dip, and slide.

They did not win, though they were good dancers. Another couple won: the man had an alarm clock tied to his bald head and numbers written all over his scalp. He was wearing oversized peg pants and pink spike-tipped shoes and a lavender shirt and jacket. His partner wore a tight black strapless gown in which she wobbled her way into the hearts of the males of the audience, her crowning moment arriving during a twirling spin in which the centrifugal forces tore free the top of her dress, revealing two plump breasts, large, quivering, and as bare as the top of her head.

Afterwards, Delores and Ana María made their way into the ladies' room, which was jammed with bald and full-headed women seriously going about the business of freshening up their eyeliner, mascara, lipstick. She sat down before a mirror to freshen up, too, and enjoyed the comings and goings of these pretty young women who were out to meet young men and have a good time.*

---

*Women worked hard to enhance their loveliness so that they could find themselves a good man for life, evade loneliness, kiss, hug, sleep, fornicate, so that each could tremble in a man's arms and find a man to take care of her, protect her, love her, a man to keep her warm against the chill winds of life. (Now a look at these women getting dressed. Quick fluff of powder around the breasts and nice nipples, quick dab down below, a flame-shaped burst of thick black pubic hair snow-powdered and nice, on with the panties, the garters, the nylons, the skirt, the brassiere, the blouse, earrings, lipstick, rouge, mascara, all to be removed later, tugged at, torn, smeared, somewhere in some bedroom or against a wall, in an alley, an apartment, in a parked car, on a rooftop, in the tranquil park. The man dancing and pressing close to her, his bone—and the bigger the better, now tell the truth, ladies

Loud big-band Latin music slipped into the room when the door opened, ladies in the stall urinating, a scent of Chanel No. 5 thick everywhere, Sen-Sen, chewing gum popping in mouths. Cuban and Puerto Rican and Irish and Italian girls lined up before the makeup mirrors, applying mascara and rouge, and fixing their lipstick. Women pulling up on their skirts and getting their garters straight, thick thighs moon-white and honey-colored in the glare of the lights.

And voices:

"Tell ya, darlin', some of these men, woooey! This fella fresh as hell, just met the guy and his bone is knocking on my door."

"You think I look all right, I mean, how do you think he'll like the way I look if I put my hair up like this?"

"And he wants me to go down to San Juan with him to a hotel there . . . Pay for it and everything."

"And the fucking bastard takes me for a walk. I'm a little tipsy and so I sit with him in the car out in the parking lot. All I want to do is sit there and just get some fresh air, and then he's all over me, like he's never been with a woman before. I don't even really know the guy, just that he's married, and I say unhappily married by the way he's grabbing at me . . . We wrestle around for a while, I don't even really mind that, but no way am I going to go to bed with a man when I don't have anything going with him, know what I'm saying? And what does he do but pulls his purple thing out of his trousers and says, 'Oh, please, honey, why don't you give it a little kiss?' and 'Oh, please,' squinting his

---

—the woman wanting the man inside her but fighting him, legs shut closed, her insides softening, the man kissing her all over and promising her things, until either he proposes to her or leaves her for someone else or she tricks him, weeping crocodile tears, and he marries her and he's earnest and gentle and courteous and sometimes they age happily together, but there are others . . . The man always looking for another woman and the woman knowing about it, but what can she do when she's been losing those precious looks that hooked him up in the first place? With a ring of fat around her gut, so tight the snaps pinch her plump skin and leave screw marks . . . What can she do, ladies?)

eyes and all like he's in the worst pain in the world. I told him, you go to hell, and left him in the car holding his thing, and so, even though I'm in the right, twenty minutes later he's back on the dance floor doing the cha-cha-cha with another girl, and from the way she looked, I'll bet she did put his thing in her mouth. I end up going home to the Bronx, number 2 line all the way uptown to Allerton Avenue by myself . . ."

"Anyway, this guy's six foot four, must weigh two hundred and fifteen pounds, works for the city, you know, and . . . he's got a thing the size of my pinkie, what a gyp!"

"As beautiful as you are, there's always some other girl out there beautifuller than you."

"I'd give it up for a wedding ring."

"Oh, God! Anyone have an extra pair of nylons?"

". . . *Qué guapo* that singer is, huh? I'd go out with him anytime."

"Well, I've *been* out with him."

"And?"

"He'd break your heart."

"His brother isn't bad, either."

"You said it."

She'd remember heading out into the ballroom again, down along the shoeshine stand, that thick row of men smoking their cigarettes like mad and trying to get a little fresh air before an opened window. Couples in phone booths and in corridors kissing and fondling each other, chandeliers that were a rainfall of crystal and light, the music coming from a distance, as if down a long, long tunnel: the string bass, the percussion, with the crash of cymbals, banging of congas and *timbales* looming like a storm cloud, from which only occasionally rose a horn line or crescendoing piano . . . Life was funny: she was thinking about Nestor Castillo and moving through the crowd toward the bar when she felt a hand gently taking hold of her elbow. And it was Nestor, as if she had wished him there. He took her over to the bar, drank down a glass of whiskey, and said, "We have to play one more set, and then afterwards we're going out, around three o'clock or so, to get something to eat. Why don't you come along with us . . . You can meet my brother and a few of the other musicians."

"Can I bring my sister?"

"*Cómo no.* We'll meet out in front."

The grand finale of the evening was the conga. The fabulous Cesar Castillo came out, à la Desi Arnaz, with a conga drum slung over his shoulder, banging that drum and leading the Mambo Kings into a 1-2-3/1-2 rhythm that moved everybody across the dance floor in a snaking conga line, hips bumping, tripping, flying forward, separating, kicking out their legs, shaking their chassis, laughing, and having a good time . . .

They ended up driving uptown in Manny's 1947 Olds and there hooked up with some of the other Mambo Kings, taking over a few long tables in the back of a little restaurant called Violeta's, which the owner kept open late so that musicians, starved after their jobs, could have a good meal. On the back wall there was a mural of a tropic sea ablaze in the colors of an eternal Cuban sunset bursting over El Morro Castle in Havana Harbor. The walls over the bar were covered with signed photographs of the Latin musicians who'd eat there regularly. Everyone from the flutist Alberto Socarrás to the Emperor of the Mambo himself, Pérez Prado.

That night, as the Mambo Kings and their companions were dining, in walked the well-known bandleaders Tito Rodríguez of the Tito Rodríguez Orchestra, and Tito Puente, who headed an outfit called the Piccadilly Boys, and although Cesar frowned and said to Nestor, "Here comes the enemy!" the brothers greeted them as if they were lifelong companions.

"*¡Óyeme, hombres! ¿Qué tal?*"

Watching the two brothers side by side, Delores got a good idea of what they were like. They were like their signatures on the framed photograph of the Mambo Kings on the wall over the bar. That picture of them posed atop a seashell art-deco bandstand in white silk suits, instruments by their side. The photograph was covered with the musicians' signatures, the most flamboyant being the elder brother Cesar Castillo's, for whom she did not at first particularly care. His signature was pure vanity. Filled with so many blooms and loops that his letters resembled the wind-filled sails of a ship. (If only she could have seen him seated at his kitchen table up on La Salle Street with a pad of paper and a pencil, and a book on penmanship open before him, practicing his signature for hours and hours.) And he was like that, Delores thought, filled with wind and meaningless gestures. He had a sly curl of experience to his lips that Delores didn't trust. Bursting with energy after a night of performance, the older Mambo King was in constant motion, joking with his fellow musicians, talking only about himself and the joys of performance, flirting with the waitresses and giving Delores and Ana María these hungry up-and-downs. It was one thing to look at her sister, who was unattached, that way, but at his own brother's new companion! *¡Qué cochino!* she thought. Rude and presumptuous.

Nestor's signature was more plainly and carefully written, almost in a nervous child's hand, as if he had taken a long time just to get his reduced, humble letters down right. He tended to sit quietly, smiling when jokes were made, nodding seriously when ordering or looking over the menu. And he tried hard to get along with everybody. He was polite to the waitress and to his fellow musicians. Courteous, almost frightened of being corrected about his table manners, even when his older brother grabbed across the table at the *tostones* platter and devoured everything hungrily, talking with his mouth full, and on not just one occasion indelicately belching in the midst of a laugh that enlarged his eyeballs and brought tears to his eyes: a man dedicated to himself, always taking more than his share: five pork chops, two plates of rice and beans, a plate of *yuca*, all drowned in salt and lemon and garlic. A bandleader's share, she was sure. No wonder the glamorous pretty-boy singer was getting a big belly and jowls! On top of that, after filling his belly, he decided to ignore everyone else at the table, and spent all his time flirting with and sweet-talking Ana María. *Dios mío*, how typical was his voracious wolfishness . . .

Nestor was more reserved, which suited her fine. And he was attentive to her, pulling out her chair from the table for her, holding doors, and making sure that she had everything she wanted. Would you like some *plátanos?* Some chicken? Pork chops? Treating her as if she was as important as any of the musicians . . . She liked him, found him a refined kind of man, the kind of poetic soul who would write songs of love. She was nervous, but, right then and there, she decided that she would let him do as he pleased with her. There was something she found immensely appealing about his solemn demeanor, his passivity, his pain.

Later, Cesar dropped Manny off on 135th Street, where he lived, and borrowing his car, drove the two sisters home to the Bronx, a perilous journey during which the girls gripped their seats in terror because he kept veering into the curb, especially while going uptown on the West Side Highway: sparks flew from the hubcaps as he went zooming past all the other vehicles, honking his horn and driving like a drunk even when he wasn't. But he got them both home in one piece and waited in the car while Nestor escorted Delores and Ana María to their apartment. Delorita would remember wishing he would at least give her a nice deep kiss, with a little bit of tongue, but he seemed so retiring and polite that she went to bed that night wondering, Is there something wrong with me? And wondering if she should have been the one to pull him close to her and slip her tongue inside his mouth.

They started going out. They would meet on those nights when the Mambo Kings weren't playing, eat some Chinese food, and then head downtown to catch a film, visit friends, or step out to a ballroom. Delorita would talk about the books she'd read and the rich man for whom she worked—"He's nice, but he's so rich he's unhappy"—and he would listen quietly, never having much of his own to say. He always seemed preoccupied about something, but he never talked about it. A man you were in love with should have a lot to say, she used to think to herself, but there was someone beautiful in there, inside that broad chest . . . Although he never said very much, she was certain that he would slowly open up. Slowly he did, speaking about his upbringing in Cuba and how he sometimes wished he'd never left his farm—he was better suited for a simple farmer's life, he used to say.

"I'm not the adventurer, like my older brother. No, sirree, I was happy to sit out on the porch at night watching the stars and living *tranquilito, tranquilito,* but I wasn't destined for that life, I was destined to come here to New York."

At first she used to believe that his pain was an ordinary homesickness for the rural countryside and that much simpler life. She always thought he smelled of the Cuban countryside, and that he had not one foul bone in his body.

But the poor man—she figured that some terrible things had happened to him when he was a kid. He had told her that he was sick enough as a child in Cuba to have the priest perform the last rites over him at least twice. "I can remember a priest dressed in a purple cloak, praying over me. Candles and oil rubbed on my forehead. And my mother in a corner, weeping."

And once on a sunny day, the day he wrenched open her heart, when they had gone for a walk in Riverside Park, he told her, "Look how beautiful it is today, huh?"

"Yes, it is, my love."

"But do you know something, as beautiful as this is, I feel as if it doesn't belong to me."

"What do you mean?"

"I sometimes feel like a ghost, *tú sabes,* as if I'm not really part of this world."

"No! *Bobo!* You're very much a part of this world."

Then they went to sit on a nice grassy hill. They'd brought a little lunch of ham and cheese with mayonnaise on seeded rolls, and cold beers. Children were playing softball in a field, and pretty college girls in Bermuda shorts and white tennis shoes were spread out here and there on blankets, studying their books. The sun up in the sky, a buzz of insects in the air, boats and barges passing on the Hudson River. Two honeybees floating over a cluster of dandelions like a young couple in love looking over a house. Then a *tling-tling,* a Good Humor ice-cream man in his squat white truck. Nestor walked over and came back with two icicle pops, his strawberry, hers orange, and they ate them, runny with sweet liquid, and then lay back. She was so happy because it was a beautiful day and they were in love, but Nestor?

He had shut his eyes and suddenly trembled. Not a physical trembling, but a shudder in his spirit. It was so strong she felt it entering her like a fume out of a gas stove.

"Oh, Nestor, why are you that way?" And she kissed him, saying, "Sit up here, beside me, *mi corazón.*"

And he started weeping.

"Delores . . . a man doesn't weep. Forgive me."

And even though his face was all twisted up, he put a stop to it and regained his composure.

"I just get so tired sometimes," he told her.

"Of what?"

"Just tired."

She didn't know what to do. She took hold of his right hand and kissed it.

"It's just that I don't feel long for this world sometimes."

Then he wouldn't say another word about it, and they went for a walk. The day ended happily with the two of them watching an Abbott and Costello double feature over at the Nemo movie theater on Broadway. Afterwards they ate pizza, and by then she had fallen in love.

She must have been lovestruck, must have looked at him with such fawning eyes, because after they'd been going out for about two months, and were kissing in the foyer of her hallway, he said to her, "You know, Delorita, I wish you wouldn't look at me that way. I'm not the saint you think I am."

And just like that he pulled her close, embracing her and forcing her to sigh with the inward shove between her legs of the burning mule bone inside his trousers.

"You see, Delorita," he was saying, "I've wanted to respect you, but now . . . I can't even sleep at nights, I'm so filled up with thoughts of you . . . And there's something else, I haven't said a word or showed my feelings because I'm a cautious man, but, Delorita"—and he shocked her, taking her hand and pulling it down over the front of his trousers—"can't you see what a state I'm in?"

They kissed for a long time, until she said, "Let's go into the apartment. Ana María's out and won't be back until late."

She wasn't nervous, stripping down before him and resting back on the very couch where her father used to fall asleep in exhaustion. Nestor had his hands all over her, his thick tongue inside her mouth, his fingers probing under the wire rim of her brassiere, and he whispered, *"Querida,* undo my trousers." And she reached down without looking and unfastened his buttons and then separated the lips of his trousers in the way that his fingers were separating the lips of her vagina, and she pulled out his thing; it was powerful and big enough that she gasped and opened her legs wide for him.

Because her undergarment was now so damp, she told him, "Pull it off, my darling," and as they covered each other's faces with kisses, she floated away again, remembering the afternoons of her youth in Havana when the house was filled with shouting, and how she would seek shelter in a room whose shuttered windows leaked sunlight, resting in her bed and touching herself so that she could forget the shouting, forget it all through the pleasant sensations, like those sensations that were overwhelming her now. Her legs opened wider and she felt herself being occupied by a tremendous force, and her insides filled with the melted wax of a large church candle, and as the sound of his frantic breathing amplified, he sounded like the wind that she sometimes heard in her dreams. Her pores opened and oozed the warm and sweet liquid of her dream and she thought, "My Lord, this is a man!" and they played for hours; Delores felt so grateful to him that she did everything he wanted. That night she went from complete ignorance to knowledge about the act of love. When she heard his moans of pleasure and saw an expression of ecstatic release on his face, a new sense of purpose descended upon her: to release this young musician from his pain.

(And poor Nestor? He thought he was with Delores and he devoured her big-nippled breasts, but when he closed his eyes and no longer saw her face, he was kissing the breast of the Beautiful María of His Soul, licking her skin from navel to toe, but when he winced at his maudlin thought and remembered how much he loved Delores and how good he felt inside her, he was pulled out of the darkness into which he had started slipping, and so he opened his eyes and looked deep into her eyes, and because he was coming and his bones were giving out inside him and his body teemed with a creamy heat that rose from his penis and exploded in his head, he closed his eyes again and felt the worst sadness about María. And yet, when he saw María, he pictured her in a room, and in that room a doorway through which could be seen the sickbed of his youth and himself, unable to move, calling out, "*Mamá!*" and waiting, waiting. And he'd open his eyes again and begin to pump Delores harder, but he could not help thinking about the other and almost slipped a few times, almost uttered, "María, María.")

By that time, Cousin Pablo and his family had moved away to a nice house in Queens and had left the apartment to the brothers. Cesar took over the big bedroom down the hall, and Nestor got one of the smaller rooms near the kitchen. He started to invite Delorita over for dinner, and because she lived so far away, she would often spend the night. Nestor would wait on the corner of 125th Street and Broadway for Delorita to come stepping off the bus from the Bronx. Or she'd head straight to La Salle Street from her cleaning job, carrying a bag with a change of clothing. She wasn't bothered by the fact that they shared the same bed out of wedlock. She thought it was no one else's business, though she was only twenty-one. And besides, she had no doubt that they would be married one day.

At first, with Pablo and the family gone, the apartment, barely furnished and crammed with musical instruments and drums, seemed drab. But Delores would bring in flowers and rolls of brightly colored Con-Tact paper. Shopping, Nestor and Delores would make trips to Chinatown, returning with vases and Chinese screens and jasmine candles. She kept the place clean and started to cook for them. They'd sometimes walk toward Columbia University and the bookstores on Broadway, and while she'd forage through the bins and used-book racks for adventure, spy, romance, and detective novels that cost a nickel apiece, he'd wait patiently. They went out a lot in those days: sometimes Cesar would borrow a car and they would go for another perilous ride in the country, or they'd go out to the Park Palace, fancy as La Conga or the Copacabana, to catch Machito or Israel Fajardo, and afterwards they would go strolling through Central Park at two in the morning. Once, after a Mambo King job in Brooklyn, they went to Coney Island. She and Nestor sat on a bench necking before the ebbing sea, and the incident with the Pepsodent man seemed as remote as the bone-white moon above them.

When she was not at night school, she would study. She'd learned her English after a long and humiliating struggle in a

Catholic school in the Bronx, where the nuns literally beat her head with a dictionary when she misunderstood or could not remember certain words. Chronic mispronunciations made her the butt of many a joke, but she endured, studied and excelled, won spelling bees and got high grades, becoming one of those *latinas* who, through a course of terrified learning, could speak English as well as anyone (and with a slight Bronxese accent, at that). She would always try to teach Nestor things, encouraged him to read a book. He would shrug and she would later find him sitting on the living-room sofa with a guitar and a pencil and paper, whistling and working out the melodies to different songs.

She was happy for the first time since she could remember and she adored Nestor for it. Sometimes she would walk into the living room, lower the Venetian blinds, and take off her dress. Or she sat beside him just to keep him company and in a few minutes found her undergarments pulled down to her knees, and her dress hitched up over her waist. She was always happy with him because during the act of love the younger Mambo King would say, *"Te quiero, Delorita. Te quiero,"* again and again. When he would have his orgasm his face would widen, as if flattening out like one of the Venetian carnival masks she saw on her employer's wall; and he'd blush during this ecstatic release from pain. There was nothing she wouldn't do for him. She'd rub baby oil on her breasts and thighs, then get a jar of petroleum jelly and smear it between her legs, find Nestor napping in the bedroom, suckle him, and then impale herself on his member.

He was a troubled sleeper and suffered from nightmares. Often, as she slept beside him, she would think of his sadness and about helping him, but there seemed to be nothing she could do to lift him out of his melancholy. Lovemaking distracted this melancholia: he'd fall asleep wedged up against her bottom at night, his erection pressed against her. It seemed they must have made love countless times in their sleep. One night when she was dreaming about picking flowers, she felt his penis entering her from behind. But not into her vagina. She was half asleep, so that the sensation of being entered there came over her body slowly: at first it felt as if her bottom were being packed with warm clay, but after a certain time the softness gave way to a widening and lengthening barb, stretching her painfully at first and then warming and softening again. She turned to facilitate his pleasure and ground her hips into him until he came. Then they were both sound asleep again and he began his uneasy dreams again.

Now, THE OPENING CHORDS TO "Beautiful María of My Soul" and Nestor in Delores's arms dreaming about 1948: In the late evenings, after finishing up with his job at the Havana Explorers' Club, where he worked side by side with his older brother, he would take walks through the neighborhoods of the city; he liked to get lost in the arcades and to wander in the marketplace among the farmers and the hen cages and gray pigs. In the alley behind a Chinese restaurant called Papo-lin's in La Marina, that neighborhood by the harbor near where they lived, he watched two red roosters, powerful machos, fight with their razor-taloned claws. Standing up in a bar in a row of bars, he would eat his dinner, a plate of rice and beans and a pork chop drowned in salt and lemon, for 25 cents, and watch the street euphorically cluttered with life: men pulling rag carts; Chinese workers in velvet shoes and long cotton smocks making their way to the tobacco factories; the poor from Las Yaguas selling their wares and services out of stalls: fortunes told, shoes fixed, *jugo de fruta* 10 cents, clocks, guitars, house tools, coils of rope, toys and religious articles, statuary and good-luck charms, flowers, love potions and magic candles, get your picture taken for 25 cents, in color! He'd look over the clothing to see what he might buy for the fifteen dollars a week he earned in those days: a good *guayabera* with fancy lace trimmings, $2; a plain shirt, $1; a pair of Buster Browns, $4; a pair of linen *pantalones*, $3.50. Hershey bar? 2 cents. Pepsi or Apur-Cola, 10 cents . . . And there were bananas hanging like lanterns off the racks, and wagon after wagon of fruit, and ice wagons, and a huddle of men throwing dice in a cool doorway. Flowers growing in pots and flowers spilling off the balconies, and lichen on the sea-rotted walls: astragal fences and antique doors, cornices brown and orange-hued, animal head and angelic door knockers. Racks of copper pots and pans, children running in and out of the stalls, sailors in the city whoring, a bicycle hanging off a rope over a row of bicycle tires; caged parrots; a shady-looking gentleman with the eyes of a turtle, sitting quietly at a narrow fold-up table from which he sold his "artistic" photographs; and then racks of dresses and pretty women moving among the racks and music coming out of the doorways. Smell of blood and sawdust, the sound of animals being butchered on the block, smell of blood and tobacco and a walk down a long alley behind the slaughterhouse that faced another slaughterhouse: a man dumping buckets of water over a floor drenched in blood and behind him, in a row, the split-open carcasses of a dozen pigs. Then the leather and carpentry and beach-goods shops . . .

Then he'd pass the prostitutes who stood in the doorways in their tight slips and robes exposing a breast, or a length of thigh, rolling their tongues over their lips, as if they'd just finished eating an ice cream: they'd check out his crotch, smile, and say, "Psssst. *Ven, macho, ¿adónde vas?*" He passed them and always waved hello: they knew him as the quiet musician walking along their street, the fellow who wasn't audacious like his brother. They would call to him and rub their breasts and once one of these ladies leapt out of the doorway and pinched his bottom: "*Guapito!* Hey, handsome, what's taking you so long?" But he never wanted to go, because ever since the days when his brother used to take him to see the prostitutes in Oriente, he had found something unbearably sad about the situation, not the touching of breasts and loins, the gushing of his sperm, or the white pan of water under the bed in which the used prophylactics floated, but the idea that he found himself feeling too sorry for these women who were forced to make love with men with whom they were not in love, spreading their legs for fifty cents and sometimes, with a really beautiful woman, a dollar.

But he was not a saint. There was one pretty girl whom he took to bed now and then, a young woman, married, as it turned out, who really needed a man to love her. He went to see her four times and had been falling in love with her when he realized that the only reason she was suckling his member and bending his back was for money, and that left him sulking with disappointment for weeks, so that he went back to his old ways. (Nothing like Cesar, who was having trouble in his marriage and would go roaring with a bottle of rum into one of those whorehouses and take up with three women at a time and come home to their little two-room apartment sated and with a glow of sly satisfaction in his eyes. Nothing like Cesar, who'd turn up in these brothels and spend the night among these women, entertaining them with his trembling, quivering baritone: he'd sing and they would cook for him and sometimes he would slip off into a room and take a woman to bed.)

So the whores of La Marina came to recognize Nestor's expression of eternal homesickness and longing for love that flourished in his face at night. Even back then, he was an insomniac, who'd only known peaceful sleep in his mother's arms when he was a baby; all other sleep was deathly, like the sleep he knew as a sick child in the days when he could not breathe and when he felt his heart churning and welts covered his back and stomach. It was the deathly sleep of opening his eyes and finding his mother sitting in a chair near his bed weeping and a priest looming over him and dabbing an oil that smelled vaguely of cinnamon onto his forehead with the back of his thumb and making the sign of the cross, and he himself thinking as a child that he was going to die. The peaceful sleep in his mother's arms was the sleep he missed, and so he would walk those streets, agonized by the night and wishing that he had never left Las Piñas or the loving grip of his mother. But he was a man, *coño!* Destined to live in the world and to take his place among the other men who were everywhere, running things and giving orders and facing life in every moment. Why should he be any different?

He would walk those streets daydreaming, and because he took no regular route and liked to zigzag in and out of the back alleys and down corridors and to follow stairways, he never knew where he would end up. This wandering sometimes made him feel an affinity with the stars. He'd sit for hours looking at them by the harbor: stars shooting across the sky, stars hanging there with their pink- and blue-tinted light and set against a sky that went on forever and forever. What were they doing up there? Murmuring and sighing and looking down at love's follies, the way they did in songs? Were they lonely, or sad, longing to break free of the darkness that nurtured them? Or were they destined to remoteness, always to search for happiness—like Nestor?

One night he went out to a park in the Maríanao district where the *rumberos* would gather under the trees by a river with their incredible *batá* drums and their bead-wrapped rattle gourds and trumpets to play music. That night he had joined them, playing the trumpet, and was on his way back home, wandering the streets. In a corner bar he drank a coffee and watched some children dancing to an organ-grinder's music. Afterwards he thought about going to a cowboy movie but then continued along a route that took him past a doorway from which he heard smashing dishes, shouts, and a struggle on the stairs. Had that argument broken out five minutes sooner or later than his arrival, the situation might have resolved itself without his intervention and the woman in the torn dress with the tears running down her beautiful face would have gone back to her apartment or made up with the man. But he happened to be walking by when he heard shouting, and then he heard quick, pattering footsteps on the stairs, slaps, then through the doorway the fighting couple, the man trying to pin her arms and the beautiful woman in tears pulling at his hair. A lot of pain on their faces, and the man violently angry.

Heroically, Nestor interceded, approaching the man and telling him, "Look, stop it, you shouldn't hurt her. She's only a woman." And then it turned into something else, the man bristling at this fairy's nerve of fucking with him, and so he said, "And who are you to tell me this?" and gave Nestor a shove, and Nestor shoved back, and then they both started punching each other, the fight ending up on the cobblestone street, with both men bloody and their clothes covered with dirt. Having watched the fight from a distance, while finishing his rice and chicken and sausage and *tostones* dinner in a café down the street, a police officer came over and pulled them apart.

When the man calmed down, he huddled with the woman, exchanged angry words with her, and then stormed off, saying: "You don't need me? Then good, you'll never see me again." She watched him leave. Every few feet he would reel around and shout something else back at her. "Bitch! Whore!" She wept, and

Nestor stood on the corner, no longer wanting to continue his walk. He did not want to move away from her, and though they did not have much to say, they stood side by side, silently. He then offered to take her to the café. "It will make you feel better," he said.

Looking at her, Nestor felt faint-headed: she was more beautiful than the sea, than the morning light, than a wildflower field, and her whole body, agitated and sweaty from her struggles, gave off an aromatic female scent, somewhere between meat and perfume and ocean air, that assailed Nestor's nostrils, sank down into his body like mercury, and twisted in his gut like Cupid's naughty arrow. He was so shy that he couldn't look at her anymore, and she liked this, because men were always looking at her.

"My name is María," she told him.

"Nestor's mine," he told her quietly.

She was twenty-two years old and had left her small *pueblo* by the sea for Havana, where she had been living for the last few years working as a dancer in different little Havana nightclubs. He wasn't surprised to hear that she was a dancer: she had a nice body and strong-looking, curvaceous legs, with muscles that were round and delicate. She was a *mulata* beauty with the high cheekbones of a starlet of the forties, a pouty, seductive double for Rita Hayworth. And the man with whom she had been fighting?

"Someone who was once good to me."

He passed the night with her in the café eating *paella* and drinking wine and telling her everything about his short life, his childhood illnesses, his sense of unworthiness, his fears that he could never be a real macho in the kingdom of machos. Her state of pain and her throbbing vulnerability spoke to his own pain. Each of his stories entered María, his new confidante, the only woman in the world to whom he had spoken so, María, to whom, in the end, these confessions would mean nothing.

That night, and many other nights, she was polite, grateful, and affectionate. At her doorway, he bowed and then turned away. She was so good-looking that he never dreamed he'd have a chance with her. But then she pulled him close to her and they kissed. She closed her eyes in some kind of sympathy, their bodies pressed together, her hand holding the back of his head. The warm softness inside her dress. The thickness of her tongue . . .

"Why don't we go out to the Luna Park tomorrow," she said to him. "Can you come here in the afternoon?"

It was his day off.

"Yes."

"Then shout up into that window there." And she pointed to a shuttered second-floor window by a balcony off which hung a sheet and some dresses.

He walked the streets home that night with his stomach in and chest out and with his *pinga* warm and bloated inside his trousers, ecstatic over the amorous possibilities. He walked around his neighborhood for hours and then finally climbed the stairs to the *solar* which he had been sharing with his older brother, Cesar. He found him cooking some pork chops over a little stove they had there. He was in his T-shirt and boxer shorts, and looked somber. It had been bad times for him since he'd moved out of the apartment he'd had with his wife and daughter. He'd been drinking, too; a bottle of Tres Medallas brandy sat on the windowsill, and Cesar seemed groggy.

"What happened to you?"

"I met someone. A girl named María."

Cesar nodded, patted his brother on the back, hoping that this woman would help with Nestor's solemn moods.

And Nestor sat with his older brother at the table, blood pouring through his veins, bursting with life, devouring another pork chop, even though he'd eaten a big meal just a few hours before. Chewing noisily like a little hungry hound. Sounds of life, of digestion, a look of happiness and hope in his eyes. Although he couldn't sleep that night, his was a joyful insomnia that buoyed his spirits, so that he felt like leaning out the window and shouting out to the world. Instead, he lay awake in bed and quietly strummed his guitar, an A-minor chord, his favorite key for writing songs. He strummed and dreamed up melodies that materialized in his mind like hard, bright pearl necklaces. He watched the window for the first signs of light. He imagined himself turning up at the farm at Las Piñas with this woman, charging across a field with her, and telling his mother: "Look, *Mamá,* this is Nestor, your son who you thought would never be happy! *Pobrecito!* Look at me, I've got a beautiful woman who loves me!"

He waited until he heard the first sounds of day and he could make out the shadowy silhouette of the outside balustrade, a wreath of flowers, on the tattered windowshade. Radio in the courtyard: "And now from the House of Socks, radio station CMQ in Havana . . ." Men in T-shirts frying sausages on their balconies. His older brother turning over in bed, sighing. Footsteps in the hallways, a little girl downstairs playing hopscotch, another jumping rope . . .

That morning and into the afternoon he was tortured by expectation. And as happy as he had felt, his self-doubts, another of the family afflictions, crept through the sunniness of his thoughts. Standing outside her window, he shouted her name for about twenty minutes, but she did not come out. By that time Nestor had become convinced that María had lied about going to the Luna Park with him and that he had been cheated of his joy. And so he began to walk away, figuring he would spend the afternoon downtown in the movie houses. He was feeling discouraged, when María came walking around the corner, breathless and hurried.

"I had to take something to my cousin and it took longer than I thought."

The day was beautiful. His faith restored, they passed the time holding hands and strolling through the crowds in the park. They played games of chance. From time to time he gazed into her eyes, thinking, I know that we're falling in love, aren't we? And she would smile, but her head would turn away, as if struck by some quick, flitting pain. She seemed cautious around him. Of course, she was getting through something with this other man. Nestor kept his distance, remained quiet, but whenever he mentioned the "incident of that day," she would say, "Don't even think about that man, he was such a *cabrón.*" Why, then, the wistful look in her eyes?

"Come," and she would take him by the hand. "Let's have fun!"

By evening they were sitting out on a pier by the sea necking, the head of his penis weeping semen tears. He wasn't bothered by the ease with which she gave herself, though old ladies and duennas gave them dirty looks. He thought, if she's kissing me so much, that's because we're in love! Why was she closing her eyes so much, as if he wasn't there? They saw each other every day for two weeks. He would go to her house, where she rented a room from a woman there, and they would head out into the street, a bounce in his jaunty walk. Their love affair came down to secret moments of hurried kissing and groping, mutual masturbation against alley walls and in movie theaters, and this inevitably led to the consummation of this love in a room filled with blue light by the harbor, on a bed white as beach sand, in the apartment of a friend.

That very day he first thought of writing a *canción* about his love for her. Sated and living in paradise, the younger Mambo King, who really had never known women, thought of this lyric: "When desire overwhelms a man's soul, he is lost to everything in the world but love . . ."

He and María feasted on each other for months. They'd go to a deserted stretch of beach outside Havana or to the apartment of Nestor's friend by the harbor. He never took her up to the *solar* he shared with his older brother, because he felt that the cheerfulness of his love would be disturbing to Cesar, who had left his wife and child, and suffered for it, too . . . And besides, what if Cesar didn't like her? His brother, his heart, his blood. In those days Nestor would rush up the stairway of their *solar*, his Cuban-heeled shoes tapping on the floor, passing images of himself and María kissing in the shadows. They'd do it on the bed and sometimes on the floor, or on a pile of dirty clothes. They seemed to love each other so much, their skin gave off a lustful heat and smell so strong that they would attract packs of wild hounds who'd follow them down the streets.

Once, when Cesar was away, she went to the brothers' flat and decided to make Nestor dinner. She was cooking up a pot of chicken and rice on the white enamel stove with animal feet, and then, ladle in hand, she stuck out her rump, pulled up her dress, and said, "Come on, Nestor."

She liked it every which way: from behind, in her mouth, between her breasts, and in her tight bottom. She would make his penis agonizingly plump and long. He used to think he would split her open, but the more he gave her, the wider she spread herself before him. He took her to the movies, where they sat in the balcony and in the midst of the crucial love scenes, he slipped one and then two and then three and then four fingers inside her. In the foyer of a building landing, he would lift up her skirt and lick her thighs. He would lean up against her like a hound, pressing his tongue against the dead center of her panties. Some days he forgot his name and where he lived and where he worked: by day at the Havana chapter of the Explorers' Club, by night in a little gambling casino nightclub called the Club Capri. She had large firm breasts. Her nipples were brown and the size of quarters, very small-tipped at first, but when he suckled them they would swell. Tiny flora of sensation blossomed and he could taste the sweetness of her milk. Livid and as thick as her wrist, his penis slid into her mouth and she reached back and opened his buttocks and stuck her hand inside, probing him. He was alive then, *coño!* Alive.

He was so in love with her that he could have died in her arms happily. Loved her so much he licked her rump hole. She came and he came and in the red-tinged silver-and-white that exploded in his brow and that shuddered through his body he felt a thready presence, like a soul entering him. He would lie beside her, feeling that his body had been turned into a field and that he and she floated ecstatically over that field on the wings of love. He thought about her as he scrubbed the hair-tonic stains off the back of the heavy leather chairs at his job at the club. He wore a short white jacket with three brass buttons and a little hat like a bellboy's, carried trays of food and drink to the club members, and he daydreamed about licking her nipples. Smell of linseed-oil-polished wood, cologne, blue cigar smoke, flatulence. The smell of leather, hair-tonic-stained chairs, thick rugs from Persia and Turkey. Nestor laughing, Nestor happy. Nestor slapping his older brother's then-troubled back. He'd work in the little kitchen behind the bar, making crustless ham sandwiches, and drinks. He whistled, he smiled, he sang happily. He'd look out across the dining room through open French doors to the patio and garden. He would think about the devastating curvaceousness of her buttocks, the sliver of thick black hair that protruded,

but just barely, from behind her spread thighs. Scent of soft violet
wisteria, falling over the garden walls, leafy jasmine and Chinese
hibiscus. The taste of her wide-open vagina, all red and gleaming
from moistness, an open orchid to his tongue.

Waiting to see her again, he suffered through evenings when
he went to work playing the trumpet and singing alongside his
brother with the Havana Melody Boys. His María worked in the
chorus line of the Havana Hilton, as one in a line of ten "beautiful
cream-and-coffee-colored dancers," and that's where Nestor
wanted to be, his eyes looking off not at the audience or the
spotlights but into the distance. He could not help thinking about
María. When he was not with her he was miserable, and after
playing these jobs he would rush out to meet her.

For his part, Cesar was curious about this Beautiful María
who had taken his maudlin, quiet brother and made him happy.
So finally Nestor arranged that they meet one night. They chose
a bar where a lot of musicians liked to go, up by Maríanao beach.
Dios mío! his brother Cesar was surprised by María's beauty and
he gave Nestor his approval, but then, so did everyone else. He
stood there trying like every other man to figure out how on earth
Nestor had landed her. Not by know-how; his younger brother
had never been a womanizer. In fact, he'd always seemed a little
frightened of women. And now there he was, with a beautiful
woman and a real look of happiness on his face. He hadn't won
her over with his looks, pleasantly handsome, with a long matador's face and a sensitive, pained expression, large dark eyes, and
large fleshy ears. It must have been his brother's sincerity and
innocence, qualities which femmes fatales seemed to appreciate.
Watching her dance before a jukebox blaring Beny More, her ass
shaking and body wobbling, her beautiful face the center of attention in that room, Nestor felt triumphant because he knew what
the others wished they knew: that yes, her breasts were as round
and succulent as they appeared to be under her dress, and that her
nipples got big and taut in his lips, and yes, her big rumba ass
burned, and yes, the fabulous lips of her vagina parted and sang
like the big kiss-me lips of her wide lipsticked mouth, and yes, she
had thick black pubic hair, and a mole on the right side of her face
and a corresponding mole on the second inner fold of her labia
minora; he knew the fine black hair that crept up gradually out

the crack of her buttocks, and that when she reached orgasm she would whip her head back and grind her teeth, her body shaking in the aftermath.

Standing by the bar proudly, beside his older brother, Nestor sipped his beer, one bottle after another, until the sea's blueness outside the club windows rustled like a cape and he could shut his eyes and drift like the thick smoke of that room through the crowd of dancers, wrapping himself around the voluptuousness that was María.

Funny, that was their mother's name too. María. María.

Remembering those days, Nestor would never think about the long silences in their conversations when they'd go for walks in the park. After all, he was just an introspective country boy with a sixth-grade education who knew more about musicians and breeding animals than anything else. Once he'd told her about himself, he had almost nothing to say. "And how are your cousins?" "How is the club?" "Nice day, isn't it?" "*Bueno,* what a good day?" "Why don't we go for a walk and get something good to eat?" What could he say to her? She was beyond human conversation. She liked it when he serenaded her in front of the opera house in the park with his guitar and crowds would gather to listen and applaud him. Some days, she seemed very sad and lost, and that made her even more beautiful. He would walk alongside her, wondering what she was thinking and what he could say to make her laugh.

Gradually, their walks turned into long vigils through the night, until they reached that place where everything would be fine: their bed. But then, somehow, even their spirited romps in bed turned into something else. She would stop and weep in his arms, weep so hard that he didn't know what to do.

"What is it, María? Can you tell me?"

"You want a good piece of advice, brother?" Cesar would tell Nestor. "If you want a woman, treat her good sometimes, but don't let her get too used to it. Let her know that you are the man. A little abuse never hurt a romance. Women like to know who's the boss."

"But abuse María? My María?"

"Take my word for it . . . Women like to be ordered around and put in their place. Then she will stop her weeping."

Trying to think what his brother meant, he started to order María around, and during their silent walks in the park he would show her that he was a man, taking her roughly by the wrists and saying to her, "You know, María, you must feel lucky to be with someone like me."

He'd watch her by the mirror, making herself up, and say, "I never realized that you were so vain. It's not good, María, you'll be ugly in old age if you look too long in the mirror."

He did other things to her which would later make him cringe with unhappiness and the unfairness of it all. Good-looking as she was, he imitated his older brother and took to looking around at all the other women on the street. He had the idea that if he could diminish her, then she would always remain by his side. When things didn't get better, their silences increased. As things got worse, Nestor became more and more confused.

But during that time when things were bad for them, Nestor sat down and wrote his mother a letter saying, "*Mamá*, I think I've found a girl to marry."

And once he'd told his mother, his romance took on a magical, inevitable quality. Destiny, he called it. At first, he made a formal proposal to her, on his knees, in a garden behind a social club, with ring and flowers. He bowed his head, waiting for an answer: he shut his eyes, thinking about all the light in heaven, and when he looked up to see her pretty face again, she was running out of the garden, his ring and flowers beside him on the ground.

When he would make love to her, he would think about the man he had seen the day they met and how she had wept afterwards. Making love, he left marks on her legs and on her breasts from gripping them roughly to show her that he was a strong man. He would get up from their bed and say to her, "You're going to leave me, aren't you?" He had a sick feeling in his gut that something inside him was pushing her away. On those nights he wished for a *pinga* so huge that it would burst her open, and let fly, like a broken *piñata*, all her new doubts about him.

Believing that persistence would win out on his behalf, he would say to her, "I'm going to ask you to marry me every day until you tell me yes."

They'd take walks, go to the movies, her beautiful face pained.

"There's something I want to tell you . . ." she'd always begin.

"Yes, María, that we are always going to be together?"

". . . Yes, Nestor."

"Ah, I knew it. I would die without you."

One night they were supposed to see a Humphrey Bogart movie and meet at their usual place, in front of a bakery called De Leon's. When she failed to turn up, he walked the streets looking for her until three in the morning, and when he returned to the *solar* he told his older brother what had happened and Cesar said that there was probably a good reason why she had missed their date. He always found his brother's advice sound and felt much better. The next day, he went to María's house and she was not there, and he went there the next day and she was not there, and then he went to the Havana Hilton and she was not there. What if something had happened to her? He kept returning to her *edificio,* but she was never there, and each evening Cesar, who was having a rough time himself, consoled him. But by the fifth day his older brother, whose life philosophy had turned into rum, rumba, and rump, told Nestor: "Either something happened to her or else she's abandoned you. If something happened to her, then you'll see her, but if she's left . . . you have to forget her."

On another morning, he knocked at the door so long that the owner came out. "María Rivera? She's moved away."

He returned again and again to the club, even when he was told that she had quit her job and returned to her *pueblo.*

For weeks he couldn't eat or drink and he lost weight and his insomnia became worse. He would sit on the rooftop of their *solar,* watching the stars over the harbor, stars of lamentation, stars of devotion, stars of infinite love, and ask them, "Why are you mocking me?" He went to his job in a disastrous state of mind, exhausted and solemn. His state of gloom was as ecstatic as his previous state of happiness.

Even the leader of the Havana Melody Boys noticed Nestor's low spirits. While the other musicians mamboed across the stage, he barely moved. Someone whispered, "He looks like he's going through a bad affair of the heart."

"Poor fellow, looks like someone has died."

"Let him alone. There's nothing that's going to cure him. Only time."

Finally he went to her *pueblo,* which was about four hours by bus from Havana. He walked the streets, inquiring about a certain María Rivera. He'd left without saying a word to his older brother and had gotten a room in a local inn. He had been there for four days and was drinking a *café con leche* in a bar when he looked over and saw the man who had been fighting with María the day they met. Now that he could get a good look at him without the distortion of fear, he was surprised to see a handsome man. He was wearing a blue *guayabera,* white linen *pantalones,* yellow socks, and white shoes, and he had strong and pleasant, manly features: dark, intense eyes, a thick, virile mustache, a wide neck. The man had been drinking calmly and then abruptly he moved out into the street. Keeping a distance, Nestor followed him. He came to a lovely street, a narrow cobblestone street that went uphill. Old orange and light pink walls, overgrown with flowering vines. Palm trees and acacias throwing their shade over the sidewalk. And in the distance, the sea's radiance.

There was a house there. A beautiful, tin-roofed house overlooking the water. A smell of pineapple and a garden. A house of happiness and voices. María's voice, laughing happily, happily.

He waited, tormentedly lingering outside like a ghost, just to catch a glimpse of her. And it made things worse. He would look into her window and hear the chatter of voices and utensils and plates and pans frying up plantain fritters, her life being joyfully pursued without him, and he cringed. At first, he didn't have the guts to bang on the door and confront her, didn't want to see the truth. But he later found his strength in a bar and returned at dusk and swaggered over to the door, belly in, chest out. A long, mournful trumpet line, rising high and looping around the stars. Scent of mimosa in the air. Laughter. He kept banging on the door downstairs until the man came out.

"What do you want?"

"My woman."

"You mean," he said, "my wife."

"Don't tell me?"

"Since a week ago."

"But she hated you."

The man shrugged. "It was our destiny."

Oh, María, why were you so cruel, when I saw the stars washing through your hair and the moon's pensive glow in your eyes?

Nestor made his way down that hill to a seawall and leaned up against a small statue of the Cuban poet José Martí, watching the sea of dusk. There he daydreamed about how happy he could have been with her, if only he had not been so cruel, or if he had been a better conversationalist or had some real ambition. If only she had not seen the weakness in his soul. As if in a dream, María appeared behind him, and she was smiling. When he went to touch her hand, it was as if he were touching air. Nothing was there. But María was there. She spoke so gently to him and so tenderly about the torments of her heart and soul that when she left his side, he felt oddly calmed.

What was it that she had said to him?

"No matter what, I will love you forever."

Forever and forever unto death.

He spent that night camped outside her doorway, sighing. In the morning he found that she had left a plate of ham and bread outside by the pavement where he had slept, but it had been overrun by an army of ember-red ants.

He returned to Havana and told Cesar what María had told him.

Around his neck was the crucifix which his mother had given him for his First Communion and which had often touched the fullness of Beautiful María's breasts. And around his chest, a sensation of stones and earth constricting him, the vague, pulsing feeling in the joints of his bones, which turned to wax, as if any second he would collapse.

"She said she still loves me. She said she thinks about me all the time. She said that she never wanted to hurt me. She says that sometimes when she's lying in bed at night she thinks about me and can still feel me inside her. She said . . ."

"Nestor, stop it."

"She said she would have married me except for one thing, this other fellow in her life, an old *prometido* from her town, where she's from. That he was just someone she was trying to forget. A country bumpkin who used to ignore her when they were together and who came here to take her back, and"— he cupped his hands over his face—"she felt that she had to go back to him and . . ."

"Nestor, stop it."

"She said she'll always remember our times together as being beautiful, but he came along before me, and, well, now our fate is sealed. She said that she married him because of an inner pain. She says she never meant to deceive me, that she really loved me. She says that her heart was broken that we hadn't met a long time before, but this man had always been her love . . ."

"Nestor, she was like a *puta!*"

"She said that I was her true love but . . ."

"Nestor, stop it. Where are your balls, man? You're better off without her."

"Yes, better off."

And what happened? After the shattering of this love affair, Nestor just wasn't the same and took on the fearful expression of his youth when he would cower in the darkness of his room at night, a feeling of doom whirling around him. He would go to his job at the Explorers' Club on Neptuno like a somnambulist, moving about the wood-paneled rooms with their maps and globes and lions' and antelopes' and rams' heads, carrying his trays of daiquiris and whiskeys for the prosperous British and Americans without ever smiling or saying a friendly word. On one of those days a shot rang out from the fancy toilets there, and the workers in the club rushed to find one of the gentlemen, a certain Mr. Jones, dead, the smoking revolver still in his hand. It would turn out that his real name was Hugo Wuerschner and he'd decided to take his life because of another club member, who had found out that Wuerschner had once acted as an agent in Havana for the Third Reich. Refusing to be blackmailed, Wuerschner, long despondent about the fall of his Führer, preferred to bring his grief to an end. The dead man's contorted and disillusioned expression was like Nestor's, so extreme was his suffering.

His older brother took Nestor everywhere, to the movies, the all-night cafés, and the whorehouses, and he told him, "She's not worth it," over and over again. "You're better off being a little hard with these women, because when you're good, it turns out bad." And: "Just forget her, she's worthless . . . not worth a single tear, you understand?"

Whenever he felt pain in his life, the older Mambo King would find himself a woman, and so he thought smothering Nestor with women was the answer. Memory of a drunken evening in the Havana of 1948 which the two brothers spent down by the harbor in a brothel called the Palace, their backs arching and exuberant sexes rising and falling endlessly through the night. Curling tongues, slapping bellies, moist thighs. They fucked and fucked and then roaring drunk made their way down to the harbor, where Nestor threw bottles at some sailors and wanted to confess his sins to a priest. Reaching the harbor, Nestor decided to steal a yacht so they might sail around the world, but when he found a rowboat and took it out thirty yards he lost the oars and vomited in the water. Standing up and laughing, he pissed into the bay, which the moonlight was chopping up into triangle reflections of the red and yellow and blue party lights of the city. In the distance, he heard the booming horn of a ship, crying out, *Castillo, Castillo,* and he shouted, "To hell with everything!" Laughing, he kept thinking, The hell with María, I am alive!

Then they went home to their *solar,* Cesar pulling Nestor through the streets and stumbling toward buildings that seemed to bow and nod like wise old Chinese men. They found the gate and the stairway up into their *solar*, up ten steps and back down fifteen, Cesar calming his brother, Nestor laughing loudly.

"To hell with everything!"

But even that night did not penetrate the glorious mask of his suffering. What powers María held over him, no one knew. That would remain a mystery to Cesar.

"You've always been that way, crying over nothing," Cesar said to him. "She's worthless, bad for you like a bottle of poison. Couldn't you see that from the beginning?"

"But I love her."

"*Hombre*, she's garbage."

"Without her, I want to die."

"Don't be stupid."

"If you knew my pain . . ."

"*Dios mío*, you've got to stop humiliating yourself this way."

(Then the voices went on until the last fading trumpet line of "Beautiful María of My Soul," inhalation of a cigarette, sip of whiskey, and the record-player arm lifts up again.)

ALTHOUGH NESTOR USED THICK World War II-issue prophylactics, he was sometimes very careless and casual about his lovemaking with Delores, doing it without a rubber and withdrawing long after the initial shudder of ejaculation. She would lock herself up in the bathroom and clean out her womb with a douche that resembled a poultry baster, which she'd filled with bicarbonate of soda and seltzer. One afternoon, while waxing the rich man's parquet floors, she had the sensation that her womb was filling up with light, like stars at dusk rising slowly in the dark sky, and it occurred to her that these intimations of light were those of a soul, a breath, life itself. A hundred-year-old Cuban doctor practicing on Columbus Avenue and 83rd Street diagnosed a pregnancy. She climbed the stairs to the La Salle Street apartment expecting that Nestor would greet the news with ecstatic, lovestruck joy. As she walked in, he was working on the very song he had been whistling when they'd met nearly a year ago. When she heard that melody, it would take her back to that day, and she believed that this bolero was now hers. She approached him, wrapped her arms around his neck, and whispered, "I have something to tell you. I'm pregnant."

Nestor took a deep breath, stared out into the middle of the living room, where sat a dolly and the black case of a bass American kit drum, blinked, sighed, and then said to her, "Are you sure?"

But when he saw the happiness in her expression wither away, he added, "No, I'm happy, *querida*. Really happy."

Then he put his arms around her, but he lowered his head and seemed to be watching the window, which was open a slit to the fire escape, and in that moment she had the impression that he wanted to walk over to the window, climb out, and never come back.

The young musician did the right thing: Nestor and Delores were married by a Justice of the Peace in a small wooded town in New Jersey. After the ceremony, Nestor remained by the table on which Cesar Castillo had placed a case of chilled champagne, tossing back one glass after the other. They had no honeymoon but threw a party that started in a Chinatown restaurant and ended up in the Mambo Nine Club, where they knew the bartender and manager and a band of their musician friends from the dance halls provided the music. In the merriment of that day, she kissed and hugged her sister Ana María and wished to God that her father were alive to see her so happy again. She thought about him and felt sad. Following the example of all the merry friends, she drank too much of that champagne. Her inexperience caught up to her and she twirled in circles to a mambo and watched everyone's face elongating, ears growing long and pointed like those of wolves, in the red and yellow lights of the club. Then things blurred and grew thick black borders. Later she woke up on the living-room couch of the La Salle Street apartment beside Nestor. He was still dressed, and with his head tilted back on the couch he was snoring and muttering to himself. She wiped his forehead with a kerchief, gave him a kiss, and thought, "My husband, my husband."

But then she listened, and like pins through her side, she heard, faintly but clearly, "María, María."

They had two children: Eugenio, who was born in '51, and Leticia, in '54. Nestor didn't quite know what to make of fatherhood, he felt so underprepared for manly duty in this world. He realized it when Eugenio was born. At first he celebrated happily. He daydreamed about walking off into the future with his wife and son down golden paths, joyful in their love. But something got to him: the utter helplessness of the baby, its crying for attention, its need for care. Holding Eugenio in his arms and examining the fresh veins under the scalp of his soft pink and sweet-smelling head, he was frightened by all the things that might go wrong. He would think about this fellow who worked with him down at the plant, who had left his one-year-old daughter in a room by herself for fifteen minutes and returned to find her dead; and he would think about this drummer he knew, a really nice Cuban guy named Papito, whose nineteen-year-old son went *pffft* out of the world because one of the veins in his head had been too thin-walled and could not sustain a surge of blood during the playing of a softball game in Van Cortlandt Park. Nestor would cover Eugenio's face with kisses, play with his toes, tickle his ribs, and sing to him. He loved it when the baby smiled and showed signs of recognizing his father, but when the baby showed any signs of discomfort, a terrible remorsefulness would overwhelm Nestor and he would walk the halls of the house as if some kind of tragedy were unfolding before his eyes. My son is suffering! And that simple fact seemed unbearable to him.

"Delores, do something with the *nene!* Make sure the *nene* is okay! Don't forget the *nene!*"

He would come home from the day job at the meat-packing plant and see how well Delores had taken care of them. Like a supervisor, he would peer down into their beds and nod pensively, examining them for the plumpness of their legs and color in their cheeks. He would feel at a loss, holding them in his arms. He was affectionate with them but never quite knew what to make of fatherhood. He was constantly brooding about them to himself, worried about their physical health. He saw them as being so helpless and so susceptible to harm that on some days he relived a terrible dream of his anxious childhood. In the middle of the day, he would think how Eugenio liked to play by the window. What if he climbed out and slammed to the pavement below? *Dios mío!* He would start pacing up and down and take five to call the apartment to make sure everything was all right. He would lift the side of white fatted beef off the conveyor belt and hoist it onto the back of a freezer truck, wearing a long smock that was smeared with blood and a pair of rubber boots. The smell of blood in the air, the carcasses and bones that were everywhere, didn't help matters.

It didn't help that Leticia developed asthma and was sickly for a long time. He felt so bad about her troubled breathing that he would come home every day with presents and candies for her. And because he was not unkind, there was always something in his pockets for Eugenio. He was astounded when they did not die, but the whole business with Leticia made him very tense. In some ways he could not stand to be around the house and the potential for disaster; in others, he could not bear to be away. Best was when the house was packed with visitors—jam sessions with other musicians and dinner parties with these musicians and their wives. And his older brother, Cesar, drunk, collar loosened, big bulge in his trousers, with his arms wrapped around a pretty girl's waist.

When responsible, mature, good-hearted people who would know what to do in a crisis were around, Nestor breathed easy. But, generally speaking, he never relaxed for a moment. His moments of release? When his penis exploded with sperm and obliterated his personality, throwing him into a blue- and red-lit heaven of floating space, and when he played the trumpet and got lost in melody. Otherwise, he didn't know what to do with himself. The responsibility weighed on his shoulders too heavily for his own good. His anxiety took on physical symptoms. Some nights, as he tried to sleep and terror lurked in the air, he would begin to sweat, and his heart would beat so rapidly he could swear he was about to have a heart attack. Other times, as it happened with his father, he broke out into terrible rashes. He was only twenty-eight in 1954, and though he didn't have very good dietary habits, eating what Cubans liked to eat, he was thin and fit. Yet the pounding of his heart would plague him night after night, and he was convinced that there was something wrong with him. But he would never think of going to a doctor.

He would send his mother in Cuba tender letters written in his simple script, speaking about his love for her and the family; heartsick letters nostalgic for the security of the home he had —or thought he had—in Cuba. He was very emotional, thinking about his childhood, about the tender care he received when he was sick in bed. He'd forget about the terrors of his solitude and dwell upon all the kisses from his mother and their housemaid Genebria, how everyone seemed to look out after him, especially Cesar. He'd open these letters with the salutation *"Querida mamá"* and finished them off with: "All of us in the household here send you a thousand, no, a million kisses. With all the love of my heart, your *hijito*, N."

He always signed these letters with a single letter, "N."

His nights were a disaster. He'd often come home to La Salle Street from a job by himself, strip down and climb into bed beside Delores, remaining awake beside her and inviting her attentions. They would wrap their arms around each other, caressing affectionately until they fell asleep. But he would always awaken in the early hours, thinking that there was something missing from his life—what, he did not know. At three-thirty in the morning, he would get up and sit in the dark living room, softly strumming guitar chords, and stirring Delores from her dreams, so that she would make her way down the hall.

"Nestor, why don't you come back to bed?"

He'd just keep strumming. He'd sit by the window, looking out. The street glowed like dusk with the light of a wrought-iron lamp.

"It's just a song."

Sometimes he didn't sleep for three or four days. He didn't know what was going on. Cubans then (and Cubans now) didn't know about psychological problems. Cubans who felt bad went to their friends, ate and drank and went out dancing. Most of the time they wouldn't think about their problems. A psychological problem was part of someone's character. Cesar was *un macho grande;* Nestor, *un infeliz.* People who hurt bad enough and wanted cures expected these cures to come immediately. Cesar was quite friendly with some *santeras,* really nice ladies who had come from Oriente Province and settled on 110th Street and Manhattan Avenue. And whenever Cesar felt bad about anything, if he felt depressed about the fact that he still had to work in a meat-packing plant to maintain his flamboyant life-style, or when he felt guilty about his daughter down in Cuba, he would go see his friends for a little magical rehauling. These *santeras* liked to listen to the radio all day, loved to have children and company around them. If he felt bad, he would just go in there and drop a few dollars into a basket, lie on his stomach on a straw mat on the floor, ring a magic bell (which symbolized his goddess, Caridad, or charity) and pay homage to the goddess Mayarí, for whom these women were intermediaries. And pssssst! his problems would lift away. Or they would lay hands on him. Or he would just go over to 113th and Lenox, to a *botánica*, and get himself a "cleaning"—the saint pouring magic herbs over him —guaranteed to do the trick. Going to confession at the Catholic church did the same job: a heartfelt opening of the heart and an admission of sins; then the cleansing of the soul. (And no death-bed confession either, no admission to heaven because of last rites. These Cubans died as they lived, and a man who would not confess his sins at age twenty-five was not going to do so at seventy.)

Nestor went with Cesar and was cleansed, paid obeisance, and felt better for a few days. Then the feeling came back to him, and he was unable to move. It was like being trapped in a tight shaft of darkness: sometimes it twisted in a labyrinth, sometimes it went straight. Moving inside it was always difficult. He even tried to go to confession when he had no sins to confess. Inside the church's big red doors and its smell of honeycomb candle wax and incense, he would march up to the communion railing, re-member how he would kneel on the cool stone floors of the church in Las Piñas beside his mother, and pray to Christ and all his saints and to the Holy Mother. He'd shut his eyes, his brow trembling with the effort to make a connection to God.

And one day when the priest's face appeared in the darkness behind the confessional screen, he said, "Father . . . I have come for guidance."

"What kind of guidance?"

"My heart is . . . sad."

"And what has made you sad?"

"A woman. A woman I once knew."

"And are you in love with her?"

"Yes, Father."

"Does she love you?"

Silence.

"Well, does she love you?"

"I don't know, Father."

"Do you want her to love you?"

"Yes, Father."

"Have you told her?"

"Yes."

"And are you in a situation that allows you this?"

"No, Father. I have a family."

"And is that why you are here?"

"Yes, Father."

"Have you acted upon this feeling?"

"In my heart."

"Your marriage makes that wrong."

"I know."

"But this temptation . . . I counsel you to pray. Do you have a rosary?"

"Yes, Father."

"Then say the rosary and you will be strengthened."

And he said the rosary, enjoying the stony companionship of the saints and Jesus; he said the rosary until the prayers were coming out of his eyes, but his guilty feelings remained. He sometimes felt so bad that he told himself, "If I had remained with María, I would have found my happiness." He would go over his romance again and again in his head, though it had ended years before. He had walked into it happily, naïvely, innocently . . . and his soul had been ruined.

Even though he loved Delores, he could not stop himself from thinking about María. A pain would throb in his kneecaps and this pain would spread upwards through his thighs and down through his ankles, a surge of melancholia, and out of this would come María. What was it that she had said to him that day in 1948?

"I will love you forever."

He would walk over to the park and secretly write her letters at least once a month, though he never received an answer. He would watch the boats passing on the Hudson River, dragging barges of piping and refuse, and think about María naked on a bed. He would have painful memories of what it felt like inside her: out of the sky would fall a silk handkerchief, warmed by the sun and dipped in honey, that would wrap tightly around his penis.

But even though he knew that it was all wrong, he couldn't get rid of this longing for her. His feelings of hopelessness always led him back to María, and thoughts of María led him back to hopelessness. He loved Delores, loved his children—why, then, were things so wrong? He tore up most of his photographs of her, save for one, and this he kept hidden in a box thick with sheet music, stuck in the living room between a bass drum and a *quinto*. He wouldn't look at this picture for months, and then he'd take it out and she always seemed more beautiful and tender than he had remembered. The fact that she had cruelly abandoned him did not temper his desire. He knew that something had to change, but didn't know how to change it.

He developed an odd habit. In the warm weather he and the family liked to go up to the rooftop for a picnic. Once when he did so, he went over to the edge and found himself leaning over it, so far that Delores cried out, "Nestor!" and the excitement and his bravery made the children laugh. For a moment, as he hung over La Salle Street watching the kids below playing stickball and the birds circling the water towers, he thought about dropping off the rooftop, as if by letting go he would fly among the buildings, looping like a butterfly until he hit the pavement. Thinking about his family, he had resisted the temptation to let go. Then he started to lean out their fourth-floor window quite a bit, as if to get rid of the feeling, and was thinking about it on the day when he came home with a present for Eugenio, who was then nearly three years old. It was a kite and they spent hours running back and forth on the rooftop, laughing and watching it rise high into the wind, its balsa cross-beams bending and the paper fluttering in the air. He stood by the edge of the roof with Eugenio in his arms. Kisses on his face and pats on the back.

Sometimes, on long walks through the city, he'd day-dreamed about meeting up with someone who would give him sound advice and have all the keys to happiness. He thought that the Italian fruit vendor knew, that those old wizened-looking Jewish men who would go walking up La Salle on their way to the Jewish Theological Seminary knew. That they would tell him what to do about those feelings which made him lower his head and want to step off the sidewalk into the path of an oncoming bus or that made him cling, with fear, to the subway walls because the edge of the platform seemed so inviting.

Lost in contemplation, he'd sometimes wander downtown amid the endless crowds that passed him on the street; people with the most purposeful and determined expressions hurrying everywhere, as if to a Dance of the Sabers. As he sat on a park bench, bums approached him and he would give them cigarettes, money. Dogs lay stretched out on the pavement, happy and panting, by his feet. And sometimes pretty women in white high-heeled pumps and feathered hats, fascinated by the soulful-looking young Latin-lover type, would sit beside him, wanting to start up a conversation.

What did he want? He only wanted to find shelter in the bosom of love, not rush anywhere, and to have the heaviness lifted off his shoulders.

One thing Nestor came to admire was Delores's habit of reading. She read huge amounts and seemed better off for it. And she had told him, in the midst of her kisses on one of his restless nights, "Nestor, you should get in the habit of reading yourself to sleep." But aside from the newspapers and the Captain Marvel books he would buy on the newsstands, he hardly read anything at all. He was curious about those books that kept Delores so occupied while sitting on the park bench rocking the children in their carriages, those cheap paperbacks whose pages she would turn while standing by the stove and boiling water to cook *yuca*. Reading gave her a vaguely absent air, though she was never lax about her wifely duties, and he had no cause to complain, because she really did look out for him.

One day, however, Nestor did buy a book. Having crossed Times Square in a gloomy mood, he stopped at a newsstand to look over the magazines and a book caught his eye. It had a simple bright-red cover and was sitting among some tattered cowboy novels and girlie thrillers in a metal rack to the side. It was a book entitled *Forward America!* by a certain D. D. Vanderbilt.

It was the jacket copy that captured the younger Mambo King's attention:

> . . . Not a human being on earth likes to admit that things aren't always as rosy as they should be. I knew a fellow who spent half his life plagued with self-doubt. This doubt had a severe effect on his outlook and on his enjoyment of life. He couldn't sleep, found himself feeling "out of the picture" when everyone else around him seemed to be having the time of their lives. He had a decent-paying job, but with a family to support, he could never put enough money away for a rainy day. On top of all this, he never exerted himself around more aggressive kinds of people. He suffered because of this fault and doubted his own manliness. Many a day he daydreamed about a better life, but he seemed completely without resources when it came to realizing it.
>
> One day, this man took a good long look in the mirror and said, "I've had it!" He spent the night awake dreaming about the possibilities for his future and came up with the principles of achieving happiness in today's busy and troubled world. *Practical secrets and principles that will work for you!* That very next day he went to his boss and presented certain ideas that he'd had about the business and was so convincing about his new approaches that his boss gave him a *big promotion* and a *bonus.* . . . Within a few months he was promoted again, and within a few years he was made a partner in the firm . . .
>
> These principles worked to solve the other problems of his life. He has since achieved the greatest kind of success with *his friends, his family.* He has won the respect and love of others and found happiness the *American Way!* Read on, dear prospective buyer. It doesn't matter what walk of life you're from. Whether you're rich or poor, Chinaman, Indian, or from the planet Mars, this book can *change your life!*
>
> I know these principles work, because I was that man!

The D. D. Vanderbilt secrets of happiness will work for you!

Momentarily uplifted, Nestor paid the 79 cents plus tax (.04) for this book and then took the bus home to La Salle Street, where he hoped to find revelation among its pages.

Life continued much as it had and yet that book became Nestor's constant companion. *Forward America!* became dog-eared in his back pocket. He needed help for the spirit but not the body: his day job in the Kowolski meat-packing plant on 125th Street left him so exhausted that he'd have to rest up a few hours before getting dressed for a night job that would last until four in the morning. But he always had the strength to bed Delores down. Young and firm Delores had skin so smooth and warm to the touch that all she had to do was open her blouse and they would soon be making love. And Cesar? Even though she used to muffle her moans of pleasure in a pillow, her brother-in-law was like a bloodhound or a Sherlock Holmes when it came to knowing their bedroom habits and he would leave the apartment to check out the girls on the street corner or head down to the park to watch the boats going by on the river, killing an hour's time before returning to the apartment to find Delorita with her face flushed and her voice humming as she happily went about the ladylike business of cooking dinner.

Once Delorita had moved in, Cesar had had to change many of his habits. He had a room on the courtyard and from his window he could see his brother's window and had the fortune or misfortune one day, while feeding the alleycats pieces of his leftover lunch and cupcakes, to look over and notice, through a narrow opening in that bedroom's curtains, his sister-in-law standing naked, looking very voluptuous and fuckable before the mirror. He knew that Beautiful María was fine, but when he saw Delores naked, he thought *Dios mío!*, took a deep breath, shook his head, and decided for the sake of his sanity and family peace to keep his distance from Delores. He did this without much trouble, as he had his own girls, but all the same he couldn't stand to walk down the hall or sit in the living room reading a newspaper or with a guitar and hear their bed shaking, the headboard thumping into the wall, his brother's loud panting and her efforts to quiet him, Sssssh ssssssssssh, because she didn't want people to hear them or to know what they were doing, a joke considering how her fecund body filled the apartment with a scent of meat, cinnamon, and blood. And so Cesar would go out for his walks, and daydreaming.

And now this ten-cent 78 rpm metal disc recorded in a "Record Your Memories" booth in Coney Island, 1954:

> (Laughter) (Static) (Laughter) (A man's and a woman's voices joking, whispering, the man's voice saying) Go ahead, go ahead . . .
> Okay. (Static) Ayyyyy! Don't grab me there! (Laughter) (In the background the roaring roller coaster as it makes a turn and a kid shouting in English) Heeeeeeey, Johnny, ahm over heah, you dumb motherfuckah. (Laughter) *Bueno,* hello out there in radio land! (Laughter) This is Angie Pérez and I (Neck kisses and slurpy sounds) (Laughter) (Static) I . . . I . . . ayyyyy! just want to say that I'm here with my new boyfriend, Cesar, that is, the famous Cesar Castillo, at Coney Island, July 10, 1954, and I just want to say that he is the freshest *cochino* in the world *aaaayyyy!* (Laughter) And we're having a great time. And he told me to say, Heeeellllo, Neessstor, and to everyone at home there! And . . . (Static) Oh, time's running out. The, the red light is flashing. We have to say goodbye. Goodbye! Good (Static and click).

Although the Mambo Kings were one of the more popular bands in New York and, one month in 1954, had made it to number 5 in a Brooklyn *Herald* popularity poll (behind Tito Rodríguez, Machito, Israel Fajardo, Tito Puente), Cesar never made much money. What could thirteen musicians plus a manager plus the union plus the IRS plus the equipment managers and drivers make if they were paid $500 for a weekend job? One of his biggest problems was that Cesar had never agreed to sign an "exclusive management contract." He'd heard too many stories about singers and bands who'd signed all their future earnings away just so they could get a good rate in a prestigious club like the El Morocco. These contracts would allow the singer to perform elsewhere but always cut the club owner in for a percentage of the earnings, regardless of whether the performer ever worked in the big-time club again. Those contracts ruined the lives of many musicians, drove a number out of the business and into the Merchant Marine, the Army, inspired name changes and, in a few instances, murders. (A song in Cesar's head? Mafia, mafia, mafia. Italian, Puerto Rican, Jewish mafia. Black tuxedos, white tuxedos.)

Because of his refusal, he was always getting into shouting matches with club owners who'd pressure him. And this behavior got him into trouble with the wrong people. When they played certain clubs, they would make less money than they deserved. Some of these joints were run by tan-suited Puerto Rican gangsters who didn't like Cubans. He was always telling them to go fuck themselves and to shove their clubs up the *fondillos* of their sporty trousers.

But, because Cesar's bad temper was putting his fellow band-members out of work, Nestor would say, "Be reasonable, *hombre,*" and the Mambo King would go back to these very same club owners and ask their forgiveness. Later he'd feel like shit.

He was always trying to hustle money so that he could have nice watches, suits, and expensive shoes, take out women like Vanna Vane, and play the sport with his friends in a bar. He liked to buy people presents, gifts for the family and his friends. He never thought twice about paying for dinner or the movies when the family went out. He was the type of fellow to walk thirty blocks to save a fifteen-cent train fare, only to buy a round of drinks at the bar. He had all kinds of expenses, mainly from his social life, but he was always betting the horses on credit, and borrowing off his friends and fellow musicians when he lost. He always needed money. It had flown out of his pockets in Cuba and it flew out of his pockets in New York. He spent generously, his impoverished youth in Cuba be damned.

There was something else, too. As much as he had vowed never to get married again, he still thought about his daughter, Mariela, down in Cuba. Now and then, if something came through for him—if he got paid for singing on a record, or a horse actually won for him—he would buy a money order and send it to his daughter. By now she was nine years old, and from time to time he'd receive a letter from her, thanking him for his gifts. Once, after some difficulty with his wife, he got permission to visit little Mariela in Havana in 1952. By then his ex-wife had remarried and was living off Calle 20 with her schoolteacher husband, an older fellow named Carlos Torres. Bent on impressing Mariela, he took her into all the big department stores —Fin de Siglo, La Época, and El Encanto—buying her dresses and toys. And he bought her everything she wanted to eat, appearing before her as a benevolent being who'd smelled of cologne on whose lap she once used to sit. This Mariela had turned out to be a nice little girl, tender and affectionate. Leaving her at the end of that trip proved much more difficult than he had planned. So he always wanted to keep his memory alive in her mind through the sending of gifts. But week to week, his pockets were empty, no matter what he did to make money.

And he wanted to get a nice new automobile. He had bought Manny the bassist's used Oldsmobile for a few hundred dollars, and while it ran well, it was quite beat up from being used for all these Mambo King jobs. Parked outside of clubs and in dance-hall parking lots, it always had people sitting on it, jumping on it, making out on its hood. Plus a few accidents hadn't helped. He wanted a 1955 DeSoto and would walk into DeSoto dealerships every few months to examine the upholstery and the dashboard and the supersonic, space-age V-8 turbo-thrust engine, "whispering" clutch, and 180-degree viewerama window. And he loved its female roundness and sheeny cream-white skin, bumper guards that protruded like breasts and dimpled hood, curvy like a fine female rump. Decked out in a pink suit with lavender shirt and white tie, and black-brimmed cane hat, Cesar Castillo would walk into the showrooms and inquire about the automobile's price, talk himself behind the wheel, and sit back, daydreaming about the fabulous days that would be waiting for him were he the owner of so fine a car.

ONE TUESDAY NIGHT IN 1955 THE Cuban bandleader and television personality Desi Arnaz walked into the Mambo Nine Club on 58th Street and Eighth Avenue to check out the talent. Someone had told him about two Cuban brothers, Cesar and Nestor Castillo, that they were good singers and songwriters who might have some material for Arnaz to use on his show. The stage of the Mambo Nine was only ten feet wide, more suited for a cabaret act than for a thirteen-piece orchestra, but somehow the brothers' group, the Mambo Kings, set up with their congas, their horns, trombones, flute, stand-up bass, saxophones, and a grand piano behind a few ball microphones. This club was where the Mambo Kings sometimes tried out new numbers on fellow musicians and composers who'd come by, people like Machito and the great Rafael Hernández, composer of *"El Lamento Borinquen,"* who'd give them advice and encouragement. It was a place where musicians from the best bands in the city came in to drink, talk shop, and see what was going on. Under the glow of red-and-white stage lights the Mambo Kings played fast dance tunes like *"El Bodeguero"* and dreamy arrangements of slow, romantic boleros like *"Bésame Mucho."* Mr. Arnaz was sitting in the back with his pretty wife, the red glow of a candle vaguely illuminating his dark, intense eyes, liking very much what he was seeing and hearing . . . In white silk suits, and performing side by side before the big ball microphone, the two brothers showed an obvious affection for each other, the audience, and the music. Arnaz, chin resting on a fist, came to certain conclusions about them.

Appearing in the light, arms spreading wide before him, a halo of aureolitic splendor around his head, it was Cesar Castillo who reminded Arnaz of the old-fashioned crooners of society ballrooms and dance halls of Cuba, men with their hair slicked down and parted in the middle, thin mustaches and butterfly-looking lace bow ties. Yes, Cesar's voice evoked for Arnaz moon-lit nights, flowers, and blue-crowned nightingales on the wing, his was the voice of the eternal *caballero* serenading a woman on her wrought-iron balcony, a man who would die for the alluring bud of love.

"Ladies and gentlemen, this next song is a little *canción* that me and my brother Nestor here started to write when we first came up to the States some years ago. It's called 'Bella María de Mi Alma,' or 'Beautiful María of My Soul,' and it's about the sadness and torment of love. We hope you like it."

Cesar nodded to his pianist, the inimitable and ever-elegant Miguel Montoya, dapper in white from head to toe, who struck an A-minor chord, and then the congas and horns came in, Nestor's opening solo bouncing off the walls and making Arnaz's glass hum. And then Cesar began to sing the verses Nestor had been writing on a cold, lonely night spent shivering by a radiator, verses inspired by the Havana beauty who had broken his heart. Among those lyrics, these lines:

> . . . How can I hate you
> if I love you so?
> I can't explain my torment,
> for I don't know how to live
> without your love . . .
> What delicious pain
> love has brought to me
> in the form of a woman.
> My torment and ecstasy,
> María, my life,
> Beautiful María of my soul . . .

Arnaz listened attentively. During the chorus, when the two brothers were harmonizing like angels aloft on a cloud and confiding their pain, Arnaz thought about his own past love, his love for his wife and others, like his family down in Cuba and old friends he had not seen in a long time. As he watched the dance floor, where young couples sighed and kissed, Arnaz leaned over to his wife and said, "I must invite these fellows to play on the show."

Later, when the brothers were drinking by the bar, Arnaz lived up to his reputation as a friendly man and introduced himself, saying, with extended hand, "Desi Arnaz." He was wearing a sharp blue serge suit, white silk shirt, pink polka-dotted tie, and a frilly fringed handkerchief that bloomed like a tulip from his breast pocket. He shook their hands and ordered a round of drinks for all the musicians, complimented the brothers on their performance, and then invited them and their arranger-pianist Miguel Montoya to sit at his table. Then they met Lucille Ball, who spoke surprisingly good Spanish. She was dressed in a pearl-button blouse with a velvet diamond-broached vest and a long skirt. Her hands and wrists glittered with rings and bracelets and she had curly red hair that had been done up in a bouffant, and beautiful blue eyes. Seated beside her husband, she had been attentively writing in a notebook densely filled with dates and numbers and names, and when the brothers approached, though she had graciously smiled, she had also tapped the face of her wristwatch, showing the time to Arnaz.

They were soon drinking champagne, the bottle kept chilled in a gold ice bucket. Lucille Ball nodded, smiled pleasantly, and every now and then leaned over and whispered into her husband's ear. But soon enough she slid into the background, allowing the men to smoke their panatelas from Havana, make their toasts and conversation. As this was a time when every Cuban in New York knew every other Cuban, the question was inevitable: "And what part of Cuba are you fellows from?"

"From a town called Las Piñas, surely you must know it, a sugar-mill town in Oriente."

"Of course, I come from Santiago de Cuba myself. I'm from Oriente, too!"

The knowledge that they were all from the same part of the world made them shake hands and nod at Arnaz in a brotherly way, as if they'd known each other for years and years.

"We grew up on the sugar mill and then we moved over to a farm when our father tried the livestock business," Cesar told Arnaz. "But I had to get out of there and bring my brother here with me. Cutting off the heads of animals wasn't for us . . .

Besides, I'd always wanted to be a singer, *tú sabes,* since my childhood, I always did my best to hang around musicians."

"It was the exact same thing for me," Arnaz said.

While talking about the dance-hall scene in Oriente, they discovered they had one more thing in common: they had both worked with the same orchestra leader in Cuba, Julián García and his Orquesta Típica.

The mention of that name had Arnaz slapping his knee. "Julián García was quite a character. Lucy, you should've seen him. He used to make us all wear white gloves and outfits in the worst heat, even those musicians to whom it was an impediment. And he carted around palm trees and Greek statues to give the orchestra a little class—was it the same for you?"

"Absolutely!" Cesar exhaled a cloud of blue smoke. "You know something, Mr. Arnaz, I swear that I saw you in Santiago. You were there that day in Julián's place, sitting on the stage . . . behind a harp or something, I don't remember exactly when, but I can recall seeing your name on the posters outside the dance hall where Julián rehearsed."

"On that steep hill from whose top you could see the harbor?"

"That was it. The dance hall on Zayas Street."

"Yes! What year was that, *coño?*"

"Nineteen thirty . . ."

". . . Seven! Must have been, because I left for the States that year."

"And Julián said that I was replacing a singer going to the States! As I think about it, that was you, sitting and strumming a guitar. Yes?"

". . . Yes, it comes back to me. I was waiting for a friend. Say, wait a minute, didn't we speak to one another?"

"We did!"

And then in the way that Cubans get really friendly, Arnaz and Cesar reinvented their pasts so that, in fact, they had probably been good friends.

"Nearly twenty years ago, can you imagine that? *Dios mío,* " Arnaz said. "Nearly twenty years just like that."

(And suddenly it was the day again when he had first met Arnaz, back in Cuba, clear as morning light: he was nineteen years old and walking up a steep hill in Santiago de Cuba, and at that time of day the westward sun was throwing toward infinity the shadows of wrought-iron balconies and the rooftops. Along the route there was a woman who always offered passersby, exhausted from the climb, glasses of cool water. On top of the hill, the burning disc of the sun, and then the dance hall itself and its refuge of shady arcades and a coolness inside its heavy oak doors. Cesar could remember looking across the dance-hall stage, through the strings of a Spanish harp, and seeing a young and handsome man sitting beside the piano; had him pinned for a *gallego* like himself. Beside the young man sat the immense Julián García, head swimming in hair dye and sweat, looking through some sheet music.

"And what will you begin with, my friend?"

"*María la O.*"

Julián began to play the chords to that *canción* by Lecuona. Cesar, black-brimmed cane hat in hand, and still nervous at the prospect of performing with Julián García, sang his heart out in a flamboyant style, using extended high notes to end phrases, arms flailing about dramatically. When he finished, Julián grunted, saying, "Good," and the young singer nodded. Then Julián ran him through some more songs and, satisfied with Cesar's singing, told him: "Come back here tomorrow and we'll rehearse with the other musicians, the full orchestra, okay?"

That was when the young man, thick pompadour of curly black hair hanging over his brow, looked over and smiled at Cesar. He had been strumming chords on the guitar to kill time while waiting for a friend with an automobile to show up and had watched Julián running Cesar through the repertoire, mostly the plaintive boleros and habaneras of Ernesto Lecuona, who was *the* Cuban composer of the day. As Julián led Cesar out, Arnaz called out to him, "Hey, that was pretty good, my friend. Name's Desiderio Arnaz," and he extended his hand in friendship. And when they'd shaken hands Arnaz, who was tired of waiting in the dance hall, suggested they go down to the foot of the hill, where there was a little bar.

"When my friend shows up here," he said to Julián, "you tell him I'm at the bar."

They drank a few beers together, talked about Julián and

women and the life of a musician, until Arnaz's friend appeared at the bar door. Then Arnaz made his way off into the future. "Hope you do well with the orchestra! As for me, I'm off to Havana.")

"So it was you. I thought there was maybe something familiar about your face. Life is funny, yes? Who would think that we would be sitting here these years later, getting reacquainted?"

He raised the bubbling champagne glass in another toast.

"I was nineteen then," Cesar told Arnaz. "A hick from the farm. Outside of a few excursions here and there in Oriente, and little trips I made by mule over the countryside, it was my first time out into the world. But what days those were! A great time in my life, singing with Julián's orchestra. It was beautiful, playing for the people."

Arnaz nodded. "I know the 'zact-same feeling, I wasn't much older than you and there I was going to Havana with a few pesos in my pocket, a guitar, and with plans of taking my act to the States. First to Miami and maybe Tampa, Hialeah, and Fort Lauderdale." He looked off, his face pained with nostalgia for youth.

"Eventually I ended up in New York, working the clubs here. Just the same way you fellows are. I had some good breaks, someone heard me singing and playing a conga and next thing I know, I'm up in New York on Broadway playing a Don Juan-type fellow in a musical comedy, something called *Too Many Girls,* it was a nice break for me, and things have gone well ever since."

But then for a moment Arnaz looked off, as if at the corner of the stage-ceiling molding, momentary exhaustion and a slight weariness in his eyes. ". . . But this life is always so much work, though." And he exhaled. "You fellows know what I mean?"

"Yes," Cesar concurred. "I know what you mean, *hombre.* One day in the tropics, and the next up to your knees in snow. One day on someone's porch in a house in the Sierra Mountains, and the next riding a subway. Here one moment and gone the next, just like that, pssssst."

At that point the other Mambo Kings, black instrument cases in hand, came over to say goodbye for the night and to thank Mr. Arnaz again for the drinks. They were all crowded around the table, laughing and nodding, as Arnaz joked with them in Spanish and complimented them on their playing. It was then that Cesar leaned over to his younger brother, consulted for a moment, and then, after the others had left, said to Arnaz, "We're going to have a late-night dinner at our apartment on La Salle Street uptown. May I invite you and your wife to join us? My brother's wife always cooks up a feast and tonight we're having *arroz con pollo*, black beans, and *plátanos.*"

"Yes?"

And Arnaz consulted with his wife. They heard her saying, "But, sweetheart, we have some business in the morning."

"I know, I know, but I'm hungry, and who feels like going to a restaurant now?"

So he turned and told the brothers, "Why not?" and soon they were out in the street in their long coats and brimmed hats, blowing into their cupped hands and stomping their feet on the sidewalk. While they had been inside, it had started snowing, and now it was still coming down, a heaven of snow falling in all directions on every street and building, awning, car, and tree. Cesar was out on the avenue calling a yellow cab, and shortly they were all huddled together in the back. Nestor and Cesar sat on the small metal flip-up seats, facing the rear window and their new friends.

Or perhaps they'd simply met Arnaz, who liked their music and, approaching them at the bar, said, "Would you fellows like to be on the show?" All business, with the fatigue of responsibility showing on his face. Or perhaps he had an air of weariness and exhaustion about him that reminded Cesar and Nestor of their father, Don Pedro, down in Cuba. Perhaps he had sadly yawned and said, *"Me siento cansado y tengo hambre*—I am tired and hungry." Whatever happened, he and his wife accompanied the brothers uptown to the house on La Salle Street.

Their taxi had made the turn off Broadway and 124th Street toward La Salle. As Arnaz stepped out of the taxi, his wife behind him, a southbound subway train tore out of the 125th Street El. Otherwise, the world was quiet. Up and down the street were rows of buildings with their yellow-lit windows and the silhouettes of people inside. Arnaz carried an Italian briefcase, Cesar a guitar, Nestor his horn. Miguel Montoya, whom they'd invited along, was behind them. With his fur-collared topcoat, delicate white gloves, and ivory crystal-tipped cane, he was something of an effeminate but dignified dandy. He was fifty-five years old and by far the most refined of the Mambo Kings. He bowed and held doors open for people, using an occasional French word— *"Merci,"* or *"Enchanté"*—impressing and winning the heart of Arnaz's wife.

The building on La Salle Street was nothing like what Arnaz and his wife were accustomed to: they had houses in Connecticut and California, and an apartment in Havana. And it was nothing like what the brothers had known in Cuba, a modest house made of pine timbers facing a field ringed by fruit trees and rhapsodic with birdsong in the late-afternoon sun, a sky bursting with bands of red, yellow, pink, and silver light and burning treetops, and orange-tinged black birds. No, it was a six-story building, the kind one would never dream about living in for the rest of one's life, situated near the top of a hill, with an ordinary stoop, basement stairs, and narrow, dim-lit entrance. Its main architectural ornamentation, a stone ibis over the doorway, was put up in 1920, during the Egyptian craze.

Opening the front door, Nestor felt a little nervous and self-conscious; he had been that way since the day of their arrival in the States, six years before. His hands shook as he tried to fit the key into the keyhole. The cold could not have helped, probably did something to the metal. They all waited patiently and finally the door opened into the narrow lobby with its solitary light bulb dangling off a thick black wire, bent like a question mark over the mailboxes. There was a dirty mirror and stairwell, and from the second doorway, the residence of Mrs. Shannon the landlady, came a strong smell of dog hair, cabbage, and, faintly, urine.

Nestor, who liked to pride himself on his personal cleanliness, puffed his cheeks and wanted to apologize for the offense to their eyes and nostrils, but then Arnaz, sensing Nestor's embarrassment, gave him a good friendly Cuban rap on the back and said, as consolingly as possible, "Ah, what a nice building you have here." But his wife rolled her eyes and gave her husband something of a double-take, then graciously smiled her famous ruby-lipped smile.

Then, as they climbed the stairs up to the fourth floor, where Cesar and Nestor and his family lived, Arnaz began to whistle the melody of the song he'd heard earlier that night, "Beautiful María of My Soul," and as he did so, he wondered about the terrible somberness that seemed to plague Nestor. He thought, "Of course, he's a *gallego,* * and *gallegos* are melancholic at heart." All the same, Arnaz felt sorry for the younger brother, who rarely smiled, nothing like the gregarious soul who was his older brother.

When his nostrils hit the good food smells in the hallway of the apartment, Arnaz slapped his hands together and declared, "*¡Qué bueno!* How wonderful!" He found himself moving along a hallway whose walls were covered with framed photographs of musicians and portraits of Jesus Christ and his saints.

---

*Who were the *gallegos?* The most arrogant Cubans, say some; the most hardworking and honest Cubans, opinionated, ambitious, strong-willed, and proud, say others. The term *gallego* referred to those Cubans whose ancestors had come from Galicia, a province of seaports, morning-mist-ridden farmlands (blue-green and foggish land, like Scotland), and rugged mountains, situated in the northwestern corner of Spain. North of Portugal —Port-of-Gauls—and jutting out into the Atlantic Ocean, Galicia had been invaded by the Romans, the Celts, the Gauls, the Suevi, and the Visigoths, who left the Galicians with a taste for fierce battle and a sometimes melancholic outlook. El Cid was a *gallego.* So were the majority of Spanish soldiers sent to put down revolts in Cuba in the nineteenth century. Another *gallego?* Franco. Others? Ángel Castro, a Spanish soldier who settled in Oriente Province, Cuba, became a land baron, and whose son, Fidel, ambitious, arrogant, and cocky, would become absolute ruler of the island.

Most recently, the term *gallego* is used in Cuba to describe light-skinned Cubans, or non-Cuban Spaniards, passing through.

"Make yourself at home, *compañero*," Cesar said in his normal friendly manner. "Now this is your home, you understand, Mr. Arnaz?"

"Sounds good to me. Now, Lucy, isn't this nice?"

"Yes, it is, Desi, just swell."

"Ah, do I smell some *plátanos?*"

"*Plátanos verdes,*" a female voice called from the kitchen.

"And *yuca* with *ajo?*"

"Yes," said Cesar happily. "And we have wine, we have beer!" He raised up his hands. "We have rum!"

"*¡Qué bueno!*"

It was around one in the morning and Delores Castillo was in the kitchen, heating up all the pots of rice and chicken and beans, and the fritters were sizzling in a frying pan. Her hair was in a bun and she had a stained apron around her waist. When they all jammed into the kitchen, Delores recognized the famous Arnaz and his wife.

"*Dios mío!*" she cried. "If I had known they were coming, I would have cleaned the house up."

Regaining her composure, Delores smiled so beautifully that Arnaz told her, "Mrs. Castillo, you're a lovely woman." The coats were left in the bedroom, and soon enough they were all gathered around the kitchen table. While the men devoured the food, Delores hurried down the hall and woke her children up. Eugenio's eyes were barely open when he felt himself being carried down the hall, his mother saying to him, "I want you to meet someone." She put him down by the kitchen doorway and when he looked up he saw the usual scene for that household: a crowded kitchen, mouths chewing, beer and rum bottles open on the table. Even the nice fellow his mother was all excited about looked just like so many of the other musicians who passed through the house. And the name Desi Arnaz meant nothing to him then, it was just a name he heard when she introduced him.

"Mr. Arnaz, this is our boy, Eugenio. And this is Leticia."

Desi Arnaz reached over and pinched his cheek, and he patted Leticia's head. Then they were taken back into their bedrooms, the kids falling asleep to a background of Spanish-speaking voices in the kitchen, the music from the phonograph in the living room, the sound of laughter and clapping, just like what they'd heard on so many other nights.

Everyone was laughing. Lucille Ball told about going to Cuba for the first time and having to cook her own Cuban meal to impress Desi's family. "I nearly burned down the house!"

"Ay, tell me about it," said Arnaz.

"But it turned out right in the end. Anyway, *señora*, I know just what you have to go through. Mashing those plantains up and everything in brown paper and getting it right."

Suddenly she remembered their walks together in the field outside the Arnaz family's *ingenio* down in Oriente. At first she was afraid of the dark countryside, but then she began to enjoy the beauty of the night sky, streaked with falling light.

"But I got it right in the end, mashing the plantains in brown paper, adding just the right amount of salt, garlic, and lemon. Just like you did with these!"

There was music on the Victrola, as Cesar still called the RCA phonograph in the living room: First he put on the fabulous Beny More, a personal favorite, and then one of the Mambo Kings' recordings, "Twilight in Havana." Arnaz seemed happy at the kitchen table, devouring the platters of food placed before him, and saying things like, "*¡Qué sabroso!* You don't know how nice it is to just relax for a change."

They were pleased to hear that Arnaz was enjoying himself. After a few drinks Cesar could care less how famous he was; he was thrilled to have a *compañero* in the apartment and matter-of-factly started, once the rum worked into his brain, to feel sorry for Arnaz.

There's a man so famous and yet he's so satisfied with the simplest meal, he thought. He's probably tired of dining out with the Rockefellers all the time!

Nestor, however, began to feel they had overstepped their privilege: he was standing in the corner of the room, playing with the fob of his watch. He had seen Lucille Ball blush when Cesar opened another bottle of rum.

"Darling, maybe we should start thinking about getting home," she said to him. But then Cesar walked in with his orange-wood Brazilian guitar and handed it to Arnaz. "Would you sing us a little song, Mr. Arnaz?"

"Why not"—and he placed the guitar on his lap and strummed a C-minor chord, flailing his hand quickly over the strings so that its soundbox vibrated like the wind hitting a shutter, and began to sing one of his biggest hits, *"Babalú."*

"Oh, great Babbbbbbaaaallllooo, oh, why did you forsake me?"

Cesar banged on the table, and Nestor, giving in to the rush of fun, started to play the flute . . . Then Arnaz began playing *"Cielito Lindo"* and by then everyone in the kitchen was a ring of arms and swaying, happy bodies.

Strummed like a waltz, *"Cielito Lindo"* was the kind of song that a loving mother would sing at bedtime to her children, and that was why the two Mambo Kings remembered wonderful things about their mother, and why Arnaz shut his eyes in pleasant contemplation of his own loving mother in Cuba.

(Nestor remembered how, as a frightened child, he used to wake up from a bad dream, covered in sweat, his heart pounding, and with a feeling of helplessness: the moon would ominously cross the window space, and the mosquito netting which hung down off hooks from the ceiling would seem to breathe like a living creature and shadows would bend into animal shapes and he would cry out so that someone would come to save him, a brother, his father, but most sweetly his mother, parting the netting and sitting beside him on the bed, whispering stories into his ear and softly singing. And Cesar remembered hearing her voice as she'd wash his hair in a metal tub in the back yard, the sunlight breaking up the flowing water into pink- and red-tinged sprays, and the wonderful sensation of her hands moving over the back of his neck and through his hair. And for Arnaz? It was the image of his mother filling the empty hours of the afternoon with songs that she'd play at a spinet in the parlor of their grand house in Santiago. Just those little thoughts made the three men feel like crying.)

But then around three o'clock Lucille Ball tapped her watch again and said to Arnaz, "Now, honey, we have to go."

"Yes, of course. Tomorrow it's work, always work. I'm sorry we have to go, but I want to tell you something before we do. That *canción* you fellows sang at the club tonight, 'Beautiful

María,' I really like it and think that you should come on my show and do it for me there."

"Nightclub show?"

"No, I mean my television show."

"Yes!" said Cesar. "Of course, you let us know what we have to do. I'll give you our address." And he rushed off into the hall, looking for a pen and a piece of paper. Later, Cesar was out on Broadway trying to flag down a taxicab for Arnaz and his wife, who were waiting on the curb. Miguel Montoya had decided to stay over, taking his chances on the Castro Convertible in the living room. They were out there for about twenty minutes before they caught a taxi, its heavy, snow-chained wheels edging their way up the snowy streets.

Arnaz shook Cesar Castillo's hand. "I'm glad we had this chance to meet, my friend. You'll be hearing from me soon enough. Okay? So, *cuídate,* take care of yourself."

Then Arnaz and his wife got into the taxi and disappeared into the night.

DESI ARNAZ KEPT HIS PROMISE and three months later the brothers were on a plane to Hollywood, California. Cesar really loved the trip, loved flying in those big four-engine airplanes and watching the clouds burn up with sunlight. But Nestor? He couldn't believe that all that metal stayed up in the air. The long eleven-hour non-stop flight frightened him. He remained in his seat, hands knotted together nervously, fearfully watching the clouds out the window. Cesar sat quietly, writing postcards and a few song lyrics, reading magazines, enjoying things. They were flying first class, which meant that the stewardesses gave the passengers the time of day. Cesar liked this one stewardess who had the nicest little pair of *nalgitas* —buttocks—the most serious-looking *nalgitas* he had seen in a long time, and when she would come down the aisle, Cesar would elbow his brother so that Nestor would not miss out on her bouncy splendor. But he was too self-occupied, too worried about how things would go, as if something going wrong would kill him. The idea of going on the show frightened him.

For Cesar, it was clear-cut and simple and he never gave it much thought, other than that it would be a good opportunity to make a few dollars and for people to see them and hear that song, perhaps get them interested in that bolero, "Beautiful María of My Soul." Turn it into the Mambo Kings' first big hit. As for the idea of appearing on television? Cesar didn't have the slightest idea about television. They watched an occasional boxing match at a friend's apartment, watched programs in appliance-store windows, but neither brother had ever dreamed of appearing on the *I Love Lucy* show.

As for the song that had captured Arnaz's interest that one night in the Mambo Nine Club? Even Cesar had to admit that it was a great song, catchy and haunting. He had gotten sick and tired of hearing about María over the years, but had walked into the living room one day when Nestor, who wrote twenty-two different versions of that *canción*, was singing it again. And it sounded as good as any of the long-time classics that make people misty-eyed in the middle of the night. Usually, hearing Nestor working on yet another version made Cesar disgruntled, but that day he told his younger brother, "You can stop now. It's perfect. It's a great song, brother." And he slapped him on the back. "Now enjoy your peace."

But Nestor didn't enjoy anything, brooding constantly like a ruined poet or an old man.

"Nestor, you're nearly thirty years old, you have a wife who loves you and two children," Cesar said. "When are you going to be a man and stop worrying yourself to death? When are you going to stop being such a fairy?"

That made Nestor wince.

"I'm sorry," Cesar told him. "Just be happy. And don't be worried, bro', you have your brother Cesar around to look out for you."

Just as he was saying that, the plane hit an air pocket, dropped several hundred feet, and started shaking.

And, like the airplane, Nestor kept shaking. Not that he was a complete wreck: playing the trumpet and singing always had a calming effect on him and he had learned to calm himself in front of his children, Leticia and Eugenio.

"Whatever you do," Cesar said one day, "be a man around your own children. You don't want them growing up fucked up."

Desilu Productions put them up in the Garden of Allah Hotel, with a swimming pool, prickly palm trees, and young starlets stretching out in the sun. Each time they would head out from the hotel for rehearsals, Nestor would belt down a glass of whiskey, sometimes two. He had gotten that way, playing in the big dance halls. The television studio was over on Selma Avenue and was so busy that no one noticed when Nestor would show up a little drunk. The actual filming of the program was to take place on a Friday and the players and musicians would have three days to rehearse. Everyone involved with the show was nice to the brothers. Desi Arnaz was especially kind and generous to the Cubans he'd hired. Ask anyone about Arnaz in those days and they'd talk about his friendliness and concern for the people working for him, like a responsible *patrón*. After all, the man was Cuban and knew how to present the proper image of a man.

They'd arrive for rehearsals at ten and spend most of the day hanging around with the musicians and watching the orchestra set up: many of its members were American musicians who'd been playing around in California big bands, but there were a few Cubans with whom the brothers killed time playing whist.

They didn't have much to do on the show. A walk-on scene and then the song. As for their acting abilities, Arnaz, who kept an active hand in everything, would tell the brothers just to be themselves—and always with a slap to their backs. But Nestor was always taking out those few pages of script with their few lines of dialogue and reading them over and over again. (A portion of this script, yellowed with age and torn, would be found among the Mambo King's effects in the room in the Hotel Splendour.) Even when Arnaz had told them, "Don't worry, even if you flub your dialogue, we'll take care of it. *Pero no te preocupes,* okay?"

All the same, Nestor seemed so worried. He was a funny

man, at times collected and reasonable about things, at other times lost and distraught.

The evening they actually filmed the show before an audience, Nestor could barely move, he wanted out so badly. He spent the afternoon pacing back and forth in their hotel room, a sweaty nervous mess. And at the studio itself he remained in the wings, leaning up against a Coke machine, watching the bustle of electricians, sound and light technicians, cameramen, and script girls all around him, as if life were passing him by. Something about singing that song, María's song, before millions, frightened him. His fear frustrated Cesar, who kept saying, "*Tranquilo, tranquilo, hombre.* And just don't forget, we'll have Arnaz out there with us."

Nestor must have looked really badly off because one of Arnaz's musicians, a nice plump baldheaded fellow from Cienfuegos who played the congas and bongos for Arnaz, went up to him and asked, "Are you all right, my friend?" Then he pulled Nestor off to the side and gave him a few swigs of rum from a small bottle that he had in his pocket. That did calm him down, and in a short time a makeup lady came over and brushed their foreheads and noses with powder. Another assistant sat tuning Cesar's guitar to a piano. A third assistant led them over to the spot from which they would enter the stage. Then Arnaz himself stepped out of his dressing room, smiled, and waved to the brothers. Then, as he always did with his younger brother before any performance, Cesar looked him over, brushed the lint off his jacket, pulled down on its hem to make sure his shoulders were straight, and patted Nestor's back. Then the orchestra started to play the *I Love Lucy* theme and someone gave them their cue, and together, guitar and trumpet in hand, they went on.

It was 1955 and Lucille Ball was cleaning in her living room when she heard a knock on the door to her Manhattan apartment, someone gently rapping.

"I'm commmmmming," she answered, touching her hairdo on her way to the door.

Standing there, two men in white silk suits and butterfly-shaped lace bow ties, black instrument cases, guitar and trumpet, by their sides, with black-brimmed cane hats in hand which they'd taken off as she opened the door. The two men nodded and smiled, but there seemed something sad about their expressions, at least in retrospect, as if they knew what would happen to them. The taller and broader of the two, who wore a slick, pimpy-looking mustache, in vogue at the time, cleared his throat and said in a quiet voice, "Mrs. Ricardo? My name is Alfonso and this is my brother Manny . . ."

"Oh, yes, the fellows from Cuba. Ricky told me all about you. Come on in and make yourselves at home. Ricky'll be out in a minute."

With tremendous politeness the brothers bowed and then sat down on the sofa, each leaning forward, not allowing himself to sink completely into its plump cushions. The younger brother, Manny, seemed the more nervous of the two, his foot tapping the floor; his darkened, somewhat tired eyes looking out into the world with innocence and apprehension. Behind them was a spinet piano on which stood a squat bowl of flowers and a porcelain figurine of a picador; then, a lace-draped window before them, a table on which the redheaded Lucille Ball soon placed a tray of cookies and coffee. All this happened in a few seconds, it was as if she had known just when they would be coming to visit. But that didn't matter—the older brother dropped a few sugar cubes into his coffee, stirred it, and nodded thanks to their hostess.

Suddenly in walked Ricky Ricardo, nightclub singer and musical impresario—the character whom Desi Arnaz played on his television show. He was a pleasant-looking man with large friendly eyes and a thick head of black hair, shiny as sealskin. Dressed in cuffed trousers, wide-lapeled sports jacket, short-collared shirt, and a slick-looking black tie decorated with piano keys and a crocodile-shaped tie clip, he definitely seemed prosperous and self-confident. He walked in with his right hand in his jacket pocket and, when he saw the brothers, rapped each on his back and said, "Manny, Alfonso! Gee, I'm glad to see you! How are things down in Cuba?"

"Fine, Ricky."

"Well, sit down and tell me, did you fellows decide which song you're going to do on my show at the Tropicana?"

"Yes," said the older brother. "We've decided to sing 'Beautiful María of My Soul.' "

"That's swell, fellows. Say, Lucy, wait until you hear the

number they're going to do with me for the finale on the show next week. 'Beautiful María of My Soul.' "

The redhead's expression changed, fell to pieces, as if someone had died.

"But, Ricky, you promised *me* the chance to sing on the show!"

"Well, I can't discuss it with you now, Lucy. I've got to take the fellows over to the club."

"Please, Ricky, if you let me, I'll never never never ask you again. Please?"

She stood in front of him and looked at him so sweetly and fluttered her eyelashes so endearingly that he began to reconsider. "We'll see, Lucy."

And shaking his head, he started speaking rapidly in Spanish to the brothers: *"Si ustedes supieran las cosas que tengo que aguantarme todos los días! Dios mío! Me vuelvo loco con estas americanas! Mi mamá me lo dijo, me dijo, 'Ricky, no te cases con una americana, a no ser que quieras un* big *headache! Esas americanas te pueden volver loco.' Mi mamá tenía razón, debía haberme casado con esa chica bonita de Cuba que nunca me puso problemas, que sabía quién le endulzaba el pan. Ella no era* crazy, *ella me dejaba tranquilo, ¿saben ustedes lo que quiero decir, compañeros?"**

And in English again, "Let's go."

The brothers put their hats on, took up their instrument cases, and followed the nightclub singer out. When he opened the door, his neighbors, a stout-looking bald man and his wife, a pretty, somewhat matronly blonde, stood before him, flattop straw hats in hand. The two brothers nodded to them and made their way out into the apartment-building hallway and left for the club.

---

*"If you knew what I have to go through every day with this woman. These American women are enough to drive you nuts! My mother told me a million times: Ricky, never marry an American woman unless you're looking for one big headache. And she was right, I should've married that girl back in Cuba! Now there was a quiet girl who never bothered me, who knew where her bread was buttered. She wasn't crazy! She always left me alone, you know what I mean, *compañeros?*"

Later, an immense satin heart dissolved and through a haze appeared the interior of the Tropicana nightclub. Facing a dance floor and stage, about twenty tables set with linen and candles at which sat ordinary but elegantly dressed people—your nightclub clientele of the day. Pleated curtains hanging down from the ceiling, potted palms here and there. A tuxedoed maître d' with an oversize black wine list in hand, a long-legged cigarette girl, and waiters going from table to table. Then the dance floor itself, and finally the stage, its apron and wings painted to resemble African drums, with birds and squiggly voodoo lines, these patterns repeated on the conga drums and on the music stands, behind which sat the members of the Ricky Ricardo Orchestra, twenty or so musicians seated in four tiered rows, each man decked out in a frilly-sleeved mambo shirt and vest decorated with sequined palms (with the exception of a female harpist in long-skirted dress and wearing rhinestone glasses), the musicians looking very human, very ordinary, wistful, indifferent, happy, poised, and ready with their instruments.

At center stage, a large ball microphone, spotlight, drumroll, and Ricky Ricardo.

"Well, folks, tonight I have a special treat for you. Ladies and gentlemen, I am pleased to present to you, direct from Havana, Cuba, Manny and Alfonso Reyes singing a bolero of their own composition, 'Beautiful María of My Soul.'"

The brothers walked out in white suits and with a guitar and trumpet, bowed to the audience, and nodded when Ricky Ricardo faced the orchestra and, holding his conductor's wand, prepared to begin, asked them, "Are you ready?"

The older brother strummed an A-minor chord, the key of the song; a harp swirled in as if from the clouds of heaven; then the bassist began to play a habanera, and then the piano and horns played a four-chord vamp. Standing side by side before the microphone, brows creased in concentration, expressions sincere, the brothers began to sing that romantic bolero "Beautiful María of My Soul." A song about love so far away it hurts; a song about lost pleasures, a song about youth, a song about love so elusive a man can never know where he stands; a song about wanting a woman so much death does not frighten you, a song about wanting that woman even when she has abandoned you.

As Cesar sang, his vocal cords trembling, he seemed to be watching something profoundly beautiful and painful happening in the distance, eyes passionate, imploring, his earnest expression asking, "Can you see who I am?" But the younger brother's eyes were closed and his head was tilted back. He looked like a man on the verge of falling through an eternal abyss of longing and solitude.

For the final verses they were joined by the bandleader, who harmonized with them and was so happy with the song that at the end he whipped his right hand up into the air, a lock of thick black hair falling over his brow. Then he shouted, *"Olé!"* The brothers were now both smiling and taking bows, and Arnaz, playing Ricky Ricardo, said, "Let's give them a nice hand, folks!" The brothers bowed again and shook Arnaz's hand and walked offstage, waving to the audience.

Nestor tried, heaven help him. Every day he read that book on self-improvement by Mr. D. D. Vanderbilt, which he'd study carefully with an English dictionary on hand. That was Nestor in that California hotel at three in the morning, sitting on the edge of the bed in boxer shorts and robe, trying hard to overcome his own skepticism about the victory of a positive attitude and of self-application over despair and defeat. After six years in the United States, he was still living with a growing dread of things. It wasn't that he feared one thing in particular; he just had the sense that things weren't going to work out, that the sky would fall in and lightning would strike him as he walked down the street, that the earth might open up and swallow him. He didn't sit around dwelling on these thoughts, he dreamed them. He had been on the same plateau of dreams for years, the same dreams that had afflicted him in childhood in Cuba, when he used to wake up in the middle of the night covered in sweat in a room swarming with crows or when he found himself entangled in burning coils of rope, when the rope mysteriously crept into his body through his ears and feasted on his insides, when he would wake up in the middle of the night and find the priest standing over him with his funeral cassock and a grim face like melted wax, his vestments and hands smelling oddly of *frijoles negros* and church incense.

Lately, he'd started dreaming again about crawling on his

hands and knees along a narrow tunnel just barely wide enough for him to fit through; the tunnel seemed to go on forever into the distance toward a faint glow of light. And as he crawled through, his shoulders and knees wedged tight, he could hear voices speaking softly, just loud enough to hear but not to understand.

He had been dreaming this and awakened as the California sun burst though an opening in the Venetian blinds, its brilliant light pouring into the room. He felt his stomach muscles flutter, a shock went through his body, and he opened his eyes. It was around noon, and the first thing he heard was his thirty-seven-year-old brother Cesar frolicking in the pool outside with his new acquaintances, three girls barely out of adolescence in scanty one-piece bathing suits, giggly and absolutely delighted that Cesar Castillo, playing the sport, kept buying them high frost-glazed drinks of fruit juice, rum, spoonfuls of sugar, orange, and crushed ice, compliments of Desilu Productions.

This was their last day in California and Cesar was having the time of his life. There he was, wearing a little tarnished crucifix on a chain around his neck, thick curling chest hair damp and streaked with gray, a long Havana cigar in his mouth, head tilted back—not in pain, but in joy—soaking up the sun, sipping his drink, and flirting with the girls. They had rushed over to him because, at first, as he strutted around the pool in his oversized plaid trunks, they had mistaken him for the movie actor Gilbert Roland. The girls were thrilled to meet him anyway, thrilled that the handsome Cesar Castillo had promised them dinner that night at some fancy joint.

"*Señoritas,*" he had said, "you name it and it's yours!"

Through the Venetian blinds, Nestor watched Cesar paddling over to the side of the pool with big splashes—he did not know how to swim. Nature was calling, and he came back into their Garden of Allah bungalow, his urine powerful and noisy in the toilet.

"It's beautiful here, huh? Too bad we have to go back so soon."

The toilet flushed and he added, "Brother, why don't you come out and join us?"

"Yes, in a few moments."

A curvaceous female shadow appeared in the frosted glass of the bungalow door and called in, "Yoo-hoo!" And when Cesar opened the door, she asked, "May I use your little girls' room?"

"Of course."

Wearing a red bathing suit with a short pleated skirt and red high heels, the blonde, all of her, rump, breasts, long legs, bounced daintily across the room. As she slipped into the bathroom, Cesar approximated the width of her hips with his hands and sucked in air through his teeth. The blonde must have felt a little self-conscious about urinating in their bathroom, for she turned on a faucet, and Cesar took this as a hint and opened the bungalow door and waited, his slightly drunken frame wedged up against the doorway, stomach in, chest out, watching the pool and the palm trees in the distance, the shrubbery behind them spilling over with flowers—joking with Nestor, he once called them "the pubic hair of nature." Happy in his thoughts, he whistled.

In a moment, Cesar and the blonde were back by the pool, jumping in and splashing water on the others. She was a good swimmer and gracefully plumed down to the deep end of the pool, gushing to the surface again, her body firm and tanned . . . Nestor supposed that he should go out, have a few drinks, and relax, but he told himself, "I'm a married man with two children." But he kept hearing Cesar, relaxed and laughing. When he looked out, Cesar was kneeling by the three girls; they were lying face-down on mats in a row: he was rubbing suntan lotion on their backs and the meatiest, sweat-beaded parts of their thighs.

Nestor winced, outraged. Why would this happy sight make him feel as if he would burst apart, as if the pain inside him was a viscous mud flowing through his veins? He was shaken by the old aches: when that happened, he would think "María," but thoughts about his wife and children sank him into a deeper gloom.

All the same, he changed into a pair of blue bathing trunks and soon was lying out by the pool. The waiter brought him a tall glass of that tropical rum punch, and the initial swallow eased his spirit. Then he started to feel friendlier about the whole business with the girls and the time away from his family, so that when one of the three girls, a brunette, sat down beside him, asking, "Are you going to come out with us tonight? We're going over to the El Morocco to catch an orchestra and dance . . ."

And she called over to Cesar, "What's that orchestra called?"

"The René Touzet Orchestra. Brother, why don't you come along?"

"I'll see," he answered tentatively, though he went everywhere with his older brother and hated to be left alone.

They had remained by the pool drinking until seven-thirty. Around four the waiter had brought them a tray of turkey, ham, and cheese club sandwiches, and they had talked about doing the *I Love Lucy* show and how everyone had been so kind to them. And they mentioned that they had a mambo orchestra in New York. One of the girls had a bit part in a Ricardo Montalban film called *Desperadoes from the Land of the Golden Sun.* Ricardo was a "dreamboat," she said. And Cesar looked at her and said, "Well, you're a fleet of dreamboats, baby."

Poor Nestor. He could not help looking at one of the girls, a brunette. Her skin was golden-brown from the sunny California life and seemed to glow with the promise of pleasure. Even though he hadn't said much to her, she seemed to have paired off with him, paying attention to him and making eyes when he'd look over. While the two others frolicked in the pool with Cesar, she had remained beside Nestor on a sun mat, and this struck him as "classier." Her name was Tracy Belair, and when they later separated so they could get dressed for the night out, she gave Nestor a sweet tongue-nipped kiss. Taking a shower, Nestor thought about that girl and it gave him an erection. But he vowed to do nothing about her.

Yet, by eight o'clock, another drink had given him a feeling of weightlessness and elation and he suddenly filled with the kind of confidence that Mr. Vanderbilt described in his book. By eight-fifteen he felt immortal.

The phone rang, and it was Nestor who picked it up.

"Hello, this is Desi Arnaz. How are you fellows? Listen, I'm just calling to make sure that everything's okay with you. You like the hotel and everything? Good." Thanking the brothers again, he added: "And let's not forget each other. Okay?"

Next thing he knew, Nestor was sitting at a table in the El Morocco, drinking champagne, the five of them grinning happily for a strolling photographer. This was a real classy joint. Everything on the menu was written in a florid script and had a French name, and many of the items cost as much as what he earned in a week at the meat-packing plant.

"Order whatever you like," Cesar told everybody.

And why the hell not? Arnaz had told them to send him the bill. Soon their table was piled high with just about every dish on the menu: a silver bowl of poor shriveled-up snails like those which used to swarm over the patio of their house in Cuba after a rain, all black, sad-looking, and cooked with garlic; platters of filet mignon, lobster, shrimps, scalloped potatoes; and bottle after bottle of champagne. This was followed up at some indecent hour by bowls of baked Alaska and Italian *baci*— chocolate and vanilla ice-cream balls dipped in dark chocolate washed down with French cognac. And there had been intermittent kisses. At one point Nestor's brunette looked at him for a long time and declared, "You know something, sweetheart, you look just like what's-his-name, Victor Mature, isn't he Spanish?" Later he became Gilbert Roland.

The orchestra sounded great, and after a while the five of them were out on the dance floor having a good time. In the midst of all this, however, Nestor decided to call New York, and that would make him wince the next day because he wouldn't be able to remember what he had said or how he had sounded. Why did he think he'd left Delores crying?

When they left the club, everything dissolved, and then he was stumbling through the Garden of Allah's door and pinching his companion's bottom through her silver-lamé gown. More champagne bottles popped. And next thing he knew, he was opening his eyes and looking over at his brother: Cesar was sitting on the floor with his back to the wall, one of the women's brassieres wrapped around his neck like a tie, toasting everybody with champagne: America! Desi Arnaz! René Touzet! And love and romance!

Making zigzags across the floor, the two brothers and their three companions tried to dance the mambo. Then Cesar started to serenade his two women and he went off with them into his separate bedroom, leaving St. Nestor with temptation herself. How had they ended up on the couch, tongue-kissing? The young woman became more and more feline with each kiss. She wore a flame-red brassiere and little red panties, and she had a black mole in the shape of a flower just over her belly button. Her glowing body seemed so perfect, so healthy, so filled with life. He went mad kissing her. Naked and wet with his kisses, she said, "Wait a minute, *amigo,* you have to take off your clothes."

And when he had his trousers off he felt a cringe of shame because, after all, he was a married man, a good Cuban, and a diehard Catholic with two children at home in New York, but that didn't stop Mother Nature, or the woman from taking a long look at him and saying, "Brother, where have you been all my life?"

Then he awoke and in the dark made his way across the room on boneless legs to the bathroom, where he vomited. He went outside to smoke a cigarette: the sky was clear, thick with swirly stars that reflected in the pool. Why was he feeling so bad? Why had he felt so bad all his short life?

About five in the morning, he woke the brunette, who smiled and embraced him, saying, "Hello, lover."

But he said, "You should go home now, huh?"

And that was that. She dressed and he sat watching her and feeling bad. Maybe it was the way he had said it, without an ounce of affection, after all he'd probably said to her when they were making love.

He tried to go back to sleep—they were to catch an eight o'clock flight home—but already the sun was rising. And so he took out that book of his and began to read an inspiring passage that he'd underlined: "In today's America one must think about the future. Ally yourself with progress and tomorrow! The confident, self-assured man looks to the future and never backwards to the past. The heart of every success is a plan that takes you forward. In moments of doubt you must remember that every obstacle is only a temporary delay. That every problem can be solved. When there is a will there is a way. You, too, can be a man of tomorrow!"

In the days after the broadcast of the show, they became celebrities on La Salle Street: gaunt, ruddy-cheeked Irishmen would step out of the shadows of the Shamrock Bar on the corner and into the late-afternoon light and say to the brothers, "Can I stand you to a glass of beer?" People would stick their heads out of the window to shout hello, passersby stopped them on the street and wished them well. Gossiping old ladies who sat in front of the stoop on frail, thin-legged chairs whispered about the fame that had abruptly descended upon those two "Spanish fellows" who lived in 500; for weeks after, the two brothers had regular fans among the Irish and Germans on the block, and even those people who hadn't seen the show knew about it and treated the musicians with a new respect. Their biggest fan was their land-lady, Mrs. Shannon, who had heard about the show from Delores and had spread the word all over the neighborhood, proud of the fact that she had them as tenants.

It hadn't always been that way. After he and Nestor had moved in with Pablo—"Now, there was a good Spanish man for you"—the parties had started, week after week and late into the early mornings, and were so raucous that she would spend half the night banging on the pipes and calling the cops to straighten them out. She had not minded the roly-poly Pablo and his de-mure, obedient wife—he had always been good to Mrs. Shannon, bringing her free steaks and chops from the plant—but not these two machos with their trail of women and wolfish-looking friends, always drinking and singing and carrying on at night in their apartment upstairs. By the time that Pablo moved out in 1950, the brothers had turned the place into a "house of sin."

The worst bit of gossip about the goings-on in that "house of sin" upstairs came from one of her neighbors, Mrs. O'Brien, who on hot nights used to go sit on the rooftop by the water tower with her husband, to catch a breeze off the Hudson River, maybe drink a few beers, and eat American cheese, ham, and mayonnaise sandwiches. One evening when they were up there, Mr. O'Brien felt restless and decided to walk around the rooftop to check out the coping. The brothers were having one of their parties downstairs: a row of six windows with the shades pulled halfway down, blaring phonograph, voices, the sight of a room thickly packed with legs and swirling hands, hands holding drinks—that's all he could really see. He was there looking down at the whole business when he heard noises—like someone panting and groaning up a steep hill. Those sounds were coming from the neighboring roof, and when he took a look, he saw what appeared to be a man and a woman on a blanket, hiding in the shadows, making love. Out of the man's shadow protruded a large and shiny penis that in the dark resembled a piece of greased pipe. His wife had joined him and they remained for a long time watching the proceedings, aghast and envious, and then decided to call the police. When they reported the incident of beastly fornication, Mrs. Shannon blushed and asked, "What will they do next?"

Despite the many complaints she had about them, she slowly became much taken with the older brother. He would often appear at her door to pay the rent, bring her little presents: food and pastries left over from the wedding and engagement parties that the brothers played; steaks from the plant. And whenever the Mambo Kings made a new record he'd give her one. And he was truly apologetic in the aftermath of their parties, saying in a polite voice: "We're really sorry if we made a racket last night. It's just that we have no way of knowing how loud things are"—and that always made her feel better. But there was something else that she liked about him. Fifty years old, stout, ragged-haired, triple-chinned, she believed that the Mambo King somehow found her attractive. Whenever Cesar appeared at her door, he gave her the sense that he found her beautiful: he'd look right into her blue eyes, pure as the morning light, and his brow would arch slightly and a smile would appear at the edge of his lips, as if to say, "My, my." She had once been an Irish beauty, who, due to a mannish temperament, flew headlong into beer-soaked matronhood. That Cesar seemed even the least bit aware of her former looks made her daydream about a little romance with him, but she kept it to that, a daydream.

Then the brothers appeared on television and she saw them actually speaking to Lucille Ball, her heart fluttered and she felt a dizziness that lingered intensely at the thought of seeing them. A few days after the show was aired, she went out and had her hair shampooed and set, bought herself a new dress, baked the brothers an apple spice cake, and later shocked her brother by announcing, "I'm going upstairs to see those two Cuban fellas."

It was Cesar who opened the door: standing before him, she

felt as if she were leaning over the edge of a steep precipice
—breathless and with a sense that she would be carried off forever.

"Yes, Mrs. Shannon?"

"I just had to tell you, you fellas were really, really great. I
saw you on the television."

"Thank you."

"And I, and I baked you a little something, see? It's a cake.
Haven't baked a cake in a long time, but I used to."

Nodding, Cesar said, "Thank you. Why don't you come in
and have a little drink, or some food if you like? Are you going
out?" he asked. "You look all dressed up."

"No, I can come in for a bit."

She followed Cesar down the hallway and past the kids'
wheel carriage and tricycles and through the kitchen into the
dining room: they had a long table still set with platters of *bacalao*
— codfish cooked with garlic—black beans, rice, a huge salad,
pork chops and steaks from the plant, and a big bowl of *yuca*:
Nestor, in a bow tie and suspenders, was sitting at the end of the
table, sucking on a toothpick. The children were playing on the
living-room floor while Delores sat at the opposite end of the
table, stone-silent, staring at her husband.

"Everybody, look who's come to visit us!"

"Would you like something to eat?"

She looked over the food and said, "Just a little chops would
be fine. And rice."

"Delores," Cesar ordered. "Give Mrs. Shannon a plate of
food."

She got up and obeyed, and piled the black beans and salad
and *bacalao* on all together: Mrs. Shannon took a seat, picking
around all the things she refused to try, but began to devour the
pork chops and steak.

Cesar watched her and said, "But you should try the *yuca*.
It's like a potato, but tastier." And clutching his heart, he added,
"In my opinion."

Mrs. Shannon chewed her meat, enchanted: Cesar complimented her again, and she inquired, "And what were they like,
Desi Arnaz and Lucy? Tell me about Lucy?"

"A really nice woman. A lady."

Then he launched into his story about the star treatment in Hollywood, the pink and light blue houses of Beverly Hills, walking down into a club called Ciro's and spying the actor William Holden in a booth with his arms around a pretty girl. She ate up every word, and Cesar, being a little bit of a ham and an exaggerater, milked their little trip for everything it was worth: visits to lush mansions, a star on every street corner, money everywhere, and there they were, two ordinary fellows, in the midst of it all. Every now and then, Mrs. Shannon would touch her collarbone, exclaiming, "It must have been something!"

Delores sat confounded over her husband's growing distance from her: he seemed restless, fidgeting in his chair, smoking cigarette after cigarette, something inside tormenting him: he inhaled deeply, at times almost gasping. Since he'd come back from California, he had been suffering from more intense nightmares, and he seemed to be spending more and more time pacing about the living room. And there was something else: he had a look of doom about him, even if he was always reading that Vanderbilt book with the crumpled pages.

Later Mrs. Shannon unwrapped the aluminum foil off the apple spice cake, which she had set down on the table, revealing a puffy-topped cake filled with citron chunks, cherries, and raisins. The children jumped up for their slices and the adults converged around the cake, admiringly. It was a delicious cake, like kissing a woman for the first time, thought Cesar; like rum-drenched pineapple, thought Nestor; like eating *flan* with Poppy, thought Delorita; like chocolate, thought Eugenio; like apple spice cake, thought little Leticia. To realize that this was made by the very same woman whose shrill voice shouted up into the courtyard at two in the morning, screaming, "Will youse fucken turn that shit down!" The same woman who came up the stairs one day and stood at the door wielding a hammer, face red and on the verge of attack. When they finished eating, Cesar said to Mrs. Shannon, "I want to give you something," and he went into the living room. He used to keep a black briefcase on top of the bass drum of an American drum kit, which sat along with other instruments on a dolly in the corner of the living room beside the couch; he snapped it open and pulled out a black-and-white photograph of himself, Nestor, and Desi Arnaz taken during the

stirring finale of "Beautiful María of My Soul"—the three harmonizing, with mouths open, teeth showing, and heads bathed in
halos of light. The briefcase was filled with about three hundred
copies of that photograph. Their friend Benny the Baby and
General Purpose Photographer had taken their studio negative
and made up the copies; he would put one in his window alongside a First Communion photo and the picture of a GI home from
the war. They had one in the hallway—the original—signed by
Arnaz: "To my good friends, Cesar and Nestor Castillo, with a
strong love *y un abrazo siempre.* Desi Arnaz 5/17/55." He came
back into the dining room with one of the photographs, addressed
it to Mrs. Shannon, and then gave it to his brother to sign. Mrs.
Shannon held this signed photograph to her breast and declared,
"Oh, thank you."

   She stayed until around ten. In the hallway, just beyond the
bookcase of the novels that Delores liked to buy, Cesar and Mrs.
Shannon stopped for a moment, and in that moment Cesar gave
her a deep and nearly loving look, as if he might really kiss her,
but he touched her elbow and squeezed her plump shoulders,
patting her on the back, as he often did with friends. Escorting
her to the door, he thanked her for the cake, and leaned over the
railing, watching the roundness that was Mrs. Shannon disappearing down the stairs. Back in the dining room, he pulled up
a chair and said to his brother Nestor, "Do you want some more
of this cake, brother?" And then, after another slice: "Imagine
that, Mrs. Shannon baking a cake for us, and a good cake. Imagine
that."

THEIR APPEARANCE ON THE
show turned out to be a good thing. Desi Arnaz so liked their
composition that he paid them a thousand dollars for the rights
to perform the song and recorded "Beautiful María of My Soul"
in the fall of 1955, when it reached number 8 on the easy-listen-
ing charts, rubbing shoulders with the likes of Rosemary
Clooney and Eddie Fisher for a week. Among aficionados of the
romantic bolero, "Beautiful María of My Soul" became some-

thing of a minor classic almost instantly, ranking up there with *"Bésame Mucho"* and *"Siempre en Mi Corazón."* Arnaz himself went on to perform "Beautiful María of My Soul" on the Ed Sullivan show, and soon enough a number of other recording artists did too, notably Nat King Cole (he recorded that song in Havana for his album "Cole Español"; it was perfect for his tender, refined voice, and his accompaniment also featured a horn solo by no less than Chocolate Armenteros). The Ten Thousand Hollywood Strings orchestra did their own cover of it, too. (You can still hear it on the Muzak tapes, stuck between an unbearably cheerful pipe-organ version of "Guantanamera" and *"Quizás, Quizás, Quizás!"* in supermarkets, shopping malls, airports, and bus-terminal lounges everywhere.) Then one day Cesar received a call from this fellow named Louie Levitt of RCA Victor, saying that Xavier Cugat was interested in doing his own instrumental version of the song. Permission was granted for the sum of one thousand dollars. With the royalties from all these recordings, the brothers suddenly had some money in their pockets. Altogether they'd make about ten thousand dollars in 1956–57 in royalties from the different recordings.

The Mambo Kings recorded "Beautiful María of My Soul" as a 45 rpm, and it was on a 33 LP album, a collection of their romantic love songs, called "The Mambo Kings Play Songs of Love." They sold ten thousand copies of this recording; it was their greatest success. As they'd never had any hits before, even near ones, Cesar was always trying to come up with new catchy dance numbers and experimented with dance steps before the mirror, his hope being to come up with a new craze the way Antonio Arcana did in 1952 with the cha-cha-cha.

They got a lot of air play on stations like WPIX and WOR radio. And they started to get bookings in first-class joints like the McAlpin Ballroom and the Biltmore Hotel, and they were able to get a few hundred dollars more for the band on weekend engagements. Jobs took them all over the city where the crowds were mixed, Italians and blacks, Jews and Latins. Then Grossinger's, the Jewish resort, hired them for a month of weekends and they had the luxury of bringing in two other bands for the underbill, Johnny Casanova Rumba Boys and an old favorite, Glorious Gloria Parker and Her All-Girl Rumba Orchestra. But their biggest honor was to play at Grossinger's on the underbill to Machito's orchestra. That was the period when teenage girls would nervously approach Cesar Castillo and his brother to ask for their autographs. These girls weren't sure if Cesar was a star, but he certainly had taken to looking like one, wearing dark Italian sunglasses, a brilliant white ascot, and eight rings on his hands. And he'd sign these autographs as if it was the most natural thing in the world. Soon they got enough jobs out of town that they scraped some money together and bought an old school bus. The first thing they did with the bus was to paint it flamingo-pink, one of Cesar's favorite colors. In the spirit of color-coordinating the group, the Mambo Kings performed for a time in flamingo-pink, black-lapeled suits. Then Cesar got his friend Bernardito Mandelbaum, the artist, to decorate the bus with palm trees, G clefs, and music notes. They kept the bus parked down in a lot on 126th, off Amsterdam. A new publicity shot was taken of the Mambo Kings: the musicians posed inside the bus with their trombones and saxophones and violins sticking out the windows. They mounted a speaker on the rooftop, through which they played music, and used the bus to get out to Jersey City, Newark, and Danbury, Connecticut. They did not travel long distances: the farthest west they'd ever performed was Philadelphia, for some Cubans there.

That all changed when they made their famous cross-country Mambo U.S.A. tour. Chosen by the Mambo U.S.A. booking company as one of the orchestras which would spread the mambo across the nation, they set out in the spring of 1956 on a two-month stint that took them to the dance halls and theaters of small towns everywhere, and major cities like Chicago and San Francisco. Typical was a dance they played in an old American Legionnaires Hall in a place called Quincyville, Pennsylvania. The town was nestled out beyond the hills, cows, and tranquil fields of the Amish country. Nestor sat in the front of the bus beside the mambo dance team of Elva and René, delighted by the green countryside and lakes and the elongating silos and trees in the sunlight. He made the trip playing cards with Cesar and reading his little book.

Whenever they passed a cemetery, Cesar would joke, saying, "Look, brother, there goes the future."

As the bus turned down the main street of Quincyville, speakers blaring mambo music, dogs barked, children whistled, kids on bicycles honked their little black horns, and the bells went *ching-ching-a-ling*. People lined up on the street to get a look at these musicians, and when they climbed off the bus at the Thomas E. Dewey American Legionnaires Hall, they were greeted with friendly nods and smiles. (Though there was that other place in New Jersey, Tanglewood, where they returned to the bus at three in the morning and found the aisles and windows smeared with excrement.)

That night they played for a crowd of redneck farmers and their wives who didn't know what was going on with their music. Behind the musicians was a banner saying in big letters: MAMBO USA TOURS PRESENTS: THE FABULOUS CESAR CASTILLO AND HIS MAMBO KINGS!

Cesar stood before the microphone, saintly under those lights, with vocal cords trembling, his wrecked-by-cigarettes voice crooning, arms spreading wide to embrace the world. The good people of the good Pennsylvania earth had no idea what to make of their music. Cesar was always a joy to watch during the fast dance numbers, the man sliding and bending, flailing his arms into odd configurations—at one moment lilting forward and stomping his heels, at the next jumping bolt-upright like an excla-mation point—his face contorting, his mouth in an "O," in a Vanna Vane "Ooooo"; his teeth set like a trap, tongue lashing the air; his braceleted and beringed hands jangling; his shoes pirouet-ting; and he'd shout, "Uhhhhhh!" while conducting the orchestra and clap and shout out the names of his musicians, *"Vaya,* Pito! *Vaya,* Nestor!" and "Uhhhhh" again.

Sometimes this was too much for more conservative crowds and then the group would launch into a mixed set of American and Latin American compositions. He crooned "In the Still of the Night," "Moonlight Becomes You," "Somewhere Over the Rainbow," then *"Bésame Mucho"* and *"María la O."* For the "Peanut Vendor," Cesar came out wearing a baseball cap and pushing a cart that had "Peanuts for Sale" written on its side. Taking to the microphone and shaking a martini mixer filled with shot, Cesar sang an English version of the song: "Oh, why don't you try my peanuts, you'll never find peanuts as tasty as mine,"

which most of the audience did not get anyway, as Cesar still had
a thick Cuban accent. But the musicians knew the meaning of
those words and always had a good laugh with the songs. Their
other big novelty number was a quasi-tango which Cesar had
composed, stealing bits of *"Malagueña"* and the *Habanera* from
Bizet's *Carmen.* He'd introduce it to the audience: "Now here's
a song about a cat who has to fight the bull all the time, and I mean
bull-you-know-what!"

In that number Xavier, their bestial trombonist, came charging like a bull toward Cesar, who played the bullfighter, waving
a large red cloth and gesturing with bows and waves of the hand
to a beautiful woman offstage. The number was set up for a few
laughs and to introduce the dance team of Elva and René. At the
end of the song, Elva in a bright red dress would come spinning
out into the brave matador's arms. Vamp and out. The audience
always broke into applause.

Whenever Elva came dancing out, Cesar would give her a
nice up-and-down, as if to see through the silk of her dress, like
Superman. He'd once seen her in a bathing suit when they were
playing in the Catskills. She was sunbathing by a lake, and when
he saw her, Cesar decided to walk over and ask Elva if she'd like
a soda. He took one look at her and blushed; a few strands of
pubic hair overrunning her bathing suit broke his heart. He was
interested in her, but thought she might be a little crazy. Poor
René, word was that he could not satisfy her, that she preferred
men with "kingly sticks," men who were really built . . . or that's
what the musicians speculated.

He was interested, but wouldn't touch her. René was his
friend and he would never fuck around with a friend's woman.
Still, he spent many a night thinking about her.

The people loved the music, but these Pennsylvania folk
who were used to country dancing had their troubles with the
mambo, and because of this, part of the evening included free
rumba and mambo and cha-cha-cha lessons.

René, the male partner, joined Elva on the stage. He was a
tiny, thin man, about five-five or so, in three-inch Cuban heels,
with big eyes, a pointy, pocked nose, thick mustache, bald head,
and soft, aristocratic eyes. He was forty-five and had found Elva
some ten years before, when she was sixteen and succulent, danc-

ing rumbas out in Maríanao Park in Havana for pennies. René hired her to join his stage act, which consisted of dancing old-fashioned rumbas at the Tropicana nightclub in Havana. They came to New York in 1947 and made a living teaching dancing at the Fred Astaire dance studios, the Palladium, and the Savoy. And sometimes they performed at the Teatro Hispano in Harlem, where René caught the stage manager feeling Elva up in the wings and attacked him with a hammer. That's when Cesar hired them to work with the Mambo Kings.

When they'd finished the bullfight song, the Mambo Kings launched into "Mambo Nocturne," one of their original compositions. The dance couple waltzed around the stage. The next number was *"El Bodeguero,"* a cha-cha-cha, and Elva and René were out on the dance floor among the crowd, showing them the steps and giving instructions: "And it's one, two, three, and slide. Stop. One, two, three, slide, and stop . . . Ah, ladies, you look great, but your husbands are stiffs!"

The men listened to her carefully and were soon bending, spinning, and lurching forward to the music, happy, red-faced, and like shy students at a high-school dance. The men doted on shapely Elva, and their pretty, thick-ankled wives were charmed by the flirtatious splendor that was Cesar Castillo.

Cesar would use the lessons as a chance to mingle with the crowd. He'd come down off the stage and dance with a dozen different women during a single song, his warm-blooded, thick hands taking the woman by the waist and spinning her like a falling flower. The evening would end with a set of Mambo Kings "songs of love": "Twilight in Havana," "Solitude of My Heart," and "The Sadness of Love." Cesar would sing about the murmuring seas, the mournful moon, scornful, mocking, deceptive, cruel, playful, entrancing love—eyes closed, his face a mask of thoughtful passion.

Everyone had a good time, crowd and musicians. The crowd was generous in its applause, and the musicians would head out thinking about the next day's journey, gather to pass along little cups of rum and prepare for the night's sleep before heading to the next day's job, a Sunday-afternoon mambo dance party at the Plainfield auditorium, Plainfield, New Jersey.

As for women? Even when he was stuck in the middle of

nowhere, in a small town where everybody watched him, the Mambo King was always up to his old tricks, dating girls wherever he could, but hardly ever with the kind of success he had back in New York, where the greater difficulties of life promoted a greater pursuit of pleasure. Still, the man never gave up! Sometimes during the dances he would discreetly ask if a certain young lady might show him around town the next morning before he left on the bus. Sometimes he made dates at night and found himself waiting on street corners with names like Maple and Vine at three in the morning, pacing up and down, cigarette in mouth, hands in trousers, waiting for these chancy rendezvous with women named Betty and Mary-Jo and Annette. Meeting these women, he would sit for hours talking sincerely with them and musing on the beauty of the stars, and then he would try to make his move: sometimes he petted, tongue-kissed, wrestled, dry-humped women in the parks of these small towns or in the back seat of a car in the local lovers' lane, but usually his restlessness and voracious ego were satisfied with the amorous tension of these dates.

(And there were other women that he daydreamed about as he sat drinking his last drinks in the Hotel Splendour. Going down on some girl on Coney Island at ten-thirty at night, the two of them huddled under a blanket. A woman with a broken leg in a cast, standing up in a phone booth during a rainstorm in Atlantic City, the gales whipping against the glass, things so dark around them nobody could see, so that in the ferocity of the winds they started to kiss, his knee pressing between her legs, and this woman saying to hell with it and pulling up her sun skirt and down with her panties, down over her legs and down over the thick plaster cast, so that he lifted her up onto him and she leaned back against the wall, laughing and thinking, This man is insane, laughing and seeing stars while people outside looked like zig-zagged pencil doodles running through the deluge. And there was that woman in the crowd watching the Macy's Thanksgiving Day parade. She was standing next to him, Leticia, and Eugenio, whose presence certainly made things easier, as this woman seemed to like children very much and smiled each time he hoisted Leticia up over his head so that she would see the bands and floats better. But he really made this woman smile when he

said, "And can I lift you up?" Ended up with them walking to
the subway together and Cesar making a date with her for a week
later. She had a nice body, really a massive woman with pendu-
lous breasts, but, *coño,* was she motherly and liked to have him
suck them and played a game of slapping his face with them, but
the woman was too serious, how could he fuck around with a war
widow with sadness in her eyes even when she looked fine in one
of those lacy Tigress of the Night brassieres, really broke his heart
to hurt her so, and she was an office manager in a place downtown, about forty years old but beautiful, she just took everything
too seriously, but, man, was she fun, another one who liked her
men "built," as she put it, men with king-sized sticks. And there
was that woman in the fancy white coat whom he watched along
Fifth Avenue one day, she was the one he followed into Saks Fifth
Avenue up to the glove department, where he stood pretending
to shop and watched her posing before the mirrors. She had one
of those elegant thin model bodies, tall and firm, and he watched
her slipping on gloves, nice soft leather gloves, and when he
closed his eyes, he imagined the way she would pull on a pair of
panties after a shower or play, with dampened fingers, with his
thing, slipping a condom on him the same way she put her fingers
into that glove. She was impossible, too snotty for him. He followed her all over the store and thought he had a thing going
because every now and then she would look deep into his eyes,
and he considered that a form of lovemaking, but just as he was
about to make his move, to approach her, these two gents stepped
out from one of the service departments, store guards, who said
to him, "We understand you're bothering one of our customers,
sir," and that was that, his face blushing with embarrassment, and
as he was being led out of the store, he got the last lick in, gave
her this look which said, "You don't know who I am or what
you've just missed, baby." And there were others, like the European lady he met on that one-night job moonlighting as a crooner
on a harbor tour boat. She was French and not even that good-
looking, but she had been staring at him as he sang on the stage.
And she was aggressive, joining him by the railing to watch the
moonswept sea, because that was when there were many lonely
European women, the war had left so many men dead. And she
said to him in a thick French accent, "I love the way you use your

hands and shake those maracas. You have lovely hands, may I look at them?" And she started to read them and said, "You have a long lifeline, if you want it, and success is here if you want it. But I see trouble ahead, something that you must be prepared for." She said, "You see that spot here that looks like an exploding star, that means something's going to explode in your life. I used to see that in Europe all the time, on many, many hands." She was so thin her Venus mound protruded like a huge fig, and when he made love to her he kept thinking about the city of Paris and the Eiffel Tower and all those newsreels he'd seen of the Free French and Allied troops marching victoriously back into the city. And there were others: Gloria, Ismelda, Juanita, Alice, Conchita, Vívian, Elena, Irene . . .)

Still, whenever Cesar came back from these dates and he found Nestor, an insomniac, waiting up in the motel-room bed, he would say something: "Oh, man, that chick I picked up, pssssshh, man, you should have seen her body!" And he'd say it to make his brother jealous, because in many ways he was jealous of his brother's marriage to Delores. Or perhaps he always had to treat Nestor like a poor soul, and therefore tormented him with tales of his amorous exploits.

. . . When I knew he was in pain . . .

Poor Nestor, when they were on the road, he would suffer at night with homesickness and ardent longing for María. In those simply furnished motel rooms, he would remain awake half the night, arms tucked behind his pillow, body racked in spiritual pain. Sometimes he would get up and take a walk, lingering against a streetlamp in the motel parking lot, or he'd find some fellows to play cards with for nickels and dimes, but played without caring if he won, outlasting even the most diehard insomniacs. On those nights the thought of looking at the same wistful moon and whispering stars as he used to during his nights of romance with María in Havana destroyed him. He would sit up in bed smoking cigarettes, then clean out his trumpet, jot down a few lyrics, or read from his book, seeking an answer to his woes. He'd feel like crumpling up. Sadness would weaken his knees. He'd pace until his older brother came in with that happy smirk on his face, his older brother whistling, his older brother yawning, his older brother falling quickly to bed. Then, while

Cesar snored away on the other side of the room, Nestor passed the time familiarizing himself with the ceiling, faces, roads, stars swirling above him.

Did he think about Delores and his children, Leticia and Eugenio? Yes, he could not bear the thought of hurting them. But what could he do? He would sit up, sighing, desperate to get rid of those feelings.

"A *cabrón,*" he would perhaps tell himself, "would have gone back to Cuba by now. A *cabrón* would have been unfaithful."

Despite his brother's constant seduction of women, Nestor wore his faithfulness like a badge of sainthood, but he sometimes found it unbearable, wanting to be held, to be comforted, to be told, "Yes, Nestor, I love you, everyone does." And those feelings would make him angry at the marriage, so that by the time he returned home, he would take it out on Delores.

He'd only begin falling asleep after the sun had started to rise. Then his dreams would take on a golden glow. "There goes the future," he would say to himself, falling asleep. "There goes the future." And he found himself stumbling through a cemetery, exulting in the obelisks, Celtic crosses, and monuments with their carved angels and bursting suns. Christ risen (Save this flesh, Lord), Christ judging (Forgive me, Lord), Christ on the Cross (Please place me in Your Heart). Then he'd wander through the cemetery, feeling very much at home, until some sound, Cesar snoring, Cesar saying, "Oh, baby," Cesar belching, would stir him from his uneasy sleep and he rejoined the world.

(And the next day, driving along the hilly countryside near the Delaware Water Gap, the bus overheated and stopped on the side of the highway for an hour. The brothers found themselves walking down a country road with Manny. They came to a field of sheep, and in the distance another field of haystacks. Nature buzzing, alive with insect sounds and birdcalls. They saw a mill and a small stone wall where they thought they might pose for a picture. Cesar had brought along a little Kodak box camera and he told Nestor to pose beside him in front of that wall. They were doing so, arms around each other's shoulder, when they heard a cowbell. Not a Latin orchestra cowbell counting 3/2 time, but a cow cowbell. Then they met the cow herself, who had come walking out of the field. Big black spots covered her hide and she moved in a swirl of a hundred flies. The spots inspired the brothers to put on dark glasses. They posed in front of the cow, looking as if they were part of the cow's family.

A farmer had been watching the brothers and said to them in a German accent, "Let me take your picture. The three of you."

And so Manny, Nestor, and Cesar, three Mambo Kings, posed for posterity.

That was June 1956.

Then the farmer invited them to his house, which was down the hill. His front garden was filled with sighing flowers, sighing as they tried to reach higher out of the ground. And the roots of the earth seemed to yawn. In the Hotel Splendour the Mambo King felt the sunniness of that day and poured himself another drink. It was a stone house and its interior smelled of dirt and firewood and cherry pipe tobacco. They drank coffee and had corn bread and ham—"*Sabroso!*"—grape jelly, and scrambled eggs. Then they drank a glass of beer each. When they offered to pay him, he refused, and when they left, he followed them back up the road to the bus, where Cesar gave him a signed copy of "Mambo Dance Party." He laughed and they were touched by his insistence that they come back any time to eat with him.)

Because of the tour, Cesar spent his thirty-eighth birthday in Chicago. They were holed up in an old twelve-story hotel called the Dover House, on the Northeast Side, overlooking Lake Michigan, and he'd had a good day walking along the shore with his brother and a few of the Mambo Kings, clowning around, eating in nice restaurants, and, as always, trying to kill time before the show. He certainly expected something more from the fellows than what he had gotten. He considered himself their father, their Santa Claus, their spiritual advisor, the butt of their jokes, and there he was, on his birthday, after a show, without any sign that his musicians would celebrate his birthday. So it was not as if he was impervious to pain. On a normal night out, he would have suggested a party, but he resisted the idea of initiating his own birthday celebration. After his fellow musicians had gone their separate ways, and Cesar and Nestor headed for their rooms, Cesar was the solemn one for a change.

"Well, happy birthday, *hermano,*" Nestor said, with some embarrassment in his voice. "I guess I should have said something to the band."

And that little incident tapped into Cesar's feeling that went back a long way to Cuba: that no one does a thing for you, so you must do it yourself.

Feeling downcast about turning thirty-eight, and about being alone on the night of his birthday, Cesar opened his hotel-room door and clicked on the light; he slept in a bed that was up against a wall of mirrored tiles. Stretched in front of those mirrored tiles was a beautiful, long-legged woman, head of thick black hair propped up on an elbow, body luscious and naked.

Taking in the spectacular curvaceousness of a body whose front startled the Mambo King and whose shapely bottom, soft and rounded as a swan's neck, was reflected in the mirror, he said, "*Dios mío!*"

And the woman, a brunette with big brown eyes, said, "*Feliz cumpleaños,*" and smiled.

She would be another acquaintance of his, an exotic dancer, Dahlia Múñez, who was professionally known as the Argentine Flame of Passion. He and a few of the Mambo Kings had watched her dancing in a club on the South Side. When his fellow musicians saw how Cesar could not take his eyes off her that night, they hired her as a present to him, and there they were: she opening her arms and her legs to him, and Cesar hurrying to strip off all his clothes, which he left in a pile on the floor. Every woman he'd ever bedded down, he would think years later in the Hotel Splendour, had something to distinguish her lovemaking. And for the Argentine Flame of Passion it was the way she enjoyed the act of fellatio, actually liked the spill of his milk inside her mouth—or so she pretended. (And her technique! She would make his spectacular member even more spectacularly huge. She'd take the root of his penis above his testicles, which resembled jowls and were the size of good California plums, squeezing so tightly that his thing turned purple with the rush of blood and then got even bigger: and then she would just roll her tongue around it, take him inside her mouth, lick him all over, pull, prod, and poke his member until he came.) She had other virtues, which kept them busy until past seven in the morning; they slept happily until around ten-thirty, when the Mambo King and this Dahlia fucked one more time, showered together, got dressed, and showed up in the hotel dining room, where his musicians were gathered to wait for their bus. When he walked in, they broke into applause. (For years he sent Dahlia postcards, inviting her to visit him in New York and saying that he might visit her in Chicago.)

The brothers loved the immensity of the United States and experienced both the pleasures and the monotony of small towns U.S.A. Of the Midwestern states, they found Wisconsin most beautiful, but they also liked the Far West. They played Denver, where Cesar, delighted all his life by cowboy movies, saw his first bowlegged, drawling cowpokes leaning up against a bar, spurred cowboy boots against the foot railing, a rinky-dink player piano jiving through "The Streets of Laredo." And it was "Howdy, pardner" and "Thank you much" and long-drawled-out English phrases. They bought the family little presents wherever they went. In Denver, cowboy hats and rubber tomahawks and little dolls, and for Delores, a "Genuine Navajo Squaw" dress. They made like tourists and sent home dozens of postcards of everything from Mount Rushmore to the Golden Gate Bridge. Aside from their moments of strangeness and displacement, they had a beautiful trip.

The guys who had it rough were the black musicians, who were treated in some places like lepers. No violence against them, just a bad silence when they'd go walking into a store, a disenchantment when they'd walk into a lodge for the hunters' special breakfast, plates slapped down on the table, drinks poured quickly, eyes averted. In one place in Indiana they had a big problem with the owner of a dance hall there. He wanted Desi Arnaz, not these ebony-black Cubans like Pito and Willy. The owner would not allow them to walk onto his premises, and the orchestra canceled, Cesar telling the man, "You go fuck yourself, mister!" In some places they had to come in through the back door and were not allowed to use the toilets with everyone else. Black musicians had to take their pisses out the back stage door. Spirits were dampened, especially when the weather was bad, because in their travels through the heartland of America these fellows sometimes felt an Arctic coldness of spirit that made New York seem like Miami Beach.

At one point, they spent two weeks on the road without ever meeting up with a single fellow Cuban, and a month when they saw no other blacks.

San Francisco was different. Cesar liked it immediately because its hilliness reminded him of Santiago de Cuba. He liked to walk up and down its streets, enjoyed looking at its pretty many-colored houses with the curlicue balconies and bay windows. That was the last stop on their tour, where the Mambo Kings were to hook up for a triple bill in Sweet's Ballroom, with the orchestras of Mongo Santamaría and Israel Fajardo. This was really important for the Mambo Kings, as they were paid two thousand dollars for a single appearance—more than they'd ever gotten before. When Cesar stepped onto the stage that night, to clamorous applause, and the orchestra opened, as they always did, with "Twilight in Havana," Cesar Castillo was positive that, from then on, things for the band would get better and better and that there would be many more nights in the future when they'd make that kind of money. Why, a fellow could live well making a few hundred dollars a week! Like a rich man. That night would always be a beautiful memory. Every song greeted enthusiastically, the crowds of dancers going wild with appreciation and happiness, and just the honor of sharing the bill with musicians of this caliber! Then, too, there was always that moment when the audience recognized the opening bars of "Beautiful María of My Soul," their one hit, the song that brought them closest to fame.

With all this money, the brothers bought themselves new suits, toys for the children, clothing. Nestor bought Delores a fur wrap. For the apartment, he bought a brand-new Castro Convertible sofa and the big RCA black-and-white television that would sit in that living room for the next twenty years. And he was always making trips to the bank, putting money away for a rainy day. His security was his blue American Savings Bank passbook, guaranteed to pay four to five percent interest annually. Manny the bassist saw a trustworthy soul in Nestor and wanted him to go into the *bodega* business up on 135th Street, but Nestor, disliking risks of any kind, backed away. He was so unsure about the future and so plagued by anxieties that he continued to work at the meat plant, reporting every so often to Pablo to pick up assignments, so that the family always had money coming into the house. Even Cesar, who always let the money fly out of his pockets, managed to put some of it away, though not much. He spent it at the racetracks and in the nightclubs and on his male and female acquaintances. For about three months, he lived a life of opulence. Even after sending a few hundred dollars to his daughter in Cuba, whom he kept promising to visit, he had enough to make a down payment on his dream automobile, a 1956 DeSoto.

The afternoons would find Cesar out on the street, proudly sponging down his DeSoto with soap and water and then polishing it with wax. Then he'd wipe the chrome with rags, until the whole machine gleamed radiantly. Cesar would go over that automobile as meticulously as he did his fingernails, with not a mark or a nick anywhere on its great windshield or over its smooth, sloping hood. He derived great pleasure from looking at it and would hold court from its front seat, playing its radio and chatting quietly with his friends until he decided to take someone for a ride up to the George Washington Bridge and back. The thing was so big and shiny that he would attract crowds of poor children, who would stand before it in awe.

"Yes, sir," Cesar would think. "That's my nice car."

He was always reluctant to leave it parked in front of the building without someone to watch over it. La Salle was a street where the hoodlum element not only sat on cars; they took flying leaps off cars to catch balls during stickball games and jumped up on top of cars to dance. He'd usually park it over in the garage on 126th Street but sometimes kept it near the building. On those occasions when he was called upstairs, he would often check out that car from the window. He loved his DeSoto. It was big. It was splendid. It was smooth. It had turbo-thrust and was fifteen feet long. It was so fabulous-looking that no woman could resist smiling when she saw it. That DeSoto was so powerful that when he roared down the street and screeched to a halt, his foot on its "touch-sensitive" automatic brake system pedal, driver and machine were one and he would feel as if he were turbo-thrusting through the dense ordinariness of the world.

He would take everybody for rides, elbow out the window, felt dice dangling off the mirror. His best friends at that time were Manny the bassist, Frankie Pérez the ballroom dandy, Bernardito Mandelbaum, artist, mambo aficionado, and Cubanophile, his fat cousin Pablo, and little Eugenio. They all got to ride around with the Mambo King. One day, he took the family and a date on an outing up north to Connecticut and stopped at a place called Little America, a memorabilia-packed log-cabin lodge whose shelves and walls were filled with animal heads, muskets, medallion-brimmed cowboy hats, tin soldiers, Mohawk Indians, rubber tomahawks, stovepipe hats, "Welcome to Connecticut" ashtrays, miniature American flags, American-flag tablecloths, American-flag pens. Cesar, a rich man, bought the children bundles of this junk. Afterwards they went into the Little America diner, where they drank sodas and chocolate malteds and came away with bags of potato chips and Snickers candy bars. Then they drove for another hour and the road opened to long stretches of meadow, streams, and woods. Cows and horses lolling behind fences, dogs barking from the side of the road. Bing Crosby on the radio singing "Moonlight Becomes You." Cesar drove his automobile, with its beautiful whitewall tires, screeching around the turns. The family gripped their seats, but Cesar laughed and whistled. Sparks sometimes flew from the friction of hubcaps hitting the highway curb. He drove into a state park, where the forest's noble pine trees towered over them. Serenely the family made their way down a corridor of these trees, carrying picnic baskets and guitars, a cooler of beer and soda. They were following signs that said, TO THE LAKE.

Bees hovered closely around Cesar and his date, Vanna Vane. He was wearing so much hair tonic that the bees swarmed around him as if he were a wildflower field. That day she wore a lot of perfume and was dressed in a red plaid dress, very plain and very matronly in its way. They were a happy couple even if they weren't a real couple. They held hands and whispered, telling little jokes and laughing. She was hoping that things would pick up with him. She liked the fact that he was generous with her. Frankly, a girl her age had to think about getting married, and even though he had told her a hundred times that they were good for a few laughs and for the Hotel Splendour, she believed there was something more to him. On a few occasions, when Miss Mambo had felt some real tenderness from him, she had started to cry in his arms. And it was as if he could not bear to see her pain, and so he told her, "Come on, Vanna. Stop acting like a little girl." So she kept her distance and waited patiently for Cesar to come around.

Cesar reminded her of the movie actor Anthony Quinn and she liked the way he would draw all the attention in a room, how other women seemed to envy her when she was out with him. And now he was on top of things, with all kinds of prospects. A Mexican film producer, Anibal Romero, had been talking to the Mambo King about appearing in a cameo part in a film in Mexico, where "Beautiful María of My Soul" was a hit. And he had been on the *I Love Lucy* show and had enough money that he bought a DeSoto and gave her a gold necklace because he was feeling successful. (Neither of them liked to think about the real circumstance of that necklace, with the Mambo King guilty about having to take Vanna Vane uptown to 155th Street, to that Pakistani fellow with the thick black hair and the inkwell eyes, a doctor who sat Vanna down for a quick surgical procedure, scraping her womb until the child of their conception was taken forever from this world. And Cesar sat outside, chain-smoking because Vanna had been crying, and pissed off about the whole thing. Afterwards he took her down to Brooklyn and bought her a banana split in a corner pharmacy and was startled that she was upset. "A lot of guys," he said, "wouldn't have even gone with you." And that made her leave the pharmacy, sadly, so that it was months before she would speak to him or share a bed with him again.) But to the family they were a regular happy couple, not at all like Delores and Nestor, who had taken to walking solemnly side by side, their remarks addressed to the children: "Come here, *nenes!*" "Don't put your fingers in your mouth after touching that!" "Give your Papi a kiss!"

It was all silence, because since the brothers had come close to fame, Nestor had begun to change. He'd go for long walks by himself, and people were always saying to Delores or Cesar that they had seen Nestor "standing on a street corner without moving." Or that "he seemed to be there but wasn't there, you know what I mean?" Then there was something else: the letters she sometimes found folded up in his jacket pockets, letters to María, whose lines Delores could not bear to read. Her eyes would skim the pages and find phrases that cut her heart like a knife: ". . . And despite all my doubts, I still love you . . . It has always been a torment . . . This love will always thrive in my heart . . . If only I had proved my worthiness to you . . ." And other sentences that made her feel like slapping his face and saying, "If your life is not good enough for you, then go back to Cuba!" But how could she? She was trapped by her love for him. The idea of this beautiful dream of their love cracking open because of jealousy would send her into despair. She would take to her books and maintain her silence. For three months this had kept the peace.

At twenty-seven, Delores was still an attractive woman. But in attending selflessly to Nestor and the family, she'd acquired a puzzled harshness around the eyes. A photograph of her with five other Cubans, the brothers and musician friends of the family, shows a woman of intelligence and beauty literally trapped inside a crush of men. (And in this photograph, taken in front of a statue of Abraham Lincoln on 116th Street, they huddled close. In the crush of machos, she seems to be waiting with annoyance to be lifted out of there.) She had never lost sight of that sad but handsome man she had met years back at the bus stop, and she loved him and the children very much. But there were days when she thought of another life outside of cooking and cleaning and taking care of the family. She sometimes went wandering around Columbia University with the children and would peer into class-rooms or stand outside a window, listening to the summer-session lecture. She'd sigh, thinking about all the college people in that neighborhood. For reasons that she was unable to understand, she derived a deep satisfaction from all this learning, but would she ever act upon this?

There seemed no way out for her. She had quit her job as a paid domestic and had finished her night classes down at Charles Evans Hughes High School, where a teacher, who was half flirtation and half sincerity, suggested that she might enroll in college at least part-time. She always got high marks in her courses and could have gotten into City College, which was only a ten-minute walk from La Salle Street. She always told her teachers, "No." But when she daydreamed about her life, her knees ached with envy of those professors who lived surrounded by books and by admiring colleagues and students.

For a time she had thought her interests were unimportant in the scheme of their family life, but whenever the apartment grew thick with Cesar and Nestor's pals from the dance halls, who expected to be waited upon, she felt like screaming. It hit her that she was intelligent and more so than anyone else she knew. A vague nausea would come over her and she would barely make it through those evenings, so cramped was her stomach.

She became solemn in the performance of her wifely duties on those nights.

"What's wrong with you? Why are you so sad?" Nestor would ask her.

"I'm sorry," she'd say. "It's my stomach. *Tengo ganas de arrojar.* I feel like throwing up."

It so distressed her that, a few weeks later, she approached Nestor to discuss the matter with him. "*Querido,*" she said to him. "I want to ask you something."

"Yes?"

"How would it be with you if I enrolled in some courses at the college?"

"And why do you want to?"

"To better myself."

He didn't say no. But his face flushed and was filled with disappointment. "You can do as you please," he told her. He let out a sigh. "You go, and that will be the end of normalcy for us!" He was up out of the chair. "Do as you please, see if I care."

"But what is the big deal, Nestor? What's the problem?"

"The problem is that I'm the breadwinner here, but if that's what you want to do, that's your business."

She was silent, hopeful that his expression would change, grow more relaxed.

Instead, he went on. "Go ahead and humiliate me before the others."

"Oh, Nestor, please."

"Then don't suggest such things to me."

"I was only trying to get your permission to go to the school."

The word "permission" calmed him. "Yes?" And he seemed more pensive about it now. "Well, maybe we should talk about this, someday. But I just want to say that a woman with two children should never spend more time than's necessary away from home."

And then he became very kind, putting his arms around her and giving her a gentle kiss. "I'm sorry," he told her. "It seems I'm getting a bad temper these days."

But after that, it became harder to accept her everyday life. She would go walking down Broadway with her kids, among the students and professors of Columbia. Some of them looked daffy, some looked like geniuses. Some held doors for her and some let doors slam in her face. Some were homosexuals and some gave her lascivious up-and-downs. Why were they students, and not she? She would sometimes leave her children with her sister, Ana María, who loved them, and then go sneaking into the big libraries of the university and sit thumbing through their books. She pretended that she was enrolled in the college and she would nod and say hello to her fellow students. She would daydream about the nature of the world and the way it was set up. Why was it that her father dropped dead on a stairway, in the midst of an exhausting work day, his heart sad from all his troubles? Why did the severe librarian with the bifocals pushed down low on his pointy nose watch her with suspicion? Why wasn't her Papi standing in one of those classrooms, lecturing about the rise of the Popes of Avignon, instead of rotting in the ground? Why was it that she would walk home, dreading the fact that her husband, whom she loved very much, was lost in his own world of pain and music? Why was it that she would spend long periods of silence around him, because he never seemed to be interested in what she had to say and in the books she read? Why was it that when mambo time came around, when the house filled with musicians and their wives and the record player was turned up, why did she act willingly like a slave, attending to all the men, and yet feel no satisfaction or closeness to the women, like her sister, Ana María, and Pablo's wife, Miriam, who went happily about the business of cooking and happily rushed into the living room with trays of food? Why did she end up sitting on the couch, watching the crowd of happy dancers, with her arms folded on her lap and shaking *no, no, no* each time someone like her brother-in-law would take her by the wrist and pull her up to dance? Why did she open the door to her apartment in the Bronx one day and find Giovanni, that nice Italian fellow from the plant, standing there with his face puffy and hat in hand to tell her that her Papi was dead? Why was it that she liked to get lost in books like the one she was reading one night, Mark Twain's *Huckleberry Finn*, when she felt her husband lying alongside her, his fingers searching between her legs and his mouth suddenly upon her breast? Why was it that she no longer felt the same compulsion to do exactly what he wanted, to lift him out of his pain? She didn't know why, and she did all the right things for him, opening her robe all the way and planting kisses on his manly chin and chest and down below, where those kisses made him dissolve quickly.

They just walked in silence, Nestor in his blue *guayabera* and checkered *pantalones*, looking at the sunlight playing between the trees of the forest. One hand on Eugenio's shoulder, the other pulling little frightened Leticia along. No words for Delores except "It's a beautiful day, huh?" And that was the way they had always been since meeting at the bus stop. The pensive and pained musician who could make simple statements about life and the world, that was all. A good man, still heartbroken over someone else, she would think to herself. And that's why he wanted me, she would think. Wanted me so that I can help him forget what he hadn't forgotten. He winced with that awareness. Nothing was ever said about it, but when he would stand close to Delores, he seemed to stop breathing from shame. He was afraid to let her go to school because he thought that she would become wiser, and see through his confusion. He did love her. He would tell her that a million times over and over again if he had to, but something kept tugging at him, and he kept thinking that it was María. Or was it something else?

As they went walking through the woods, Nestor and Delores were tense. The children felt it, though they were too young to know why, and Cesar knew it. He was always walking over and joking with them. He came across some daisies and picked them for Vanna Vane and for Delorita. A flower slipped from his hand and for a split second was suspended between them, floating there. Like a magnet trick in the circus, Nestor stepped back, and the flower dropped to the ground. Later, Nestor thought he had seen a deer in the forest and went to look for it. As the family watched, he walked into a shaft of sunlight and for a moment he seemed invisible. Then he shouted, "It *is* a deer!"

Over a hill was the lake, and in the distance, mountains. There were a few summer vacationers spread out here and there along the shore, and a bathhouse, where the family changed into their bathing suits. The children played in the shallows of the water. Eugenio was five years old, but he'd remember how good the roast chicken tasted that day, the long-legged insects which seemed to float on the surface of the water, and his mother, looking fine as ever, sitting on the side of the blanket, and his father on the other, Nestor repeating, "Why is it that we are being this way? Don't you understand? *Yo te quiero.* When you understand that, you will be happy again!"

But each time she turned away from Nestor, he would look around for support from the others, as if someone should step forward and say, "Yes, don't be so hard on him, Delorita, he's a good man."

Cesar and Vanna Vane were inseparable. They jumped into the water, which was cold, and charged back to shore, stretching out on towels, drinking Rheingold beer, and enjoying the sunshine. Nestor, the younger Mambo King, watched them attentively, and each time Cesar's bottle emptied, Nestor would bring him another. Now and then he would say to Delores, "Forgive me?"

Then, Vanna Vane, in a green bathing suit, nipples pointy, limbs chilled, ran into the water. Cesar followed her, but because he couldn't swim, he mainly splashed around and laughed like a child. Vanna, being a city girl, really didn't know how to swim either, and they both went bobbing under the water, held each other by the waist, and played touchy-feely. Enchanted, they kissed. Delores remained on the shore, reading. Nestor was playing with the children when he suddenly felt determined to prove himself a man. There was a small island in the middle of the lake, a few hundred yards out, and he decided to swim there. But he'd only get so far and then sink into the water, churning frantically, his face contorting with the effort to stay afloat. When he started to go under, he felt a fierce constriction in his chest and gut, and from his mouth gushed a stream of bubbles. A few times it looked as if he might drown, as no one there swam well enough to save him, but when Delores put down her book and started to cry out, "Nestor! Nestor! Come back!" he kicked swiftly and with Herculean effort made his way toward the shore. Wrapping a towel around him, Delores covered his shivering body with her own. A chill wind had started to blow across the lake surface, and the greenish water, as if filled by shadows, darkened into black. Then heavy black-bottomed clouds started booming like conga drums in the distance, and just like that, the sunny day, with its hot sunlight brilliant against the lake, grew cold, the air charged up with static energy, and it started to rain. Everyone huddled under the bathhouse awning, watching the rain for about a half hour, and then they got dressed and made their way back to the car. Cesar Castillo took the family back to La Salle and then, with Vanna Vane, drove over to the Hotel Splendour.

THEY WERE GOING TO PLAY A JOB out in New Jersey. Cesar was standing before the living-room mirror, looping his tie into the shape of a crouching butterfly. As he started to brush back his slick hair, he noticed the window curtains wavering, and from down La Salle Street he heard fire sirens wailing. Then in the cool air he smelled smoke: in a building down the hill, a burning apartment and three little children screaming at the top of their lungs for help (black smoke swirling through the rooms, the floors growing hot from the fire raging underneath). Just out of the bathtub, Nestor went to the window, too. Then the whole family gathered by the windows to watch the brave firemen with their hooked pikes and fire hoses, balancing themselves on their high ladders. Glass melting, windows bursting from the heat, glass shattering on the street—people were everywhere watching this. The fire made the brothers nervous and they went into the kitchen and poured themselves a few drinks. Something about the screams, the billowing clouds of smoke. A night of smoke and crying in the air. A sadness filled the apartment; death was in the air, and they drank up two beers and two Scotches.

Cesar, with his thickset face, shrugged his shoulders and tried to forget about the whole business, and Nestor remembered certain principles of positive thinking, but through their minds echoed those children's screams. The shadows along the walls were jagged, cutting up the light.

They got dressed and ready to go, black instrument cases by their sides. It was the usual parting, no different from any of the others. Cesar had his black guitar case and a small box filled with percussion instruments out in the hallway by the door. Nestor followed behind with his black trumpet case in hand, hat pulled low over his brow. With his look of intense sadness, he knelt down and called over Eugenio, entranced by the glow of the RCA television, for a goodbye kiss. (You can see that look on his face that time he appeared on the *I Love Lucy* show, and sometimes you can see that same Cuban melancholy breaking through Ricky Ricardo's expressions, at once vulnerable and sensitive, the expression of a man who'd been through the mill and wanted no more pain in his life.) Eugenio kissed him goodbye and then hurried back to the television. He was watching *Superman*. And as Eugenio ran off, Nestor tried to hold on to him for one more kiss.

He had spoken to Delorita in the kitchen. *"Bueno,"* he said. "We're going now."

"When will you be back?"

"Well, you know it's a coming-out party in New Jersey, *una fiesta de quince.* We'll try to be back by five or six."

She was smoking a cigarette and, exhaling softly through her nostrils, gave Nestor a desultory kiss. Leticia, who was standing beside her, sank back into the folds of her dress and apron. What could Delores do but nod "Yes."

"Okay, *Mamá*," Nestor said to her. "See you later."

Later she would sit in the living room while the kids watched TV, happy to have the evening more or less to herself so that she could read and do as she liked, maybe take a nice long bath.

By eight o'clock in the morning she would be damning herself for not having shown him more love. She would watch the walls fall away and like a character in a novel move down the hall amid a swirl of shadows.

He was whistling—or that's the way everybody would remember him—whistling "Beautiful María of My Soul." Already he was fading away, though, his being compromised by memory, like a ghost. It was cool enough outside that the brothers stomped their feet on the ground and wisps of frosty air blew out their nostrils and mouths, the time of the year when some Christmas lights were still blinking in the windows, some still alive in that building. Survivors huddled in coats and blankets below, a spray of water falling in an arch in the glow of the black wrought-iron streetlamps. The moon over the rooftops, a mambo-singer moon with thin pencil-line mustache, stars shiny like glittering dots of gold lamé. They made their way down the stairs and stood for a time among the crowd watching the fire, waiting for Manny in his wood-paneled Studebaker station wagon. Cesar and Nestor would follow in the DeSoto. Breath from Nestor's lungs, tail-pipe clouds of steam, black and swirling into the dark night. (Like the sky in Cuba from the porch, the Mambo King would reflect in the Hotel Splendour, the stars going on forever and forever.) An hour and a half later they were still thinking about the fire, how things go up in flames. They had arrived at their destination in New Jersey: a caravan of five cars had pulled up to the club, and from the car driven by Ramón the *"Jamón"* from Brooklyn, out came Vanna Vane, who had gotten a ride so that she'd have a chance to hang around with that "big lug of a guy," Cesar.

The Mambo Kings set up inside the club, on a stage under a battery of red lights. Helium balloons everywhere bobbing softly against the ceiling. Half the room was cluttered with long tables and with relatives and friends of the girl of honor. Set against the wall opposite the horseshoe bar, a table of grandmothers in rhinestone brooches and with tiaras in their hair, each throwing back glasses of sangria and maintaining a strict watch on the goings-on of the younger couples in the crowd, slick *suavecitos* and their young girls, the teenagers at another table looking bored and anxious for the proceedings to begin. Two cooks carried in, as if on a stretcher, two large suckling pigs, their skin brown and crispy, and set them down on a long table that had been covered in a red cloth. Then out came more platters of food, followed by the crowning touch, a three-foot-high choco-late-éclair cake drenched with a honey glaze and topped with the number 15. The guy who was throwing the party was named López, and he handed Cesar a list of songs he wanted the band to play, numbers like *"Quiéreme Mucho,"* "Andalucía," and the song of his courtship of his wife, *"Siempre en Mi Corazón."*

And he added, "And can you play a little of that rock-'n'-roll for the *nenes?*"

"Seguro."

"And one more thing, that song you sang on television?"

" 'Beautiful María of My Soul'?"

"Yes, that one."

In came Mr. López's daughter, wearing a five-layer silk dress with an old-fashioned hoop skirt and tottering on high heels, a procession of her girlfriends and aunts behind her. She carried a large bouquet of flowers, wore a crown on her head, and exuded, as she turned to look at the crowd, a blue nobility that was both haughty and grateful.

In green wrap-around sunglasses, Nestor stepped up to the microphone and, with head tilted back, raised his trumpet and began to play—for the last time in his life—the haunting melody of "Beautiful María." Then, beside him, the fabulous Cesar Cas-tillo pulled from his pocket a frilly perfume-scented handker-chief, and this he passed over his dampened brow. Eyes shut, Cesar waited for his pianist, Miguel Montoya, to finish his tremolo-pedal-choked introduction, and with his arms spread wide before him, face noble and grinning like a horse, he began to sing.

With that, Mr. López took hold of his daughter's slender, white-gloved hand and led her out to the middle of the dance floor. Elegantly, he swung her in circles, eyes proud, a big smile on his face. The crowd applauded and converged upon father and daughter. Then everyone danced.

During the break, Nestor went off to lean up against a corner to watch the children attacking a *piñata*, fat with *caramelos*, toys, and coins; one by one, the children whacked the *piñata* with a stick, the hitting sounds taking him back to when he was a kid (and he would hear beatings in the other room, his older brother, Cesar, huddled in a corner, his arms held over him, to fend off their Papi). But these blindfolded children were happy, and a strong boy smashed open the *piñata*, and the children swarmed over the prizes. Eating noises, elderly voices lecturing the young, champagne bottles popping, and on the stage, different acts: a juggler from the local Knights of Columbus, cigarette smoke tearing into his eyes, spinning three torches into a pinwheel of light. Then there were the two little girls in their Shirley Temple hairdos and little red bows, tap-dancing across the stage. Then a comedian in a big red wig and bulbous fake nose presided over a raffle. The prizes were a box of Havana Partagas & Co. cigars, a case of pink champagne, a two-pound box of Schrafft's chocolates, and many smaller prizes, enough for just about everyone to come away with something: ballpoint pens, compact kits, small purses, cigarette cases each stamped with "Congratulations, Carmencita López, Feb. 17, 1957."

Miss Vanna Vane won a little seashell compact kit with a pop-up mirror, which she brought back to the table to show her man, Cesar. The Mambo King was drinking that night. Lately he had been that way at some jobs, just belting down a few glasses of booze every so often, when he could get to the bar or would join people at one of the tables. With his arm wrapped around Vanna Vane's waist, he kissed her behind the ear and then took hold of her chair and pulled it close to him so that he could feel her warm thigh through her slitted skirt against his leg and the slightest pulse there. The pulse in its silent way saying, "Cesar, we're going to have fun, and I'm going to show you how much I love you."

She was a nice and affectionate woman, a great dancer who never gave Cesar a hard time except when it came to her looks. She had little complaints about what going out with him was doing to her figure. Cesar was always taking her to restaurants and parties and she'd end up eating all kinds of fattening things. She could tear through a platter of chicken and rice, another of crispy *tostones,* and follow up with a few bottles of beer, and yet the next day she would spend hours before a mirror sucking in her belly and later squeezed herself into a Maidenform girdle. That she'd get depressed about it astounded Cesar, who enjoyed her maturing plumpness and the way her body quivered. (He winces, remembering how, when she climbed on top of him, she would like him to squeeze her *nalgitas* really tight, each squeeze timed to when she'd taken all of him inside: and then she'd grind her hips and everything would feel creamy. Wince again: she'd spray atomizer perfume on her neck, cleavage, and in the damp center of her Lily of Paris panties. In the room in the Hotel Splendour, she performed private stripteases for him and wrapped his member up in her nylons and capped it with her panties. Wince again.)

Vanna sat between the brothers and then she jumped because she felt Cesar's hand settling on her lap. She wriggled, but he left it there. Then, without saying a word or looking at her, he started rubbing her thigh. She wriggled some more, took another sip of her drink, and smiled again. Finally she whispered to Cesar, "Please, there are people here. Your brother's right here."

He sipped his drink and shrugged.

Nestor was sitting pensively watching people on the dance floor, the chaos of the tables, daydreaming. He'd been in a bad mood since earlier in the evening; it was as if he knew. While he was onstage and playing the solo to "Beautiful María," a bad sensation had started in his kneecap and risen slowly, rib by rib, through his chest and neck before settling in his thoughts. It was the simple feeling that his desires somehow contradicted his purpose in his life, to write sad boleros, to lie sick in bed, to mourn long-past loves, to crave what he could never have.

Later in the evening, when their work was done, the musicians attended to the tedious business of packing up their instruments and waiting for their pay. Then they collected bags of leftover food and pastries. And Nestor stuffed his pockets to overflowing with *caramelos* and chewing gum, marbles and small toys. Cesar took a bottle of rum with him and collected Vanna and made his way out to his car.

"Brother," he said to Nestor, "you drive."

Nestor had taken his last piss, eaten his supper, played his last trumpet line. He had scratched his itchy nose, winced at an off-key note, taken his last swallow of rum and, unwrapping one of the cellophane candies, had tasted his last sweet. In the men's room of the club, he had washed his face with cold water; he had inadvertently looked down Vanna Vane's cleavage while reaching across the table to get a light from a candle. He had felt like calling Delores but changed his mind. While thinking about the principles of positive thinking, he had noticed a stain on the left lapel of his suit jacket. Before the mirror and looking himself over, he had imagined that his insides were filled with a thick dark fluid like octopus ink. He had felt himself lifting off the ground while leaning back during his trumpet solo, felt himself passing through a wall. While pissing, he had ached, thinking about Beautiful María naked in bed, ached with a lack of understanding about things.

He had almost swatted a fly but decided against it, the poor thing was half dead and clinging to the corner of the bathroom mirror, and had watched some machos arm-wrestling at a back table. He had examined the intricacies of a dime. He had blown his nose. Sweating because it was so hot in that club, and wanting to feel the cool night air on his face, he had opened the back door and looked up into the sky, which seemed to be hanging low to the earth, and identified a constellation, Cygnus. He had watched the snow falling behind the club and had noticed the way the snow collected on the lower branches of the tree and then fell softly off. He had wondered what it would be like to go walking off into an eternal distance. He had thought of the past as going on forever. He had wondered if there were angels, as his mother used to say there were. Remembering how she'd point up to the Milky Way and say, "Look at all the people there," he daydreamed about a heaven dense with souls. He had been aware of the crucifix hanging around his neck and remembered the day his mother gave it to him. He was twelve years old and kneeling, trembling, at the altar railing to receive the Eucharist. And that night, years later, he had felt a slight pain behind his left ear. He had wished he had bought a spicy girlie magazine off the newsstand on 124th Street a few days before. He had remembered promising to take Eugenio and Leticia to the museum again to look at the dinosaur bones. He had remembered pressing up against Delores in the kitchen as she cooked over the stove. She was reading a book with cowboys on the cover. He had started to get an erection, three-quarters of the way up, and she had started to push herself into him from behind. Then the children came in, and his brother came in. And the steam pipes rattled and it sounded like people were trapped inside the pipes, rapping at them with knives and spoons. He had wondered about Jesus Christ, when He was up on the Cross, had wondered if Jesus, who could see everything in the world, past, present, and future, could see him walking across the club floor. He had remembered how much he loved to think about Jesus fishing in the Sea of Galilee. He had remembered to buy his sister-in-law, Ana María, twenty pounds of center-cut lamb chops from the meat-packing plant at a special bargain price. He had remembered the taste of his wife's nipple. He had decided to lose a few pounds because his stomach was getting fat. He had thought about a melody he had been fooling around with. He had dreamed about undoing things, not his children, or his wife's happiness, but of somehow going to Cuba again and into the arms of María. He had remembered thinking, Why do all these pains swirl around inside of me, when will all these pains end?

Then the part that for the Mambo King or anyone else was hard to imagine. Seated in the back of the DeSoto, Cesar Castillo was fooling around with Vanna Vane: they were both drunk enough that he kept sliding his hand up into the warm upper reaches of her skirt, to where the nylons hit the garters, and she was pure pleasure, kissing him affectionately and laughing, the two of them sipping their rum while Nestor, in the front seat, kept his eye on the road and tried not to be thrown by the icy curves or by the lovely snow which had continued to fall everywhere. Vanna was sliding her hand along the inside of Cesar's thigh, and he pressed his face against hers, telling her all the dirty things they would do once they got back to Manhattan. The back seat was thick with perfume and cigarette smoke, noisy with kisses and laughter, and they were so wrapped up in each other that they sometimes forgot Nestor was driving. He became an anonymous driver for them, as they got lost in each other; he was the man in the overcoat, black-brimmed hat, and scarf, with a trumpet case beside him on the front seat and a box of percussion instruments on the floor.

Nestor had been quiet for a long time, paying more attention to the road than to the kissing behind him, when he thought to ask, "Would you like me to turn up the heat?" But then, just like that, the car began swerving and slid over a patch of ice and he panicked, hitting the brakes and jerking the wheels so that the DeSoto flew into a dense wood and crashed into the trunk of a massive oak. There was a boom and then a loud yawning sound, like a ship's mainmast cracking, and the sturdy V-8 turbo-thrust engine tore loose from its bolts and slammed the steering wheel into Nestor's chest.

And that was all. He passed out behind the wheel, letting out a deep sigh. He closed his eyes and felt someone pouring hot oil onto him and he had to ask himself why were his insides filled with wetness: wet palm fronds, rotting flowers, stems mashed and bloody; wet sheet music, wet toilet paper, wet condoms, wet pages from a Bible, wet pages of a television script, wet pages of D. D. Vanderbilt's *Forward America!* The wheel had hit him like a hard punch in the chest, not even a terribly powerful punch, and he had heard the yawning and after the yawning a ringing of faraway bells. Then black-and-white stars floated around on the insides of his eyes, as if he'd just stared into a camera flash, and he opened his eyes and the falling snow had parted like a curtain and he could see the sky as it had looked from the porch of his family's house in Cuba: there were the constellations of Cygnus the Swan, Hercules, and Capricorn, and countless other stars, more radiant than he had ever remembered, the stars blinking like a child's happy eyes. And then started to swirl around like dancers in a crowded ballroom. He closed his eyes and felt like crying but could not cry. He tried to speak. "Tell the family they were in my thoughts," he wanted to say, but then even thinking became more difficult and he started to fall asleep, and though he was trying his best to stay awake, his thoughts became dreamier and darker, and then he daydreamed that someone was stroking his thick, wavy hair, and did not wake.

Thrown off their cloud of romance, Cesar and Vanna passed out for about ten minutes. The others, who had been following behind, came upon the scene. To free Nestor, the men pushed back the seat and carried him into the snow, where they laid him down on a blanket. Steam oozed from his nostrils and lips, steam and smoke and a smell of burning rubber and gasoline. They would say that Nestor opened his eyes and looked up at the sky, smiling sadly. Cesar was revived by a swig of rum and for a moment thought he was waking up on a Sunday morning in the Hotel Splendour with a terrible hangover. But Vanna Vane was weeping, and there were some of the Mambo Kings with flashlights, then policemen and strangers and sirens in the distance. Kneeling down by Nestor, the Mambo King surprised himself by making the sign of the cross over him. He remained there for a long time, touching Nestor's face and repeating, "Just wait, brother. Just wait." But nothing else happened—or there was nothing else that the Mambo King cared to remember.

He did remember Nestor rushing up the stairs to the apartment, happy as a small boy, carrying a Santa Claus gift-wrapped guitar as a present for Cesar, something hot he had picked up off the docks. He remembered the man sitting on the edge of the couch and, when he thought no one was looking, burying his face in his hands. He remembered the first time he heard the name María and the first time his brother played the chords to that song when they were living in Cousin Pablo's house. And somehow he could not separate Nestor's death from that song. He daydreamed that Nestor had heard him kissing Vanna lasciviously —and the truth was that he'd already started playing this game with her, nudging the opening to her vagina through her panties with his thumb, the man glorified by the moistness gradually accumulating there—and that Nestor couldn't bear to have so many others living in a world of pleasure while he existed in a world of pain; that, because of that feeling, instead of heading straight on the icy road, he jammed the wheel to the right abruptly, wanting to hit a tree. Then his brother's words, which

he'd never paid much attention to, came back to him, to everybody: "Sometimes I don't feel long for this world."

He remembered something else too, the medical man in the
hospital where they'd taken Nestor saying, "It wasn't that bad.
Just a little vein near his heart got crushed, just bad luck."
"Bad luck."

The worst was breaking the news to Delores. She knew
something was going on when Cesar turned up with Manny at
nine-thirty the next morning. She had been asleep when she
knew: her book, *Double Indemnity*, fell off the night table at
three-thirty in the morning and she could feel a slow sucking
mercury passing through her bones, as when she had answered
the door to her apartment in the Bronx and learned that her father
had died. So what could she do but pace the halls and stand vigil
by the window, waiting to hear the news? What could she do but
stare at herself in the mirror and wish that things had been better
between them?

When Cesar conveyed the news, "There's been an accident
involving Nestor. He's gone," she said, "Would you repeat what
you just said, *cuñado,* brother-in-law?"

He did.

Then, calmly and impressively, she said, "I must call my
sister, Ana María, and tell her."

Cesar said he would tell the children. Eugenio and Leticia
shared a little room at the end of the hall, and around the time
of the crash they had heard some of the boiler-room pipes below
twisting and churning as if about to burst or tear loose from the
walls. And this was followed by a metallic yawn that caused
Eugenio to sit up in bed. They were sleeping late Sunday, waiting for their mother to fetch them for eleven-o'clock High Mass
at the church. But that day Cesar pushed open the door, still in
an overcoat that smelled of snow. He touched their faces and said,
"Your Papi's gone far away."

"To where?"

"Just far away."

And he pointed toward the west. It seemed to be a good direction.

"And will he come back?"

"I don't know, children."

He reached into his pocket and brought up some of the hard red and orange candies his brother had gotten for the children from that party in New Jersey. And he gave them some, saying: "Your Papi asked me to give you these candies.

"Now get dressed, some people are going to be coming here."

Those people were the priest, Father Vincent, from the church, and Bernardito Mandelbaum and Frankie Pérez and Miguel Montoya and Ana María and Manny, and then there were the other Mambo Kings, turning up with their wives and kids or with their girlfriends, or just standing solitarily in the hall, hat in hand, head bent low. The priest sat in the living room, speaking about "grace," and the children, without knowing why, had to get dressed up in their Sunday best. Still, it was nice with every visitor to their home treating the children with kindness, patting their heads, and giving them money for comic books and candies.

Why, if the atmosphere had not been so unbreathable from grief, it might have been like a real party for the kids!

They decided against a wake but waited two days for the arrival of one of the three brothers from Cuba, Eduardo, who was as thin as a rail and had never flown on an airplane before. New York looked black and gray to him. He'd walk around the apartment at night in a terry-cloth bathrobe, white socks, and thin-soled shoes. He was quite tentative about everything. He seemed confused walking down the street, his senses bombarded by the noise of traffic, construction sites, subways. He was in his forties but seemed older. His hair was streaked with white and he was so soft-spoken that no one could hear half of what he was saying. His face was sun-beaten and he would pass through the household shaking his head, as if to say, "Poor Nestor," and, "This doesn't make sense."

Nestor's death and funeral lingered in memory, like clouds of pain. No one wanted to remember.

Even in the Hotel Splendour, the Mambo King had to fight the impulse to replay "Twilight in Havana" or "Beautiful María of My Soul," and to head back into the past, circling around the most painful event of his life, the loss of his brother. Maybe play "Manhattan Mambo" and bring back the early club days, or get down to things again with the Julián García Orchestra.

A detail that was easy and pleasurable to remember? That on the day before his brother's funeral, he slipped off to the Hotel Splendour for an hour with Vanna Vane. For an hour they pretended that nothing terrible had happened. She wanted to forget and he wanted to forget. So he threw her onto the bed and lay on top of her. They were too fucked-up to even take off their clothes, but he hitched up her skirt, pulled his weeping thing out of his trousers, and jammed it between her legs. They didn't even really fuck, he just kept rubbing it against her opening, just wanting to think about being alive.

He couldn't help thinking about the plump-thighed Vanna Vane. She kept imposing herself upon him, the image of Miss Vane pulling her nylons over her thick, shapely legs, Miss Vane snapping her garters. Clean cool bed sheets against his skin rubbing against her skin. Endless kisses and Miss Vane's big ass up and down over him.

"You know what I like that you do to me sometimes?"

"What?"

"I like it when you bite my breast hard as I'm coming."

"Okay. And you know what I like? I like it when we're doing it the regular way and then I'm about to come and I pull out and then you take me in your mouth and then I'm about to come and I pull out and go back inside of you and we keep doing it until I can't contain myself anymore."

Eugenio figured it out from the funeral. So many people just kept patting them on the head and giving them quarters. They hadn't known what "die" was. Until then, only Christ had died on the Cross, but that only meant that he flew up into paradise and returned to the earth. The Dominican nuns gave them rosaries, and a lot of the kids of that street, Irish and otherwise, turned up at the funeral, even when they hadn't always spoken or thought kindly of the family. Ana María told them all about guardian angels who would protect them in the event that they were threatened by the devil. They heard that God in heaven was looking over them. But they never dreamed that their Papi was dead. Leticia supposed that he had gone over the hill to Grant's Tomb and across the river, westward. What is it that they heard their Papi saying one day, "You see over there, children? You keep going in that direction and you end up in California. That's where me and your uncle went that time."

(And in California? Desi Arnaz came pulling up to his home near San Diego. He was driving a car like Cesar's, a DeSoto. And when he got out, he went walking through a garden whose bougainvillea walls reminded him of the flower-covered walls of Cuba. He lived in a large pink-walled ranch-style house with a tin roof, a garden, a patio, and a swimming pool. He entered the house through the patio, where he would sit drinking coffee and reading his mail. There was a letter from a friend of his, a letter that mentioned the untimely passing of that Cuban songwriter Nestor Castillo. Just happened like that! Remembering the younger brother who'd had a rough time on his show, he felt saddened and tried to think what he could do for the family. His face contorted in the way that a Cuban's face will contort when he's reading bad news, his lips turning down and his mouth widening, like a mask of pathos. You know what he wished? He wished he could walk across a room and find Cesar and his brother's family lined up by a bar and buy them dinner and drinks and reach into his pocket, come up with his wallet, and give the family five or six crisp $100 bills. But what he did was this: he sat down and in a simple script wrote the family of Nestor Castillo a condolence note. It was very direct: "I am saddened by the bad news that has reached me here in California. If there is anything I can do for you, please let me know. Your friend always, Desi Arnaz.")

The church was jammed with musicians. Machito and Puente and Mongo Santamaría had turned up for the funeral. And there were many lesser-known musicians, ordinary men who came in wearing long coats, heads bowed, hats in hand, fellows who'd visited the apartment at one time or another with their wives and girlfriends. There were a few co-workers from the meat-packing plant. Elva and René stuck in the thick of things, and wishing they could run away and dance. Manny the bassist stood by the red church doors greeting the mourners.

Miguel Montoya attended the funeral with an old woman, his aunt.

The organ played the "Te Deum." The altar was covered with white flowers, as was the coffin, its white ceremonial cloth embroidered with chrismata.

The family and their closest friends took up the first few rows in the church. Cesar stood beside Delores and she beside the children. Cesar's face was red, as if someone had slapped him hard. His hand rested on little Leticia's shoulder. She was only three years old and had no idea what had happened. Even when it was explained that Papi was away, she expected him to come back in through the door. Squirming in her seat, she kicked her black patent-leather shoes against the pew rail; sucking on her fingers, her hands dripping red from the hard cherry candies that Cesar had given her before the service. Patting the top of Leticia's head, her uncle kept pointing to the altar, where the miracles took place. And Delores? She seemed to be controlling her feelings, her cheeks sucked in and her mouth tense, so tense you could imagine her teeth shaking at the effort of containment. In her head, a storm of thoughts: she had lost her father young, and now she had lost her husband.

(For a time, other people ceased to exist. Faces were like pale masks floating before her; voices seemed to come out of nowhere. Hands pulled on her hands. Her children seemed like oversized dolls. She would have liked very much to be anyone else in the world, even Nigger Jim in that book she read. She would have the vague memory of being led up and down the steps of the church. Lots of people saying nice things to her, wishing her and the family well. Yes, you fall in love, you give your heart, you long for their kisses, they break your heart and die. They leave you locks of hair and old hats and memories. That's how men did things. Shower you with affection when they want something from you, and then vanish just like that. *Men! Qué cabrones!* Her father collapsing on a stairway, Nestor disappearing into the night with his black instrument case in hand. It hit her: I was in love, for all our differences. Oh, hold me, hold me, God, hold me.)

Ana María stood beside Delores. Then there was Eduardo, up from Cuba. He kept touching the bridge of his nose and squinting as if he had a terrible headache. Cousin Pablo, nervous behind the family, with his wife and children. Then there were others, Frankie, Pito, and in the back of the church, among all the Irish, Vanna Vane sobbing.

There were wreaths and bouquets of flowers from Maurio Bauza, "Killer" Joe Piro, "Symphony" Sid Torrin, and others.

"To the Castillo family with deepest condolences, Carlos Ricci and the management of the Imperial Ballroom."

"With sincerest regrets, Tito Rodríguez."

"We feel in your hour of sadness . . . Vicentico Valdez."

"May God bless and strengthen you in your time of sorrow . . . The Fajardo family."

Benny the baby photographer had turned up with his fiancée, with whom he was deeply in love. He was a short, pleasant-looking man, with a close-cut head of smooth black hair, the kind of head babies and children love to rub. He had been happy because he was in love, laughing and writing love poems to his girl. But now his friend was dead and it seemed so tragic, because Nestor was only thirty-one years old.

The sermon was given by Father Vincent, a tall, balding Irishman. During his sermon he spoke about the fate of men: ". . . Those of us who understand the tragedy of human souls who live only for the physical world also know about the splendor that awaits us. Here was a man who gave of himself to all. He was someone who came to us from Cuba and now he has gone on to a more glorious ancient kingdom, the kingdom of everlasting light, brilliant with the love of God who is everywhere in His infinite universe. God who is everywhere because He is the universe."

"Nestor," someone cried.

Over the altar there was a triptych which seemed to have a life of its own, "The Story of Man." Naked Adam in a beautiful garden, head hung low in shame, naked Eve behind him. Birds fluttered all around and the trees that receded into the narrow, olive distances were thick with fruit. Around an apple tree coiled the serpent of temptation, forked tongue oozing from his mouth and happy because he'd gotten them to sin. Adam and Eve were passing through a gate and entering a wood of dark trees. A golden-haired angel after them, brandishing a sword. Sadness and despair, Adam's expression saying, "We'll never reenter that happiness." And, next to this scene, a cave-tomb. A large boulder had been moved away from the entrance, before which two Roman soldiers, swords and spears by their side, lay writhing on the ground in fear, muscular arms and hands covering their faces. In the foreground, the crucified man, Jesus, in a white robe, hands held aloft for the world to see that it was he who had been dead and returned. The wounds in his hands and feet are deep red and shaped like eyes; his face is calm. (And the children can't help wishing that they could see what was inside that cave or over the rolling hills toward which Jesus walks.) And in the third panel, Christ risen, and sitting on a throne, the glowing dove of the Holy Spirit over his head, and Jesus judging all men: throngs of angels and penitent men and the saints huddled on cypress-tree clouds—was that where Papi went?

"Nestor."

The pallbearers carried the coffin out. It was the first time that anyone in the family had ridden in a limousine. There was something vaguely thrilling about that trip out to Flushing, Queens. There were more words over the grave, and with the grayness of the city looming in the distance and flowers being tossed into the grave, the children felt like playing games of tag among the tombs.

S ITTING IN THE HOTEL SPLEN-dour, the Mambo King winced because he could not get those thoughts of his brother's death out of his head. Somehow he had wandered from those happy images of quivering female thighs and was now trying to return to them. He sipped whiskey, looked over the funny cover of "Mambo Inferno" with its cartoon depiction of male and female devils on the tiered ledges of hell, everybody dressed in red and with horns and tails. Flames leaping upward! He took the record out of its sleeve and put it on the spindle. He was racked with pain: not an hour had passed in the last twenty-three years when he did not think about "poor Nestor." That was the end, he supposed, of his "happy, carefree life."

"Nestor."

"In the name of the Father and the Son and the Holy Ghost."

He wondered what time it was and then realized, while trying to look at his watch, that he was really drunk, because the numbers floated around the clock face, as if they were children riding on the hand. He had another drink anyway. He made his way to the toilet again to urinate, leaning his weight on one hand against the wall and watching his big thing and the flow of urine, curious as to just when it might turn pink with blood.

He remembered when he used to masturbate five, six times a day, a long long long time ago.

He remembered those parties they used to have back in the happy days, the tug of the past so powerful. In the living room: tables abundant with food, red-bulbed lamps, piles of records, lines of suave, unruly, boisterous, polite, bashful, arrogant, tranquil, and violent young men spilling out of their apartment and down the stairs past the cooked-cabbage smells of the hallway and into the street, where fights sometimes broke out; while beautiful women turned up in packs with their scents of perfume and sweat in that apartment, the loud record player heard for blocks, the lady downstairs terrified that the sagging floors would fall in, the Irish cops requesting with some hesitation that they turn things down and stop stomping on the floor, and in the early morning the last of the partyers leaving, singing and talking loudly as they made their way down the street.

The record started playing, lilting horn lines and frantic drums in his room in the Hotel Splendour.

In the name of the mambo, the rumba, and the cha-cha-cha.

Now he was going through his dead brother's effects, his nephew Eugenio sitting on a chair watching him. Over the last month they'd given away all Nestor's size-ten shoes, his hats and clothing, some nice stuff, too, which they'd left out in boxes in the living room of the apartment on La Salle Street. Lots of people turned up and Cesar, taking care of things in those days, was very matter-of-fact about the giving away of those items. He sat back in an easy chair, chain-smoking cigarettes and saying, "All that stuff is first class, we were never cheap about clothing." He managed to keep a few items for himself: a few of his brother's jackets, which he took to the shattered-looking Jewish tailor on 109th Street, who let them out around the middle. Bernardito Mandelbaum got Nestor's white silk suit, the one he wore on television. Frankie kept his cream-colored jacket. Eugenio would regard the piles of clothing and feel a strong desire to throw himself on them, to swim through the heaps on the floor and glory in the lingering smells of cologne and tobacco that he identified with his father. For a time, Eugenio played a game: sitting out on the stoop, and trying to identify his father's shoes or some other item of clothing worn by the male passersby.

Cesar also kept his brother's trumpet and the sheets of paper on which he had written down his lyrics and chords, kept the crucifix and chain that their mother had given Nestor for his First Communion.

Then there was that book, *Forward America!* That was something else the Mambo King had found in Nestor's jacket pocket.

And at that time Eugenio took to napping side by side with his uncle, the two holding each other tight, day in and day out for months. Whenever footsteps sounded in the hallway, like the tap, tap, tap of Cuban heels on the floor, Eugenio almost expected to hear the door opening and then Nestor's clear whistle, the melody "Beautiful María."

The sad business of memory came over Cesar in waves like the initial symptoms of a bad winter influenza, and this led to a plague of melancholia that was blood-red and spread quickly through his psyche. It brought on a paralysis of ambition and feelings of self-contempt, so that he took to spending many of his days in the apartment. This fierce melancholia exerted for a time a hallucinogenic influence. Many an afternoon, while standing by the window, he would hear the El shaking with the arrival of a train and then he'd happily watch the people flooding out of the kiosked stairway. Near that corner was the narrow, gloomy doorway of Mulligan's Bar and Grill and then a stretch of wall against which the kids on the street played "Chinese." Then kids on the street playing "Three Steps to Germany," kids playing "Cow in the Meadow." One day he looked out the window and saw a slick-looking character leaning against that wall. He was wearing a black-brimmed cane hat and a long coat. There was a black instrument case by his side.

"I'm going to get some cigarettes," he said. Then he put on his coat and headed down the street toward the slick man, who made his way to the stairway. Cesar rushed up the stairs and managed to get on the downtown train just as the doors were closing. Then he moved methodically from car to car looking for the man with the black-brimmed straw hat and black instrument case. He never found him. Once the Mambo King rode the train down to 59th Street, where three different lines, running to the boroughs of Brooklyn and the Bronx, converged, and he saw this same man standing against another wall, beside a magazine stand. He blinked and the man was gone. The same thing happened again, except this time Cesar rode the A train into Brooklyn, got off after half an hour, and found himself drinking and ravenous in a bar. He was so worked up, his heart pounding so loud, that he had to calm himself down. But he got so calm that a gang of leather-jacket thugs followed him across this stretch of street, which passed in front of a deserted construction site, and about five of the gang members, who had sailors' caps on and Marlboro cigarettes rolled up inside the sleeves of their T-shirts, swooped down on him, knocking him to the pavement and giving him a bad beating. It didn't help that he was wearing his flamingo-pink suit and a pair of cream-colored Cuban-heeled shoes, and not only did they rob him, one of the fellows tried to kick his temples in. (He was saved because someone in the gang felt compassion and pulled his friends away.)

When he woke up, Nestor, or the man or spirit who looked like him, was standing under a lamppost across the street, smoking a cigarette. Cesar held his arm up and cried for help and then blinked his eyes and the man was gone.

Those were days of confusion for him—and for everybody. Something odd was going on with Delorita, too.

She seemed to be taking Nestor's death in stride, spending her evenings with the children and with Ana María and her *novio*, this fellow Raulito, who worked for the Merchant Marine union. Ana María was staying in the apartment then. At night, the two sisters slept together, the way they had as children, in flannel nightgowns, with their arms wrapped around each other. And if Delores could not sleep, she read her books. Neighbors who knew about her literary bent of mind rained books down on her, and a pile of them were stacked beside her bed. She was happiest when she'd walk down toward the university bookstore, where she would forage through their bins and used-book racks, coming home with shopping bags of novels. And there were also the books she'd acquire at the church bazaars. She liked to spend two or three hours a day with these books, propelled forward by a dictionary and the simple desire to possess more knowledge. She made her way slowly through the driest landscapes of biological, agricultural, and historical prose. Although she read about everything, she still preferred detective novels. She'd fall asleep with a small reading lamp on by her side, one arm hanging off the bed, a paperback or hardcover book in hand. Reading reminded her of the nights when she waited up late for her father or her trumpet-playing husband to come home.

Cesar knew how much she liked books and in his journeys around town he would walk into bookstores and browse for Delores in a way that he never did for himself. He gave her at least two novels at that time, *Moby Dick* and *Gone with the Wind*. Inscribed by Cesar "To my lovely sister-in-law, with love and affection, Cesar," they sat in the bookcase. He bought her other gifts: a pretty fake-pearl-buttoned black dress, a Chinese scarf, a blue velvet hat, a new hand mirror, and, because of a persuasive salesgirl at Macy's, Coco Chanel perfume from Paris. And he got hold of a nice photograph of Nestor and Delores, posed in the park on a nice spring day, and had that put in a good frame so she could keep it in the bedroom. (Not that they needed more pictures. Their walls were covered with photographs of the band and the two brothers with Cugat, Machito, and Desi Arnaz, alongside pictures of the saints and Jesus with a fiery heart.) While he had become wild and moody in his public life, in their household Cesar behaved in a courteous and almost meek fashion,

especially when he was around Delores. There was very little he
wouldn't do for her, he would say.

They would go out shopping together, take the kids to the
park together, go to the movies.

Neither Cesar nor Delores knew what was happening. She
not only began to look forward to her days spent with Cesar, but
she would get all dressed and made up for their excursions. Holed
up in the apartment together on a rainy afternoon, they would
pass each other in the halls and their skin would give off a faint
scent of cinnamon and cooked pork. There were times when he
would find himself in the kitchen standing behind Delores and
he would want to put his arms around her waist, pull her close,
move his hands over her body, and touch her breasts. Brooding,
he would sit there daydreaming about when his brother was alive.
He remembered the time when he looked across the courtyard
into his brother's window and saw Delores standing naked in
front of the mirror, her body bursting with youth and loveliness.
It didn't help that she had become careless about the way she
dressed and would spend her days in a pink terry-cloth robe,
without a stitch of clothing underneath. It didn't help that he
would walk into the bathroom and find her frilly undergarments
hanging off the shower hoop, dainty brassieres, panties, and nylons. It didn't help Cesar that her body quivered when she walked
across the room or that he would stare at her, tortured, when she
leaned over the table to wipe away a stain and he could glimpse
the plumpness of her breasts. Nor that he walked by the bathroom
one day when the door was open a crack and saw her standing
naked, dripping wet, just after a bath. He dreamed about her. He
would be resting in bed, pressed up against the mattress, his body
wrapped in the sheets, and the door would open and Delores
would be standing there in her robe. She would open her robe
and move naked toward the bed: a thick vegetable-and-meat smell
would fill the room and he would find himself kissing Delores and
then she would lie down beside him and open herself to him. Her
legs spread wide, a shaft of sunlight would come flowing out from
her. Then they would make love and his thing would burn up,
as if he were jamming the sun. But often the dream ended sadly.
He would walk through a dense wood of his desires, thinking

"Delores" and then "Nestor." That connection always startled him and he would wake up feeling ashamed.

Taking the situation badly, he would sit in the living room, hands folded on his lap, remembering that Nestor was gone, killed while driving his own fancy DeSoto, and the doctor saying, "Just a little vein near his heart." His legs would go hollow, as if they'd suddenly been drained of their blood and sinew and bone. He'd imagine that his legs were made out of tin piping, and he would feel so weak-kneed he'd have trouble standing up.

He tried to cheer himself by getting the hell out of the house and started to chase women again as never before in his life. Then he fell in with a rougher crowd, a lot of hoods whose violent temperaments struck him as diverting. Night after night he'd make his way around town to the various dance halls and supper clubs in the company of flirtatious dames and stacked floozies, women who might have stepped out of the record cover for "Mambo Inferno"; long-nailed, big-rumped, these women had wicked expressions, immense mouths, teeth streaked with lipstick, hair puffing upwards like flame, and eyes in dark teardrops of mascara. He lived for that life of fleshly distraction. Whereas women used to go for him because he was a good-looking, brash pretty-boy singer, they now found themselves with a more maudlin master of seduction. The agony in his expression, his heavy-lidded eyes, his sad demeanor, and the story of his grief brought out the charitable side in women, so that practically every night Cesar found himself necking in alleyways, in apartment foyers, in the back rows of movie houses. At first, in the name of making Delores jealous, he brought a few of these women to the apartment, but he stopped because he sometimes heard Delores weeping at night and thought she was doing so because his behavior was disrespectful.

So for a time his life was a rainfall of frilly panties, bursting girdles, camisoles, slips, brassieres, gartered nylons, thick condoms, baking soda and Coca-Cola douches, curly blond, red, and black pubic hair. He enjoyed the company of pear-bottomed, sweaty-thighed Negresses with silken interiors, powerful *mulatas* whose legs lifted him up off the bed. He banged Italian beauties who danced in the chorus at the Mambo Nine Club and spinsters whom he met on the dance floor between sets at the Catskill resort hotels where the Mambo Kings sometimes played on the weekends. He made it with cigarette and hatcheck girls, hostesses and twenty-five-cents-a-dance girls from the ballrooms of 43rd and Eighth. He made it with three of the musicians who played with Glorious Gloria Parker and Her All-Girl Rumba Orchestra, among them a Lithuanian trombone player named Gertie, whom he made love to against a wall of flour sacks in the storage room of the Pan-American Club in the Bronx.

His lovemaking, which was never a delicate operation, be-came more blunt and violent. He'd drag Vanna Vane up the stairs of the Hotel Splendour, taking her roughly by the wrists. Usu-ally, by the time he'd opened the door, his thing was already hard. He'd walk behind her, bumping his enraged penis into the dead center of her ass. Then he'd press her up against the wall, sliding his hand into the slit of her silver-sequined skirt, his sensitive musician's fingers prowling lasciviously over the rough head of her nylons, up onto her thighs, and then under the waistband of her panties and into the tangle of her pubic hair. She was so wiped out by Nestor's death that she allowed him to do whatever he pleased. They'd get naked: he fucked her in the mouth, between her legs, up her ass. She sometimes wondered if Cesar was crazy, the look he'd get making love to her frightened her, as if not only his penis but also his heart would burst. They must have been crazy, coupled in each other's arms, it was "I love you, baby," and "And I love you," again and again. And he found comfort in it until he'd climb the stairs to the apartment on La Salle Street and realize, once again, that it was Delores and not Vanna Vane he wanted.

(And poor Vanna, she'd put up with the Mambo King for another three years and then marry this nice guy who worked for the post office. In the last days of Cesar Castillo's life, spent holed up in the Hotel Splendour, she was living with her husband and two sons up in Co-op City in the Bronx. She had put on a few pounds, but she was still pretty. A lot of people used to tell her, "You look like Shelley Winters." She would be the first to tell you that she was happy now, especially after all those years of being a wild girl, abused by men. But even though she would say that, Miss Vane, now Mrs. Friedman, would remember those chaotic and dense nights with affection, wondering, like so many others, what ever happened to Mambo King Cesar Castillo.)

But when he found no release from his pain through women, Cesar started to drink too much. Inside the Palladium, he was the man reeling by the horseshoe bar, the man unable to clearly recognize the faces of the people who came to greet him. Marlon Brando stood next to him for five minutes at the bar, and the Mambo King did not recognize the famous movie actor. He mistook people. A musician named Johnny Bing, who had a thick head of wavy black hair, came over, and Cesar thought he was Desi Arnaz. "If you knew what the family's been through, Desi," and he reeled backwards and then forwards, laughing, so ecstatic was his pain.

Next thing he knew, he would be dragging himself up the stairs to the apartment. When he'd finally reach the landing, the tile floor would be spinning around like a 78 rpm record. Then he'd try to put the key into the lock, but the keyhole kept fading in and out and doubling up like a mirage. When he finally got the key by the hole, it wouldn't go in, bending all up, like a drunkard's flaccid penis. Finally he'd have to ring the bell and Delores would come to the door and help him to his bed, a wall-crashing struggle down the hall which always woke and frightened the children.

His continuing grief was a monument to *gallego* melancholy. He would struggle down the hall, a heavy weight on his shoulders, as if he were carrying on his back the weight of a dead man. He didn't understand, he longed for the days when he just did as he pleased. These things will pass, he told himself. He fell asleep and found himself waking in the meat-packing plant, among the hanging, white-fatted sides of beef, moving a startled and frightened Nestor out of that cold place and toward the door where there was sun. He dreamed of examining the U.S. Govt. stamp of approval and within the circle read, "You can love a woman so much it sometimes breaks your heart."

He fell in and out of these drunken sleeps longing for Delores. Laughing at himself. He felt he was paying for his brother's death. He wanted to suffer, he pushed people away from him. He was confused: how could he have known that he was trying to keep his brother alive by becoming like him?

When they had held something of a memorial dance in Nestor's honor down at the Imperial Ballroom, which raised fifteen hundred dollars to help with the funeral expenses, Delores turned up looking like a young Hollywood voluptuary. Still young and fine, she had borrowed a sexy black dress from Ana María and came in tottering on three-inch stiletto-thin heels. The men parted before her as if she were the Queen of Sheba. (It was a nice benefit, too. Everything fell into place, notice of the event going out in handbills and ads in *La Prensa,* the *Daily News,* and the Brooklyn *Herald.* The dance was emceed by the disc jockey "Symphony" Sid, and the orchestra consisted of some of the best musicians in the city, Maurio Bauza, Mongo Santamaría, and Vicentico Valdez being the most prominent. The ladies, many of them musicians' wives, brought food—pots of *arroz con pollo,* black-bean soup, and suckling pig—and they made a vat of sangria, another of the Mambo Kings' favorites. And there were kegs of beer from the local Rheingold brewery. A big crowd paid $1.04 each to get in the door, and money baskets were passed around.) Followed by her children and Ana María, Delores sat near the stage, surrounded by flowers, her expression pouty and sullen, like a spoiled movie actress.

At her table she met and greeted family friends. She sat fanning herself and taking an occasional bite from the good food that would appear before her on the table. Well-behaved Eugenio and Leticia were fairly stoic about the whole thing. Leticia was pretty in a pink dress and with a bow in her hair. She watched the bandstand happily and waited for her Papi to appear on the stage. Cesar performed that night. As the orchestra plucked, banged, and blew on their instruments and Cesar stepped to the microphone to sing a bolero, his eyes would settle longingly on Delores.

That night there was one man to whom Delores paid special attention. Not the Emperor of the Mambo, Pérez Prado, who bowed before Delores and paid his respects, nor Ray Barretto, who sat Leticia on his lap and gave the kids a dollar to buy

candies. No, she paid special attention to a bookkeeper by the
name of Pedro Ponce. He was a baldheaded, stern-faced fellow
of about forty with a toothbrush-bristle mustache. He wore a
checkered jacket, a lace bow tie, and suspenders that hoisted his
oversized brown trousers halfway up his chest. His sole item of
fashionable attire was a pair of tan-and-cream-colored shoes.
Pedro lived over on 122nd Street and used to give the brothers
advice about keeping books and paying taxes. They had known
Pedro from "just around," as he sometimes went to have his cup
of double espresso in the same little Cuban joint where the brothers went for their coffee. The night of the benefit he approached
Delores at the table, hat in hand and heart brimming with respect.
The fact that he stuttered when he spoke and that he averted his
eyes, staring over her shoulder and up the stage, touched her. She
thought, "Now here is a man who would never give me trouble."

"I share in your pain," he said to her. "It's a dreadful thing
that has happened to you. My heart and sympathy go out to you."

And he reached into his pocket and pulled out an envelope
containing two twenty-dollar bills.

"A small amount . . . to help," he said.

"*Que Dios te bendiga,*" Delores replied. "May God bless
you."

That night Cesar had it really bad for Delores. When they
returned home and the children were put to bed, he asked her to
make a cup of coffee for him, and while she was standing at the
stove he surprised himself, stepping up behind her and putting his
arms around her waist.

"Delores . . . Delores."

Naturally, she turned around and pushed him away, repeating, "*Déjame tranquila!* Leave me alone."

"I'm sorry, Delores. I'm drunk, can't you see?"

"Yes. Now go to sleep."

She helped him into his room. He sat on the edge of the bed
and, rubbing his eyes, said, "That baldy fellow likes you, huh?"

She helped him off with his shoes and pulled off his socks.

"Delorita . . . I want to ask you something." It took him a
long time to get that sentence out.

"Tell me," and she tried to lift his legs up off the floor and onto the bed. Right then she wished she had the strength of a man. "Lean back," and with a great heave she got his legs up.

"Just one question, I only want to ask you one little question, sister. Do you hate me?"

"No, *hombre,* I don't."

"Then what is it that you feel for me, sister?"

"I feel sorry for you sometimes, *hombre.* I worry about you. Why don't you go to sleep."

"But do you see how I feel for you?"

"Yes, I can see it, but it doesn't make sense. Now go to sleep."

"A lot of women have liked me, Delorita. I've satisfied them all."

"Go to sleep."

He had curled up and she put the covers over him and then he put his hand around her waist again and said, "Just stay like this with me for a little longer, just show me a little love."

Then he started to touch her all over, fondling her breasts, and she told him, "No, *hombre,* now let me go!" And when he wouldn't let go, she slapped his face as hard as she could, and was on the verge of getting the broom when his eyes suddenly popped open, in a moment of pure soberness.

"Okay, okay, okay," he repeated. Shaking his hands in the air as if everything had been a terrible mistake.

"Okay?"

I was so *jodido* in those days, the Mambo King thought in the Hotel Splendour. I was so fucked up with sadness that I may have crossed the boundary of good manners, but if I did, that was because I wanted so badly to give to her all that God had chosen to take away.

There was something else. He lost his heart for music and his soul withered. He wrote no songs, picked up neither guitar nor trumpet. And while the Mambo Kings continued to get work, his heart wasn't in it. The band's morale was low: it wasn't a question of finding a replacement trumpet player—there were a hundred trumpet players who could have played the same lines and solos—but his brother's absence just took Cesar's spirit out of everything. He tried hard to be a professional about it, but his performances were so withdrawn and tentative, no one would have guessed he was the same aggressive king cock strutting singer of just a few months before. He suddenly had the look of a man who had not slept in a long, long time. On top of that, he really started to drink, just so he could get up onstage. And that started to show: he'd flub his lyrics and screw up his solos. Sometimes, while trying to dance, he'd fly backwards, as if someone had tipped the stage. He sang entire songs with his eyes shut, repeated the same lines, forgot about turnarounds, and stopped giving and taking cues.

He would think about his brother, dead in the ground, and say, "If I could change places with you, bro', I would."

Audiences noticed this change and word started to get around that Cesar Castillo was getting a little fucked up.

Despite this, some nights he'd have a big horse grin, sing and play the trumpet, and even loosened up enough to joke around with the audience. Those were his reefer nights. But they didn't last long. Once, in the middle of performing at the Imperial Ballroom, Cesar forgot where he was and wandered off the stage in the middle of a song, with a startled expression, as if he had seen something in the wings.

The worst was that Cesar started to become foul-mooded around others. The Mambo Kings Orchestra went through two replacement trumpet players, who quit because Cesar would deride their talent, making faces at their solos and stopping songs before they were done, shouting insults at them. Then he started picking fights with strangers. Some poor guy had the misfortune of bumping into Cesar while walking out of the men's room at the Park Palace, and that was it: Cesar was on the man, pounding the shit out of him on the floor. It took four men to calm him down. That kind of thing happened again and again in clubs around the city where the Mambo Kings were playing.

"I was lost," Cesar thought as he sat in the Hotel Splendour. "I was fucked up and didn't know what to do with myself."

His behavior seriously upset Miguel Montoya. They went out one night and dined at Violeta's and that's when Miguel Montoya said, "Look, everybody knows you're upset about Nes-

tor—we all are, you know that—the fellows in the band think it
would be good for you to take a break for a while."

"You mean, leave the band?"

"For a time."

"Yes, you're right, I have been a son of a bitch lately."

But "for a time" turned out to be forever, because the
Mambo King Orchestra would never perform again with Cesar
Castillo as their singer and leader.

AFTER LEAVING THE BAND, HE
went back to Cuba to visit his family. He had to get out of New
York, he told himself. He wasn't behaving in a correct manner
and his enjoyment of life—booze and women and love—was
going out the window.

He retraced the journey he'd made with Nestor back to
Cuba: he took the train down to Miami Beach for a few days,
visiting with musician friends who worked one of the big hotels
there. And then, with his heart in his gut, he made his way back
to Havana. The big news down there in 1958 was the revolution
against the Batista government. On the afternoon when he went
over to Calle 20 to visit his daughter, he stopped to brace himself
with a few drinks. It was a beautiful calm street, sunny and quiet
—the other Havana of his dreams. The revolution, that's what the
men were talking about in that bar.

"This fellow Castro, they say he and his men are being
beaten out in Oriente. Do you believe it?"

"Yes, he's being beaten. You don't see Batista leaving the
country."

That's what the official version was on the radio. And the
only change he'd noticed at all was that there were more police
and military personnel at the airport. And on the way in from the
airport he'd noticed two big military vehicles, a tank and a personnel carrier, on the side of the road. But the soldiers were
sitting out on the street beside the vehicles, metal helmets by their

side, having lunch. (And here he can't help imposing a conversation he'd had years later with a woman who had worked as a domestic in Batista's household: "The problem with Batista was that he wasn't cruel enough and a little lazy. He could've had Fidel executed in '53 but he let the man go. He was lazy and liked to have a good time with high-society people. He was so out of it that when the revolution came he didn't have the slightest idea what had really happened, *sabe?*") Otherwise, things seemed to have been the same all over the city, from what he could see. The men in their *guayaberas* and linen jackets leaning at the counter. Cesar smoking a cigarette and sipping from his *tacita de espreso* and his two Tres Medallas brandies, sunlight bursting against the limestone-and-brick walls across the street, beyond the shade of the awning. And he noticed, as he looked over his *tacita*, a pretty woman in pink slacks.

Cuba was making him feel better already. He'd called up his ex-wife from New York, announcing his intention to visit his daughter, Mariela. Luisa, who had married a schoolteacher, was good about extending him that privilege, and soon he was making his way to the *solar* where they now lived. He'd purchased a big stuffed rag doll for Mariela and a bunch of flowers, hibiscus and chrysanthemums, for Luisa. As he passed into an inner courtyard, entering a winding wrought-iron stairway through a gate, he ached with regret that he'd fucked up things with his wife. So, standing before her door, he looked like a wrecked and exhausted version of himself. But they were both surprised by how happy they were to see each other. That is, Luisa opened the door, let him into a nice, big, airy apartment, and smiled.

"Mariela's taking a bath, Cesar," Luisa told him. "She'll be out to see you soon."

And they sat talking by a little table in the kitchen. On the wall, a crucifix and a photograph of Julián García. (Looking at Julián and thinking of his kindness made Cesar go "psssssssh" inside.) Things were well with Luisa. She was newly pregnant. Her husband was running a big school in Havana and they had high hopes when it came to this fellow Fidel Castro.

"*Y Mariela?*"

"She's a precocious child, Cesar. Artistic."

"In what way?"

"She wants to be a ballet dancer. Studies it at the Lyceum."

A few minutes later, intense and pretty, Mariela came out to greet the father she had not seen in so many years. They went out, as they used to, Cesar taking her around to the different stores and for a nice lunch in one of the harbor restaurants. Thirteen years old, she had kissed him, but kept her head bowed as they'd walk along the streets. She was an awkward, thin girl, with wild eyes, and must have been afraid, the Mambo King thought, that he was finding her plain. That's why he kept telling her, "Mariela, I'm so proud that you turned out so beautifully." And: "You have your mother's pretty eyes." But she also had some of the family's sadness and did not have much, or know what, to say to her father, who'd abandoned her. He alluded to this abandonment a few times as they walked along Galiano, a street lined with shops.

"You understand that what happened between me and your mother had nothing to do with you, child . . . I have always cared for you, haven't I, child? Written you letters and sent you things. Yes or no? I just don't like to think that you see me in a bad light, when I'm not that way. Do you see me that way, child?"

"No, Papi."

His spirit bolstered, he began to speak to her as if he would be back the next day and the next to see her.

"Perhaps next time we can go to the movies?" And: "If you like, we can make a little trip to Oriente one day. Or you can come to see me in New York."

Then: "But you know, child, now that you're growing up, maybe I should come back here to Havana. Would you like that?"

And she nodded that she would.

When he took her home later, she was happy. From the doorway he could see a pleasant-looking man sitting in the parlor, a book open on his lap.

"Can I come back to see her tomorrow?"

"No. Tomorrow we're going away."

"Then when I come back from Oriente?"

"Yes, if we're here. But you know she's not your child

anymore, Cesar. She's the daughter of my husband now, and her name is Mariela Torres."

The worst telegram he had ever sent in his life, to Las Piñas shortly after the wreck in which his brother was killed, saying: "Nestor has been in accident from which he will never recover," a message it took him a long time to word, unable as he was to say the blunt truth. He imagined his mother reading and reading those words over and over again. He could have written: "Nestor was driving and I was fucking around with a girl, but I would have been a fool to pass her up, she was so good-looking: my fingers were playing with the buttons of her blouse, my fingertips were touching her breasts, her nipples were taut between them, her hands were touching me, when things got out of control. He was drunk and the car slid off the road, hitting a tree."

And he imagined it again: a kiss, laughter, the honking of a car horn, the words *"Dios mío,"* a terrific groan of metal, smell of gasoline, smoke, blood, the mangled heavy chassis of a sporty 1956 DeSoto.

(And behind that? An inkling, since he was close to death himself now, of what his brother felt like. Inside a doorless room and wanting to get out, his brother pounding on the walls, hurtling against them.)

Two of his older brothers, Eduardo, who had come to New York for the funeral, and Miguel, were waiting for him at the Las Piñas station. He embraced them with all the strength in his limbs. They were wearing *guayaberas* and linen *pantalones.* The song *"Cielito Lindo"* was playing out of a radio in the stationmaster's office. The stationmaster was leaning forward over the ticket counter, reading a newspaper. On the wall, a framed portrait of Batista, President of the Republic of Cuba; an overhead fan.

He'd always planned a triumphant return to Las Piñas. He used to joke with Nestor about how, in emulation of the Hollywood movies, he would drive into Las Piñas in a fancy automobile, laden with nice gifts from the States, pockets filled with money. Regret in his heart that he hadn't returned to Las Piñas in eleven years, though he had been back to Havana for carnival a few times and to play Mr. High-Life around his friends. And now? He had returned out of guilt: his mother had written him letters saying things like "At night I pray to God that I see you again before I am too old. My arms feel empty without you, my son."

They made their way to the farm by a dirt road, their carriage taking them along the river. A column of palm trees and houses built out over the water on one side, and dense wood on the other. The trees were thick with black birds and he could not help remembering that day when he was a kid and he and Nestor were away from the farm, walking through the forest, looking for hollow tree trunks that they might make into drums. They were walking in the wood for twenty minutes without hitting light, and then they came to a clearing, where they heard a rustling in the trees. Above them a few birds were flying from the high branches of trees on one side to the high branches of trees on the other. And they were followed by about twenty more birds. Then fifty, then a hundred birds. Then a rustling in the distance, as if a strong wind were blowing through the treetops, but it wasn't the wind: the treetops were shaking, leaves and fronds shuddering as if they were being whipped, and then the shuddering grew even louder and then clarified: it was a river of black- and blue- and light-brown-winged birds rushing through the forest in migration. As the brothers stood there, the sky over them grew dense with the flight of a million birds fluttering their wings, shooting between the treetops as if storming through the world, so many that they could not see the sunlight anywhere in the forest and the sky turned nearly black for an hour, that's how long it took those birds to pass.

Remember that, brother?

Then there was the old hut where that lanky black man Pucho, who used to play the guitar and lord over his hens, first gave him music lessons. They passed an abandoned water mill, walls half collapsed, and then the old stone tower from the time of the *conquistadores*. They passed the road to the Díaz farm, the road to the Hernández farm.

Then they came to their farm. He remembered the approach well. As a young man he used to make the three-mile trip from Las Piñas by mule, a guitar slung over his shoulder, a cane hat pulled down low over his brow. When they turned into the farm road, he saw his mother for the first time in many years. She was on the porch of their simple, tin-roofed house, conversing with Genebria, the woman who'd wet-nursed the Mambo King.

They had about ten acres of land, a pen where the gray pigs played gaily in their swill, a few tired horses, and a long, low hen coop. And beyond it, a field of wild grass ringed by fruit trees.

When he saw his mother, he thought she would say, "Why did you let your brother die? You know he was the light of my world?"

But his mother had much love in her heart for him, and she said, "Oh, my son, I'm so happy you've come home."

Her kisses were tender. She was thin, almost weightless in his arms. She held him for a long time, repeating: "*Grandón! Grandón!* You're so grown!"

He was happy to be home. His mother's affection was so strong that for one brief moment he had an insight into love: pure unity. That's all she became in those moments, the will to love, the principle of love, the protectiveness of love, the grandeur of love. Because for a few moments he felt released from this pain, which had withered the coil at the bottom of his spine; felt as if his mother was an open field of wildflowers through which he could run, enjoying the sunlight in his face, or like the night sky cut by the planets and the mists of far away—"That veil over the hidden face of *Dios,*" as she used to say. And as she held him, the only words she had to say: "Oh, son, oh, son of mine."

(On top of this, the memory of how he felt a few years later, in 1962, when he heard that his mother had died, at the age of sixty-nine. The telegram shot out black threads that flew into his eyes, stinging them like dust motes, so that he, the man who never cried, began to weep. "My mother, the only mother I'll ever have."

He kept rereading that telegram as if his concentration would rearrange the meaning of the words. He wept until his body shook and his stomach was in knots, until his desire to repress the sadness drew into his chest and he felt an iron band tightening around his heart.)

"Oh, son, I'm so happy you've come home."

Being around them again brought back a few of his child-hood longings, and mostly these had to do with the ladies of the house. In his dreams of youth—and later, when his mother was dead—she would be represented by light. His happiest hours as a boy were spent on the porch or in the back yard, napping with his head on her lap, the sun burning silver-white through the treetops above them. His mother, María, saying, "Pssssssh, *niño,* come here," and taking him by the hand into the yard to that tin tub set out on the patio under the immense acacia tree, where she would wash his thick, curly hair: that was when the Mambo King had sweeter ideas about women, when his mother was the morn-ing light. Genebria, whose breast had tasted like cinnamon and salt, would bring the boiled water, and this water, tinged pink and yellow and blue by the sunlight, would drip down over his head and onto his privates, what a pleasure that was, looking up into the attentive and loving eyes of his mother. Now, dirty from his long journey, he went to his old room near the back patio, where he stripped down to a pair of boxer shorts and a sleeveless T-shirt and called out to his mother in the kitchen: "*Mamá,* do me a favor and wash my hair."

So the old scene was reenacted, with the Mambo King bent over a tub in the yard, eyes squinting with the pleasure of simple affection: not a thing had seemed to change then: his mother, now older, poured the water on his head, scrubbed him with soap, and massaged his scalp with her tender hands.

"*Ay, hijo,*" she repeated like a horn line, "I'm so happy that you're home."

Genebria was there to wipe the water off his head. After all those years apart, the Mambo King couldn't pass her in the hall-way without giving her bottom a little pinch. He'd always had a special fondness for her, thankful for the complimentary way she'd gasped one afternoon many, many years ago. He was at that age when he would fall asleep and dream about the stretching of his bones, when his body was an expansion of flesh and organs, when pleasure hummed in his spine, wrapped around his hips, and burst out through his sex. He was at the age when he wanted to flaunt his newfound virility before the world like a boy dragging a crocodile through a house. He was in the bathtub going about the rubbing and cleaning of his private parts when his thing, ready to burst with redness and milk, came up, bobbing like a bottle of wine in the water. Genebria was cleaning the house, and when he heard her singing, he called to her, "Genebria, can you come here?" And when she did, the future Mambo King stood up and, pulling his thing, said, *"Mira! Mira! Look! Look!"*

"Stop that, you beast! You little pig!" She gasped and ran back into the house.

Smiling, he held on to it and sank down under the water, his milk oozing out like white octopus ink. Then a silver-edged redness exploded inside his shut eyelids and he had the sensation that the world had abruptly tipped over. He spent many of those days in a dream of pulling, prodding, choking, banging, wetting, and exploding this new instrument. As for Genebria, what was her new nickname for Cesar, that name she'd say with fondness and curiosity?

"Hombrecito," at first, and then, *"El macho."*

Now, when he saw her and said, *"Mira, mira!"* it was with great sadness.

"Here, Genebria, I've brought you some perfume."

And he gave her a little bottle of Chanel No. 5.

It was perfume and a hat for his mother, and Italian wallets and Ronson lighters for his three brothers. And, yes, a bundle of recordings and some photographs of Nestor and the family.

His mother sat on a rattan rocker on the porch, looking through the bundle of records. The smooth, modern 1950s design of some of the record covers, with flowing musical notes, New York skylines, and sharp cut-out conga drums, made her smile.

And the lettering was in English, and on three of the covers Nestor was posed side by side with his older brother.

"Nestor," she called him. "My son who is in paradise."

In his room he dressed slowly, knowing that before long he would see his father, Pedro Castillo, again. He heard horses outside, and his father chewing out one of his sons, "I'm not going to pay you for doing nothing," and in the same indignant tone he'd always used around him.

What was it that the old man used to say? "You want to waste your life in the dance halls? Suit yourself, but when you need money, don't come back to me. You become a musician and you'll be a poor man all your life."

He heard the porch screen door and his father's boots on the parlor floor. In a moment he would go into the parlor and embrace the man, who wouldn't give a damn that Cesar, despite their past troubles, was still trying to show him respect and affection.

As he stood before the mirror rubbing a lilac lotion into his thick hair, he heard his father's voice again. "María, you say he's back? Well, then, where is he? Has he come back to do some work around here?"

And he shut his eyes, not quite sure just how he would remain calm, because to hear his father's voice was to invite bodily disaster. Feeling a flutter of restrained violence just below his heart, he dallied by the mirror, telling himself, *"Tranquilo, hombre, tranquilo."*

He took a swig of rum and made his way to the parlor to see his father again. He was forty years old.

Sitting in the Hotel Splendour, good and drunk, Cesar had the worst trouble thinking about his father; even remembering his appearance was difficult. He had a picture that he'd always liked, one of those thin, cracked photographs, yellow at the edges, with the back stamped "Oliveres Studios, Calle Madrid no. 20, Holguín." The only one he had of his father. It was a humorous picture taken around 1926 or so, the man in a bow tie and a linen suit, a big cowboy-looking hat, and a thick, droopy *guajiro*'s mustache, sad Castillo eyes, stiffened expression—leaning his weight on a cane. And right behind him, a movie poster of Charlie Chaplin from *The Gold Rush,* Chaplin in the same pose.

"The golden time . . ." he thought.

He had one beautiful memory of his Papi taking him and his brothers into Las Piñas, where they spent the morning in a café among the men, eating sandwiches and drinking *batidas*— fruit malteds . . . Farmers in that café, caged hens by the doorway, and the man chopping up fruit on a counter dripping with juice. That day his father, Don Pedro, had lifted him off the ground and had stood talking with the men in the bar, the future Mambo King in his arms. He was a gaunt man, smelled of tobacco, and when he drank his *tacitas* of coffee, he'd have to wipe his mustache clean of froth. He had huge knuckles and his cheeks and forehead were burned Indian-red from his countless days in the fields.

But that was the only time it was so beautiful. When he would think about his early childhood, he'd remember cringing like a frightened animal when he was near his father. He would see red and black and silver birds streaking across space in swiftly forming arcs, and his face, his ribs, his back, his legs would sting from beatings with fists and a stick. His older brothers, who were better behaved, got beatings, too—in the name of respect and authority and because their Papi did not know what to do with his anger and foul moods. They grew up into more or less respectful and weary sons, with shattered expressions and broken spirits. While Cesar, in his father's words, "got worse." But he never understood why the man beat him. He used to cry out, cringing in a corner, "What have I done to you? Why are you doing this?" He felt like a happy little dog that only wanted a little kindness from that man, but he got beat and beat and beat. It used to make him cry for hours, and then after a while he couldn't cry anymore. He tried to be happy, playing jokes on his brothers and running through the house, a continuous burst of energy, like his dancing, like his music, from too many slaps in the face. He'd gotten so used to the man beating him into the ground that after a while he seemed to enjoy it, taunting the man and challenging him to beat him again and again. He would roll on the floor laughing because his father sometimes hit him so much that the man's fists ached. His father would beat him until a strange look would come over Pedro's face, a look of sadness and futility.

"Son," he would say, "I only want your love and respect."

"You know your father came to Cuba without so much as a penny. He never had a father to look after him, the way he looks after you. He's known only work, *hijo*, sweat."

"Your Papi was cheated by fate. He's too trusting. People have robbed him because he's always had a good heart. God was not generous. Tomorrow he'll change. God will pardon him. He's a worker and a provider. You must be tolerant of him. Forgive your father. He loves you, *niño*. His heart is made of gold. Never forget that he is your father. Never forget that he is your blood."

No softness in Pedro's face, no kindness, no compassion. Pedro was a real man. He worked hard, had his women on the side, showed his strength to his sons. His manliness was such that it permeated the household with a scent of meat, tobacco, and homemade rum. It was thick enough that their mother, María, would fill the house with flowers, which she put in vases everywhere. And eucalyptus in pots to swallow up this scent of manliness that wafted through the rooms in wavy bands like heat off a steaming street.

He didn't have much money and had never learned how to read or write, signed his name with an X. But he claimed a high standing in the local society of Las Piñas because of his *gallego* blood and his white Spaniard's skin, which placed him above the mulattoes and Negroes of town.

The Mambo King remembered a hurricane that drowned many of the horses and cows and pigs, who were found floating in the water the next morning, with bloated bellies and distended tongues. He remembered someone knocking on the door of their house one night, and when his father answered the door, a knife was plunged into his shoulder. He remembered the military men with whom his father dealt in Holguín. Over the years he'd been cheated more than once and considered himself, after all his efforts, a "poor man."

His Papi was so tense that he suffered from a plague of maladies that had to do with his bad moods, debts, and hard work. He sometimes suffered from a hysterical eczema and prurigo that so dried his skin it became as hard and brittle as parchment. The Mambo King could remember days when Pedro's body looked as if he'd just finished running naked through a forest of thornbushes, all scratched up and covered with sores. On hot days he would become so agitated that the only thing he would wear was a pair of *calzoncillos*. His father would come in from a stone house at the field's edge, where he sometimes holed up, racked with the pain of hot salty sweat on those tormented limbs. Without a good word for anyone, he would head out to the tub in the back yard, where he would soak in a bath to which María had added a rose-scented lotion, with an alcohol base, that only made his condition worse. Soaking for hours in the shade of a pomegranate tree, he'd rest his head on the tub's rim, sip rum, and in agony watch the sky.

Those were the days when his Papi worked in the fields taking care of his animals. Off in the distance, standing in the shade of breadfruit, papaya, and plantain trees, the stone house where he slaughtered livestock. At midday, one of his boys would carry out a pot of food, which he'd angrily devour. Then he would go back to the business at hand: if he had to slaughter a pig, his white linen *pantalones*, his cotton *guayabera*, his skin, his nails, his thick *campesino*'s mustache smelled of blood. The poor animals kicked and sometimes they ran into the field, galloping for a distance before collapsing to the ground.

(And now he cuts through everything else, remembering the day when his Papi came after him with a machete. He couldn't remember what had started the trouble. Was it one of his indignant looks, his usual lack of respect, or was he sitting out on the porch, strumming his guitar?

All he knew was that his father was chasing him across a wild sugarcane field, the machete raised over his head, shouting, "You come back here." He ran for his life, ran as fast as he could, down the corridors of sugarcane, his father's shadow, one hundred feet long, behind him. He was running toward the forest when he heard a terrible scream: his father lay on the ground, clutching his leg.

"Help me, boy!" his father called to him. "Help me!"

Then: "Over here, boy. I've jammed my foot on a stake."

He wanted to help his father, but what if it was a trick? What if he went to his father and the man struck him with the machete? His father called again and again, and slowly the future Mambo King moved closer. Then he moved closer and closer until he could see that his father was telling the truth, saw the bloody stake protruding out of the instep bones of his right foot.

"Pull it up," he said to Cesar.

When he did, pulling up on the foot with all his strength, his father let out a scream that sent all the birds flying off the treetops.

And when he'd gotten to his feet again, limping, his arms around his son, Cesar thought that things would be different.

Then they were back in the house and his father was stretched out in a chair. He called to Cesar, saying, "Come here."

As his son leaned close, he slapped Cesar in the face, hard, with the back of his hand.

His father's face was red, eyes cruel—that's how he remembered him now.)

But in 1958 the Mambo King was in such pain that he embraced his father. He did love the man. After so many years away from that house, he hardly felt like a son around his father. The man walked with a limp, from the time he'd impaled his foot on a stake in the field, and he surprised the Mambo King by giving him a strong embrace back. Then they sat in the parlor, in silence, as they used to. His mother waited on him, and the Mambo King sat there drinking. Later that night, he tried to comfort his mother, who'd gotten all weepy about Nestor, holding her in his arms.

It had been the records. She had listened to his trumpet playing and remembered her sons when they were boys, remembered when Nestor had been so sickly as a kid, pale with asthma.

"He worshipped you, Cesar," she told him. "He was always

so happy when you did anything for him. Happy to go places with you and to sing and dance and play for the people . . ."

Then her silence, her tears.

What else could he remember?

Visiting his friends in town and riding horses again. He was the rage in the local bars, talking about New York and inviting everyone he knew to come and visit him. He went to see the first woman he'd ever taken to bed ("This was just to see if you like it. Next time you'll pay, okay?"). And he walked beyond the cemetery, where his old music teacher, Eusebio Stevenson, a movie-pit house musician, used to live. The man had been dead for a long time. ("Mister! Mister! Can you show me how you do that on the piano?") He walked among the tombstones and felt exhilarated, talking to the spirits.

Out on the porch those nights in 1958, he sometimes felt that the universe could be peeled away like the skin of an orange, revealing paradise, where his poor brother had gone. The paradise of his mother, his religious mother who believed in all that. Paradise, where the angels and saints and the good souls go, up to the swirling heavens among the luminescent stars and the perfumed clouds . . . Why, then, did she weep? During the day that question would accompany him to town, where he would visit friends, hang around the street corners. He would make the journey back to the farm along dirt roads on a borrowed mule and with a bottle of rum tucked under his arm. This bottle he would drink at night. He drank rum until God hung low in the heavens like a heavy cloak. He drank rum until the rims of his eyes glowed with a pleasant pinkness, like the wing of a nightingale in a flash of light, and until the trees that ringed the farm breathed in, the way that only drunkards can hear. He drank until it was time to get up, and then he would cheerfully make his way into the house, shaving before a mirror in the room of his youth, and afterwards sitting with the women, enjoying the industry of the kitchen.

It was on one of those mornings that he heard his mother

saying to Genebria, "Take this plate of food to my poor drunkard of a son."

Then the memory of saying his goodbyes: to Miguel and Eduardo, whom he would not see again for nine years; to Pedrocito, and to his father and his mother, none of whom he would ever see again in this life.

Holding his mother, he maintained his macho composure, but whispered, "One thing I want you to know about me, *no soy borrachón.* I'm not a drunk."

And his mother nodded, "I know," but she had a different look in her eye, complacent, stoic, and perhaps convinced that things were destined to go a certain way. But the lingering doubt in her eyes, and his sense that many other things were wrong, too, and that he was at their center, disturbed him.

This disturbance followed him home from Cuba on the Pan Am flight on which he ate American-cheese sandwiches served in wax-paper bags, and on which he flirted with the stewardess, smiling and winking at her each time she came by, followed him off the train in New York and up the steps to the apartment on La Salle Street, followed him when even his beloved nephew, Eugenio, answered the door and wrapped his arms around his leg, followed him even when Leticia, who was pure affection, came charging down the hall, pigtails bobbing, to embrace him and to see the gifts he had bought for her, followed him on his visits to the Hotel Splendour with Vanna Vane, to the side of his brother's grave, through many things, through many years, and to the very moment when he sipped yet another glass of whiskey that steamy night in the Hotel Splendour, years later, an indelible and thorny line, memory, forever present.

DECIDING THAT HE HAD TO DO something to change his life, Cesar went into the Merchant Marine. His connection was Ana María's boyfriend, Raúl, who worked for the union.

He worked on a ship for eighteen months and returned in the spring of 1960, looking weather-beaten and sporting a grizzly beard. Around his eyes clustered the swirly deep lines that had formed on those countless nights he spent at the deck railing fighting the queasiness in his stomach and his disappointment over the monotony of his days. He had become nearly bulimic by then. He had a monstrous appetite from his day's labors as a stoker's mate, feasting on the ship's cookery and heaving it over the side by late evening. His illness was enhanced by the huge quantities of Portuguese wine and Spanish brandy that cost the sailors pennies and that the ex-Mambo King guzzled down like water with his meals: it would take a few hours for the acids to wreak havoc with his stomach lining, and then, out on deck to gaze at the stars and to dream, he vomited his suppers into the pretty and phosphorescent Sardinian waters, into the Mediterranean, the Aegean. In Alexandria, Egypt, where he spent three days' shore leave, he had his picture taken in a Stanley Bay bar, sporting a gleamy-brimmed captain's hat and sitting on a rattan throne, flanked by a Puerto Rican chum named Ernesto and a cheerful Italian named Ermano, and surrounded by the potted palms that so reminded him of Havana (this, too, in the Hotel Splendour).

His eyes seemed to be filled with a black liquid of sorrow; they were contrite, curious; they said: "I have seen a lot." The Cesar Castillo who looked wistfully into the camera was gaunt, dark-eyed, and world-weary. Now he seemed to have somehow acquired his dead younger brother's melancholy. He went to an Egyptian bazaar, where in the midst of a surging crowd he saw the ghost of Nestor looking through a street vendor's table heaped with onyx bracelets and scarab necklaces.

And in that sweaty brow would also swirl the memory of names of ports-of-call: Marseilles, Cagliari, Lisbon, Barcelona, Genoa, Tangiers, San Juan, Biloxi. (Women, too. He remembered the misty night in Marseilles when he met Antoinette, a delightful woman who loved to suckle his member. Some women didn't know what to make of it, but she treated his thing like a favorite rag doll. Exhilarated by its elasticity and thickness, she'd rub her big stretchy French lips over its head, as if its seepage were some kind of lotion, until her lips became sheeny with his semen and her nipples, taut as cork, stood out from her breasts and her hot ass left a line of moisture down from his knees to his toes. Viva la France!) He had lost a lot of weight but walked with a bounce in his step. In the duffel bag slung over his shoulder, he'd brought back lots of presents from his journeys: silk scarves, ebony candlesticks, a small Persian rug, a roll of Oriental silk that he had bought for practically nothing from the mate on his tanker, a gift for Ana María, who liked to make dresses. By that time he had been at sea for a year and had not sung a note or touched an instrument.

Music was far behind him, he would tell himself. Walking up the hill, duffel bag over his shoulder, Cesar Castillo was another man. His hands were callused and cut: he had a scar down his right shoulder from a boiler valve that had burst and scalded him, and though he didn't like to admit it, the strains of the last few years had made him slightly myopic, because now when he read the newspaper or that book by D. D. Vanderbilt he had to squint, the words were so blurry.

The biggest item of news in his absence was that Delorita had married the bookkeeper, Pedro, in a quiet City Hall ceremony; the man was now part of the household. He was not a bad fellow; neither flashy nor particularly friendly, he would install himself on a big easy chair in the living room of the apartment on La Salle Street, feet up on a stool, and occasionally glance up from the newspaper at the television. The only sign of Nestor's previous life in that household were a few photographs left here and there in the hallway and on the mantel in the living room. Otherwise, the apartment on La Salle Street had adapted to the presence of another man, a non-musician, reliable and steady, whose instruments were not congas, or guitars, or trumpets, but rather, ledger books, rulers, and mechanical pencils. Although he was dull, Pedro was nice to the family. He took Delorita and the kids out every Saturday night to a restaurant or a movie: and sometimes he would rent a car and they would take a Sunday drive. He was a private, snippy man with odd bathroom habits. The john was where he would go in the office for peace and quiet, and it was where he would go in the household when Eugenio, trying to torment him, banged and threw his toys against the wall, shouted, gave him dirty looks, and otherwise tried to disturb his leisurely peace. He was not a bad man, but he was also not Nestor, and this provoked in the children a certain weariness and distrust, which the poor beleaguered man stoically accepted and tried to offset with gentleness and demonstrations of concern.

Cesar came back to all this. No one recognized him on the street. He did not look like the Cesar Castillo who had posed on the cover of "The Mambo Kings Play Songs of Love," nothing like the Alfonso Reyes of the *I Love Lucy* show. The children were happy to tug on his beard. Eugenio was now nine and had more or less adjusted to the new situation. He had developed something of an introspective, pensive demeanor, not too far removed from his father's. When he came down the hall and saw his uncle, who smelled of tobacco and the sea, Eugenio's expression, suspicious and serious, gave way to pure exaltation.

"Nene!" his uncle called out to him, and Eugenio charged down the hall. When Cesar lifted him up, Eugenio's feelings of emptiness went away.

That night the family and friends from the neighborhood gathered to greet his return. He went into the bathroom, where, with Leticia clinging to his side, he shaved off the great beard, and emerged with his face a bright sunburnish red and all squiggly with deep lines, and his slick mustache restored.

Of course, the family passed the evening hearing about Cesar's adventures. At nearly forty-two, the man had seen a little bit of the world. He would think about the way he and his brother used to walk down by the docks around Christmastime to buy boxes of Japanese toys, the most exciting items being battery-operated, cable-controlled green-and-white New York City police cars, which they'd pay a quarter apiece for and give out like Santa Clauses to the children they knew on the street and in the building. They'd look at the great steamship lines with their smoking chimneys and the elegant French porters and daydream about something as fanciful as playing the café society of Gay Paree, as his pianist Miguel Montoya called it.

"Salud!" and a worldly nod were his greetings to the household in those days, his nephew, Eugenio, clinging to his side. Emptying his duffel bag, he offered Eugenio some nice presents: an African ivory-handled hunting knife, purchased in Marseilles and attributed to the Yorubas of the Belgian Congo, and a light

Italian silk scarf, which Eugenio would wear for years. Then his uncle gave him a crisp twenty-dollar bill. (Eugenio, looking through the bag, found something startling, a French magazine called *Le Monde des "Freaks,"* with wavy, out-of-focus photographs of pretty, big-rumped women sucking off and fornicating with sailors, circus performers, and farm boys all over Europe.) This, with a wink and an index finger pressed to his lips, and a rap to his nephew's shoulder.

Eugenio was proud of his uncle, having kept close tabs on his journeys. Eugenio had borrowed an atlas from his pal Alvin so that he could look up the cities and ports named on the postcards which would arrive from time to time. (Nearly twenty years later, Eugenio would find one of those postcards and remember how the messages rarely varied, saying, more or less, "Just to let you know that you are always in my thoughts, and that your Uncle Cesar loves you.") Eugenio kept those postcards in a plastic bag under his bed, with a few hundred rubber cowboys and Indians and a page from a *Life* magazine article about the Folies-Bergère of Paris (this showed a row of beautiful French women kicking in a line, their pointy, sparkle-covered breasts provoking a concupiscent interest from him) and his collection of baseball and Christmas cards.

One Christmas card from 1958 was a family portrait of Desi, Lucille, Desi Jr., and Lucie Arnaz, posed in front of a fireplace and a thickly ornamented evergreen tree, prosperity and Christmas cheer glowing all around them. The card for 1959 was more subdued: a wintry scene of a sleigh moving over a countryside —signed, "From the Arnaz family" in bold Roman print. And written under that the words, "With much love and concern, Desi Arnaz." Cesar always gave the cards to Eugenio, who saved them because Mr. Arnaz was famous: all the kids on the street had made a big deal about his dead father's appearance with his uncle on that show: this card was further proof of the event. What struck him most and the reason why he showed it around was the word "love."

That first night back, his uncle drank until four in the morning, and his face was droopy and livid from the rush of blood and thoughts in his head. When his friend Bernardito had asked the ex-Mambo King, "So tell us, Cesar, when are you going to get another orchestra together? Everybody at the Palladium asks for you." Cesar, red in the face, answered in an angry voice, "I don't know!"

Then it was "Come on, don't be that way, Cesar, sing us a little bolero," to which he answered, "I don't feel like singing much these days."

By the time Delores had gone into the kitchen to chase Frankie and Bernardito out because it was already past midnight and Pedro had to go to work the next morning, time had dissolved and the point of existence was to drink down rum and to feel that inward radiance which passed for love.

"Why do you want to chase my pals out of the house?"

"Because it's getting very late."

"And who are you, anyway? It was me and Nestor who got this apartment in the first place. It's my name on the lease!"

"Please, Cesar, be reasonable."

But then Bernardito and Frankie got up from the kitchen table, where they had been sitting for hours, pouring drinks and patting their old friend on the back, and with their manly talk about women, Cuba, baseball, and friendship. They got up because Delorita was shouting now, "Please go."

Later that night, Pedro the accountant told Delores, "It's okay if he stays for a time, but he has to get his own place to live, as soon as he can."

When his friends left, Cesar slumped at the table as if he had been betrayed. Eugenio, sitting across from his uncle, loyally remained by his side. While Delorita went down the hall, Eugenio listened to his famous, worldly, slumped-over, macho uncle imparting his little observations about life: "Women, boy, will ruin you if you're not careful. You offer them love, and what do you get in return? Emasculation. Orders. Heartbreak. Now, everyone, I know what they think about me, that I hurt your father in some way. It was the other way, he put me in a bad way with his unhappiness."

Now and then he would realize to whom he was speaking and stop, but then Eugenio, through the gauze of half-shut eyes, vanished.

"Men should stick together, boy, to avoid suffering. Friendship and a few drinks, that's good. Friends. You know who was good to me? A good guy? Let me tell you, boy. Machito. Manny. There are others, I can't remember their names now. Everybody good to me. You know who was a swell guy, a hell of a man, who loved me and your father? Desi Arnaz."

Then Pedro appeared in the doorway, calmly walked over, and in a quiet voice said to the Mambo King, "Come on, *hombre.* You've had enough, and it's very late."

Pedro had taken hold of his elbow. "I'll go to bed," Cesar told him, "but not because you threaten me, but because you're a man and I respect the request of another man."

"Yes, *hombre,* I appreciate that. Now let's go down the hall."

"I'll go, but just remember, don't push me, because I can have a temper."

"Yes, yes, sleep, and tomorrow everything will be fine."

In her bedroom, lips pursed tightly, one hand formed into a fist, and rapping at her knee through the pink flannel nightdress, Delorita was waiting, waiting for the ex-Mambo King to sleep.

Pedro was trying to be a nice guy about the whole thing.

And Eugenio? When the bed had been extended out of the sofa, and his uncle was lying down, still dressed, Eugenio went about the business of removing his socks and shoes.

No one wanted Cesar Castillo to suffer, certainly not Eugenio. He looked forward to waking his uncle in the mornings. Would creep down the hall from his room to find the man squirming around in the sheets and speaking to himself in a mangled voice, like a man chewing out the side of his mouth on a great big black *puro,* or Cuban cigar: "Cuba . . . Nestor, you wanna meet a really nice broad? . . . My *pinga*'s big and hungry, baby . . . And now, ladies and gentlemen, a little *canción* that me and my brother here, that pretty boy trumpeter, wrote—take a bow and let the ladies get a good look at your mug, bro'. In the imperious night all the joy in my heart radiates like starlight. Brother, why are you crying out so painfully? . . . I should've married a long time ago and behaved myself, right, bitch? Someone, quick! Put out the fire! Yes, I'm very well acquainted with Mr. Arnaz, you know we're old pals from Oriente Province,

Cuba. You know, if it wasn't for that fucking revolution down in Cuba now, I would go back."

Face twisted in his sleep and tormented, as if inside him there was a hell, his uncle filled with caverns and flames and whirls of black smoke. A cool man's hell, however, just as on the cover of "Mambo Inferno." Bernardito the artist drew it (and "Welcome to Mamboland," too). Hell with conga-playing devils and horn-headed women in red leotards, the musicians themselves depicted as black silhouettes perched on ledges in the distance. That hell inside, something painful there so that he moaned, turned in bed, and then abruptly, as if sensing the good intentions of his nephew, eyes popping open . . .

He fit in with the household but knew that he would soon have to move. He didn't have much money saved, though from time to time a check could be expected to turn up, royalties mostly from "Beautiful María of My Soul," which had been published jointly in Nestor and Cesar Castillo's names. Although musicians came over to the house to see if he wanted to jam or head out to a club, he either agreed and failed to turn up or simply told his friends that he preferred to eat dinner and have a few drinks.

For all his sorrow and confusion, he was fairly social. His little appointment book, in which he used to keep business numbers and club and dance-hall dates, filled with dinner dates. He went out nearly every night for three months. Each afternoon found him restlessly taking a walk through those six blocks from La Salle Street to the shadow of the West Side Highway. He still liked to go out with women, but found the consumption of large meals almost as pleasurable. He was happiest when he would go to someone's house for dinner and find himself on a blind date. He was always walking down to the plant to get some free steaks from Cousin Pablito. He got big-bellied and had to let out his many suits at the tailor's. He started to develop his first double chin and his fingers grew thicker, his hands wider. He used to go down for a *tacita* of coffee in a little joint around the corner from La Salle Street, and the cup would seem like a doll-house coffee cup in his hand.

He did not sing, he did not write or play music and took to standing around on the street corners. At hepcat bongo-player parties he smoked reefers and slipped into a pretty springtime, then into a deep gloom. He still liked to let loose, dancing and trying to put the make on as many women as possible, drinking his heart out, but when he did so, he also tended to get out of control. His memory on some nights? Of being led by three or four men down a stairway. Of standing on a subway platform, unable to read the numbers on the train. Behind all that, there was always Delorita reminding him day in and day out that he would have to find his own place.

"Yes, I know. Today," he would say.

He would turn up at parties and people would wonder how he could have let himself go. Didn't he know that people still wanted to hear him sing? Didn't it mean something that his picture was still up on the wall of Violeta's restaurant, alongside Tito Puente, Miguelito Valdez, and Noro Morales? And what could he have thought, walking by the window of the Paris Beauty Salon, Benny's Photography Studio, and the hardware store and seeing himself in that white silk suit, posed with Nestor and Desi Arnaz? He certainly didn't forget about Mr. Arnaz. Every now and then he would head downstairs and sit on the stoop, writing letters. Letters to Cuba, in a state of political change; letters to his daughter, letters to old girlfriends, and letters to Mr. Arnaz.

But what of it? One day he got tired of his inactivity and hooked up with a friend and got himself a cart, selling *coquitos:* ice-sludge cones served up with *mamey,* papaya, and strawberry syrup for fifteen cents each, a business he foolishly got into with two hundred dollars of his savings. He spent the summer out on the corner of 124th Street and Broadway selling and giving away these ices to the kids from the projects, whose affection he relished. He would keep himself cool by drinking down Rheingold beer. Some days, he would stare off into the distance, his forehead warmed by the incredible sunlight, his attention caught by the sound of some young guy in his apartment practicing scales on the trumpet, his mind drifting off to the past, his body shaking from that past's influence over him. One day he got tired of the *coquitos* cart and gave it away to a kid named Louie, a lanky

Puerto Rican who took his place on the corner, making good money so that he could buy himself some nice clothes. Another day, he sat on the living-room couch without moving for an hour. Leticia, who adored him, climbed all over his shoulders and back, a thin little pigtailed creature who kneaded his thickening flesh as if it were a heavy mass of potter's clay. Eugenio made it his habit to play wherever Uncle Cesar happened to be. It made him feel good to be around his uncle, a simple feeling of connection like a thread in the air.

Pablito was really concerned for his favorite cousin and, on one afternoon when Cesar came by to buy some more meat, offered him his old job back, on a temporary basis, filling in for men who were away on vacation. He took it and worked like an animal for the month of September 1960, carrying on his shoulders half carcasses of beef weighing one hundred and fifty pounds, that sensation of weight on his back not very different from what he'd feel sometimes in his dreams when he carried the corpse of his brother, whose arm Cesar would tug as if to awaken him. (His brother, who sometimes opened his eyes and said, "Why don't you leave me in peace.")

He wasn't sure what he wanted to do with himself. From time to time, with a few drinks in him, he would head uptown to 135th Street to hang around with Manny, his old Mambo King bassist, who would try to talk Cesar into starting up another *conjunto.* The Mambo Kings only lasted out the year Cesar left. Miguel Montoya went off to California to find his fortune recording piano Muzak albums, and the other musicians, like Manny, their moment of glory gone forever, settled into solving the ordinary problems of life.

Things were working out for Manny. He was one of those practical fellows who kept sober at parties and frugally saved his money. After seven years with the Mambo Kings, he'd saved enough bread to buy himself a *bodega,* which he ran with a brother. Truth was that the scene was slowing up and jobs were fewer and harder to come by. There were enough low-paying jobs at Saturday-night church dances, graduation parties, and in uptown social clubs and Latin Exchanges, but the resort gigs went to the biggest musicians like Machito, Puente, and Prado, and, in any case, the season was limited. The same thing happened with the big dance halls, joints like the Palladium, the Tropic Palms, the Park Palace. And as for cities like Havana? Castro had kicked the Mafia out and closed down all the big clubs, the Club Capri and the Sans Souci and the Tropicana; and those musicians who were now leaving Cuba for the States were also hustling, the scene getting even tighter. With a wife and three kids to support, he was happy to own that business. In the afternoons, Cesar would walk uptown and sit with Manny behind the counter, helping out with little chores like going into the storeroom to get more *chorizo* links or another case of shortening. Or if a kid came in to buy a *guava* pastry or some gum balls out of the round plastic containers on the glass case over the meat display, Cesar would pick these out with tongs, wrap them up in wax paper, and hand them over to the customer. A radio played. Manny had his own copy of that Mambo Kings photograph, hung up behind the counter, the thirteen musicians pictured in white silk suits atop that art-deco seashell bandstand, once again smiling through the squiggles of signatures for all the world to see, but Cesar liked to keep a low profile, getting some salty *bacalao* or cooking up on a hot plate behind the counter some *chorizos* and eggs for them to eat for lunch.

When customers recognized him—"Aren't you Cesar Castillo the singer?"—he would nod yes, and then shrug; he had maintained an elegant manner. In a cotton shirt and pleated linen *pantalones* from Mexico, he wore golden bracelets on his wrist and three rings on each hand, a black-brimmed panama pulled low over his brow. When people asked him what he was doing, he just shrugged again. His face would turn red. But then he decided to fall back on the explanation that he was putting together another orchestra, and that seemed to satisfy people.

Sometimes Manny came up with some business proposition. He was always pushing for Cesar to use his talents: his looks, his charm, his singing ability.

"You know, Cesar, if you don't want to go through the grind of an orchestra again, maybe we could do something on the other end, like put together a supper club. A quiet place, not so much for a younger wild crowd but for people our age. Where they could get some dinner, and maybe we'll have some musicians, too."

"Maybe sometime," Cesar would say. "But for now . . . I don't know."

But the truth was that hearing a melody, humming a song, thinking of a lyric reminded him of Nestor. Never happy in life, his brother had died. Period. *Punto,* end of the *canción.* The few times he had started to consider Manny's offers to put another orchestra together, his interest would peak and then his bones would grow hollow, whistling with a grief over the rotting corpse of Nestor.

Wince, swallow of rum. The melody of "The Cuban Cha-cha-cha" playing in the Hotel Splendour, and the Mambo King feeling an ache in his sides, getting up from the chair to stretch; itch between his legs, and those voices from next door again, voices creamy with pleasure.

He was still in the habit of going to the park in the nice weather with Eugenio to throw a ball; sometimes he went by himself, a solitary figure sitting up on the grassy hill watching the river and thinking. He sometimes sat for an hour. The river went by, and on the river, boats passed. The water curled in waves sidewise, foam rippled. Light glistened in triangulated waves, like silver dust being sprinkled by the wind. The wind pushed the clouds. Birds passed overhead; the river flowed. Traffic in two directions on the highway. The wind blew through the trees, the grass wavered, dandelions dissipated, the grass parted under the snouts of hounds. A white butterfly. A leopard-winged butterfly. A multi-knobbed centipede crawling down a tree. The knots in the tree, oozing tiny arrowhead-shaped bugs. People walking, kids throwing a ball, college students playing cricket, folksinger sitting on the stone wall playing a steel-stringed guitar and kicking his feet up, bicyclists in two directions, baby carriages, mamas in curlers and chinos pushing strollers, then the *rrrring rrring* of the Good Humor truck and children running, the ex-Mambo King giving in to the pleasure of observing life around him and leaning back on the ground and breathing softly and slowly enough that he could begin to discern the circular movement of the earth, the pull of the continents and the surges of the ocean, everything in motion, the earth, the sky, and beyond, he thought one afternoon, the stars.

He'd started to read Nestor's book, the only book he'd ever

seen Nestor reading. While going through Nestor's effects, Cesar had decided to hold on to it, why he did not know. He'd thumb through the pages, reading the passages that Nestor had underlined and starred: passages about ambition and personal fortitude, about overcoming odds and seizing the future.

"Why, Mr. Vanderbilt," he asked the book, "did my brother accidentally or not so accidentally take his life?"

The book didn't reply, though the passages were generally positive about life management.

He thumbed through more of the pages and for a moment he felt a jolt of ambition. For a moment he enjoyed the prospect of having a plan in motion, no matter how vague it seemed then. Something to look forward to in the future. Something to keep him busy. He knew now that he had to do something with himself or he'd turn into one of the bums on the street. He read more of the book and its encouraging passages and soon began to fall asleep. It was a sleep in which all sound from the world fell away, a deep, sturdy sleep.

One afternoon, the landlady's brother, Ernie, fell down a stairway and broke his back. Within a few weeks, a sign made with black marker on a piece of cardboard appeared in the corner of the window by which Mrs. Shannon perpetually sat, smoking cigarettes and watching television and the street. Now her brother had taken to a bed and the normal duties of the building were proving too much for this lady. The sign said: "Superintendent wanted. See Apt. 2."

She was watching *Queen for a Day* when she heard a knock on her door.

Cesar was standing in the doorway, hat in hand, hair slicked back and sweet-scented with cologne and Sen-Sen. She thought he might be there with some complaint about the water, which had been acting up, but instead of complaining he said: "Mrs. Shannon, I saw your sign in the window and wanted to speak to you about that job."

A tingle went through her body, because when Cesar said "job" he pronounced it "yob," just like that Ricky Ricardo fellow.

She smiled and let him into the chaos of her living room, which smelled of mildewy rugs, beer, and cabbage. She was excited, even honored, that there was something she could do for this man. Why, he was practically a celebrity.

"Are you really interested in this?"

"Yes, I am." He pronounced "jes" instead of "yes," and "jam" for "am."

"See, things have been a little slow for me on the music end, and I would like to have a regular income."

"Do you know anything about superintending, electricity, plumbing—any of that?"

"Oh yes, when I first came to this country I worked," he lied, "as a super for two years in a building downtown. It's on 55th Street."

"Yeah? Well, it's not the best work, but not the worst," she said. "If you really want to do it, I can give you a trial, and if it doesn't work out, you know I don't want any hard feelings."

"And if it does work out?"

"You get paid and your rent free. There's an apartment rented by some college students opening up next month. You would get that and twenty-five dollars a week. If everything's all right." Then she added, "It's not union, you know." Then: "Would you like a beer?"

"Yes."

She went into the kitchen and he looked around. He wasn't one to criticize apartments, but Mrs. Shannon's living room was dense with newspapers and butt-filled bottles, glasses of beer, and yellow-tinged milk. One pretty picture caught his eye, however: a hand-tinted photo of a clover-covered meadow in Ireland, the country of her ancestors. He liked that.

As she came out of the kitchen with two glasses of beer, she felt enchanted and somehow elated at getting Cesar Castillo to work for her.

She sat in her easy chair, saying, "You know, I still think about how you and your brother were on that *I Love Lucy* show. You wouldn't believe it, but I once saw Lucille Ball on the street in front of Lord and Taylor's around Christmastime. She seemed like a nice lady."

"She was."

"And Ricky, you were pals with him?"

"Yes."

She looked him over admiringly; he didn't know what she might be thinking. He wanted everything to be over with quickly. He didn't want to go through any long route to find a new life for himself. No way would he go back, despite his longings, into the life of a bandleader. Walking down the hill from the park, and feeling buoyed by the practical advice of Mr. Vanderbilt, he had seen the sign in the window and decided that he would take the first step toward security. Better than dealing with club owners, and petty gangsters, and with the agony of pure memory. Besides, it all seemed to make sense. There wasn't so much work involved, and he would always have a roof over his head. And if he changed his mind and wanted to play music again, he would have the time to do so. He could not recall that the superintendent of his building had ever worked particularly hard, only that he often saw the man heading underground to the basement. Somehow he found the idea of the basement appealing.

"Yes," he continued. "Mr. Arnaz is a gentleman."

He milked it for everything it was worth, delighting her. Then she offered him another beer.

She came back into the living room a few minutes later, holding a beer and an old cheap Stella guitar with a warped neck. "Would you sing something for me?"

He wiped the strings of the guitar clean with a handkerchief; the thick gritty strings left traces like gunpowder on the cloth. Pressing down on the fret board hard, he struck an E-minor chord and, clearing his throat, said, "You know, I don't sing very much these days. It's a little rough for me now."

He started to sing *"Bésame Mucho"* in a voice that, if anything, was more soulful and vulnerable than it had been before: now his baritone really quivered with melancholy and a desire for release from pain in this life, and his singing made Mrs. Shannon, who'd always had her eye on the musician, absolutely happy.

"Oh, delightful," she said. "You should make more records."

"Maybe, one day."

By the time he had finished the beer, she had told him, "Well, we'll try you out," and then, with a broad smile and her huge body, that eternal mass under the soup-stained dress, shaking: "But you gotta promise that you'll sing every now and then for me. Promise?"

"Okay."

"Now, just let me get my slippers on and find the keys for the basement and I'll take you down and show you the works."

Down the stairs and into the basement, and following the hallway past the boiler and washing-machine rooms, he went. Then for the hundredth time—or was it the thousandth?— Cesar Castillo, ex-Mambo King and former star of the *I Love Lucy* show, found himself before the black bolt-studded fire door that was the entrance to his workroom. A solitary bulb, its filament burning like a tongue of fire above him, the lunar-looking walls filled with cracks out of which seemed to sprout long strands of human hair. He was not wearing a white silk suit or a frilly-sleeved mambo shirt, or sporty golden-buckled shoes, ladies and gentlemen: instead, a gray utility suit, plain thick rubber-soled black shoes, a belt off which dangled a loop of keys for twenty-four apartments, various storage rooms, and electrical closets. In his pockets, crumpled-up receipts from the hardware store, building-complaint slips, and a sheet of yellow lined paper on which after two years of musical inactivity he had started to write down the lyrics for a new song.

In the basement, his spirits flourished. He whistled, he happily pushed brooms, he liked the idea that metal things like wrenches and pliers hung off his body, clanking like armor; he found himself walking about the building in the same attitude as his captain at sea, arms folded behind him, eyes inquisitive and proprietary. He liked the happy-looking row of electrical meters and the fact that they ticked off in 3/2 time, claves time, that the multiple rows of pipes with their valves whistled, water whirring through them. He liked the crunching noises when faucets were turned on, the conga-drum pounding of the washroom dryer: the thunder of the coal-bin walls. In fact, he was so elated by the perfect realization of a purgatorial existence that better spirits came to him.

"*Me siento contento cuando sufro,*" he sang one day. "I feel happy when I'm suffering."

In the foyer outside the bolt-studded door to his workroom, his dog Poochie, a wiry, corkscrew-tailed mutt who resembled the famous movie hound Pluto, with his droopy face and long hooked paws, nails like black sea mussels. On the black door itself a calendar, a big-hipped pretty girl with green eyes in a scanty bathing suit, wading in a pool and lifting to her mouth a frosty-tipped, fluted bottle of Coca-Cola.

Inside, his worktable, a chaos of screw-and-nail, washer-and-nut-filled jars, tin cans, spools of wire and string, dollops of wood compound, solder and paint drops; tagged apartment keys on a wire hanging across the wall; then another calendar, from Joe's Pizzeria, featuring Leonardo's *Last Supper.* Wooden boxes were everywhere, and one paint-speckled telephone into which he would say, "Speak, this is the super."

He set down tools everywhere, and these congealed with a resinous-looking paste, so carelessly did he take care of them. A dusty, rusty-bladed fan sat atop a stack of old *National Geographics*, which he sometimes liked to read. There were two large storerooms, a deep and narrow-shelved room in which he was always finding items of interest: among them, a six-stringed lute, which he now added to the instruments in his apartment upstairs, and a spiked German helmet from the First World War, which he kept on a beauty-salon manikin head as a joke. And he had all kinds of magazines: nudist magazines with names like *Sun Beach California* which featured sling-shot-testicled men and strawberry-faced women, pictured with watering cans and little plaid sun hats in the garden of life, a strange race, to be sure. Then a stack of scientific and geographical surveys, refuse from the apartment of Mr. Stein, a scholarly fellow from the sixth floor. And Cesar had a big stuffed chair, a stool, an old radio, and a record player salvaged from one of the workrooms.

A stack of records too, including the fifteen 78s and three long-playing 33s he'd made with Nestor and the Mambo Kings. He never played them, though he heard them from time to time in jukeboxes or over the Spanish-language radio station, the disc jockey introducing a *canción* in this manner: "And now a little number from that Golden Era of the mambo!" He kept some of those records upstairs, too: up in the small apartment he'd gotten with the job, that joint crammed now with instruments and with the odd collection of souvenirs from his travels and his musician's life and with the pieces of mismatching furniture which he more or less stoically brought up out of the basement.

His apartment reflected the bad habits of a jaded, lifelong bachelor, but he would pay Eugenio and Leticia to come down once a week and sweep his floors, wash his dishes, wash his clothes, and so forth. His sister-in-law, happy that he was no longer in the same apartment and willing to forget many things, made it clear that he could take his meals upstairs at any time. He did so three or four times a week, but mainly to make sure that he was around his dead brother's children and that their stepfather, Pedro, was good to them.

Settled in, he went about his business happily. He came to know the neighbors, to whom he had rarely said more than a few words. Some people knew that he had been a musician, others did not. Most of his chores involved minor repairs of faucets and electrical sockets, though on occasion he had to bring in outside help, as when Mr. Bernhardt's living room caved in. He learned his job little by little: he applied himself to an apprenticeship in faucet fixing, boiler maintenance, spackling, plastering, electrical wiring. He would stand before the burning incinerator once every few days, watching the flames consume the cardboard and paper and wax milk containers, hear the bones crackling, singed skin evaporating, all turning to smoke. He tended to remember things, to get a look of lost contemplation as he would stand in front of the open incinerator door, stoking the dying larvae of the embers.

Often Eugenio wondered about his uncle then. The man staring into the fire and not moving. It wasn't so much that Cesar Castillo stared into the embers or sometimes murmured to himself; it was that he seemed to be somewhere else.

What did he see in these ashes? The harbor of Havana? The fields of Oriente? His dead brother's face floating amid the burning junk?

It didn't matter. His uncle would come out of it, tap his nephew's shoulder, saying: "Come on." And he would shovel the ashes into the trash cans, dragging them down the cracked concrete floor and up the stairs with mighty heaves and onto the sidewalk to await the garbage truck.

And he had made the acquaintance of other superintendents. Luis Rivera, Mr. Klaus, Whitey. His tenants were Irish, black, and Puerto Rican, with a few scholars and college students thrown in. His plumber was this one-eyed man named Leo, a Sicilian, who used to play jazz violin with the Tommy Dorsey Orchestra, lost the eye and the will to play during the Second World War. Cesar was never beyond the generosity of offering a man a drink, so that when Leo finished a job, he and Cesar would retire to the workroom to drink beer while Leo would relate his sorrows.

The flamboyant Cesar Castillo became a good listener and got the reputation of a man to whom one might tell one's troubles. His friends who came to visit him were either beset with woes or looking to get something from the ex-Mambo King. Men wanting to borrow money or to pass the night drinking his booze. People on the street and in the clubs who used to talk about what a womanizing and insensitive man he had been before his brother's death now talked about how, perhaps, this tragedy had helped to reform him into a more noble character. Actually, most people felt sorry for him and wished the Mambo King well. His phone was always ringing; other musicians, some of them famous too, were always trying to check him out: the great Rafael Hernández inviting him over to his place on 113th to talk music and have some good food; Machito inviting him to raucous gatherings in the Bronx; and so many others, wanting to see if the ex-Mambo King would perform again.

SİDE B

Sometime later in the night in the Hotel Splendour

SOMETIME IN THE MIDDLE OF the night the noises started in the room next door again, chair legs scuffling against the floor and the man's voice gravelly with self-satisfied laughing. The Mambo King had nodded off for a few minutes, but a pain in his sides jolted him awake and now he sat up in his chair in the Hotel Splendour, the steamy world slowly coming into focus. Two of his fingers smarted because he'd fallen asleep with a cigarette burning between them, and a blistery welt had risen there. But then he noticed the worse, more edemic welts and blisters up and down his arms and on his legs. *"Carajo!"*

He got up to urinate, and by the toilet, he could hear the voices from next door. Listening for a moment, he realized they were talking about him.

The woman's voice: "Come back here, don't bother no-body."

"But I've been hearing music all night from that room next door. I'll just inquire."

Soon there was a knock at the Mambo King's door. The black man was big-boned and thin, wearing lumpy pinstriped pajamas and a pair of velvet slippers. He had a big pompadour and black-and-blue bite marks on his neck.

"Yes, what is it that you want?"

"It's me, your neighbor. Can I ask you something?"

"What?"

"Look, I've just run out of booze. You got any you can spare until tomorrow, I'll pay you for it."

The Mambo King had pushed open the door just enough to see the man. He considered the request and felt sorry for the couple, stuck in the Hotel Splendour without enough to drink. He could remember a night with Vanna Vane when they'd drunk all their booze. Naked and in bed and too lazy to leave the room, he had leaned out the window of the Hotel Splendour and called down to a little kid passing by: "Go to the corner and tell the liquor-store man that you need a bottle of Seagram's whiskey for the mambo musician. He'll know! And get him to give you some ice, too, huh?"

Gave the kid five bucks for his trouble, later paid the liquor-store owner—that's how he solved his problem.

What the hell, he told himself.

"Just wait a minute."

"That's nice of you, sport."

Then the black man looked in and saw how Cesar had trouble walking across the room. "Say, you all right?"

"No problem."

"All right!" Then: "How much?"

"Don't worry about it. *Mañana.*"

"Yeah? Well, shit, you're a gentleman."

The Mambo King laughed.

"Looky here," the black man said in a really friendly manner. "Come over and say hello to my baby. Come on in for a drink!"

While "Beautiful María of my Soul" played once again, he slowly pulled on a pair of trousers. It would only take three, four hours of drinking to tighten his muscles. Screwing the cap onto the half-full bottle of whiskey he had been drinking—he had two others left on the bed waiting for him—he followed the black man to his door.

"Baby, got some!" to his woman, and to the Mambo King: "What's your name, pal?"

"Cesar."

"Uh, like Julius?"

"My grandfather's name."

Cesar had shuffled into the room, noticing the faint smell of fucking on the sheets. It was funny, he could barely hold his head up. His shoulders felt as if they were being forced to slump forward; his whole posture was that way. He saw himself in the mirror, saw an old man, jowlish and tired. Thank God he dyed his gray hair black.

"Babe, this is our neighbor come to say hello."

On the bed, in a violet negligee, the man's female companion. Stretched out like that dancer in Chicago, the Argentine Flame of Passion. Her nipples dark, bud-tipped flowers against the cloth. Long-legged, wide-wombed, her hips smooth and curvy like the polished banisters in the Explorers' Club in Havana. And her toenails were painted gold! There was something else he liked: she'd brushed out her black hair so that it almost touched her shoulders, and looked as if she were wearing a crown or a headdress.

"You resemble," said the Mambo King, "a goddess from Arará."

"Say what?"

"Arará."

"You all right, man?"

"Arará. It's a kingdom in Africa where all magic is born." He said that, remembering how Genebria had told him this, sitting out in the yard in Cuba when he was six years old.

"And when the man dies, he enters that kingdom. Its entrance is a cave."

"In Africa, he said!"

The black man instructed her, "That's what all them spiritist shops are called. Arará this, Arará that."

"You're very beautiful," Cesar said, but he could hardly hold up his head to look at her. Then, when he managed to, the Mambo King smiled, because even though he felt sick and knew that he must look pathetic, he'd caught her looking and admiring his pretty eyes.

"Here's your drink, my friend. You want to sit down?"

"No. If I sit down, I won't get up."

If he were a young man, he was thinking, he would get down on his knees and crawl over to the bed, wagging his head like a dog. She seemed the type who would be amused and flattered by that. Then he'd take hold of her slender foot, turn it just enough so her leg was perfectly shaped and then run his tongue up from her Achilles' heel to the round of her dark buttocks: then he'd push her toward the wall, open her legs, and rest his body on hers.

He imagined an ancient, unchanging taste of meat, salt, and grain, moistened and becoming sweeter, the deeper his tongue would go . . .

He must have drifted off for a moment, looking as if he

might fall, or perhaps his arms started shaking, because suddenly the black man was holding him by the elbows, saying, "Yo? Yo? Yo?"

Maybe he reeled around or seemed as if he would fall, because the woman said, "Mel, tell the cat it's two-thirty in the morning. He should go to sleep."

"No problem."

At the door he turned to look at the woman again and noticed how the hem of her negligee had just hitched higher over her hips. And just as he wanted to see more, she shifted and the diaphanous material slid up a few inches more until he could see most of the right side of her hip and thigh.

"Well, good night," he said. *"Buenas noches."*

"Yeah, thanks, man."

"You take care."

"You take care," said the woman.

Walking slowly to his room in the Hotel Splendour, the Mambo King remembered how, toward the end of the year in Cuba, during December and into January, the white men used to form lines into the houses of prostitution so that they might sleep with a black woman, the blacker her skin the better the pleasure. They believed that if they slept with a black woman at that time of year, their penises deep inside those magical wombs, they would be purified. In Las Piñas, he used to go to this old house —*bayu*— with an overgrown garden at the edge of a field, and in Havana he would visit, along with hundreds of other men, the houses on certain streets in the sections of La Marina, where he and Nestor had lived, and Pajarito. They came back to him, the cobblestone streets closed off to traffic and dense with men knocking on the doors. In every instance, at this time of the year, a huge bull of a man, usually a homosexual, would let the customers in. Their lights low, the houses had dozens of rooms and smelled of perfume and sweet-scented oils, and they would enter a parlor where the women waited for their customers, naked on old divans and enormous antique chairs, anxious to be chosen. At that time the white prostitutes sulked because business fell off for them, while the *mulatas* and the black queens swam in rivers of saliva and sperm, their legs wide open, taking in one man after the other, each man's bodily hunger sated, each man's soul cleansed. And it was always funny how, in those days, he would stick his thing back into his trousers and make his way into the street, feeling strong and renewed.

Now, as he shut the door behind him and made his way toward another bottle of whiskey, the room thick with the trumpets, piano, drums of his old orchestra, the Mambo King, weak of body, daydreamed of making love to the woman next door, and it was then that he could hear their voices again:

"Pssssst, oh, baby."

"Not so hard, honey."

"Ohhhh, but I like it!"

"Then wet me with your mouth."

The Mambo King was hearing the bed again, the mattress thumping against the wall, and the woman moaning, the softest music in the world.

He drank his whiskey and winced with pain, the stuff turning into brittle glass by the time it reached his stomach. Remembered when he could play music and drink all night, come home and devour a steak, a plate of fried potatoes and onions, and finish that off with a bowl of ice cream, and wake up the next morning, four or five hours after the meal, feeling nothing. The thing about one's body coming apart was that, if anything, you felt more. Leaning back in his chair, he could feel the whiskey burning in the pit of his stomach, and leaking out through the cuts and bruises that he envisioned his ulcers looked like, oozing into his liver and kidneys, which throbbed with pain, as if someone had jammed a fist inside. Then, too, there was the column of heat, long as his penis, shooting back up out of the pit of his stomach and skewering his heart. Sometimes the pain was so bad as he sat drinking in that room in the Hotel Splendour that his hands would shake, but the whiskey helped, and so he could continue on.

He'd had a boyhood friend in Cuba, a certain Dr. Víctor López, who had turned up in the States in 1975 and set up an office in Washington Heights. One night, three years later, when the

Mambo King was playing a job in a Bronx social club, he found this Dr. López among the crowd. They had not seen each other since 1945 and had a happy reunion, with the two old friends kissing each other and slapping each other's back, remembering and laughing over their childhood in Las Piñas, Oriente Province.

Afterwards, his old friend noticed that Cesar's hands trembled and he said, "Why don't you come along to my office one day and I'll give you an examination, gratis, my friend. You know we're not so young anymore."

"I will do that."

The doctor and his wife left the crowded, red-lit social club, and the singer made his way over to the bar for another drink and a tasty fried *chorizo* sandwich.

He didn't go see his old friend, but one day, while walking down La Salle Street, he felt certain pains again, like glass shards cutting inside him. Usually, whenever these pains, which he'd been experiencing on and off for years, came to him, he would drink a glass of rum or whiskey, take some aspirin, and take a nap. Then he'd go upstairs to see his brother's widow and the family, or he'd head out to the street, where he would hang around with his old pals, Bernardito Mandelbaum and Frankie Pérez, *"El Fumigador"*—the Exterminator. Or if his nephew Eugenio happened to be around, he would take him out for a drink. Best was when he'd hear his doorbell ringing in quick, enthusiastic spurts, because that meant his girlfriend was waiting in the lobby.

But that day the pain was too much, and so the Mambo King went to see Dr. López. Because he had known the doctor from his old *pueblo,* he felt all the trust in the world in the man, and thought his fellow cubano would produce a few pills that would make his pains go away. He expected to get out of there in a few minutes, but the doctor kept him for an hour: took his blood, checked his sputum, his urine, listened to his heart, thumped at his back, took his blood pressure, looked in his ears and up his ass, felt his testicles, peered into the dark green eyes that had made him such a lady killer in his youth, and in the end said, "I don't know how to tell you this, my friend, but your body is something of a mess. I think you should go into the hospital for a while."

He turned red, listening to the doctor, felt his pulse quicken.

He thought, Víctor, how can this be? Just the other day, I screwed the hell out of my young girl . . .

"You understand, your urine is pink with blood, your blood pressure is way too high, dangerously high, my friend, you have the symptoms of kidney stones, your liver is enlarged, your lungs sound blocked, and who knows what your heart looks like."

You see, she was screaming. I was making her come, me, an old man.

"Look here, Víctor, you want to know how I feel about this business? It's just that I'd rather go out like a man, rather than slowly rotting away like a piece of old fruit, like those *viejitos* I see in the drugstores."

"Well, you're not so young anymore."

He answered the doctor insolently, with the same kind of annoyance as when he was a kid and he'd heard something he didn't want to hear.

"Then, *coño*. If I'm already at death's door, I'll die and then I'll find out a lot of things, won't I?"

"My friend, if you don't do something now, you will rot away slowly like a piece of old fruit. Not today, and maybe not tomorrow, but all these things, unless taken care of, mean the beginning of a lot of physical suffering."

"Thank you, Doctor."

But he didn't really believe in his old friend's advice, and that was why two years later he had said his goodbyes, had written his letters, and had packed up to pass his last days in the Hotel Splendour.

Now the Mambo King had trouble standing. When it was time for him to get up and turn the record over, his sides ached. But he managed to turn the record over and to make his way across the room in the Hotel Splendour to the little toilet: could have been the same little toilet where Vanna would be standing in front of the mirror, stark naked, dabbing lipstick on her mouth and cheerfully saying, "I'm ready!" He wished his sides didn't ache so much, that it wasn't so hot outside, that his brother was not dead. Standing over the toilet, he pulled out his big thing, and his urine went gurgling in the water. Then he heard something, like a man's fist pounding on the wall, and when he finished, he stood by the dresser and listened carefully. It wasn't anyone pounding on the wall, it was that couple next door going at it! The man was saying, "Das right, baby. Das right, yeah." The man was going to have an orgasm and Cesar Castillo, Mambo King and former star of the *I Love Lucy* show, had shooting pains through his body. Bad kidneys, bad liver, bad everything, except for his *pinga,* which was working perfectly, though a little more lackadaisically these days. He sat by the bed again and clicked on the record player. Then he took another long, glorious swallow of whiskey, and during that swallow he remembered what they had told him at the hospital some months ago:

"Mr. Castillo, you're going to be all right this time. We've reduced the edema, but it's the end of drinking for you, and you'll have to go on a special diet. Do you understand?"

He felt like a fool, sitting on a hospital bed with only a smock on. The nurse standing beside the doctor was shapely, though, and he tried to play up to her sympathy, and he did not mind letting his thing show through the slit when he got back into bed.

"No more," the doctor said in English. "*No más. ¿Comprende?*"

The doctor was a Jewish fellow and was trying hard to relate to the Mambo King, and Cesar nodded, just so he could get the fuck back out. He had been there for a month and been prodded and probed, very much convinced that he was going to die. He'd pulled through, though, and now he had to live with the humiliation that his body was rotting on him. He'd gone through long periods of sleep, then, under the medication. Daydreaming about Cuba, daydreaming about himself and *el pobrecito* Nestor when they were kids, and about women and booze and good fatty fried foods. He figured that's what a dead man would think about. That and love. The oddest thing was that he kept hearing music in those deep sleeps. So Dr. Víctor López, Jr., was right when he had warned him, as had the doctor in this hospital.

"You have two choices, only two. One is to behave yourself and live. The other is to abuse yourself. Your body is incapable of processing alcohol, you understand?"

"Yes, Doctor."

"It's like taking poison, you understand?"

"Yes, Doctor."

"Do you have any questions?"

"No, Doctor. Thank you, Doctor. And good night, beautiful nurse."

When he finished emptying the first bottle, he opened a second and filled up his glass. Then he sat back, enjoying the music, a little number called "A Woman's Tears," an earnest ballad written out on the fire escape of Pablo's apartment during the old days. He always enjoyed Nestor's trumpet playing, and just then, as the bongos were playing like claps in the forest, the man next door had started to groan, his orgasm deep and rich, and she was moaning, too. The Mambo King decided to light another cigarette.

When he had gone into the hospital, forcibly taken there by Raúl and Bernardito, his limbs were bloated and he couldn't keep food down. Even so, it still surprised him, as if all his years of drinking and eating and doing just as he pleased would never catch up with him. He'd had the symptoms for a long time, going back years (to 1968), but he'd always ignored them.

When he'd think about that hospital stay, he'd remember how much he had slept. For days and days and days, it seemed. He had a lot of dreams at first—dreams about the basement, few about his life as a musician. In one dream the basement walls had started to peel badly and were covered with bubbles that wept a light pink liquid. And he went to work, much as he had for years in his building on La Salle Street, mostly plumbing jobs in the dreams. Pipes burst inside the walls and the softened plaster and ceilings came down or crumbled at his touch. He'd open closets and a wall of insects, prickly and black, would fall onto him. Investigating a clanking noise in the boiler room, he'd find himself crawling down a tunnel which narrowed, so that, while searching for the pipe, he would find himself wedged into a space, so constricted he could barely move. (These were the straps around his wrists and legs.) When he'd finally find the loose joint, dirty water would drip down on his face and often into his mouth. In his dreams, when he'd touch either metal or wood surfaces, he would feel a shock.

At times, things seemed very normal. He would be sitting in his basement workroom looking over all the apartment complaint slips that he would accumulate during the day: "Mr. Stein, fix window." "Mrs. Rivera, toilet." And, in a good mood, he'd begin to sing, his voice carrying lovingly into the courtyard, the neighbors hearing him.

And there was always Mrs. Shannon to stick her head out the back window and say, as he'd cross the courtyard, "Ah, you know that you sound just like that Ricky Ricardo fellow."

Then he'd go about his business.

He would sing, "My life is always taking a funny turn."

In his dreams (as in life) he'd find junkies working the back windows with screwdrivers and icepicks, he'd shovel snow, fix clogged toilets. Then he'd go to a job and something drastic would go wrong (as in life). A Handi Wipe caught inside a drain beneath a sink, Cesar down on the floor trying to get it out with a bent wire hanger, and then, desperate (as it seems to crawl farther and farther into the pipe), he gets a snake, a whirling cable that will break up anything but which struggles against the cloth: finally, when with a great yank he gets it out, he's covered with grease and hair and food bits and wants a bath but cannot move.

He remembered another dream when Mrs. Stein's kitchen pipe burst, flooding her apartment and caving in the ceiling below, just as it had really happened once, but in the dream he stood out in the courtyard laughing as all the water gushed out of her windows like a waterfall.

Then there was always the dream in which he felt like a monster. He was so heavy that his feet as they hit the floor sounded like drums being dropped out of the back of a moving truck, the ground beneath him cracking. He was so cumbersome that when he climbed the stairs to the fourth floor he snapped every step in half and could barely move in sideways through his door.

A more pleasant dream? When all the walls fell away and he could see everything going on inside the building. Beautiful naked college girls (whom he'd sometimes spy from the roof) preparing to take showers, chatting on the telephone, sitting their fine asses down on the toilets and performing the delicate act of defecation. Men urinating, couples fucking, families gathered around their evening meal: life.

Lots of dreams about music, too, but mainly he dreamed about things crumbling: walls coming down, pipes turning brittle, floors rotten and insect-laden, everything soft and mealy to the touch.

Once, on a night when his body felt filthy with medication and with sweat and uncleanliness, his mother came to visit him. Sitting beside him, she held a white *palangana* filled with soap and water and cleaned him slowly and lovingly with a sponge, and then, luxury of luxuries, she washed his hair, her soft, soft hands touching his face again.

For the first three days he had done nothing but sleep, and when he opened his eyes, his nephew Eugenio was sitting beside his bed.

The kid was in his late twenties by then. Unmarried, he had the same sad expression as his father. Sitting by his uncle, Eugenio passed the time reading a book. Now and then he would lean close and ask in a loud voice: "Uncle, are you there? Are you there?"

And even though he could hear his nephew he could not respond, could do no more than open his eyes and then instantly fall back to sleep.

"Uncle!"

A nurse: "Please, sir, don't shout."

While thinking about this, Cesar wished he could have said something to the kid. He almost came to tears, touched by the way his nephew sat near him, even when he was feeling impatient, getting up every few minutes to pace in the ward among all the machines.

"Nurse, can you tell me what's wrong with my uncle?"

"Speak to the doctor."

"For one thing, his electrolyte functions are out."

"Will he wake up?"

"Time will tell . . ."

Then one day he noticed the pretty Puerto Rican nurse bending over to give some poor man whose skin had turned yellow an injection. That's when he sat up for the first time and wanted to shave and wash, to get back together and walk out of there like a young man.

"We're all so happy that you feel better," Delores told him. "I brought you some books."

Books on religion, saints, meditation.

"Thank you, Delores."

And when he saw his nephew sitting nearby, he called the boy over—well, he was a man, wasn't he?—grabbed him by the shoulder and squeezed. "Well, you glad I'm okay? It was really nothing."

His nephew was silent.

(Yes, Uncle, nothing. Just three days of being sick to our stomachs that you were going to die, of sitting beside you and feeling the whole world was going to fall away.)

"Come on, smile, boy? Smile for your uncle." But then he grimaced with pain.

Eugenio's face passive, unmoved.

"Help me, boy, to sit up."

And silently Eugenio helped him, but not the way he used to as a little kid, when his eyes were sick with worry. Now his expression was cold.

Eugenio, looking very much like Nestor, left the hospital room without saying a word.

(And what was it that the others brought him? Some girlie magazines from Frankie, a roast-beef sandwich with mayonnaise, lettuce, and tomato from Raúl, a little pink transistor radio from the Aztec-looking lady who owned the bakery across the street, a bouquet of flowers from Ana María, a new black-brimmed cane hat from Bernardito. And his girlfriend Lydia and her children brought him some crayon drawings of children running, with a bright yellow-and-orange sun in the sky. Lydia sitting with him and trying to nod happily.)

Then, like sunlight filling the ward, he felt more of his strength returning. A heat thickened around his waist, as if he were wading in tropic water, and he woke up one day with an erection. He was wearing only a smock, because of the bedpan business and all the tubes, but when the blond nurse came by to look after him, she was startled by the old musician's sexual apparatus. Blushing as she went about the business of straightening up the bed sheets around him, she could not help breaking out into a slight "Oh, you bad boy" smile, and it so pleased him that when she left the room, he called out to her: "Thank you, nurse, thank you! Have a good day!"

That's when he noticed the other guy. Not the legless man; the bloated man who'd turned up in intensive care, wired up with tubes—liver, kidneys shot, bladder blocked and completely incapable of processing his bodily fluids. For five days he lay next to this man, and despite his own pain, the Mambo King kept thinking, God, I'm glad I'm not him.

The man kept getting worse. His fingers were puffed up with fluid, his limbs so bloated that his fingernails oozed. His face, too, was like a pink balloon on which a makeup artist had composed a pained expression; fluid dripped from his lips, from his nostrils, from his ears, but nothing from anywhere else. With his own edema problems, the Mambo King would open his eyes to the sight of that poor man, and shake his head over the man's living nightmare.

"See him," one doctor said. "Keep on, and you'll be like that."

Now the pain was very bad, but what the hell, at least he was going out with style. Forget that a few of the veins on his ankles had started to bleed through the skin, forget that he was dizzy and knew, knew for sure, that he was on his way out. Nothing that another belt of whiskey wouldn't fix up. And to celebrate this drink, he turned up "The Mambo Kings Play Songs of Love."

At least he had gotten out of the hospital and would never return. That had been in June, and he laughed despite his pain, remembering the nurses. There had been a young Puerto Rican nurse who had seemed like a bitch at first, never smiling at him or even saying hello, but then he softened her up with compliments, and in the days when he seemed to be getting better told Frankie to buy her a bouquet of flowers. (It had nearly killed him when she would lean close to his bed to take his pulse or to check all the tubes and needles they had stuck into his arms and legs, as she wore one of those modern blouses with a zipper down the front that always seemed to open just enough to torture him with her cleavage, slipping all the way open one glorious afternoon as she struggled to shift him over on the bed. The zipper slid down and he could see the front clips of her pink brassiere, its material thin and nearly transparent, and struggling to contain her breasts, squeezed snugly inside and overflowing the soft material, so nice and big and round.) The other nurse, an American girl, and blond like Vanna Vane, had seemed nice from the start, didn't catch any attitudes when he tried to flirt with her, just smiled and went about her business, perhaps a little shyly in fact, as this nurse was quite tall, nearly six feet in height, with long hands and limbs and broad shoulders, and probably considered herself unfeminine and awkward, but he wouldn't have thought twice about going to bed with her, all six feet of her shapely nursiness. And she would have felt loved and beautiful and so fucked-out that she would not be able to walk for days. That's why, when he was awake and his medication had not made him forget how to speak, he'd flirt with her, happy because she would put her hand on her big hips and flirt back, calling him "My favorite and most handsome patient," and "Sweetheart." That kept him happy for a while, but the guy next to him, a diabetic fellow who'd lost the use of his legs, kept telling Cesar, "Forget it, *hombre.* You're too old, what would a young woman want with you?"

Thank you, my friend.

AND NOW NOTHING BUT DRUMS, a battery of drums, the conga drums jamming out, in a *descarga*, and the drummers lifting their heads and shaking under some kind of spell. There's rain drums, like pitter-patter pitter-patter but a hundred times faster, and then slamming-the-door drums and dropping-the-bucket drums, kicking-the-car-fender drums. Then circus drums, then coconuts-falling-out-of-the-trees-and-thumping-against-the-ground drums, then lion-skin drums, then the-whacking-of-a-hand-against-a-wall drums, the-beating-of-a-pillow drums, heavy-stones-against-a-wall drums, then the-thickest-forest-tree-trunks-pounding drums, and then the-mountain-rumble drums, then the-little-birds-learning-to-fly drums and the-big-birds-alighting-on-a-rooftop-and-fanning-their-immense-wings drums, then a-boat-down-the-river-with-its-oars-dropping-heavily-into-the-water drums, then a-man-fucking-a-woman-and-jamming-the-bed-frame-into-the-wall drums and then someone-jumping-up-and-down-on-the-floor drums and then a-fat-man-slapping-his-own-belly drums, and then a-woman-smacking-her-ass-down-on-the-floor drums and then Morse-code drums and then the-sky-breaking-up-and-all-the-heavens-falling-down drums, and then a-bap-bap-bap-like-dialogue drums and children-running-through-an-empty-church drums and a-conquistador-firing-cannons-at-an-Indian-village drums, then slaves-being-thrown-into-the-hold-of-a-ship, the-heavy-weather-worn-oak-doors-crashing-clumsily-shut drums and then the-beating-of-pots-and-pans drums and then lightning drums and then an-elephant-rolling-on-the-ground drums and then heartbeat drums and a-hummingbird-drone drums and then tick-tock-and-stop drums, then a-hurricane-through-the-shutters-of-a-hundred-houses drums, then the-jalousies-flapping-in-the-wind drums and sails-pushed-by-a-sudden-gale and breasts-pumping-against-a-male-stomach, the-sweat-farting-through-belly-buttons drums, rubber-trees-bending drums, forest-winds-blowing, black-birds-flying-through-the-high-branches drums, plates-and-coffee-cups-shattering-in-a-pile drums, wild-native-banging-on-a-row-of-human-skulls, bones-flying-through-the-air drums and beat-on-the-tortoiseshell drums, beat-on-a-fat-wriggly-ass drums, Chinese-chimes drums, and men-hitting-men drums, belts-hitting-faces drums, thick-branches-against-the-back drums, and then rapping-coffin drums, all drums, *batá,* conga, bongo, *quinto, tumbadora* drums booming like storm clouds, beautiful-women-shaking-their-life-giving-hips drums, a-million-bells-falling-out-of-the-sky drums, a-wave-assaulting-the-earth drum, *comparsa*-lines-twisting-through-town drums, celebrational-marriage drums, firing-squad drums, a-man-moaning-

with-orgasm drums, and shouting, yawning, laughing, crying
drums, drums from across a field and deep in the forest, the drums
of madmen onstage letting loose, good old Pito on the *timbales*
and Benny on the congas for a little ten-second interlude in the
middle of one of those old Mambo King songs.

So WHY HAD THE MAMBO KING
started playing music again, after losing so much of his heart? It
had to do with the family in Cuba, his brothers Miguel and
Eduardo writing him letters and asking for money, medicine, and
clothes. This had become his "cause." Even if he had never given
a shit about politics before, what could he do when someone in
the family asked him for help? At first he took on any kind of
extra work, plastering and painting apartments to make more
money, but then after being urged on by his old bassist Manny,
he started accepting pickup jobs here and there around the city.
(The first job back? Hilarious, a wedding out in Queens in 1961,
a Cuban fellow who got caught by his bride pinching the
bridesmaid's ass. Later, while they were packing up their instruments, out into the parking lot spilled bride and groom, the
bride slapping and kicking at him.) The money that survived
his generous and spendthrift ways went into buying food and
medicine which he'd ship to Cuba. With Delores's *Webster's
Dictionary* open before him, he would carefully draft letters to
the government, inquiries as to the procedure for getting his
family out, and then show these to one of the smarter tenants,
a certain Mr. Bernhardt, who had once been a college professor.
Reading through bifocals, Bernhardt, a portly and distin-
guished-looking fellow, made the proper corrections and then
he'd redo the letters carefully on an antique British typewriter.
(And Cesar would look around his living room. Bernhardt had
worked as some kind of history teacher and his tables were covered with papers and books in Latin and Greek and clumps of
photographs of archaeological sites, as well as a collection of
thick, impossibly old books on witchcraft, and file folders containing pornographic photos.) The replies to his letters said that

it all came down to getting permission from the Castro government; but those letters to Cuba seemed to go floating from office to office, rotting in bins filled with thousands of others. In the end, it would take them five years to get out.

There was more to it. On some nights, while listening to music, he'd remember his childhood in Cuba and how he'd go out to the sugar mill to hear the famous orchestras that toured the island: orchestras like Ernesto Lecuona's Melody Boys. In 1932, admission to hear Lecuona cost one dollar and everybody in Las Piñas would go, that being the grandest cultural event of the year. Families would make their way to the sugar mill in carriages, automobiles, and wagons, and the roads would be jammed with travelers from nearby towns. Some made the journey on horseback. Conversations cutting through the night, the chirping of the crickets, and the clop-clop-clop of horses. The stars humming like delicate glass bells. In the sugar-mill concert hall, there was a high-ceilinged ballroom with chandeliers and arched windows with great pleated drapes, Moorish wainscoting, and floors so polished they glimmered as if in sunlight. One night, nearly fifty years ago, Ernesto Lecuona came out onto the stage and Cesar Castillo, then a boy, was there to hear and see him. He was not a tall man and resembled, at first glance, a more thickset Rudolph Valentino. He wore a black tuxedo, a pearl-buttoned shirt, a bright-red bow tie. He had dark, penetrating eyes and long, slender hands. Seated before the piano, his face serene, he played the first ebbing chords of his famous composition "*Malagueña.*"

Later, during the intermission, the revered Lecuona came down off the stage to mingle with his audience. That night, as he saw Lecuona moving through the crowd, Cesar Castillo, fourteen years old, pushed forward to shake that grand gentleman's hand. That was the evening when Cesar introduced himself, saying, "My name is Cesar Castillo, Mr. Lecuona, and there's something I've written that I'd like you to hear. A ballad."

And Lecuona sighed, giving off a scent of lemon cologne. Although he seemed a little weary, he politely nodded and told the boy, "Come and see me afterwards in the parlor."

After the concert, in a large parlor adjoining the ballroom, the young Cesar Castillo sat down before a piano, nervously playing and singing his *canción*.

Lecuona's reaction was honest and gentle: "You have a good singing voice, your verses are monotonous, but you have written a good chorus."

The name of the song? Nothing that he could remember, just that one of the verses mentioned "wilting flowers."

"Thank you, Mr. Lecuona, thank you," Cesar remembered saying, "thank you," as he followed him back toward the crowd, that image fading almost instantly, but not the desire to slip back inside that music which had sounded so beautiful.

In time, he was working joints like the Sunset Club and the 146th Street Latin Exchange (A cabdriver: "You know who I took up there one night? Pérez Prado!") on Friday and Saturday nights, dispensing with the hard business of running a band and just taking jobs as they came along. He didn't charge very much, twenty or twenty-five dollars a night, and this tended to get him work, because (whether he realized it or not) he was still something of a name.

He just never knew it.

Even took work as a strolling guitarist and singer in restaurants like the Mamey Tree and the Morro Castle in Brooklyn.

Of course, it was a pleasure to perform for the people again. Got his mind off things. And it always made him happy when someone would come along and ask him for an autograph *("Ciertamente!")*. It felt good when he'd go walking along the 125th Street markets on a Sunday afternoon and some guy in a sleeveless T-shirt would call out to him from a window, "Hey! Mambo King, how's it going?"

Still he felt his sadness. Sometimes when he played those jobs with Manny, he would get a ride back home. But most often he rode the subways, as he didn't like to drive at night anymore. Having scrapped his DeSoto, he had bought a '54 Chevrolet, but whenever he took it out, he would feel like jerking the car into a wall. Now he took it for occasional spins up and down Riverside Drive on nice days, washed it on Sundays, playing its radio and using it like a little office, to greet pals. Mainly, it was a pain in the ass; he was always paying parking tickets and lending it out to friends. That's why he'd sell it in '63, for $250. In any case, he liked to drink, and taking the subway meant that he didn't have to worry about wrecking the car or hurting anyone. The only setback was that he sometimes felt nervous waiting on the platforms late at night—New York had started to get bad in the early 1960s; that's why he would walk all the way to the end and hide behind a pillar and wait there for the train.

Anonymous in a pair of sunglasses and with his hat pulled low over his brow, guitar or trumpet case wedged between his knees, the Mambo King traveled to his jobs around the city. It was easy to get home when he worked restaurants in the Village or Madison Avenue bars, where he would serenade the Fred MacMurray-looking executives and their companions ("Now, girls, sing after me, 'Babalooooooo!' "), as those jobs usually ended around eleven at night. But when he'd play small clubs and dance halls out on the edges of Brooklyn and the Bronx, he'd get home at four-thirty, five in the morning. Spending many a night riding the trains by himself, he'd read *La Prensa* or *El Diario* or the *Daily News*.

He made lots of friends on the trains; he knew the flamenco guitarist from Toledo, Spain, a fellow named Eloy García, who played in the Café Madrid; an accordionist with a tango orchestra in Greenwich Village, named Macedonio, a roly-poly fellow who'd go to work in a gaucho hat. ("To play the music of Matos Rodríguez is to bring Matos back," he'd say.) He knew Estela and Nilda, two *zarzuela* singers who would pass through matronhood with wilting carnations in their hair. He knew a black three-man dance team with conk hairdos, friendly and hopeful fellows, resplendent in white tuxedos and spats, who were always heading out to do auditions. ("These days we're hoping to get on the Ed Sullivan show.") Then there were the Mexicans with their oversized guitars, trumpets, and an accordion that resembled an altar, its fingerboard shiny with hammer-flattened religious medals of the Holy Mother, Christ, and the Apostles, bloody with wounds, hobbling on crutches, and pierced through with arrows to the heart. The men wore big sombreros and trousers that jangled with bells, and high, thin-heeled cowboy boots, leather-etched with swirly flowers, and traveled with a woman and a little girl. The woman wore a mantilla and a frilly dress made of Aztec-looking fabric; the little girl wore a red dress and played a tambourine on which an enamel likeness of John the Baptist had been painted. She'd sit restlessly, unhappily during the rides, while Cesar would lean forward and speak quietly to her mother. ("How is it going with you today?" "Slow lately, the best time is during Christmas, and then everybody gives.") They'd ride to the last stop downtown, to the Staten Island Ferry terminal, where they would play *bambas, corridos, huapangos,* and *rancheras* for the waiting passengers.

"*Que Dios te bendiga.* God bless you."

"The same to you."

There were others, a lot of Latin musicians like himself on their way to weary late-night jobs in the deepest reaches of Brooklyn and the Bronx. Some were young and didn't know the name Cesar Castillo, but the old-timers, the musicians who had been kicking around in New York since the forties, they knew him. Trumpet players, guitarists, and drummers would come over and sit with the Mambo King.*

Still, there were the tunnels, the darkness, the dense solitude of a station at four in the morning, and the Mambo King daydreaming about Cuba.

It made a big difference to him that he just couldn't get on

---

*Always a nice hello and sometimes a reunion, the fellows inviting each other out to jam sessions. In the Hotel Splendour he remembered that one of his favorite jam sessions took place when Benny the conga player invited him over to the Museum of Natural History, where he worked, in his reincarnated life, as a guard. Around nine one night, when it was really dead, Cesar showed up with a few other musicians and they ended up playing in a small office just off the Great Hall of Dinosaurs, Benny playing the drums and a fellow named Rafael strumming a guitar and Cesar singing and blowing the trumpet, this music echoing and humming through the bones of those prehistoric creatures —the Stegosaurus and Tyrannosaurus Rex and Brontosaurus and woolly mammoth, breathing heavy in the vastness of that room and click-clacking onto the marble floors melodies caught in their great hooked jaws and in the curve of their gargantuan spinal columns.

an airplane and fly down to Havana to see his daughter or to visit the family in Las Piñas.

Who would ever have dreamed that would be so? That Cuba would be chums with Russia?

It was all a new kind of sadness.

Sitting in his room in the Hotel Splendour (reeling in the room), the Mambo King preferred not to think about the revolution in Cuba. What the fuck had he ever cared about Cuban politics in the old days, except for when he might play a political rally in the provinces for some local crooked politician? What the fuck had he cared when the consensus among his musician pals was that it wouldn't make any difference who came to power, until Fidel. What could he have done about it, anyway? Things must have been pretty bad. The orchestra leader René Touzet had fled to Miami with his sons, playing the big hotels there and concerts for the Cubans. Then came the grand master of Cuban music, Ernesto Lecuona, arriving in Miami distraught and in a state of creative torpor, unable to play a note on his piano and ending up in Puerto Rico, "bitter and disenchanted," before he died, he'd heard some people say. Bitter because his Cuba no longer existed.

God, all the Cubans were worked up. Even that *compañero* —who never forgot the family—Desi Arnaz had scribbled a little extra message on one of his Christmas cards: "We Cubans should stick together in these troubled times."

What had a friend called the revolution? "The rose that sprouted a thorn."

The great Celia Cruz would come to the States, too, in 1967.

(On the other hand, Pala de Nieve—the musician "Snowball"—and the singer Elena Burke chose to remain behind.)

When his mother had died in 1962, the news came in a telegram from Eduardo, and a funny thing, too, because he had been thinking about her a lot that week, almost a soft pulsing in his heart, and his head filled with memories. And when he first read the line "I have bad news," he instantly thought "No." After reading the telegram, all he could do for hours was to drink and remember how she would take him into the yard as a child and wash his hair in a tub, again and again and again, her soft hands that smelled of rose water scrubbing his head and touching his face, the sun down through the treetops, her hair swirling with curls of light . . .

The man cried for hours, until his eyelids were swollen, and he fell asleep with his head against the worktable.

Wished he had seen her one more time. Told himself that he would have gone back the previous year, when he'd first heard that she had gotten sick, if it hadn't been for Castro.

Sometimes he got into big arguments with Ana María's husband, Raúl, about the situation down there. A long-time union man, Raúl kept himself busy organizing union shops in factories in the West Twenties, where most of the workers were immigrants from Central America and Puerto Rico. They were still friends, despite their differences of opinion. But Raúl kept trying to persuade the Mambo King about Castro. On a Friday night he went so far as to bring him down to a club on 14th Street where old Spanish and Portuguese leftists held meetings. He sat in the back listening as the old Spaniards, their expressions and politics shaped by beatings and jail terms in Franco's Spain, gave long, heartfelt speeches about "what must be done," which always came down to *"Viva el socialismo!"* and "Viva Fidel!"

Nothing wrong with doing away with the world's evils. He had seen a lot of that. In Cuba there had been rotting sheds made of cardboard and crates, skeleton children and dying dogs. A funeral procession in a small town called Minas. On the side of the plain pine coffin, a sign: *"Muerto de hambre."* On the street corners where the handsome *suavecitos* hung out talking, some guy who'd lost a limb while working at the sugar mill, in the *calderas,* begging. When he pictured suffering, he thought of a dead dog he'd found lying on the cobblestone road near the harbor of Lisbon: a tiny hound, with a sweet face and pleasantly cocked ears, stiff on its back, with its belly torn open, its dark purple stomach bloated to the size of a fifteen-pound melon.

He had no argument with wanting to help others, Raúl. Back in Cuba, the people took care of their own. Families giving clothing, food, money, and, sometimes, a job in the household or in a business.

"My own mother, Raúl, listen to me. My own mother was always giving money to the poor, even when we didn't have very much. What more could anyone ask?"

"More."

"Raúl, you're my friend. I don't want to argue with you, but the people are leaving because they can't bear it."

"Or because they haven't the strength."

"Come on, let's have a drink."

A letter, dated June 17, 1962:

To my dear brother,

We may have been apart these years, but you have never lost our hearts. The truth is that the situation down here has become bad. Pedrito is the only one of us who has any sympathy for the Castro government. I feel so depressed just writing those words. Just a year ago I was able to help the others out with the money I was making from the garage, but the government's taken that away, chained up the doors and informed me that I was welcome to work there if I wanted, but to forget about being the owner. The bastards. That's Communism. I refused to go back and [crossed out]. I know that you've prospered and hope that you can see your way to sending us whatever you can. Bad enough that we've had to endure the tragedy of losing Nestor, but now all this seems to just make things worse. I wouldn't ask you if I didn't think you had the money. If you could send us fifty or a hundred dollars a month, that would be enough to help us live decently until our applications for exit visas are approved—if ever. But that is a whole other matter. May God bless you. We send you our love.

Eduardo.

So he raised money for his brothers and also sent money and gifts to his daughter, Mariela, even though she didn't really seem to need them. A headmaster during the days of the revolution, Mariela's stepfather had edited an underground pro-Castro newspaper and, after the revolution, was rewarded with a good post in the Ministry of Education. Living in an airy apartment on Calle 26 in the Vedado section of Havana, the family thrived, enjoying the privileges of his position, while she studied ballet.

(Among the photographs which the Mambo King had taken

with him into the Hotel Splendour, a favorite picture of his daughter in leotards and tutu, beneath an arched window in a room with pilastered walls and ornate tiles. This was at her ballet school in Havana. The picture, taken in 1959, shows a thin, genteel girl with large brown eyes and a teaspoon-shaped face, lively and elegant, in ballet slippers and with a dreamy expression, as if listening to beautiful music. Another picture, taken in 1962, shows her dancing during a rehearsal of *Giselle;* watching her, Alicia Alonso and her ballet teacher, a pretty Cuban woman named Gloria.)

Sometimes he found himself hanging around the bars and *cantinas* of Washington Heights and, on occasion, Union City, New Jersey, where in the early sixties many of the feverish Cubans had settled. Sipping his *tacita* of *café negro,* he would listen quietly to the political chitchat. The newly arrived Cubans, bitter and forlorn; the old, established Cubans trying to figure out what was going on in Cuba: a man with a shaking right hand whose older brother, a jeweler, had committed suicide in Havana; a man who had lost a good job as a gardener on the Du Pont estate; a man whose cousin had been sent to prison for walking down the street with a pound of sugar hidden in his shirt. A man who lost his farm. A man whose uncle was sentenced to twenty years for shouting "Fuck Castro!" at a town-hall meeting. A man whose precious and beautiful niece was abducted to frigid Moscow, where she married a humorless, barrel-chested Russian. A man who had been shot through the elbow during the Bay of Pigs invasion.

Voices:

"And they call us 'worms.' "

"Castro came to the island owning ten thousand acres of land and now he has the whole thing!"

"I smuggled arms for that son of a bitch."

"Who thinks he would have succeeded had we known he was a Communist?"

"They say the reason Castro was released by Batista in '54 was because they castrated him."

"They reduce our discontent to our stomachs. They say we have left because we can't find a good meal in Havana anymore. That's the truth, because all the Russians are eating the food. But there's more. They have taken our right to sit with our families in peace, before tables bountiful with the fruit of our labors."

"So we left, *hombre,* and that Castro, *mojón guindao,* can go to hell!"

"He's like Rasputin."

"Let them eat cake is his attitude."

"He made a deal with the devil."

"We've been betrayed all around."

"Yes, I know it," the Mambo King used to say. "I have three brothers and my father still living in Oriente, and they all say the same thing, they want to get out." Sip of coffee. "Except for my father. He's very old, in his seventies, and not well."

And he couldn't resist: "I have a daughter in Havana. It's my opinion that her thoughts have been tampered with."

The Mambo King would walk up the hill of La Salle Street, head bowed, back slightly stooped, belly hanging over his belt, and thoughts clouded with Cuba. In the clutter of his basement workroom, he would read the anti-Castro pamphlets that his friends gave him. Stuck between the pages of his younger brother's book, *Forward America!* ("For whatever your problems may be, remember where there is fortitude and determination there is a way!"), this portion of a pamphlet from 1961–62, circled in red ballpoint ink and set on the table in that room in the Hotel Splendour:

> . . . We cannot deny that in the era of republican government we had political leaders who did not always, through honesty and patriotism, implement the just and splendid laws of our Constitution. Yet we could not have known or even imagined the kind of tyranny unleashed by Fidel Castro and his hordes. Former comic-opera dictatorships at least tried to seek democratic solutions to their moral failings. Their methods only became dictatorial when provoked by Communists, who disturbed the public peace and drove innocent, stupid, and fanatical young people out into the streets, using them as cannon fodder. Some people say Cuba is going to flourish anew under Fidel Castro, that malnutrition, prostitution, illiteracy, corruption, and poverty are going to be stamped out forever, that the island will

become a paradise of equality, with a truly humanitarian government. Ask those who have been brutally tortured and lie dead in unmarked graves if this is so. The truth is different: Fidel Castro and his gang of robbers and murderous convicts, like the odious Argentine Che Guevara, the Spanish criminals Lister and Bayo, and expert torturers and killers like Raúl Castro and Ramiro Valdés, the head of G-2, have traded off Cuba to Euro-Asiatic powers. Powers that are geographically, spiritually, and historically far removed from everything Caribbean and that have turned Cuba into a tropical colony and military base for Russia. Since January 1, 1959, Cuba has become a miserable pauper state without resources or freedom and the sincere, happy spirit of Cubans has become replaced by tragic gloom. The gaiety of everyday Cuban life and commerce with its rum and good cigars and its bounty of sugar and all that springs from sugar has been reduced by a severe rationing in the name of Soviet-Cuban trade relations. The average Cuban citizen must brace himself stoically for the bleak future while Fidel himself smokes only the best twenty-dollar Havana cigars, drinks rum, and stuffs his gut with Russian caviar. While thousands of Cubans have begun to live in exile, one hundred thousand others rot in prisons for political crimes. The remaining population is divided up between the Cuban traitors who support the tyranny and those who have chosen to remain behind for personal reasons or cannot leave because the government will not allow them to. Let us not forget them! Long live Jesus Christ and long live freedom!

Inspired by the fiery prose of these pamphlets and by news from Cuba, the Mambo King would hole up in his basement workroom, drink beer, and write to Mariela—letters which over the years became more imploring in their tone.

The heart of them said this: "From what I hear about Cuba, I can't believe that you are happy there. I am not one to tell you what to do, but the day you want to leave and come to the United States, let me know and I will do everything I can, and do it willingly, because you are my flesh and blood."

He'd sign them, "Your lonely father who loves you."

Never receiving acknowledgment of these offers, he thought, Of course the letters are intercepted and cut to ribbons before she can read them! Instead, her letters spoke about her dance training—"They say I am one of the more promising students"—and about high-toned cultural events, like a performance of Stravinsky's *Firebird* by the Bolshoi Ballet on the stage of the opera house (which left him blinking, because the only ballets he had ever attended were the pornographic ballets at Havana's notorious Shanghai Theater).

Sometimes (daydreaming, nostalgic) he believed that he would feel some new happiness if Mariela came up from Cuba to live with him, escaping by boat, or miraculously with the permission of the government ("Yes, the poor thing wants to be with her true father. Give her our blessing to leave"). Then she'd look after him, cook his meals, help keep house, and, above all, would receive and give him love, and this love would wrap around his heart like a gentle silk bow, protecting it from all harm.

In a way, thinking about Mariela helped him to understand why Nestor used to sit on the couch and torment himself for hours singing about his "Beautiful María," even if it was all a pipe dream. Something about love and the eternal spring, time suspended—so that the Mambo King daydreamed about himself sitting in his living room by the sunny window, head set back and eyes closed while his daughter, Mariela, cut his hair, the way his mother used to, Mariela's lovely voice (he imagined) humming into his huge ears, her face radiant with happy love for him. Now and then he would feel so inspired by all this that he would take the train to Macy's and, guessing at Mariela's size, buy her a half-dozen dresses and blouses, lipsticks, mascaras, and rouge, and, on one occasion, a long silk scarf, yellow like the sunlight in old paintings—rushing hurriedly through the store as if the right choice of gift would make things different. With these items he would enclose a note: "Just to let you know that your father loves you."

And for each November 17, Mariela's birthday, he'd put together a package of goods generally unavailable to Cubans, things that he thought a teenager would like: chocolate bars, cookies, jam, chewing gum, potato chips, sure evidence of the diversity and abundance of life in America.

She never came running into his arms.

ONCE HE GOT OUT OF THE HOSPI-
tal in June, his strength on the wane, he didn't care about anything. Yes, everybody was nice to him. Machito came over to the house to pay his respects, and so did many other musician friends. But he felt so weak, walked so slowly (because of the medications), he didn't want to get out of bed. Was that a life for the fabulous Cesar Castillo? And forget about his job as superintendent. He had to get Frankie and a few other friends to fill in. When Lydia, his young woman, with whom he had been having his troubles, wasn't over to take care of him, he would head upstairs to eat with Pedro and Delores, the tensions now gone between them, as he wasn't a frisky bull anymore but an old hound on his way out. On top of that, he had to maintain a boring, low-fat, low-salt, grainy diet, while deep down he craved *plátanos* and pork and a heaping plate of rice and beans, with a glass of beer or wine or whiskey on the side.

What pleasures did he have left? Hanging out and going fishing up around Bear Mountain with Frankie, sitting in Bernardito's house listening to music; hours and hours of watching TV, and reading spicy magazines like *Foto Pimienta!*, with their grainy black-and-white pornographic photographs and their advertisements for the "Revolutionary European System to Lengthen the Size of Your Penis!" ("My old lady never really thought I was 'stud' enough for her, *pero ahora la penetro muy profundo*—but now I go in really deep—and she can hardly wait to go to bed with me!") and with their ads for lotions and love potions ("Lubricante Jac-Off, Loción Peter-Licker"), and the personal ads in the back, male and female. ("Honest, clean man from Veracruz, Mexico, 38 years old, with a youthful appearance and a penis of nine inches length and two and one half inches thickness seeking lonely female companions between the ages of twenty and sixty for a love affair." "Bisexual man from Santurce,

Puerto Rico, with a six and one half inch penis, seeking out couples for weekend entertainment, am willing to travel." "Lonely Cuban man, fifty years old but youthful and well en-dowed—*superdotado*—living in Coral Gables and homesick for Cuba, seeks a female partner for romance and life." "I am an abandoned thirty-four-year-old woman with a six-year-old son, very romantic and feel alone and sad. I am an American citizen, white, *gordita*—chubby—with big breasts, and I am a passionate lover. If you are a healthy male between the ages of 35 and 50, with a good job and decent character, please send information and photograph." Her photograph, of a naked woman bending over, was below the ad.)

"Dios mío!"

And of course he liked to watch the variety shows on Channel 47 from New Jersey, a Spanish broadcasting station, his favorite being the incredibly voluptuous Iris Chacón, whose jewel-beaded hips and cleavage made the Mambo King a little delirious, and he liked the old musicals from Mexico, like the kind that his former arranger Miguel Montoya used to compose scores for: vampire Westerns and masked wrestler/detective/nightclub singer films and the soap operas about love and family, the women young and beautiful, the men virile and handsome, while he was just an old man now, sixty-two years old but looking seventy-five. Hollywood movies also made him happy, his favorites featuring the likes of Humphrey Bogart, William Powell, and Fredric March, Veronica Lake, Rita Hayworth, and Marilyn Monroe. (Though he also seemed happy whenever a Laurel and Hardy film turned up. He used to like watching them in the movie house in Las Piñas. But there was one he really liked, *The Flying Deuces:* Mr. Laurel and Mr. Hardy escape from the French Foreign Legion in a biplane that crashes, killing Oliver Hardy. At the end of the film Stanley is walking down a road on a beautiful spring day, with a hobo stick and a bundle over his shoulder, sad and wistful that his old pal is dead. Butterflies, trees bending in the breeze, birds chirping, the sun shining, life all around him, and he says, "Gee, Ollie would like a nice day like this," and just then, as he turns the corner, he comes upon a mule, a mule with a mustache, bangs, and a hat just like Ollie's, and as Stanley recognizes that Ollie has been reincarnated as a mule, tears come to his eyes, he pats the mule's back and says, "Gee, Ollie, I'm happy to see you," and Ollie answers something back like "This is another fine mess you got me into," but it's a happy fade-out, and the Mambo King, thinking about resurrection and the way Christ burst through the tomb door, radiant with light, imagines how beautiful it would have been for his younger brother to have returned, and he gets teary-eyed, too.)

Now and then, he watched the *I Love Lucy* show, and saw that episode one last time before he made his way to the Hotel Splendour. Saw his brother and wept, thinking how life had become very sad because of his death. Closing his eyes, he heard the rapping at Ricky Ricardo's door, stood in Lucy and Ricky's living room one more time, and could swear that if he reached over to his side he could touch his brother's knee and nod as Lucille Ball came into the room with their coffee and snacks, and it would give him the worst craving for a nice little glass of booze, but he kept thinking about what the doctors had told him and knew that the logical thing would be to improve his health, but he was desolately bored, it seemed that all he had were memories, that where his pleasures resided now was in the past. Everything else was too complicated, even walking across the room, what with arthritis aching in his joints and his fingers still so bloated and stiff that he couldn't even play the guitar or trumpet anymore.

(There were countless other episodes besides the one in which he had appeared with his brother. At four in the morning, just a few weeks before he had left for the Hotel Splendour, he had sat up watching two old *I Love Lucy* reruns:

The first was an episode about Lucy getting all nervous because Ricky's sweet mother is coming up from Cuba to visit and Lucy doesn't know more than a few words of Spanish, which she always botches, and so, when Ricky's mother turns up, demure and tranquil, to see her loving son, they sit quietly in the living room together, each without knowing what to say and waiting for the other to speak, and they seem to live in this world where everything happens because of the door, and Lucy keeps looking toward the door, waiting for her husband to help her out, and they sit on the couch for a long time, just smiling at one another, Lucy fidgeting and the Cuban mother perfectly content to sit on the couch waiting for her nightclub singer son, of whom she is proud, and you just know that when he walks in she'll rise and give him a tender kiss, that she will hold him in her arms. Feeling embarrassed because even her four-year-old son, Ricky Jr., speaks better Spanish than she does, Lucy's really trying to figure out a way around this, because not only has Ricky's mother come to visit but now some of their cousins from Cuba, other cousins, are coming to join them for dinner. It happens that Ricky has booked a mentalist act for the Tropicana nightclub and this mentalist, a classy fellow with a beautiful Cuban accent, does all his "mind-reading" with a listening device, which Lucy borrows from him, so that the mentalist, hiding in her kitchen, can feed her lines through a microphone. When the family comes over, Lucy's sudden knowledge of Spanish at first impresses everyone, but then the mentalist has to leave because his wife has just had a baby, and right then and there Lucy begins to fuck everything up, fumbling her Spanish and making a fool of herself. Yet the episode ends happily, with all the Cubans touched by her effort, with everyone embracing, and with Ricky Ricardo lovingly kissing her.

In the second, Ricky and Lucy are living up in the country far away from the troubles of the city, when Lucy gets the idea to raise chickens and buys a huge supply of eggs, but because she doesn't have an incubator, she brings them into the house and turns up the temperature, without realizing that all the eggs will hatch suddenly, so that when Desi Arnaz, alias Ricky Ricardo, with his wildly expressive eyes, comes home, the living room's filled with ten thousand chicks, chirping and crawling happily over everything, under the sofa and on top of the tables and chairs, and so Ricky stands astounded in the doorway and does a double take, slapping his forehead with the palm of his hand and his eyes brimming out—his "Lucy! *No me digas que compraste un mink coat que costaba $5,000!*" expression. And he starts mock-cursing in a thousand-words-a-minute Spanish, and Lucy's afraid, until Desi's good mood returns and everybody's happy again . . .

Good and funny episodes! he told himself, while drinking in the Hotel Splendour.)

And Lydia, his last love, whom he'd met in a Bronx nightclub in 1978, could not bring herself to make love to him anymore. That hurt the most. She would come over to check in on him every few days, and he was always happy as a young pup to see her, but when he touched her now, she'd pull away.

"You're still not well," she'd say to him.

But he'd persist. She'd cook his meals and he would stand behind her, pressing against her back until the heat of her rump aroused him. And without thinking twice, he would undo his trousers and show her his hound-snouted thing, not even fully erect but still able to put many a younger man to shame. "Please," she'd say, "I'm here to take care of you."

He persisted. "Just touch me there."

"*Dios mío*, you're like a child."

And she took hold of his thing, giving him hope, but put it back into his trousers.

"Now sit down and eat this soup I made for you."

She'd clean his house, cook his meals, make his bed, tidy up the magazines and newspapers in his living room, but all he wanted was to strip off her clothes and make love to her. Nothing he tried worked with her. No singing, no jokes, no flowery compliments. Finally he resorted to pitiable behavior. "You never loved me. Now I feel so useless, I may as well die." That became his song for weeks, until, worn down, she took pity on him, stripped off her dress, and in a black brassiere and panties, kneeled before him, pulled off his trousers, and began to suckle his aged member. Holding her thick black hair and brushing it away from her eyes, he appraised the expression on her face and realized that it was one of pure revulsion and he wilted, asking himself, Am I so old and far gone that she doesn't want me anymore?

She kept at him until her mouth and jaw were tired and then settled into a rough masturbation of him, finally producing the tremor that he had been waiting for. But when she had finished, it was as if she could not bear to look at him, this old, thickset man with white hair, and she turned away, both her fists pressed against her mouth and biting her knuckles in some agonized judgment of what she had just done. And when he touched her gently, she pulled away, like everybody else in his life.

"Are you being like this because I haven't been able to give you and the children money lately? I have money in the bank I can give you. Or if you can wait until I start working again or if a royalty check comes in, I'll bring you money, okay? If that's what you want, then I'll do whatever you want to make you happy."

"*Hombre,* I don't want to touch you anymore because touching you is like touching death."

And then she just started weeping.

Dressed, she kept saying things like, "I'm sorry I told you this. But you've pushed me so much. Please understand."

"I understand," he said. "Now please leave this death house, this sick old man, just go."

She left, promising to return, and he stood up, looking at himself in the mirror. His huge, red-snouted *pinga* hanging down between his legs. Belly gigantic, skin saggy. Why, he almost had breasts like a woman's.

He thought: It's one thing to lose a woman when you're twenty-five, forty, another when you're sixty-two years old.

He thought about his wife, Luisa, in Cuba. His daughter, Mariela.

The many others.

Oh, Vanna Vane.

Lydia.

"*Mamá.*"

". . . like touching death."

It took him a long time to make his decisions, the first being "Fuck this shit with special diets and no more booze!" Getting nicely dressed in a white silk suit, he went up to that little joint on 127th Street and Manhattan Avenue and had two orders of fried plantains, one sweet, one green, a plate of *yuca* smothered in salt, oil, and garlic, an order of roast pork, and a special dish of shrimp and chicken, bread and butter, all washed down with half a dozen beers, so filling and bloating that making his way back up to La Salle Street was one of the great struggles of his life.

That was when he decided to hell with everything. Took his savings out of the bank and bought everybody presents (among them: a set of false teeth for Frankie, a plumed hat for Pedro, who had been too shy to buy one for himself, an old Don Aziapaú recording entitled "Havana Nights" for Bernardito, and for his nephew, Eugenio, who liked to draw, something he'd learned in college, the thickest art book he could find, one on the works of Francisco Goya), and then spent a month visiting friends here and there. What a bitch to say goodbye to old pals like Manny and Frankie. What a bitch to say goodbye to Delores, to travel out to Flushing, Queens, with a box of pastries and gifts for his cousin Pablo, to eat a nice meal with the family and then give him an *abrazo* for the last time.

NOW HE LAUGHS, THINKING ABOUT grinning Bernardito Mandelbaum again and what he had been like when they first met in 1950: skinny, with a thick head of tousled black hair, in baggy hand-me-downs from an older brother, plaid shirts and a pair of scuffed brown Sears, Roebuck shoes and white socks! That's how he'd dress for his job as a clerk in the office of the Tidy Print plant where Cesar had also worked in the stockroom for a time. In a cavernous room noisy with printing machines they had become friends, Bernardito immediately liking Cesar's lighthearted and suave demeanor and always doing him favors. In the mornings he'd get the Mambo King coffee, bring him homemade pastries for a snack, and whenever the Mambo King had to leave early for a job, Bernardito would take care of punching out his time card. In exchange for these favors, the Mambo King let Bernardito into his circle of friends at the plant, Cubans and Puerto Ricans and Dominicans, who'd sit around at lunch conversing and telling bawdy stories. And Bernardito, an aspiring cartoonist, with his high-school Spanish, would listen attentively, later picking Cesar's brains about certain words and phrases which he'd collect into a notebook.

He seemed like a nice enough kid, and that's why the Mambo King approached him one afternoon and said, "Listen, boy, you're too young to be missing out on all the fun. Why don't you come with us tomorrow night after work. Me and my brother, we're playing this dance in Brooklyn—near where you live—I want you to come with us after work, okay? Just get a little better dressed, wear a nice tie and jacket, like a gentleman."

And that was the beginning of a new life, because the next night Bernardito joined the Mambo King and his brother for the evening, eating a steak and a platter of fried sweet plantains and then driving down with them to the Imperial Ballroom, where he fell under the spell of the music and found himself gyrating wildly before the stage like a living hieroglyphic, confusing the ladies with his cryptic moves and strange mode of dress— brown jacket, yellow shirt, green tie, white pants, and brown shoes.

Taken in by the excitement and glamour of the dance halls, he forgot all about Bensonhurst and started to hang around with the Mambo King on the weekends, rarely coming home before three in the morning. Slowly, under Cesar's—and Nestor's —wing, Bernardito became transformed into a high-stepping ballroom *suavecito*. The first thing that changed was his way of dressing. On a Saturday afternoon, Cesar met Bernardito and they made the rounds of the big department stores and clothing shops. Out went the hand-me-downs from his older brother. With his savings, Bernardito bought the latest in fashion: ten pairs of pleated trousers, wide-lapeled puff-shouldered double-breasted jackets, Italian belts, and sporty two-toned shoes. And he had his hair shaped into a pompadour and grew a wisp of a mustache, after the fashion of his newest friends.

Then he started to collect Latin records. His Sundays were spent haunting record shops in Harlem and on Flatbush Avenue, so that in time this kid who hadn't known Xavier Cugat from Jimmy Durante started to accumulate rare recordings by the likes of Ernesto Lecuona, Marion Sunshine, and Miguelito Valdez. And he would have hundreds of these records, enough to fill up three bookcases, one of the best collections in the city.

He was happy until he started to have fights about his new life with his parents. His parents, he'd told the Mambo King, weren't too happy about the hours he was keeping and were worried about his new friends. His mother and father, who had emigrated from Russia, must have been quite surprised when, on a Sunday afternoon, they heard their doorbell ring and found the two brothers standing there. They had dressed up in suits, bought flowers and a box of chocolates from the Schrafft's on 107th Street and Broadway. That afternoon the brothers sat with them, sipping coffee, eating cookies, and behaving so agreeably that Bernardito's parents changed their minds.

But, soon afterwards, Bernardito went to a Mambo King party and met Fifi, a thirty-year-old hot tomato, who soon won his heart with affection and with the carnal pleasures of her body. He moved into her apartment on 122nd Street and would spend the next twenty-five years trying to make peace with his parents. Settled in with her, Bernardito began to live his life much as he always would, holding a full-time job by day and working as a freelance illustrator at night: he was the artist for *The Adventures of Atomic Mouse* comics and had also drawn three Mambo King covers, among them "Mambo Inferno."

Then Bernardito's life fell into the tranquil Cubanophile track of his days. For thirty years he and Cesar Castillo would be friends. And in that time Bernardito not only learned a Latin life-style, speaking a good slangy Cuban Spanish and dancing the mambo and the cha-cha-cha with the best of them, but he also slowly turned his and Fifi's apartment into a cross between a mambo museum and the parlor of a Havana mansion of the 1920s, with shuttered windows, potted palms, an overhead mahogany fan, animal-footed cabinets and tables, tropical-fish tanks, wicker furniture, a parrot squawking in a cage, candles and candelabra, and, in addition to a big modern RCA television and stereo, a 1920 crank-driven Victrola. Lately he had started to look as if he had stepped out of that age, parting his hair in the middle, wearing wire-rim glasses and a thin mustache, baggy, suspendered *pantalones,* bow ties, and flat, black-brimmed straw hats.

And he had signed photographs of some of the greats: Cesar Castillo, Xavier Cugat, Machito, Nelo Sosa, and Desi Arnaz.

The day the Mambo King had gone to Bernardito's house to say goodbye, he found his friend sitting by the window, hunched over a drawing table with a pencil in hand, working out some advertising drawings. A staff artist for the *La Prensa* syndicate, he also earned extra money as a freelance artist, spicy cartoons for girlie magazines being a quick and easy specialty

—a big-assed chick bending over to pick up a rose, her butt out in the world, some man gaping at her, and his matronly wife, beside him, saying, "I didn't know you liked flowers so much!" That afternoon, he sat beside Bernardito as he worked, the two men talking and drinking. Usually Bernardito listened to music while he worked, and that day had not been different: Nelo Sosa's orchestra came out of his speakers, sounding beautiful.

For an hour or so they talked, and then, feeling the sadness of that day, the Mambo King presented his old friend with a package of rare old records from Cuba by the Sexteto Habanero, five 78s he had found in a sidewalk shop in Havana during the 1950s.

"These are for you, Bernardito."

And the Mambo King took a good long look at his friend. The man was in his late forties now but still had this goofy grin of enchantment he'd get when he was nineteen.

"But why are you giving me these?"

"Because you're my friend," the Mambo King told him. "Besides, I never listen to them anymore. You may as well have them."

"Are you sure?"

"Yes."

Happily, Bernardito Mandelbaum placed upon his old KLH stereo, which had a 78 rpm gear, the Sexteto Habanero's famed recording of *"Mamá Inez."*

And then he played all the others, and as he did he kept asking, "Are you sure you want to give these to me?"

"They're yours."

Then they just sat for a time and Cesar asked, "And your *señora?* When is she coming home?"

"She should be here soon."

Yes, and that was another thing. After waiting twenty-five years for his parents to pass away, he had finally married Fifi.

It was another hour before Fifi came home, offering to cook the Mambo King a nice healthy dinner of fried steak and plantains, and planting a kiss on his cheek that made him blush.

But he refused the dinner, saying that he wasn't feeling well.

At the door, he said goodbye to Bernardito, giving him a strong embrace and holding it for a long time.

"Come back on Sunday," Bernardito told him as the Mambo King made his way down the stairs. "Don't forget. Sunday."

The worst goodbye had been with Eugenio. He didn't want to leave the kid "behind," without seeing him one last time. And so, one day, he called Eugenio at his job as a bookkeeper in an artist-supply store on Canal Street, a joint called Pearl Paints, and invited him out to dinner that night, so they could hang around like they used to. They met on 110th Street and ended up in this Dominican place on Amsterdam Avenue, ate a nice meal. Afterwards they made their way out to this little bar called La Ronda, where beers were five dollars apiece but where the stripper dancing in the cage had a nice compact body. They'd come in when she was down to nothing. (Now and then she would go into the back with customers for a price, lie down on a bed, and open her legs.)

"*Mambero,*" she called to him when she noticed he had come in. "Are you feeling better?"

He shrugged. Then she gave Eugenio an up-and-down, and the Mambo King leaned over to his nephew with a twenty-dollar bill in hand, saying, "Do you want to go with her? Makes no difference to me."

"You go with her, Uncle."

The Mambo King looked at her up in the cage with her firm legs and nice smooth thighs. She'd even shaved her vagina, the slit like a sidewise mouth, which she had made gleamy with some Vaseline and who knew what else. It was tempting, but he said, "No, I'm here to spend the time with you."

By then, everybody in the family knew that Cesar had abandoned his special diets and medicines, putting on weight and getting teary-eyed and sluggish. It hit Eugenio bad. As he sat beside his uncle, certain old desires came over him—to run away, go somewhere else, be someone else.

They listened to music and then there were long periods of silence: the kid seemed so unhappy.

"Do you remember when we always used to go to places and music jobs together?"

"Yes, Uncle."

"Those were good times, huh?"

"They were okay."

"Well, things change. You're not a *nene* anymore and I'm not a young man."

Eugenio shrugged.

"Do you remember when I took you to that woman up on 145th Street?"

"Yes!"

"Eugenio, don't be so cross with me. She was a dish, huh?"

"She was a pretty woman, Uncle."

Then: "Are we going to be here for a long time, Uncle?"

"No, just for a few drinks, boy." He sipped. "I just want you to know that . . . you mean a lot here," and he tapped his chest.

Eugenio scratching his brow, the dancer leaning forward in her cage and shaking her breasts.

"I hope you believe me, boy. I want you to believe me."

"Uncle . . ."

"I just wanted to tell you one little thing, man to man, heart to heart." His whole face was red and immense, his breathing heavy. "*Que yo te quiero.* I love you, nephew. You understand?"

"Yes, Uncle, is that why you told me to come here?"

Then: "Look, Uncle, I really thought something was wrong; I mean, it's one in the morning and I have to get home."

The Mambo King nodded, wanting to let out a cry of excruciating pain. "Well, I appreciate that you have come to see your old *mambero* uncle," he said.

And then they sat in the bar awhile, watching the stripper and not saying much. The jukebox loud with the latest Latin hit-makers' songs—musicians like Oscar de León and perennial favorites like Tito Puente.

Later, they were both standing by the subway on 110th Street and Broadway.

Eugenio had to get down to East 10th Street, where he lived, while the Mambo King would catch the uptown local. The last words he said to his nephew repeated the words he used always to say when he was drunk. "Well, don't forget about me, huh? And don't forget that your uncle loves you." Then he embraced his nephew for the last time.

Waiting for his train, he had watched his nephew across the

platform. Eugenio was sitting on a bench reading a fancy paper, *The New York Times*. His nephew, who had gone to college, was as melancholic as his father and becoming more so as he got older. As the Mambo King's train approached, he whistled across to Eugenio, who barely looked up in time to see his uncle waving. Pressed against the window and squinting through his dark green glasses, the Mambo King watched his nephew out of the rushing car until he was swallowed up in the dark tunnel.

That had been a few nights before, the Mambo King remembered as he sat in the Hotel Splendour.

Remembering something else, too, he went in this little suitcase and took out some envelopes and letters so that he might look at them one more time, and then he fished through the soft cloth pockets of his suitcase and withdrew a fine black-handled straight razor, the gift of a friend many years ago, and placed it before him on the table, in case he found himself lingering too long into the night in his room in the Hotel Splendour.

MUSICIAN, SINGER, AND SUPERINtendent, he had also become a teacher in the early 1960s. Most of his classes, which would gather on Sunday afternoons, consisted of five or six students, and for a few years included Eugenio, who started trumpet lessons at about the age of twelve. In the nice weather he'd sometimes hold the lessons out in the park, but in the cooler seasons they'd gather in his apartment. He gave these lessons for free, because it made him feel a little bit like his old teacher Eusebio Stevenson and the kindly Julián García, who had looked out after him many years ago.

And because he didn't like to be alone.

Happy to have these kids around, he'd usually spring for sodas and cupcakes, but if he had a few extra dollars in his pocket he would send Eugenio out to the *bodega* across the street with five dollars to buy a few pounds of cold cuts and some loaves of Italian bread and bags of potato chips, so that these boys, some of whom did not always have much to eat, might have a nice lunch afterwards.

Gathered in his living room, the boys would wait for the maestro to come out with an armful of records and his portable record player. Depending on his mood, he would just teach technique or, as he did on this day, play some mambos and old *canciones* and drift off into memoryville, relating to them some of the very same things that his teacher, Eusebio Stevenson, had once told him:

"Now, the rumba is derived from the *guaguancó*, which goes back to long ago, many hundreds of years ago, when the Spaniards first brought the flamenco style of music to Cuba, and this Spanish style, mixed up with the rhythms of the Africans, played on the drums, led to the early forms of the rumba. The word 'rumba' means magnificence. The slaves who first danced this were usually chained up at night by the ankle, so they were forced to limit their movements: when they danced their rumbas, it was with much movement of the hips and little movement of the feet. That's the authentic rumba from the nineteenth century, with drums and voices and melody lines that sound Spanish and African at the same time . . . And what is the African? The African always sounds to me like people chanting in a forest, or shouting across a river. These rumbas were first played with only trumpets and drums. When you hear modern music and there's a drum jam session, a *descarga*, it's called the *rumba* section. In any case, these rumbas became popular in the nineteenth century; the small military bands in the towns of Cuba used to spice up their bland waltzes and military marches with rumba rhythms, so that people could let loose and have a good time.

"The mambo, that's another dance. That came along in the 1940s, before you were all born. As a dance it's like the rumba, but with much more movement of the feet, as if the chains had been removed. That's why everybody looks crazy, like a jitterbug on fire, when they dance the mambo."

And he'd show them a few steps, his lumbering body moving nimbly across the floor, and the kids laughed.

"The mambo's freedom comes originally from the *guaracha*, an old country-style dance of Cuba, always played cheerfully.

"The stuff we have now like the *pachanga* is really just a

variation. Most of what you are going to play, if you should ever play with a *conjunto,* will be in 2/4 time, and on top of that you'll hear the claves rhythm in 3/2, which goes one-two-three, one-two.

"Now, most orchestras are going to play their arrangements in the following way, the songs being divided into three sections. The first is the 'head' or the melody; the second is the *coro,* or chorus, where you get the singers harmonizing; and then finally the mambo or rumba section. Machito often uses that way of arranging."

Then he would go on about the different instruments and time schemes, this whole erudite discussion covering up the fact that he did not know how to read music himself.

After this, the actual lessons and playing of instruments, with the most attentive pupils being Miguelito, a stringy Puerto Rican, who wanted to learn the saxophone; Ralphie, Leon the one-eyed plumber's son, and Eugenio, with his decent ear and careful demeanor. Both played the trumpet. Taking turns, each student would get up and play a song and the Mambo King would comment on his technique, and show the student how to correct a flaw. And this method worked, as some of his students excelled and moved on to other teachers who knew how to read music. This was one shortcoming of which the Mambo King was ashamed. While he could sit them down and identify the notes in a written piece, he'd never learned how to read quickly. His face would flush and he would avoid looking into his students' eyes; and forget about playing through complicated jazz scores like the books that Miguelito would turn up with, thick with Duke Ellington arrangements.

Still, there was no shortage of new students. There was always some poor kid from La Salle or Harlem or the Bronx who had heard about a Mambo King who gave free music lessons, and sandwiches, too! And the Mambo King never regretted taking them in. His only bad experience involved a kid with a pock-marked face and gruff, fast-talking manner à la Phil Silvers in the Sergeant Bilko television series. Cesar knew Eddie from the neighborhood. In the middle of his second lesson, the kid went into the kitchen to get a glass of water: later, while getting dressed to go out, the Mambo King couldn't find a gold-banded Timex watch and about twenty dollars in cash that he had left in the drawer of his bedroom dresser. Missing, too, was a Ronson lighter from another drawer and a silver ring which the Mambo King had received from one of his fans. Eddie was caught trying to peddle the ring in a Harlem pawnshop, and did an afternoon in the juvenile pen. He was never allowed back into the house, but the Mambo King continued giving lessons to his other students, a handful of whom ended up as struggling happy professionals.

Now he was listening to Eugenio practicing his trumpet and it was raining. Under a blanket of late-afternoon drowsiness, he listened carefully to the kid, whose playing sounded so distant: at times he confused the raindrops on the window ledges with those which used to fall in Cuba, and turned happily in bed, as if he were a kid again, when sleep was beautiful and the world seemed an endless thing. Slowly he came out of this—his dog Poochie had started barking because a fire alarm down the street had gone off—and he sat up and lit a cigarette. He'd been out real late the night before, working some job in the Bronx, and his head was pounding. Something about a woman in a short green dress kissing him in front of a jukebox, and then something else about a horrendous time trying to get a cab in those dead Bronx streets at four in the morning. Then what could he remember? Last thing he knew, he was resting in bed and could feel his tie being slipped off from around his neck, someone unbuttoning his shirt and trying to pull it off his back. Then the pleasure of his shoes slipping off his feet, and those tired soles refreshed by the cool night air. Then: "Good night, Uncle," and the light clicking off.

Well, he had to get up, had another job to play up in the Bronx, any other night, dear God, but tonight. He would have preferred to stay in bed and fall asleep again to that nice rush of water out the rain gutters, which always reminded him of tropical storms like those he was ecstatic about in Cuba. (A crack of lightning reminded him that he had once been a little kid dancing on the patio tiles and spinning in circles, euphoric under the downpour.) He didn't want the rain to stop, didn't want to get up, but finally left his bed. Eugenio was playing *"Bésame Mucho,"* and as the Mambo King took care of business in the toilet and later shaved, he reflected on how, after nearly two years, the kid was finally starting to show some real improvement. Not that anyone in the family thought he should settle on a musician's life, no way, boy! You had better go to school so you don't have to slave your ass off working with your hands or playing jobs in the middle of nowhere until four in the morning. And understand, there's nothing wrong with entertaining the people or with the enjoyment of playing itself. No, it's everything else eating at you, the long trips home so late, the tiredness in your bones, the kind of dishonest people you have to deal with sometimes, the feeling that one night is going be like another, forever and forever.

Unless you're very very lucky, he'd tell the kid, you have to work hard. Unless you're like Frank Sinatra or Desi Arnaz with a beautiful house in California, you know, kid? I advise you to be sensible. Get yourself a nice girl, get married, have kids, the works. And if you try to have a family on a musician's salary, you better believe that you're going to have to get a regular job before you know it. So if you want to play, go ahead, but just remember that for you it should be a hobby. I mean to say, boy, you don't want to end up like your uncle, do you?

(The kid would always lower his head.)

Later, when he went upstairs, the kid had already eaten his dinner and was waiting anxiously for his uncle in the living room. In the kitchen, the Mambo King joined pretty Leticia and dour Pedro at the table and ate his meal while listening to Delores carry on about the boy: "You must tell him to calm down. He's going to get in trouble. Do you understand?"

They'd been having trouble with him for the last year. He still wasn't getting along with his stepfather and had started to run in the streets with some bad kids. They'd tried everything: they'd gone after him with a belt, taken him to the priest, to the youth counselor, and on one occasion Delores had called the police. But none of it worked: the kid reacted by running away and hopping a train that took him in the dead of winter to Buffalo, New York, where he holed up in a rail yard for three days and nearly caught pneumonia. And she wasn't even happy about him going off on those late-night jobs with the Mambo King, but at least that was better than hanging around in the street.

"Just talk some sense into him," Delores pleaded with him. "Tell him it's not good for him to be like that."

"I will."

On their way to these jobs he'd tell Eugenio to listen to his mother, to forget about the kids on the street. "You know I'd never lay a finger on you, boy, but if you keep going this way, I'll have to do something about it."

"Would you do that to me?"

"Well, I, I, I wouldn't want to, because you're my blood" —and he'd be thinking about the beatings he'd once received —"but you should absolutely respect your mother."

"I don't respect her no more."

"No, no, nephew, don't be that way."

But he could see how the kid might be pissed at Pedro. The guy was a stiff.

"Eugenio, think what you want to think, but just remember that your mother's a good woman and that she'd never do anything that's not right. I mean, you shouldn't be so angry just because she chose to marry again. She did it for you, do you understand?"

And the kid would nod.

"I heard you today," he said. "You sounded good."

Then: "Let's go."

The club was up a steep hill, a narrow stairway, past a NO GUNS PLEASE sign, a little old lady selling admission tickets by the door. By the time they'd arrived, they were chilled to the bone. The warmth of the crowd, comforting.

Voices:

"Hey, look who's here!"

"*Mambero!*"

"Nice to see you. This is my nephew, a giant, huh?"

Then: "Good, everybody's here."

Sometimes, when he'd rap Eugenio on the back, hitting the frame of a solid man, he would marvel at the passage of time.

When they reached the little wooden platform that was their stage, he met with his musicians, all of whom he had played with before, but who had never met Eugenio.

"He's learning the trumpet," the Mambo King said to their pianist, Raúl.

"Then let him sit in."

"No, he's happy just to play the bongos."

And just to be with me. When he was younger, a few years back, the kid used to stay in my apartment all day, watching television and doing as he pleased. Once he asked me, "Uncle, can I come and live with you?"

And I answered him, "But, *chico,* you almost do."

That night the Mambo King sang well. He played his usual sets, mixing fast and slow songs, joking with the audience and sometimes stepping out onto the floor. Spinning around (as he used to in the rain, how he sometimes wished to be under that wind-torn tree), he would catch sight of his nephew sitting on a black drum case, tapping away on a pair of bongo drums set between his knees, and looking nearly like a grown man. Soon enough, that would be the case and the kid would leave their household and things would never be the same again. Was that why he always hung around his uncle? What could that kid be thinking? Maybe he just concentrated on the music or day-dreamed—but about what?

"Do you want to play the trumpet later? We can do *'Bésame Mucho,'* would you like that?"

"No, I'm happy just sitting here."

He let him have his way, never forcing the kid. Still, he couldn't understand why his nephew practiced so much, if he didn't want to play.

"Are you sure?"

"Yes, *hombre!* Come on," said another of the musicians.

But he kept to the bongos. And just then the Mambo King thought that Eugenio was even more reserved than his father, his poor father.

Playing a trumpet solo, during *"Santa Isabel de las Lajas,"* he realized that he simply did not understand Eugenio. Delores kept telling him that the boy was angry, that he would throw things down from the walls, had scattered Pedro's bookkeeping ledgers and his stamp collection all over the floor, that he had been caught running through the streets breaking windows. That in the street he was quick-tempered, starting fights over nothing.

"Don't you see that, Cesar?"

If that was so, why was the boy so gentle with me?

There he was, tapping the drums, how could anyone say that things weren't right with him?

You know, boy, I'll be sorry when you're out of the house.

Tilting his head back, he drifted aloft on the flow of notes, drifted into his vision of Eugenio:

A boy who used to fall asleep on his lap in midafternoon, a boy who would hold him steady on some nights when they walked along the street and he needed someone to help him on the way. A hand touching his face, the quiet boy who preferred television in his uncle's apartment, rather than in his own. (The boy loving that program on which me and my brother had appeared.) And he was a respectful boy, a boy he'd take to Coney Island and to the Palisades amusement park or to visit friends like Machito or to the market on 125th Street. A boy who knew how to say "Come on" to him, when his spirits were low as they were on that afternoon three years ago when, standing on the stoop and looking around at the world, he shuddered with longing for his mother, whom he would never see again. A boy who took his hand that day and led him over to the market, where the vendors had set up stalls selling everything from Barbie dolls to Hula Hoops, a boy who had pulled him free of his sadness, running happily from booth to booth and finding him, of all things, a secondhand store that had a rare mambo record by one of Cesar's favorites, Alberto Iznaga!

That was all he had to know, all that he knew, all that he would ever know about the kid.

If I could give you anything in the world, I would, boy, but I don't have that power.

He leaned back from the microphone, touching Eugenio's head.

Later he stood by the window watching the street, with a drink in hand, whiskey that made him ache a little less.

I would have brought your Papi back in a second if I could.

"Eugenio, do me a favor and get me another drink?"

"Yes, Uncle."

I would have snapped my fingers . . .

And when he got the drink and started to belt it down, he

tried to reassure the boy: "Don't worry, I'm too tired to stay out late tonight."

Around one-thirty, they played a final set: *"El Bodeguero,"* *"Tú,"* *"Siempre en Mi Corazón,"* *"Frenesí,"* and *"Qué Mambo!"*

And there they were at three o'clock in the morning at the 149th Street station, waiting for the express into Manhattan.

The stillness in the station, the boy leaning up against his uncle, and his uncle against a column, black instrument case by his side.

THE MAMEY TREE RESTAURANT, a huge place on Fifth Avenue and 18th Street in Brooklyn, with two dining rooms and a juice and sandwich bar that wrapped around the corner and opened to the sidewalk.

Its owner, Don Emilio, would pass his days seated in a wheelchair by the cash register, sternly scanning the dining room. He wore gleamy metal-rim glasses and his *guayabera* shirt pockets were stuffed with panatelas and red-nibbed, shiny ball-point pens, always arranged neatly in a row. His legs dangled, hopelessly, in a pair of black *pantalones*.

The poor man had arrived in the States, settled in Brooklyn, and like many other Cubans worked like an animal to save money and start a business, the restaurant, which flourished, and then boom, a stroke filled his legs with sawdust and he ended up in the wheelchair, paralyzed below his waist. "Used to be a nice guy," the waiters told Cesar. "Used to be proud of the whole works and treat us good, only now all he thinks about is that people are robbing him . . . the same way that God robbed him of his legs."

Walking into the crowded dining room this Saturday afternoon, the Mambo King sheepishly removed his hat and with head bowed said, "Good afternoon, Don Emilio."

"How are you, my friend?"

"Good, Don Emilio. I've come for my guitar. I left it here last night."

(Because he had been drunk and did not want to take it on the subway.)

"My wife told me. I think she put it in the back."

"Yes?"

Through a pair of double doors he made his way into the bustling kitchen, where three cooks were working over huge, many-burner stoves and ovens, baking chicken and pork chops and making pots of rice, broth and fish soup, frying plantains and boiling *yuca*.

"The boss sent me back here for my guitar."

"Carmen's taken it upstairs. She said she didn't think the heat would be good for it."

Then the cook, in a long, sauce-stained apron, pointed out to a back door that opened into a yard. "Up those stairs, on the second floor."

Across a small back yard where a tree and flowers had managed to grow through the cracked concrete floor, he made his way into another doorway and up the steps to Don Emilio's apartment on the second floor. When his wife opened the door, the apartment was glowing with sunlight and smelled like roses. Inside, set out on every table, desk, and sill, bouquet after bouquet of flowers, so many that their colors floated through the room.

(And he remembers again how his mother in Cuba used to fill the house with flowers.)

The Mambo King took off his hat and, flashing a warm smile, said quietly, "Carmencita, I've come to get my guitar."

A pretty woman in her late thirties, with a vaguely defeated air about her, Don Emilio's wife, Carmen, was wearing a clean, matronly, pink sleeveless dress. With her coiffure of hair-sprayed curls, long eyelashes, thick lipstick, and mascara, she seemed ready to step out. No children in the apartment, a few photographs set out here and there in the room, including a wedding picture taken down in Holguín, Cuba, in a plaza, before the revolution, when Don Emilio had the use of his legs. (He was this tall, grinning fellow, holding his wife close.) An antique crucifix over the couch (And, Jesus, promise to help me), electric sun-rayed clock, a big color TV set, a plastic-covered couch. It was an old apartment with a brand-new bathroom, where there was a fancy-looking hospital-style commode with handles fitted onto the seat.

"Please come in, Cesar."

"Okay, but I only came to get the guitar."

In its black case, the guitar was leaning up against the radiator.

"I wanted to talk with you," Carmen said.

The Mambo King shook his head. "I'll listen, but if you're going to talk to me about your husband, I want no part of it. I have nothing against Don Emilio and . . ."

"And I have nothing," she said desperately. "When I'm not working downstairs, I'm here, alone. He won't even let me go out on the street unless he's with me in the wheelchair."

Then: "*Hombre . . .*" and she undid the front buttons of her dress, from her neck to the hem of her skirt, and spread it open. She wasn't wearing anything underneath. She had a short and plumpish body, her bottom nice and round, and large stretch-marked breasts. Resting back on the couch, she told him, "Cesar, I'm waiting."

When he hesitated, she sat forward, undid his trousers, and fondled him so that his thing unwillingly (he liked Don Emilio) sprang into the world and she wrapped her fingers around him and fed upon him as if she were a small creature of the forest seeking honey from a hive.

Mother Nature took over, and with his trousers and drawers pulled down below his knees, he made terrified love to her, afraid that Don Emilio or one of his brothers might find out about them. The first time he had been down in the cold-storage room, a year ago, when Don Emilio was sick in bed with the flu, and it was very late and he had been playing his usual night's work (strolling among the noisy tables playing "*Malagueña*," singing "*Bésame Mucho*" and "*Cuando Caliente el Sol*") and was waiting around to get paid, when she told him to come back with her to the office so that the waiters would not see how much she was going to give him; and then she pushed open the door of the cold-storage room, hitched her skirt up over her waist, and that was that, as he was a little drunk and her panties had fallen down nicely over her black-nyloned, red-high-heeled legs. The phone in the office next door kept ringing—Don Emilio calling to see when she would come home—and the melody of Beny More's "*Santa Isabel de las Lajas*" came in faintly through the walls, his knees scraping against fifty-pound burlap sacks of lentils, and Doña Carmen's face crushed against his chest (and biting whatever she could reach), and then everything ended quickly. It hadn't taken her more than two minutes to get what she had wanted. Afterwards he had felt bad, for in the days when he had first started playing music again and would go from restaurant to restaurant looking for work, to raise money for the family in Cuba, Don Emilio had been one of the first to hire him.

But he had to admit that once they had started, there wasn't much chance of stopping . . . Just her hand on him would have been enough, and she had done more than that; thick as a sink J-joint, his thing was slowly entering her. (She kept stopping him every three inches or so and would throw back her head and grind her hips until the tight hot space blossomed with moisture and unfurled like silk and then she would let in more, whipping her head from side to side and grinding her teeth to suppress her moans.) Once he was all the way inside her, it took him only seven strokes, his immense body smothering her, her pelvic bone hitting hard against his, everything squirmy underneath, the tip of his penis licking her cervical flower, and Carmen saying, "Don Emilio was once built like you. I used to call him *caballo.*"

Then it was all over; she broke into pieces and kicked over a lamp and he barely had time to get dressed, say "Good day," and drink down a glass of water. His livid bone tucked back into his trousers, he found himself standing outside her door, anxiously, as if he'd just narrowly avoided being hit by a bus.

Downstairs, with his guitar case in hand, and into the kitchen, and crossing into the dining room, and thinking about Carmen's rump and how she had placed his hand over her mouth as she came, flicking her tongue in and out between his index and forefinger, and Cuba and Don Emilio and the crowded room, smell of pork chops and black beans and rice and fried plantains, and wondered if they'd smell Doña Carmen on his hands or his face. Making his way toward the door, he buttoned his London Fog overcoat, and was waving goodbye to his friends until next week, when Don Emilio called him over.

"Cesar, do me a favor while you're here," Don Emilio said to the Mambo King, holding him firmly by the wrist. "Sing that nice little number for those newlyweds over there. He's the son of a good friend of mine."

"Yes, if you want me to, Don Emilio."

"It would make me happy."

And Don Emilio gave Cesar a friendly rap on the shoulders and the Mambo King got out his guitar, slung its velvet strap over his shoulders, and walked over to the newlyweds' table. First he sang the Ernesto Lecuona song *"Siempre en Mi Corazón,"* and then, strumming two chords softly, an A-minor and an E-major (the opening chords to "Beautiful María of My Soul"), he spoke these words:

"Children, may God bless you on your journey. Now you are entering a special time in your lives, precious but difficult . . . There will be trials and happinesses awaiting you, and there will be times when you, as wife, and you, as husband, will perhaps quarrel with the other and wish that you had never made this bond. And your hearts may wander, and sickness may bring despair. But if these things should ever happen, remember that this life passes quickly and that a life spent without love is lonely, while the love that a man and a woman feel for each other and their children shines like sunlight in the heart. And this sunlight accompanies you forever, protects you all your life, even unto the final days when you are old together and the days are not so long, when you may fear the time when your Maker calls you from the world. But just remember your mutual love will always preserve you and it will be your comfort forever."

And when he finished, Cesar bowed and the young couple, aquiver with joy, thanked him.

"Bueno," he said to Don Emilio. "I have to get back to Manhattan."

"Thank you, my friend"—and he patted Cesar's back and gave the Mambo King a five-dollar bill. "For your trouble, my friend. We'll be seeing you next week, yes?"

"Yes, Don Emilio."

Nervous and vaguely elated, he rode home to La Salle Street. Inside his bathroom, he undid his trousers to wash himself over the sink: even though he felt like a traitor, the image of Carmencita's furious passion was like the lick of a thick female tongue over his member, and just like that he watched, as if from the mouth of a dolphin, spout three clear drops of semen, stretched like a silver wire between the tip of his thing to that point in the air where it snapped free of his dense finger.

Aᴺᴰ ᴛʜᴇʀᴇ ᴡᴀꜱ ᴛʜᴀᴛ ᴍᴏʀɴɪɴɢ when he had gone upstairs to have a nice Sunday breakfast with Delores and the kids. He was enjoying a *chorizo*-and-fried-egg sandwich when he heard Frankie the Exterminator honking his horn from the street.

"Yo!" Frankie called up into the window.

Down below, Frankie was happy with excitement.

Cesar went downstairs.

"You know my friend Georgie from Trinidad?"

"Yeah."

"Well, he wants us to go down there for carnival."

He started to think that he hadn't had a nice vacation lately, trips everywhere to the Bronx and Brooklyn, but nowhere else.

"Thing is, Georgie's got a house there, and all we would have to pay is the airfare and whatever we eat, which is cheap there."

By the following Thursday night, Cesar, Frankie, and Georgie were dancing in a carnival line. Wearing a sheet and a bull's head, Cesar danced, blowing his trumpet. Frankie was the devil; Georgie, a naughty harlot. They stormed through the crowded streets, climbed onto the back of flower-covered floats, threw pennies and candies at the children, flirted with the pretty women in their one-piece bathing suits and bikinis, by day enjoying the tropical sun and by night the lantern-lit porches, party houses out of whose windows blared the music of that incomparable Trinidadian, the Mighty Sparrow, whom Cesar had admired since the mid-1950s.

The crowd was so merry and drunk that the women took off their tops and the men, being swinish louts, lost control, pinching asses, grabbing breasts, and stealing kisses. The masks helped, as they did away with the lines and the sagginess of the men's once handsome faces. Flirting back, the women shook their hips and, audaciously rolling their tongues around their lips, grabbed their most audacious parts, grabbed the men, too. In every alley there was at least one drummer, one trumpeter, one blaring speaker, and a half-dozen couples shamelessly fornicating. There was so much lovemaking going on, so much dancing and cavorting, that the streets smelled of sweat, perfume, and sperm. Packs of wild hounds barked and howled their joy. Then they spilled into their friend Georgie's little house, with its pink and light blue walls, and rolled around on the floor, laughing and kissing their new lady companions.

The men were having such a good time they hardly slept. The first night, a half hour's worth of sleep was all that Cesar had. They'd bought two cases of rum and filled the house with women, soft and delicious girls of sixteen and overripe but willing ladies of fifty. Georgie turned up his record player as loud as it would go: everybody danced some more. Hour after hour they listened to the Mighty Sparrow and his celebrated calypso orchestra, and when they weren't dancing and drinking, they were back on the streets howling like the roaming packs of wild hounds.

It would have been a dream vacation save for the frailties and limits of endurance of the human body in men approaching their fifties. All the flowing blood, the rum-sludge-filled stomachs, the dizzying heads, the spurting sexual organs, the bubbling digestive systems continuing without respite. These were fellows who had never read health magazines with their articles and medical studies about how many times a man was supposed to get an erection. But these three got it up, breathing the heady air of miasmic, stupefying vapors and living for fun.

AND WHY SUDDENLY REMEMBER another friend who worked as a caretaker in the cemetery near Edgar Allan Poe's house up in the Bronx?

"No easy job working here at this cemetery," the man told the Mambo King. "Tell you that, *coño*. A lot of voodoo and *santería* people come here to hold ceremonies because it's conse-crated ground, and I know this because sometimes in the morn-ing I find blood on the ground, ashes and small-animal bones strewn about the graves: sometimes the tombstones are splattered with blood."

"I would be frightened."

"No, these people are not so bad, personally they are quite nice. I see them sometimes coming by in the mornings. Tourists too, people from Europe. See"—and he pointed across the way. "Just down that way stands the cottage of the writer Edgar Allan Poe, that's where he lived for a few years. That's the house where his wife died of tuberculosis in the wintertime. They were so poor that he didn't even have a cent for firewood and he had to cover her up with newspapers, and he would put his house cats over her so that she might be warmer. But she died anyway, the poor man by her side. In any case, the *santeros* say that his house emanates a great supernatural force and that spirits hover around it, and so that's why they especially like this cemetery: the care-taker of Poe's house, who also works for the city, told me that he sometimes finds bones and blood and bird feathers scattered over the ground by the entrance."

He remembered more:
There had been the *pachanga* in 1960.
The bossa nova in 1962.
The Mozambique and the bugaloo in 1965.
After that, he couldn't figure out what was happening.
One thing he never got used to in those days was the change in fashion. It certainly wasn't 1949 anymore. It seemed that ele-gance had gone down the toilet and the young people of that time were dressing in circus costumes. The men wearing Army fatigues and big thick boots, the women plaid lumberjack shirts and formless, loose-hanging dresses. It was all beyond him. Then it was bell-bottomed trousers, paisley jackets, and impossibly wide-collared shirts. And the hair. Sideburns, muttonchops, wal-rus mustaches, hair down to the shoulders. (Even Eugenio had been that way, wearing it in a ponytail down his back and looking like a forlorn Indian.) He'd shake his head and in his humble way

try to maintain the elegance of his youth, even if Leticia called him "Mr. Old-fashioned." But, turning around, he saw that even many of his fellow Latin musicians had changed, wearing their hair long and sporting beards and thick Afros. *Carajo,* they were going with the times!

That's why, when he attempted a recording comeback in 1967, he put out a 45 rpm called "Psychedelic Baby" on the Hip Records label out of Marcy Avenue, Brooklyn, a basic Latin bugaloo, with a hybrid Latin-rock improvisation on the flip side (he was using young musicians) built upon a twelve-bar blues progression, a boogie-woogie spiced up by congas and 3/5/7 harmonies on the horns. (For that record he used a young Brooklyn pianist named Jacinto Martínez, Manny his bassist, a sax player named Poppo, Pito on drums, and three unknowns on the horns.) The record sold two hundred copies and was most notable for its black-and-white cover, the only photograph of the Mambo King in a goatee à la Pérez Prado. Dressed in *guayabera,* wrap-around shades, matching blue linen trousers and white golden-buckled shoes, he had posed for the photograph in front of the old 1964 World's Fair Unisphere in Flushing Meadows, Queens.

(There was one more recording comeback that same year, a 33 LP called the "The Fabulous Cesar Castillo Returns!" which included a new bolero "Sadness" and a new version of "Beautiful María of My Soul" done with five instruments accompanying Cesar on the guitar and vocals. A memorable recording that rapidly disappeared into the 39 cents bins of Woolworth's and John's Bargain stores everywhere.)

Soon afterwards Cesar tried to audition for a spot at the Cheetah discotheque and was passed over for an act called Johnny Bugaloo.

And 1967 was the year that his brothers Eduardo and Miguel and their families finally left Cuba and settled in Miami, leaving one brother, Pedrocito, and their father behind. (The old man, white-haired and cantankerous in his seventies, still worked the farm with his son. The very day that the Mambo King sat in his room in the Hotel Splendour years later, he was still going strong, an old, bent-over man cursing and talking to himself and perhaps daydreaming about his youth in a place called Fan Sagrada in Galicia, Spain.) They were in their late fifties, but their sons were young and ambitious and eventually ventured out into their own businesses—a dry-cleaning service and clothing store. When the Mambo King went down to visit them, they were pure gratitude, as, by then, he had been sending them money for over five years. They told the Mambo King that he could come and stay with them in their crowded and cheerful households any time he wanted to. He did so on four different occasions over the years, but became a little saddened by the sight of his two hickish brothers growing old on chairs in front of the stores in Little Havana, their faces heavy with the jowls of daily monotony and their eyes dreamy, while their sons charged forward, selling the latest Malibu and New York fashions to rich jet-setting South Americans and filling their houses with appliances and putting enough money away so they could send their kids off to law and business school! Visiting them, he always had the feeling that he had stepped into a retirement home as his older brothers moved through the bustle of family life and enterprise like ghosts and drove with their sons to get a little cup of *café negro* in the evenings in cars with .38 revolvers stashed in paper bags under the front seat—who could be happy with that? (Then, too, there would be their visit to New York, when the cousins met the cousins, the newly arrived young Cubans checking out long-haired Eugenio and quiet, beautiful Leticia, neither party saying a word to the other the whole evening.)

The following year he dented his trumpet while he and a pickup group were playing a block party in the Bronx. That was a period of "racial unrest," as the newspapers called it. Martin Luther King was dead, Malcolm X was dead, and young black people were restless. (The day after Martin Luther King, Jr., was shot, the stores all up and down Broadway and Amsterdam closed up and burly Irish policemen stood on every corner waiting for the riots to spread south of 125th Street.) They were performing in the Roosevelt High School playground and found themselves surrounded by a crowd that wanted to hear a song called "Cool Jerk" and were clapping and chanting that name, while the group of seven musicians continued to play their mambos, cha-cha-chas, and old standards like *"Bésame Mucho"* and *"Tú."* But some in the crowd were drinking and soon started throwing bottles to where all the Puerto Ricans, Dominicans, and Cubans were hang-

ing out, what the newspapers would call the "Spanish contin-
gent," and they threw bottles back and someone had a knife, zip,
and people started to shout and rush the bandstand, and zip, the
conga player was slashed in the arm and the bass player was
kicked in the stomach by someone trying to steal his wallet.
When this started, Cesar was in the midst of a mellow solo,
sounding nice and feeling good because he and his old pal,
Frankie the Exterminator, and his bassist, ex-Mambo King
Manny, had killed a case of Rheingold beer before the show.
Some kid came toward Cesar to steal his guitar, which he had set
down behind him, but he took his trumpet and bopped the kid
on the head with it. Then things were calmer. The cops came.
The representative from Rheingold, one of the block party's
sponsors, pleaded for order, was booed down, and El Conjunto
Castillo packed up and went home. Things like that happened to
musicians from time to time, and made them laugh.

AND NOW THE MEMORY OF THAT
woman again struggling down the escalator of Macy's department store, overloaded with Christmas packages. The Mambo
King had bought his niece and nephew their Christmas toys, a
slim-banded watch for his sister-in-law, and a Japanese transistor
radio for her husband, Pedro. *La Nochebuena*—Christmas Eve
—was one of his favorite times of year: the man would make trips
downtown to the docks and over to the big department stores, to
Chinatown and Delancey Street, accumulating boxes of scarves,
gloves, socks, hot watches, record albums, and bottles of imported
perfume and cologne that he would give out to his acquaintances
and friends. And he loved receiving gifts: the year before, the
"family" had given him a white silk scarf. He loved the way it
looked when he wore his overcoat and black-brimmed hat and
soft Spanish-leather gloves. He was wearing that scarf and looking very dapper when he saw the woman's shopping bag split
open, her presents tumbling down the stairs. A gentleman, he
stooped over, helping her with the packages and, as it turned out,
got on the same train with her, an uptown number 2.

He lied to her, saying that he was going that way, and asked her if she'd need help getting those packages home. He charmed her with his politeness, and when he told her that he was a musician, she liked that very much, too. She lived up on Allerton Avenue, an hour out of his way, but he accompanied the woman to the door of her building, anyway. By her doorway she thanked him and they exchanged addresses, wishing each other a Merry Christmas. A week later she called him from her job with the telephone company—she was an operator—and one night they went on a date, ending up in a Sicilian restaurant where everyone knew her. Later he escorted this woman home—her name was Betty, he recalls now in the Hotel Splendour—politely bidding her farewell and bowing. She struck him as an Old World type of woman, with whom he couldn't be forward. He took her out to the movies, to restaurants, and one night she turned up at a dance he and his pickup musicians were playing, where she spent the evening dancing with strangers. But she would not pass in front of the stage without giving him a big smile.

When he seduced her at three in the morning, in a bedroom decorated in Mediterranean colors—aqua blue, passion pink, Roman orange—she removed her white black-felt-buttoned dress, then her slip, and beneath that a pair of flowery-crotched panties and garters. When he'd taken his clothes off, his erection leapt out into the world and he started to kiss her and his hands went all over her body; each time he was about to mount her, however, she'd push him away. So he turned off the light, thinking that she felt inhibited, but then she flipped it back on. He got to the point where his member was weeping copiously as he pressed against her clamped-shut legs. Finally he sprang back, sitting against the bed frame. His penis, which he'd wedged under her leg, leapt free and smacked his belly.

In his room in the Hotel Splendour, he laughed, shaking his head, despite the pain. The Mambo King had looked at her, saying, "Jesus, I'm only human, woman. Why are you torturing me so?"

"It's just that I've never done it before."

"And how old are you?"

"Forty."

"Forty—well, don't you think it's about time?"

"No, I'd have to be married first."

"Then what are we doing here?" And he turned red in the face and was about to get dressed and leave. But then the woman showed him what she liked to do, taking his big thing ("It feels heavy") into her mouth, and went at him like a pro, and when he started to come, Betty squirmed and twisted, grinding herself into the bed, and then, as her body flushed and her face turned the color of a spring rose, she came, too.

Heartened, the Mambo King thought the woman had to be joking about her virginity, but when he tried to mount her again, she locked her legs and solemnly told him, "Please, anything else but this." And then she grasped his thing and began sucking him again, and when he came, she did, too, the same way as before. Then they fell asleep, but he woke around five-thirty because she was suckling him again. It was strange, waking up in the dark of the room, to find her moving up and down over his thing. Her mouth and tongue, wet with saliva, felt good on him, but she'd bitten him up so much and stretched and pulled and bent his thing to the point where he was feeling sore. He never thought he'd ever say this to a woman, but he did: "Please give me a rest."

On Christmas, Cesar held a raucous party in his apartment. First he spent the day with the family upstairs, eating the roast turkey that Ana María and Delores had prepared, and fulfilling his avuncular duties. By the evening, he was back in his apartment playing host to musician and dance-hall friends who turned up with their families, so that by six-thirty in the evening Cesar's bachelor apartment was overflowing with children and babies, pots of food and pastries, and eating, dancing, singing, drinking adults.

Bongos playing, Bing Crosby, cha-cha-cha out the phonograph, and the living-room floor sagging under the feet of happy dancers.

When the woman called him around eight-thirty to wish him Merry Christmas, he was dizzy with fantasies about making love to her. Drunk and infused with the holiday spirit, he found himself saying, "I love you, baby. I have to see you again, soon."

"Then come here, tonight."

"Okay, baby."

Leaving Frankie and Bernardito in charge of the proceedings—"I'll be back in two hours"—he made his way to the northeast Bronx. With the determination of an aviator about to circumnavigate the globe, he appeared at her door, vibrant with energy, and holding a bottle of champagne and a carton of food from the party. All the way up he had been thinking, "I'm not going to let her get away this time."

And within a minute of walking through her door, they were on the bed kissing and fondling one another—she was feeling a little tipsy and amorous after attending a family party that day—and then events were about to unfold again in the usual way when he started to wrestle around with her on the bed, both laughing as if it were a joke, until he decided to part her legs, and this time, when she shut them close as a vise, he really used his strength and forced them apart and so wide that the inevitability of penetration was like heated breath flowing out of her vagina, and even though she had started to plead with him, saying, "Cesar, I mean it when I say stop, so please stop," he couldn't. With the smell of her femininity thick in his nostrils and his skin feverishly hot, he didn't hear her or didn't want to hear her: lowering himself and bringing the weight of his body to bear, he entered her and she felt as if she were being occupied by a living creature the weight and length of a two-year-old cat. When he had his climax, the Mediterranean colors of that bedroom swirled inside his head, and when he calmed down, he thought that he might have been a little rash in his impetuosity, but hell, he was just being a man. Besides, he'd treat her well, touch her hair, call her pretty, make everything all right with compliments.

But she was crying, and no matter what he tried, kissing her neck and brushing her hair away from her eyes, kissing her breasts, apologizing to her, and offering never never to force himself on her that way—"It was passion, woman. Do you understand? A man like me can't help himself sometimes, do you understand?"—she kept on crying. Cried for the two hours that he sat beside her by the bed, feeling as if he were the cruelest man in the world, yet unable to understand why she was so upset.

"It was about time for you," he said, patting her shoulder and making things even worse.

The Mambo King remembered that she continued to cry as he dressed and was crying as he left for the street. He never saw her again. As he sat drinking in the Hotel Splendour, he sort of shook his head, remembering her and still puzzling over how a woman, voracious with her mouth, could be so offended and hurt when all he wanted was that she take care of him in the more normal, natural way.

I N THOSE DAYS HE ALWAYS seemed busy with his superintendent's duties, busy with music and with women, though not as many as he used to find, but enough that every few months Delores or Ana María would see him walking out of the building in a blue suit and looking dapper, on his way to meet his latest flame. There had been some nice ones like Celia, one of Ana María's friends, who had overwhelmed the Mambo King with her strength and her powers to control men and who had him figured out—"What you have to do is learn to be content with what you have in this world, *hombre*"—but he never wanted to hear that. They were together for about six months and the family had hopes that she would calm the Mambo King down, slide him into a life of domestic tranquillity, and help him stop drinking.

But he broke off that love affair, saying, "I wasn't meant to be tied down." And he meant it literally, because Celia refused to take shit from him. She was a hard Cuban woman who'd lived in New York for most of her life and had always fended for herself. She smoked cigars if she felt like it, cursed with the best of them, and was always hustling around with different businesses, turning up at Christmas to sell the ladies perfume and with shopping bags of discount Korean and Japanese toys. And she was always out on Broadway in a wool cap and lumberjack's jacket selling the semi-dry Christmas trees which she would buy in Poughkeepsie and drive back herself in a black pickup truck. Scandalous in bed—"Let's see if you can satisfy me!"—she carried herself like a man and liked to give Cesar orders, all in the interest of helping him out. She was known locally as something of a clairvoyant and was always sensing presences in the house —his mother, his dead brother—and had wanted to take charge of his life, push him forward, play up his nearly glorious musical past, and encourage him to cultivate people in power like Machito and Desi Arnaz.

"Why don't you go to California, see if he would give you a job. You say he's so nice. You have to use your connections to get ahead in this world."

Why wouldn't he? Because he never wanted to bother Machito or Desi Arnaz, didn't want them to think he might use their friendship for personal gain. And while he knew she was well-intentioned, he just couldn't stand, after so many years of bachelorhood, to be told that he should change his ways. One night, when she had come over to watch television with him, he got drunk and then wanted to go out dancing. And when she told him, "It's too late, Cesar," he said, "To hell with this domesticity nonsense, I'll go out alone!" That's when she pushed him down into his easy chair and tied him up with a fifty-foot piece of laundry line, and told him, "No, *señor*, you're not going anywhere."

At first he laughed and had a change of heart and said, "Come on, Celia, you know, I promise you I won't go anywhere."

"No, this is to teach you a lesson that when you have an engagement with someone, as you do with me, that's it. No going out, no doing as you please. You may have been able to do what you wanted with these other *fulanas*, but forget about that with me."

So he remained still and then told her to release him, but quite seriously, with the laugh gone out of his face, and when she refused, he wanted to probe the limits of his Herculean physicality and tried to break the rope by expanding his biceps and chest, but the rope did not break. Then he gave up and, defeated, fell asleep. In the early morning, both Celia and the rope were gone.

That was it, as much as he liked her, as much as everybody thought that she and he could be happy together, as much as he felt like bringing her flowers and liked the way she looked out for him; she had pushed him too far: "You crossed a line with me, Celia. No woman"—and he was pointing his finger around at her face—"can be allowed to do that to a man. You have humiliated and dishonored me. You have tried to reduce me in my stature. This act is something I cannot tolerate or forgive! Ever."

"Forgive? I was trying to keep you from hurting yourself."

"I have spoken, woman. Now you must live with the consequences of your act."

That was that, and he found himself another woman, Estela, who would walk her two miniature poodles in the park and who drove the Mambo King crazy with the pleasant way she'd address those doll-sized canines, whose coats she had dyed pink and on whose heads she had affixed enormous red ribbons and bell collars, the dogs absolutely despising him and scratching at the bedroom door and yipping and jumping up and down whenever he started to carouse with her. It would take a long time to arouse Estela, to turn the leathery firmness between her legs into the soft down of dewy rose petals, and by then the animals would have given up and would stretch out before the bedroom door, morose and defeated. And it always seemed that the moment he had penetrated Estela—she was a trembling, tense woman who worked in the principal's office of the local Catholic school —the hounds would begin to weep and whine so sadly that their squeals of displeasure always brought out Estela's maternal nature, and she would disengage herself from him and, naked, attend to the poor little things, while the Mambo King would lie back and daydream about throwing the beasts out the window.

Then there had been the professor of Spanish language from the university, whom Cesar had met one morning while getting a haircut over at the beauty salon. (He loved it when Ana María or Delores pressed close to cut his hair.) She was named Frieda and had once been badly hurt by a love affair in Sevilla, Spain, a few years before he met her, and so she accepted when the Mambo King asked her to go out to a restaurant, loving the opportunity to practice her Spanish and to see a little bit of his world. She was about thirty-five years old and the Mambo King was already in his early fifties, slightly plump around the center, but definitely on the dapper side, holding doors for her and always treating whenever they'd go out. He would take her to nice restaurants and dance halls, teach her how to *merengue,* and she would haul him off into thickly carpeted and chandeliered rooms at the university, where they would attend readings and lectures by the leading intellectuals of Latin America and Spain. He never knew what was going on, but had very much liked hearing the writer Borges, who had a very pleasant, avuncular manner about him, the kind of fellow, Cesar figured, who would go out and have a few drinks with you. And that's why he shook Borges's hand (the poor man was blind). Another thing about the woman was that she was very fastidious in bed. The first time they made love she took a tape measure and figured out the Mambo King's length from the bottom of his testicles to the tippy-tip of his member and wrote this happy figure down in a book she used as her diary. Then, frantic from the Spanish brandy and flamenco music, they made lascivious love. She was very serious and very nice, he used to think, but he had no use for her friends and always felt like an aborigine at those cultural gatherings. When that one ended, it had really hurt Delores, who sometimes accompanied them to those lectures. (She, too, saw Borges and went out to the library the next day and read one of his books.)

There were others. One of these ladies was just for fun. Every year or so, he would fly down to San Juan, Puerto Rico (wincing as the pilot would announce they were flying over the eastern tip of Cuba), and from there take a rickety shuttle plane to Mayagüez, a beautiful city way out on the west coast of the island. He'd take a public car up into the mountains, where time seemed to dissolve, where farmers led their animals down the roads and men still rode horses, until he reached the town where this woman lived. He'd met her at a dance in the Bronx in 1962 and that was the year he first went to bed with her, first walked the dirt road of her town and saw the powerful river rushing downstream from the Dole pineapple cannery. He always had a nice time. She had two grown children and didn't want anything from the Mambo King but companionship. He would bring her gifts—dresses, earrings and bracelets, and perfume, and transistor radios. One year, he made her the gift of a television set. Nice times, he'd remember, playing cards, watching television, and conversing with the family, eating, napping, eating, napping. Around three-thirty it would rain for half an hour, a torrential downpour that would get the river really churning, and he would sit on the porch dozing in enjoyment of that sound (the rain, the river) until the sun came back out and he would bathe, wedging himself against some rocks, as there was usually a powerful and swift current, float on his back and daydream. Kids swimming all around him, kids jumping in from the bank and from the sweet-smelling trees. He'd stay there until it got too crowded for his taste. Around five-thirty the workers from the cannery would come down and jump in and that's when he would gather up his things and go back to the house.

So for two weeks he'd rest. Her name was Carmela and she liked to wear flowery dresses. She was five foot two and must have weighed one hundred and eighty pounds, but she was a pleasure in bed and as sweet-hearted as any woman could be. She owned a record player, which blared out her windows, and whenever he bought her some item of jewelry, she would sit out on the porch waiting for passersby to whom she could show it off. One funny night they went to see the film *Ben Hur* in the small chaotic tenth-run movie theater that had been overrun by light green insects which had come swarming up out of the floorboards after an especially heavy rain. The insects were everywhere, on the chairs, on the customers, flying across the scenes of Judah Ben Hur racing in the Circus Maximus. These insects forced them to leave early. On the way home she tightened her grasp on his hand, as if she never wanted him to leave, but he always had to. When they'd part there were never any troubles.

Then there was a woman named Cecilia, and María, and Anastasia, and on and on.

As if all the music and women and booze in the world would have made a difference about the way he felt inside: still sick to his heart over Nestor.

This sorrow was so adamant five years, ten years, fifteen years later that he was almost tempted to go into a church and pray, when he wanted a hand to cut down through the sky, to touch his face the way his mother used to, soothing him, forgiving him.

Walking up La Salle Street, his head bowed, back slightly stooped—those years of hauling the incinerator-ash-filled cans were starting to get to him, he had some days when he sought repentance through suffering. Sometimes he was unnecessarily rough with himself, driving a wood chisel into his hand one day, or carelessly grasping a hot steamy pipe while working on the boiler. The pain didn't bother him, for all his scars, bruises, and cuts. Because he was a diehard macho and because the pain made him feel as if he were paying his way in this world.

Once, when he was coming home from a job, walking along Amsterdam Avenue, three men swooped down on him, pushed him down on the sidewalk, and started kicking him. The Mambo King rolled over and covered up his head the way he used to when his Papi beat him . . .

A loosened half row of teeth, split lip, aching jaw and sides, somehow all so soothing . . .

Many of his friends were that way, troubled souls. They would always seem happy—especially when they'd talk about women and music—but when they had finished floating through the euphoric layer of their sufferings, they opened their eyes in a world of pure sadness and pain.

Frankie was one of those men. Frankie with the worst breaks in life. He had a son whom he loved very much, but as the kid got older he spit in his old man's face. Cesar was always separating them when they'd fight in the street, and he'd accompany Frankie downtown to the juvenile pen to get the kid out. Then the Vietnam War came along. His son had grown up; six foot one, broad-shouldered and handsome, the big-dicked healthy wise-ass son of a Cuban worker.

And what happened? Came home one day, walking down the street in high jackboots, uniform pressed, and the brim of his military cap a shiny black. Out of his mouth came "Gook this, gook that," and it was off to Vietnam, where on his first jump he landed on a mine and was shipped home in a metal container the size of a Kleenex box. On top of his closed coffin with swirly brass rails, a small American flag, a Purple Heart, a photograph of his handsome face. Cesar held Frankie by the arm throughout the funeral, looked out for Frankie, kept him drunk for a week.

He found some comfort in wrapping his arms around his friend's shoulders and saying, "Now, now this will pass." He found some comfort in feeling the man's pain, as if it somehow aggrandized or glorified his own.

Sometimes there were three or four of them down in his apartment or in his basement workroom, drinking until their faces peeled off and all that was left was shadows.

Sad expressions, twisted mouths, voices so slurry no one could understand what the other was saying.

IN THOSE DAYS HE HAD A FRIEND who was a petty gangster with a reputation for sponsoring businesses. His name was Fernando Pérez and for a long time he had been considered a respectable member of the neighborhood. He'd been around for a long time and ran most of the numbers shops on Amsterdam and upper Broadway. He was squat, square-faced, short-limbed, and stubby-fingered. Gentlemanly in gray leisure suits, he liked to wear a white black-brimmed hat and pointy white crocodile-leather shoes with three-inch heels. He used to dine regularly at Violeta's downtown and at another little place on 127th and Manhattan, where he would sometimes run into Cesar. Although he went around with two rough-looking men, he was the picture of civility. He kept an apartment on La Salle Street, a house in Queens, a house near Mayagüez in Puerto Rico, and a fourth, legendary apartment on 107th between Broadway and Amsterdam. This was known locally as the fortress, and rumor had it that the man kept all his money in a huge safe built into the wall, that to get to that safe you had to break down three heavy doors and fight off numerous bodyguards posted on the stoop, in the hallway, and then in different rooms.

He had been a big Cesar Castillo fan back when. He had courted his wife, Ismelda, at the dance halls where the Mambo Kings played, and on those nights Pérez had always sent the Mambo King a good bottle of champagne to drink at his table. They'd greet each other by the bar of joints like the Park Palace, send greetings to each other's families. Their only dispute, now forgotten, had happened years ago when the Mambo Kings, after their appearance on the *I Love Lucy* show, had been closest to fame. Fernando Pérez had wanted to put them under contract, but Cesar and Nestor wanted nothing to do with him. It had hurt his feelings enough that for about ten years he never said a word to the Mambo King.

One day in 1972, as Cesar was sitting in Violeta's restaurant, Pérez walked in with an entourage of friends. He was flashing a wad of bills and dropping twenties on the head of a young and delighted woman, who squealed and sent kisses flying through the air as she gathered up the money. And he announced, with grandiosity: "I'm buying dinner for everybody in here tonight."

So the patrons applauded him and he sat down. His party dined on suckling pork and platter after platter of rice and beans, *yuca,* and *tostones.* Cesar had noticed him when he walked in, had nodded respectfully. Later, Pérez came over and they embraced as if they were the oldest friends in the world.

"It's good to see you, my old friend," Fernando Pérez told the Mambo King. "We shouldn't lose more time in our friendship. Life is too short."

They talked: Pérez had just gotten over a heart attack, and in the flush of appreciation for finding more time in this world, he had apparently turned into a more magnanimous soul. And there was something else: around Pérez's neck there was a large, glittery, rhinestone-encrusted crucifix, the kind widows wear. This he touched continuously during his inquiry about Cesar's life.

"What am I doing?" the Mambo King said. "I'm working with musicians, nothing that will make me rich, you understand, but I bring in my few dollars here and there. And I'm in the building over there on La Salle Street."

He was saying all this with shame, because long ago Pérez had told him: "Unless you act now to insure your future, people will forget about you just like this." He had snapped his fingers.

Now that he had some distance on all that and he could tolerate things again, the Mambo King began to feel disturbed by what he did not have in this world. He was getting older. He was fifty-four and had been throwing his money away on women, gambling, and friends for years.

He had no health insurance, no security, no little house in

the Pennsylvania countryside, as a violinist friend did. No little *bodega* like Manny's.

What did he have? A few letters from Cuba, a wall filled with autographed pictures, a headful of memories, sometimes scrambled like eggs.

(Again, he remembers back to long ago and his Papi in Cuba saying, "You become a musician, and you'll be a poor man all your life.")

Cesar nodded. "Well, you seem in good shape," he said to Pérez.

"God bless you, that is what I say to the world now." And Pérez startled him by kissing him on the neck.

"I nearly died, did you know that?" he said to Cesar. "And when I was on the brink of death I had a revelation: lights showered down on me from heaven and for one brief moment I saw the face of God. I said to him, 'Allow me the chance to do good for mankind, allow me to be your humble servant.' I am here now because of that, *sabes?* and I can tell you I want to help you. What is it that I can do for you, Cesar? Do you need money? Do you need help with your music? Please tell me, I want to know."

"There's nothing I want, Fernando. Don't worry about me."

"At the very least," Fernando said before returning to his diners and the pretty young girls whose breasts were spilling out the tight bodices of their red ruffled dresses, "you must come and visit me at my house in Queens. Will you do this?"

"Yes."

"Good, and may God bless you. *Que Dios te bendiga!*"

And he dropped a five-dollar bill on the counter, saying, "Give my friend here a drink."

Then he embraced Cesar and made his way to his table: "Now don't forget."

Thereafter, the two men were friendly again. Pérez would drive up in a white El Dorado Cadillac and park in front of the *bodega* from which he conducted his business of loan-sharking and numbers running. He did so with an air of reverence and saintliness, making the sign of the cross over his customers and sending them off with his blessing. And when he saw Cesar on the street, Pérez would honk the car horn and wave the Mambo

King over. It was always: "When are you coming out to Queens for a visit?" And: "Why are you so distant with me, my friend?"

"No, no, I'm not that way," he said to Pérez. Then he leaned into the car window, making small talk, and usually walked away with a Havana cigar (Pérez would get them from a friend in Toronto).

One Thursday night, he went out to Queens, where Pérez lived in a three-story twenty-room house. In every room, pleated French curtains, a color TV set, and a telephone. Tropical-fish tanks and a big abstract painting in his living room, a stereo, bar. And he had three Cadillacs parked in front of the house. But what impressed the Mambo King the most was the swimming pool in Pérez's back yard.

They dined in a screen-enclosed sun porch in the back, Pérez and his wife sitting at each end of a long, platter-covered table, and Cesar between them. Ismelda would ring a little bell and in would come the Peruvian maid, to whom they both gave orders: "Take the beans back, they're much too cold." "Don't we have fresher bread?" "Bring another bottle of wine."

They sat talking about the old days. Fernando would get up and reach across the table to touch his wife's beringed hand.

"Our love started," Fernando said to him, "one night at that place your orchestra used to play in Brooklyn."

"The Imperial Ballroom," his wife tenderly said.

"Man, you were great that night, up there on the stage. What was that song you used to start with? I have it on one of your recordings."

"We used to begin our performances with an instrumental bolero called 'Twilight in Havana.' "

"Your brother, may God rest his soul, used to open it with a long trumpet run, right? Something between Chocolate Armenteros and Harry James. I remember this well because I was at the bar watching the orchestra. I remember that song so clearly"—and he hummed part of the melody. "I remember it because it was during that song that my brother introduced me to my little wife here. That was almost thirty years ago, and look, we're still together and prospering."

He made a toast.

"You know what our plan is for the coming year? To go to

the Vatican this next Easter and turn up at one of those audiences with the Pope. I want to have that honor and satisfaction before I finally enter the sunset years."

And he went on about the prosperity of his children: two sons had gone into the business with him and flourished, two others were in college; he had seven grandchildren and enough money for the rest of his life.

"But my greatest gift is that I have my health." Pérez rapped on the table. "Money, women, possessions mean nothing in the face of death. It all comes down to shit in the end. That's what I thought, in any case, before I saw the light."

They'd dined on pork chops and fried chicken, rice and beans, fried plantains, a huge mixed salad, tripe soup, toasted Italian bread, and for dessert they had espresso and caramel-glazed lemon-cream and rum-filled pastries. Then came out the bottle of Courvoisier, which was so smooth and so delicious that Cesar could not resist drinking down glass after glass.

Afterwards, in the living room, they sat listening to the dulcet music of the Ten Thousand Hollywood Strings, Miguel Montoya's group. Eating from a box of French bonbons, Cesar relaxed and felt an immense nostalgic gratitude for knowing the gangster Fernando Pérez. He was also touched by the huge mahogany crucifix that took up most of the wall opposite the couch.

"I guess we do go back a long way," the Mambo King said tearfully. "I guess we are really good friends, aren't we, Pérez?"

"Yes, we can thank the Lord Jesus Christ for that."

Cesar had spent most of the night feeling that there was something vaguely unjust about the fact that the shady Pérez, who'd once dealt in prostitution and drugs, was so prosperous. The brandy did its work, however, changing the Mambo King's opinion of the whole enterprise. And he was touched when Pérez, taking the Mambo King by the hand, led him before the crucifix, asking that he kneel down and say a prayer with him.

"I don't know, *hombre*," Cesar said, laughing. "I haven't said too many prayers lately."

"As you like, my friend."

Pérez and his wife knelt down and shut their eyes: almost instantly, their faces turned a deep red and tears flowed from their eyes. Pérez was speaking rapidly. A few words which the drunken Mambo King picked out: "Oh, the passion, the passion of Our Lord who died for us worthless souls."

After this, they watched television until eleven, and then Pérez called a private taxi to take the Mambo King home.

"Don't you ever forget, my friend," Pérez told him. "If there's anything you ever want or need from me, you tell me, okay?"

"Yes, yes."

"*Vaya con Dios.*"

The taxi, whose driver seemed cynical and leering, drove away.

The next day he ached with a sense of failure. It would hit him from time to time, and had seemed to subside now and then, especially when he was busy with music and women, but his life had been slowing down lately. His body was changing. Now he was getting jowls, his eyes ended in a burst of viny wrinkles, and, worst, his hairline had started to recede. He felt much more cautious about women, set his sights on the pleasures of memory, though from time to time he would get bored and call up an old flame. Miss Vanna Vane had become a Mrs., but he would sometimes meet her downtown, where she worked as a secretary, take her out to lunch, reaching out under the table to touch her thighs. He saw other women, but was slowing down. Though his thing got big as ever, it was more lackadaisical. Just walking down the street to say hello to Eugenio on the corner, to meet up with Manny the bassist seemed to take it out of him. And sometimes when he was resting in bed he felt terrible aches in his heart, aches in his kidneys and liver; headaches between his brows.

Hard to take that he wasn't a young king cock anymore. Delores, who read everything, had told him that he was going through a "middle-life crisis."

"You feel that way because you don't think you have much to look forward to, but the truth is, you could live another thirty years."

(He laughed in his room in the Hotel Splendour.)

And it came down to something else: What would he do when he was too old to earn a living? So he played those jobs, and there was always someone to talk about his making a comeback, like that fellow Pérez, but he was so out of what was happening, jazz-rock-fusion, acid *salsa*, disco boleros, it seemed hopeless. He mostly worked, in those days, when younger bands canceled. The old-timers liked him, but who else remembered him? All this gave him regrets.

Wished he had hooked up with Xavier Cugat.

Wished he had stayed married.

Wished his brother was alive.

Wished he had some money.

On the workroom door, the girlie calendar with the big-tit broad in a clingy wet bathing suit, shoving a fluted Coke bottle in her mouth, did nothing to him. He lay his head down on the paper-covered table for half an hour, got up, strummed his guitar. Then he thought he might revive his spirit by dwelling on his virility, pulling from a drawer a pornographic magazine, and then unzipping his trousers and masturbating. In his workroom easy chair, he drank a beer and started to doze again. Hearing the softest music in the walls, made by the water shimmering through the pipes, he realized that it was the *I Love Lucy* theme. And when he opened his eyes he found himself standing beside Nestor, poor nervous Nestor, as they were preparing to leave the stage wings to make their appearance on the show.

"*Óyeme, hombre,*" he said, straightening Nestor's bow tie. "Be strong. It'll be great. Don't be nervous, just do as we did during the rehearsals with Mr. Arnaz."

His brother nodded and someone said, "Your cue's coming up, fellows."

And Nestor said, "Brother, you don't be nervous. Read that book."

And then they proceeded, as they had many many times before, to walk into Ricky and Lucy's life and to sing "Beautiful María of My Soul."

When he woke from this "dream," he remembered his brother's advice, searched his worktable, finding his brother's old copy of *Forward America!* under a pile of building-complaint and hardware-store slips. Flipping through the pages, he reread one of the lines that Nestor long ago had underlined: "In the worst circumstances, never retreat. Keep your eyes on the horizon!

Don't look back and always march forward . . . And remember:
It is the general with the advancing army who *wins the war!*"

Feeling restless, he was unable to get much work done that
Saturday. The Mambo King hung around the workroom, listening to the radio and organizing the papers in his desk, until about
three, when he decided to go out to the Shamrock bar.

It was while drinking a whiskey that he heard the owner, a
fellow named Kennedy, tell someone that the bar was for sale.

"And how much do you want?" someone inquired.

"Thirty-five thousand."

The Mambo King remained there, drinking and occasionally paying attention to the baseball game on the television. Usually he never stayed for very long; but by his second glass of
whiskey he was feeling exhilarated, didn't really want to go back
down to the basement.

Then this Irish man came in, sat beside Cesar. His face was
covered with Xs, little cuts from this guy who had slashed him
up. A mugger had attacked him and cut his face up one night as
he staggered home. Thing was, he kept going home by the same
route and it kept happening again and again.

"Now, you must take care of yourself," the Mambo King
said to the man.

"Nah, nah," Dickie said. "I know what's coming to me."

He sat in the bar for another hour, watching the owner, Mr.
Kennedy, a bony, flush-faced man with shaky hands and a huge
age-spot-mottled nose, washing dishes and making drinks. After
buying himself and Dickie another drink, he decided to go home.
That was the afternoon when, climbing the stairs to his apartment, Cesar found his second-floor neighbor Mrs. Stein standing
outside her door.

"My husband doesn't want to wake up," she told him.

Good thing he had been fortified by drink. When she took
him into the bedroom, Mr. Stein was sitting up in bed with a
bundle of papers in his hand, his mouth half open, tongue just
slightly out between his teeth, as if he were about to say something. A scholar, he was always preoccupied but polite and never
impatient with Cesar in his duties. Once, while repairing an

electric socket in that room, the Mambo King had wanted to ask Mr. Stein a question. He'd been inspired by all the papers with odd writing on them—"Hebrew and German," Mr. Stein had said. "And this is Greek."

And so he had asked, "Do you believe in God?" And without hesitation Mr. Stein said, "I do."

That's what he remembered about him.

Now he was covering the man's head with a sheet. But not without first shutting his eyes, clear and blue and looking at a crack in the flecking walls.

"Mrs. Stein, I don't know how to tell you this, but you must call an ambulance. Or do you have a relative I can talk to?"

Then it hit her: "Now I have been sent to hell," she said.

"Now, please just sit, I'll take care of everything."

That night he had trouble sleeping, spent hours in tortured thought. Why was he, a cocksure and arrogant macho in his youth, now relegated to fearful thoughts of lifelong loneliness? Why were his knees aching? Why did he feel at times that he walked around with a corpse slung over his shoulders, as if the days after his brother died were somehow repeating themselves?

Now and then he thought about the bar. For years (since his return from the Merchant Marine) Manny had been after him to go into a partnership, start something up, like a dance hall or a club. And now he was thinking: Wouldn't be so bad for a fellow like him who knew the music business to set something up, like a Latin cabaret or dance club. The biggest problem would be money. In his head he went through all the prosperous people he knew, people who'd promised to help him out in a jam. There was Miguel Montoya, now living in Arizona; Bernardito, Manny, his cousin Pablo. They all had a few thousand dollars put away. And Pérez. But thirty-five thousand? And beyond that, how much more would he need? That bar was run down, but he could fix it up, repaint the walls, get some lighting, build a little stage. It could be done inexpensively. Certainly he could get a lot of his musician friends to work cheap. Acting as an MC, he'd get up before a microphone and graciously introduce young and old talent. And what if it caught on, becoming as popular as the

Havana San Juan or the Tropicana, then everything would fall
in place: money, women, and good moods.

Then he thought about the kind of people who would go to
his club. Young, respectable, and fun-loving couples with a few
dollars in their pockets, more well-to-do middle-aged people who
liked a mix of the old standards and the new . . . His speculations
went on until the early morning, and then finally, thinking that
there might be something to his idea, he fell asleep.

Everybody told him he was crazy to get involved with Pérez,
even if Pérez walked around, and went to church, wearing a
crucifix around his neck. And he knew it, too, but he didn't care:
he put it in the back of his mind. When he daydreamed about the
place, he saw it done up as a lush little tropical paradise. Saw
himself making like Desi Arnaz as MC and singer (and on the
edge of this thought, Nestor) and perhaps becoming more than
just a superintendent and pickup musician. But he ignored everyone's advice. Even after he had a dream about what would happen: that it would open fine and go along nicely for a while, but
that Pérez's people would take it over and turn it into something
else. Still, he went for it. Manny and other friends sprang for
seven thousand, with Pérez putting up the rest, half as an invest-
ment for himself and the rest as a loan to Cesar.

"I said that I would help you, my friend."

By June he had assumed the ownership of the Shamrock and
its ice machines, meat freezer, meat grinder, horseshoe bar, lunch
counter, jukebox, tables and chairs, cash register, speckled mirror
and bar stools. Out of his basement he dragged the tinny upright
piano, had the thing tuned, and set it against a wall: there was a
dining area which had seen much better days. The walls had been
covered with wood paneling and light green Con-Tact paper.
These he tore out in favor of mirrored tiles, which he purchased
for next to nothing from a friend in the Bronx. Then he set out
to build a small stage. He wanted it to be about the size of the
stage of the Mambo Nine Club, as if that might invite success. It
measured six by twelve feet, just large enough to accommodate

a small band. He covered the plywood construction with a plush red carpeting, painted the doorway an ebony black.

The Irish in the neighborhood knew things were permanently changing when they saw Cesar scraping the shamrocks off the front window. When he finished with that, he got his friend Bernardito the artist to come in as his art director, filled the joint up with rubber palm trees and papier-mâché pineapples. On one of the walls, he stuck a big painting of Havana that he had purchased in New Jersey. Then he put in a flamingo-pink awning that reached the curb, and a fancy neon sign with the words *Club Havana* flashing in two colors, aquamarine and red, for the window.

Finally he brought over a few of the hundreds of photographs he had in boxes from his heyday in the mambo era, stuck a few in frames over the bar, signed photographs of everybody from Don Aziapaú to Marion Sunshine. And with them went the framed photograph of Arnaz, Nestor, and himself.

He decided to charge two dollars' cover, a dollar a drink, and to offer a simple menu that would feature such dishes as *arroz con pollo*, rice and beans, fried plantains, and Cuban sandwiches, for which he'd find some poor woman as a cook. Then he had a thousand promotional fliers made up and hired little kids for a buck an hour to tack them up on lampposts, in building lobbies, and under car windshield wipers. When all this had been done, he got into the habit of turning up there after work. He'd walk around the premises, as if it were some kind of dream come true, smoking a big blue cigar and nodding to himself, tapping the counter, posing in front of the bar mirror, and pouring himself drinks.

Of course it was more complicated than that: he had to apply for licenses, liquor, cabaret, restaurant. He had to have everything inspected by the buildings commission and by the Board of Health, which would not let him open until Pérez took care of the inspectors. There were no problems after that. Pedro advised Cesar about bookkeeping and Pérez provided the "security."

"May God bless us, but you know, my friend," Pérez told him, "if you don't take the right precautions now, all kinds of trouble may follow."

It was decided that Pérez would keep a man around the club, and he gave Cesar a present that he had wrapped up nicely in shiny blue paper: a .38 Smith & Wesson revolver, which the Mambo King bundled in a towel and left jammed behind the boiler in his basement.

It was a funny thing. Just about a week before they were going to open the club, Cesar had a visitor. He was sitting in the little back room that he used as his office when Frankie, who had been mopping the floors, told Cesar, "Some lady's here to see you."

She was a young hippie woman, maybe thirty. She walked in wearing a suede cowboy jacket and rattlesnake boots. She described herself as a filmmaker and said she was working on something around the theme of "alternate life-styles in the melting pot of the city."

"Yeah?"

"We just want to come in here one night and film. Would that be okay with you?"

"Will you pay for this?"

"No, no, it's not for pay. I don't make any money on this. It's for a film about Latins in New York City. I'm doing it for a friend of mine from Columbia."

"Not Professor Flores?"

Flores was a Cuban friend who taught Spanish there.

"No."

She told him that all she wanted was to get a small crew with camera and microphone in one night, film the dancing, and do a few interviews.

He thought about it and then told her, "I have to talk to my partners about this, but I'm going to tell you okay. We're opening next Saturday night. And if you want, you can come and make your movie then."

Once word got around that the opening of the Club Havana was going to be filmed, it took on something of the air of a glamorous Hollywood event. The filmmaker turned up that Saturday night with her crew. With free music, food, and drinks, people from all over showed up: old friends from the dance halls, musicians and their wives, friends of the family, patrons of the beauty salon where Ana María worked part-time, friends from the street. Soon the men escorted their beautiful women into the place. That first night, Cesar acted as both MC and singer, using an eight-piece band of pickup musicians to back him. In a white silk suit with a carnation in his lapel and a thick cigar in hand, he sang, he shook his hips, patted backs, laughed, urged his friends to enjoy the free food and the big open bar, and found it hard to believe that he had not thought of all this before. And the people seemed to love the place.

Cesar had asked good dancers he knew to turn up that night. In fact, Bernardito of Brooklyn had become quite expert at dancing the mambo. And Frankie, middle-aged and worn, was still a professional in his writhing, grinding movements. Spotlight and cameras set out on the dance floor, the dancers went crazy, and the orchestra got into long, epic claves-beat jams, the two drummers, the pianist, two trumpet players (including Cesar, a sweaty mess behind his dark green glasses), flute, saxophone, and bassist played their hearts out. And when the camera turned on him, the Mambo King hammed it up, a trumpet in one hand, rump out, feet turning, his mouth pouting "Oh, baby!" and his hands flailing the air as if his fingertips had caught fire, his body, despite his heft, nimble and bending in all directions and shapes. (Then, during a later song, he performed like a robot, moving his limbs and head as if his joints had been stuffed with gears and cotton.)

Everybody clapped and laughed, the music sounded great. Even the jaded neighborhood kids who preferred groups like the Rolling Stones or Smokey Robinson and the Miracles were having a good time. Even Eugenio, who'd long since stopped dancing regularly, came in, and, fortified with a few drinks himself, danced the mambo and the *pachanga,* though not nearly as well as his uncle or most of the others.

After a while Cesar and his friends got used to the camera, but not to the fact that a woman was giving the orders. She was tall, with a great head of hair and fierce-looking, intelligent eyes. Frankie referred to her as *"señorita jefe"* and bowed with mock deference when she would pass condescendingly by.

That night, the most touching dance couple on the floor

turned out to be fat Cousin Pablito and his wife. Although he was only about five foot four, he cut a dashing figure in a blue suit, white shirt, and red tie. He and his wife never used to go out, but now, with their kids grown up, they were free. (Their two daughters had married, and their son, Miguel, had a good mechanic's job and lived in the Bronx.) Pablito and his wife's specialty was the *pachanga* and at one point during the evening the whole nightclub crowd surrounded them as they danced: when the camera fixed on them, Pablito really let loose, showing off every step he knew. In the end, even the hippie camera crew were touched and applauded, whistling and hooting, too.

The opening turned out to be a grand success. Unbridled in their enthusiasm, the crowd danced and drank from nine in the evening until four-thirty in the morning. Even the sidewalk was jammed with people. It was as crowded as the sidewalk outside a funeral parlor during a wake, and as noisy, too. When the band inside wasn't playing, the jukebox put the music of Beny More right out into the street. With their bellies full, heads woozy from booze, feet danced out, the customers left, happily promising the proud owner that they would return.

And the filmmaker thanked the Mambo King for his help, too, and while the festivities were still going strong, she and her crew packed away their equipment into metal cases and went home.

(And the film? The night's work resulted in only ten minutes of footage that would be shown at a festival in the Whitney Museum, and included a brief interview with Cesar, who appeared with the caption "manager of the club" floating beneath him. Seated at the bar, with a big cigar in hand, and dapper in his suit, he was saying: "I came here with my younger brother in the late 1940s and we had a little band, the Mambo Kings. I composed with my brother a song, 'Beautiful María of My Soul,' and this caught the attention of the singer Desi Arnaz, who asked us to appear with him on his TV show *I Love Lucy,* do you know it?"

And that ran in the film in a loop, jerking back to a point where he's first saying, ". . . Desi Arnaz, who asked us to appear with him on his TV show *I Love Lucy.*" Jerked back, it showed about ten times in quick succession.

Then it cut to the same kind of loop of Pablito dancing the *pachanga* with his wife, the same steps being repeated over and over again in a jerky manner. It was shown many times in the viewing room of the Whitney, and then later in France, where it won a prize.)

Then, around five that morning, a Sunday, when most people's thoughts were turning toward God and the Eucharist, Pérez bid everyone good night. At that point the opening party had dwindled down to Cesar, Pablito, Manny, Bernardito, and Frankie, who had manned the bar for the night. And there was Eugenio, twenty-one years old and attending college, who had worked in the kitchen. As Pérez left, he told them, "I have something for you. Just stick around for a few minutes." And so they did, and for all their exhaustion and yawning, they were suddenly awake again as three comely young women in glittering silver-sequined miniskirts walked into the club, removed their garments, and started to dance.

The club ended up doing its main business on Saturday nights. For the rest of the week, the Mambo King depended on the local beer drinkers and college students who would come in for his dinner specials. He also rented the club out for private parties, gave the space free to the local church for special cabaret nights, and on several occasions held fund-raisers. But Wednesday nights were reserved for jam sessions. Eating and drinking and paying cheap prices, the musicians who'd turn up at midnight used the Club Havana as a second home, jamming until four in the morning, just like the jam sessions Cesar used to attend at the little beach clubs near Havana. Sitting up on one of the high stools by the bar, cigar burning blue between his thick thumb and index finger, he smiled and nodded at his customers, applauded loudly for the young musicians who would take the stage. Over the years, the bright stage lights had sensitized his eyes, and so he always wore his green sunglasses. Behind the dark lenses, his eyes looked as if they were underwater, and though his jowlish face seemed languorously absorbed in the proceedings, he often drifted off into a reverie of songs that he might write, about love, women, family.

From this club he earned a humble living. The late-night hours left him exhausted for his day's work as superintendent. This exhaustion, the ache in his bones, the flutters in his stomach, the more lackadaisical rigging of his penis, made the Mambo King realize he was aging. Gray hair appeared in his sideburns (to which he applied Grecian Formula). The sharp pains in his gut, the acidity in his esophagus—hot in the throat of his dreams at night—and the dull, stony pains in his sides—symptoms of liver and kidney maladies—proliferated.

In the name of the mambo, the rumba, and the cha-cha-cha of youth, he ignored all this.

And still during this time he attended to his work in the building, though now he had the luxury of hiring friends to perform certain jobs for him. He paid Eugenio, who had washed out as a musician, to take care of things. For the first year of that club's existence, it was Eugenio, down from his studies at City College, who'd turn up at tenants' doors with a wrench and pair of pliers.

DURING THIS TIME CESAR HAD A reputation as one of the Cubans in New York who would put up exile musicians in his apartment and help them find work. Every now and then, trumpeters and *congueros,* pianists, balladeers, and bolero singers, fresh from Cuba, would come to live in one of the Mambo King's spare rooms. Before he had opened the club, he would try to find them jobs at anything in the neighborhood and through his connections: Pablo at the meat plant; Bernardito, who knew the printing and magazine business; and club and restaurant owners like Rudy López of the Tropic Sunset, or Violeta, who might need dishwashers or waiters. Finding music jobs was harder. Even if the Cuban population in New Jersey was growing and there were more jobs than before, there still weren't enough to go around. So he'd let these Cubans stay with him, often lent them money and helped them find instruments in Harlem pawnshops. (Or he'd lend them one of his own.) He did so in the same spirit as he would help his own family. With the average stay being about a month, new faces were always turning up at his apartment.

But one thing about having the club—Cesar could put people more easily to work, taking them on as waiters usually, or sending them into the back to wash dishes. Paid them out of his own pocket even when the club was dead. And he had some good musicians working with him. There had been Pascual Ramírez, a pianist, who was adamantly political and hated the revolution, the man pounding the tables when he'd get worked up about it. And then this other fellow, Ramón, who played the saxophone and spoke sincerely and hopefully about things changing in Cuba. (The poor man hanged himself in Miami in 1978.)

Usually Cesar would just bring these visitors upstairs to meet the family, but between the club and the building, his days were long and full and he had little time to relax, to visit Delores and Pedro and the kids, to watch Delores adoringly whenever she walked across a room. If he worked until four in the afternoon, he was lucky to get an hour's nap. Then, dressed, he'd make his way over to the Club Havana. Although he was often tired, he'd gotten used to the routine.

One of those afternoons, while getting ready to go to work at the club, he received a long-distance telephone call from Miami, some fellow, a friend of a friend from Cuba, by the name of Rafael Sánchez, who told the Mambo King, "Me and my younger brother, Rico, we're coming to New York and were wondering if you might be able to help us with a place to stay?"

"Of course," the Mambo King said.

A week later, he found the two brothers, cane suitcases and black instrument cases, a trumpet's and a saxophone's, by their side, standing before his door.

"Señor Castillo?" the older brother said. "I'm Rafael Sánchez and this is my brother, Rico."

The older brother was a slightly balding man of thirty, thirty-five, with a handsome face and a startled expression. He was wearing blue dungarees, a white shirt, a worn blue blazer, a black overcoat, and a black-brimmed, brown felt hat. Bowing, he shook hands with the Mambo King, as did his younger brother, Rico. He was about twenty-five and thin and gaunt, with a thick head of black hair and clear blue eyes. He wore dungarees and a dark sweater, an overcoat, and a wool cap on his head.

"Come in," the Mambo King said. "You must be hungry."

So they went down the hall to the kitchen, where he served the brothers steak sandwiches, French fried potatoes and onions, *pasteles*, and salad, drowned in oil and salt. They drank beer and beer and beer and played the radio, and Cesar stuck his head out the courtyard window and whistled to Delores, so she might come down and meet them. She came along with Leticia, who was now eighteen years old, quivery and fine like the *flan* they served the brothers.

"And how was your trip?"

"Tiring, we came up on the train. But we got to see the scenery," said the older brother. "This is my second time in the States now, but for my younger brother this is the first."

The younger brother said, in a quiet, quiet voice: "I can see how someone can get lost here."

The Mambo King nodded. "You mean in spirit or on the streets?"

"In spirit."

And he poured more beers, as beer made him feel more relaxed and friendly. He patted them on their backs, and then came the stories about how they'd gotten out of Cuba via Spain, spending three months in Madrid and then making their way to a cousin's house in Miami for another three-month stay. They both had been jazz players in Cuba, the older brother playing the saxophone and guitar, and the younger, the trumpet.

"Back in the old days before the revolution," said Rafael, "we used to listen to jazz in Havana on CMQ, sneak around to all the big hotels to hear the big bands and jam sessions with people like Dizzy Gillespie . . ."

"He's great," said Rico.

"In this one bar we knew up at La Concha"—he was refer-ring to a beach popular with young people and musicians, about forty minutes' drive out of Havana—"we'd listen to music and meet other musicians. Nice days. But then we had the revolution and what we hear is this jive Eastern European jazz like pompom waltz music, and sometimes we'd be lucky, and get our hands on a short-wave radio and listen to the real stuff from the States and Mexico. In any case, we were both working in Havana, Rico in a cigar factory and myself driving a bus around the city, and we both just wanted to get out of there. I mean, what was there for us? Fidel closed down so many of the clubs and hotels, and what work we got, playing weddings and dances for the Russians, was not to our liking. To tell the truth, we could see that he was doing some good things with the poor people, but for us? What was there? Nothing. In any case, it was Rico here who pushed that we leave. But it wasn't easy."

The brothers' expressions? World-weary exhaustion, fol-lowed by healthy, appreciative smiles.

Then the story of a friend, a bassist, traveling with the Tropicana Review out of Havana in Mexico City, climbing out the second-floor window of a hotel bathroom and running for blocks and blocks and catching a taxi that took him to the Ameri-can Embassy. Another traveling performer, a male singer, leaving his dressing room in London disguised as a woman.

". . . But, as not to let this nice little gathering slip into a maudlin state of affairs," the Mambo King remembered the older brother saying, "I make a toast to our friend Cesar Castillo."

"And to the lovely ladies who have brought us tender *flan* and warm smiles," said Cesar. "And to our new friends."

"And to Dizzy Gillespie and Zoot Sims and John Coltrane," said the younger brother.

"*Salud!*" all around, even for Leticia, who drank a glass of wine, which made her cheeks turn red.

Enjoying the role of *patrón,* Cesar lifted his glass for a final toast: "To your future!"

Then it was good night to Delores and Leticia, and the Mambo King set the brothers up in one of the rooms in the back and went off, a little drunk, to the club.

The next afternoon, he showed them around the neighborhood, introducing the Sánchez brothers to his friends. And he pointed across the street, saying: "See that place across the way? That's the Club Havana. That's mine." Then: "We'll see what work I can find for you. Maybe in the kitchen, if you like."

Within a few weeks, the brothers were working in the Club Havana as dishwashers and waiters. Now and then, when things were slow, they'd jam, Cesar sitting in on the piano, and the brothers beside him on the stage playing their instruments. Cesar had heard a lot of jazz in the fifties, and while he could make his way around a few lilting blues riffs, as he got older he definitely preferred living in boleroland and melodyville. But the brothers played wild and looping music, crows and nightingales in a cage, around which he circled, while cheerfully trying to keep up.

He remembered that.

One night, he had this dream: The brothers were shouting up to his window from the street, and when he looked out, they were down below in *guayaberas* and white linen trousers, their faces tormented with the cold. The city was covered with snow and he called out the window, "Don't be worried, I'm going to let you in." He screamed in his sleep so loud that the older brother appeared at his bedroom door, asking, "Are you all right?"

(And another night, a glimpse of an eerier dream: the entire neighborhood trapped inside a glacier, everything frozen in its tracks, but music piping through the ice.)

"Yes, yes. It's the club. Sometimes I think too much about the club."

(And sometimes he would shut his eyes and imagine that it was 1949 again.)

Liking them, he went out of his way to make both brothers comfortable and to help them get work. He called bandleaders and club owners to put out the word that the musicians were available. He took them down to Macy's and Gimbels and bought them nice suits, new shoes, took them over to the beauty salon, where Ana María cut their hair. He felt bad when they had to wash dishes, but paid them even on slow nights when there were hardly any dishes to wash. When he heard that the older brother had a thing for the singer Celia Cruz, he went out and bought an armful of her recordings, and when he heard Rico say that he missed having his own phonograph, he went out to a pawnshop on 116th Street off Manhattan Avenue and bought him one. (Now, at night, he would hear Rico jamming along with the recordings of Machito and Miles Davis.) He took them along with him to meetings of the Cubans of Washington Heights, brought them every Sunday to Delores's, where they enjoyed the hospitality of the family. ("Anytime you want a meal," Pedro told them, "you're welcome.") And he was concerned for them. He blamed himself whenever he saw Rico, homesick and claustrophobic, yawning before the television, blamed himself on the grayest days when Rico or his older brother would stand before the window, heartbroken. Not one to lecture others, he found himself pointing to the 123rd Street projects and saying, "You don't want to go in there." He identified the junkies on the street and the lowlife drug dealers who sometimes popped up on the corner. When he looked into Rico's or Rafael's eyes and found sadness, he would say, "Do you want a drink, my friend?" And in an hour they would be halfway through a bottle of rum.

Once he almost told the brothers about his brother Nestor. They'd seen his picture on the curvy-glass-front cabinet in the corner of the living room, and they'd seen the Mambo King pictures in the hall. He didn't tell them because why should he share his sadness.

On the other hand, he might have told them about Nestor a dozen times, and couldn't remember.

Sometimes he found himself staring at Rico and thinking about Nestor, wondering where so much time had gone. Then he would sit at the table, lamenting the pleasures, the main ones being affection and comfort, his brother was missing out on, the pleasures his brother would never have.

On a Sunday night, he fell asleep on the living-room couch after visiting with Bernardito and Frankie and their women in the chatty, lively household upstairs. He had another dream, this one beautiful.

He was in a field in Cuba, wading in wildflowers, with his brother at his side, picking them for their mother.

He hadn't had so beautiful a dream in a long time.

They remained with the Mambo King for three months, helping him out in the club and here and there in the building, while also trying to find work as musicians. They got along with everybody, and only Leticia had her heart broken by one of them: Eighteen years old and agonizingly fine, she had given up the matronly dresses and books that her mother bought her and taken to wearing a silver-lamé miniskirt and pink blouses and sunburst-pattern brassieres, all to impress Rico, who hardly noticed her. The Mambo King was so oblivious of Leticia's life that his discovery of this drama, which had been going on for several months, came to him as a complete surprise. He'd seen her crying from time to time but blamed her tears on the monthly female cycle, overheard Delores lecturing Leticia about the essential unworthiness of men, heard Delores threatening Leticia with convent school if she didn't straighten out, and, still, he remained dense about the particulars of his niece's existence. He became aware of the situation only when Leticia came to visit Rico at the Club Havana, wearing so seductive a red dress that Delores came after her with a belt and beat her. Intervening as a peacemaker, the Mambo King sent Delores home and held the weeping Leticia in his arms, wondering, "Who is this woman brimming over with emotion?"

For a half hour he listened to Leticia's laments: how she felt as if she were a dog on a leash, as her mother never let her do anything by herself, that all she wanted was a little life of her own. And tears and more tears, and the Mambo King not knowing what to say except "These things will pass."

Later, while standing alone by the bar, he tried to reconcile his memory of Leticia as the skinny, affectionate little girl who would come running into his arms years ago with the love-throttled raven-haired beauty whose ample femininity and dense emotions now confused him. He had tried to stop her crying by offering to buy her infantile presents—an ice-cream cone, a doll, a jump rope—but she kept crying. Something about her tears

took him back to lots of other women whom he seemed to identify with tears—his mother crying in bed, his wife weeping on
the street, Delores crying in bed—and still he did not know what
to do. In the end, he gave her a hug, a ten-dollar bill, and took
her home to the apartment, without saying another word.

And the brothers? While Rafael, the older brother, liked to
go downtown on his nights off, visiting friends (they would
sometimes come up to drink cheaply on evenings when Rafael
was waiting tables) and going to jazz clubs in the Village (the
Half Note on Spring Street being a favorite), Rico would put on
his blue pinstriped Macy's suit and head off to the subway, smelling all sweet from a rose-honey cologne; a nice story really, a
romance involving a girl he had known back in Cuba, with whom
he hooked up again. She lived in New Jersey with her family.
He'd go out to see her a few nights a week, slicking back his hair
and preening himself before the mirror. He'd ride home on the
PATH trains at four in the morning, moving quietly through the
house, not wanting to disturb anyone. Usually the Mambo King
would be awake and sitting at the kitchen table with Frankie or
one of his other friends, speaking quietly, the man fighting sleep,
or he might be sitting in the living room watching television or,
pad in hand, going over some old arrangement that he was trying
to remember. Or he'd be trying to write a song.
    One night, Rico came home and joined the Mambo King at
the table and related that he was going to marry this woman, that
he and his older brother were going to be living in her family's
house in Elizabeth.
    The Mambo King shrugged. "Let me know what I can get
you as a present," he told Rico. And he patted the younger
musician on the back. And, smiling, he said, "I knew I smelled
love in the air!"
    There was something else: he asked the brothers to perform
at the club.
    It was arranged. One night Rafael and Rico Sánchez ap-
peared on the stage of the Club Havana, backed by Manny the
bassist, a pianist named Eddie Torres, and good old reliable Pito
on the drums. They played a lot of jazzy-sounding instrumentals,

some old dance standards. Now and then, the older brother would step to the microphone and sing a bolero, and in the tradition of bolero singers, his vocal cords quivered, his eyes closed, and his expression became pained and sincere. Seated at a back table, Delores, Leticia, Eugenio, and Pedro. And at the bar, drinking shots of rum, the Mambo King, listening attentively and feeling pleased by the repetition of certain events.

"*Adiós,* my friends," he recalled telling them when they left.

AFTER THIS, THINGS STARTED TO change at the club. Even though Cesar owed Pérez thousands of dollars and seemed to be doing a decent business, he made no payments, claiming that he just didn't have the money. And why? Because he was still playing the big man, hiring friends, like the brothers from Cuba, keeping two waitresses on salary, a cook named Esmeralda, Frankie behind the bar, and dishwashers, and, on top of that, giving meals and drinks away, and paying his musicians decently, regardless of the take at the door.

Hearing reports of this conspicuous generosity, Pérez one day called a meeting of the partners.

"I don't know how to relate this to you, my friend," Pérez told him. "But it's my opinion that you think you're running a social club, yes?"

"No, but it's my club."

"Yes, run with my money."

In total, Pérez claimed to have put over forty thousand dollars into the place. Manny, who had put in five thousand, didn't really care how Cesar ran the club, as long as it made the Mambo King happy, but Pérez stated the case that, as a businessman, he had to look out for his own interests.

"All I want is that you leave the management to me, okay? Otherwise, you can continue as you like, bringing in bands and greeting the patrons. That is what you do best, understand?"

Then he gave Cesar a hearty *abrazo.* "Believe me, as God is my witness, this is the right thing to do."

Eventually Pérez sent two of his men in. One resembled the

boxer Roberto Durán and possessed his piercing black eyes just before the kill. The other seemed more easygoing, low-keyed, until he spoke to you and then he'd smile, lips curled with sarcastic intent. They called the Mambo King Papi and humored him when he gave them orders. They didn't much like Eugenio or his friends, didn't like "dead-beat" Frankie, measured out the drinks, gave no buy-backs, and never fed the jukebox with quarters from the register.

They fired one of the waitresses, making Cesar look cheap, which depressed him.

But with this new management came a whole new clientele. Sports from Brooklyn who would double-park their lavender Cadillacs out on the street and who wore thick gold chains around their necks. They'd sit at their tables and pull out thick wads of twenty-dollar bills, and they favored "soul" music whose bottom-heavy bass lines nearly blew out the jukebox speakers. Bands were featured only one night a week now, Saturdays. Slowly the number of old Latin standards began to dwindle, and so did the number of older customers. And they were generous, giving out big tips and always buying the "boss," Cesar Castillo, drinks. By midnight he would find himself leaving the club with Frankie by his side, so drunk that he sometimes could not see across the street. It was on one of those nights that he had another beautiful dream: the Club Havana was burning down, but it was a silent fire, like embers in the incinerator, without sirens or shattering glass, just the place burning up with all the bad people inside. Sometimes he would just make it to his stoop and sit there wishing that the club would burn.

Sitting in the Hotel Splendour, he did not like to think that those men had used the Club Havana to sell drugs, as the neighborhood gossip said. But even back then, he knew that something was wrong, because of the way people looked at him. The old Irishman with the strawberry-red chin who always tipped his crooked gray hat looked the other way when Cesar passed by. Even gentle Ana María, cutting his hair, did not smile. And there were the stories, or coincidences, that did not sit well with him. Nice black kid, "one of the better ones," as he used to say, named Alvin, falling off a rooftop. Irish kid named Johnny G., found slumped and fucked-up in some Broadway tavern, dead. Other Irish kid dead in some basement. Italian kid named Bobby wrecked while joyriding, high on drugs; black kid named Owen sucked into a Far Rockaway sewer. Kids yellow with jaundice and who-knows-what, nodding at the Mambo King and saying, "How are you, Mr. Castillo," a dead look in their eyes. Kid named Tommy, funniest guy on the street, gone with hepatitis. Blind lady newsdealer on 121st slashed straight down the middle of her face for a few dollars; radio-repair man slashed from ear to ear. Then the others he heard about, slipping from memory because he didn't want to think about them. Just that a lot of the kids used to hang out in front of the Club Havana at night, noisy and exuberant in their black chinos, V-neck sweaters, and double-laced Converse sneakers. He could have made a lot of money if he had stayed in the partnership, but one day he and the other partners approached Pérez, wanting to sell out. Debt paid, Cesar walked away from the club with five thousand dollars to show for it—Pérez had been generous. Then he flew down to Puerto Rico for two weeks and holed up in a mountain town near Mayagüez with some old friends. By the time he returned, he felt somewhat detached from the whole business, though while walking up the street he could hear the jukebox through the doorway and a murmur of voices. He'd taken all his pictures out from behind the bar, and Pérez was kind enough to change the name from Club Havana to the Star Club. A year later it was changed again, to Club Carib, and the year after that, when Pérez died (lifted to heaven by angels), it shut down for good, its front doors and windows whitewashed and covered up with boards.

AND JUST LIKE THAT, ANOTHER line of music brings back a Guatemalan man, a tall, macho-looking fellow named Enrique, whom Cesar had known from his Park Palace dance-hall days. Ran into him one afternoon in the street, years later, and they ducked into a bar, where he related

to the Mambo King the story of his "first intercourse," as he put
it. He was a teenager walking home from school along a dirt road,
when he heard a voice calling to him from the bushes, a female
voice saying, "Come here," and when he stepped closer and
parted the leaves, he saw an Indian woman on the ground, her
skirt hoisted up and legs open for him.

"She had a nice body," he told the Mambo King, who nodded and smiled. "And said to me, 'Show me what you have,'" and
she fondled him and his thing got big, "very big," he said with
a macho's attention to that kind of detail. And then they "coupled"—that was his word—right by the road, and while he had
enjoyed himself and had left her satisfied, he said that if the truth
be told, he would have preferred the company of a good-looking
boy who lived down the road, a good friend.

Now, this boy had a sister named Teresa, who was always
making eyes at Enrique. They flirted with each other, even
kissed, but in the end they both knew that, amorously speaking,
he preferred the company of men. He didn't even have anything
going with her brother, but everyone knew. That was the first
part of the story. And then he picked it up fifteen years later, with
Enrique living in New York and receiving letters from Teresa
pleading with him to marry her so that she might get American
citizenship: that after they were married they could then arrange
for the arrival of her brother. Loving Teresa like a sister, Enrique
wrote her that he would take care of everything, that he would
be waiting for her at the airport. A month after her arrival they
were married at City Hall and lived more or less as husband and
wife for a year, though they did not share their bed carnally.

The Mambo King nodded.

By that time she had started to make friends, inviting other
couples over to the house, and now he really had to behave like
a good husband, and that meant that he could not have any of his
male companions around. In fact, she began to forbid that his
friends come to the house, as she had begun to find them distaste-
ful. And there was another thing: she was tired of going to bed
at night and waking up beside Enrique, who tended to sleep, he
kept telling the Mambo King, with powerful and virile erections.
And even though she knew he was indifferent to women, she
would fondle him night after night, until they became lovers,

enjoying each other. This idyll lasted for several months and he began to barter with her, the company of his friends in exchange for his virile services, a proposal that made things worse between them, because with that she told him, "Enrique, but you don't understand, I love you. I've always loved you," and, "If I can't have you, I don't know what I'm going to do," like an actress in a bad Hollywood movie—his words again—but then, when he did not believe her, she stepped things up and went with whatever men she met on the street, and got a reputation as a harlot, so that Enrique, a huge man, had to go out and fight for who knows whose honor, but he did so. And then he tried to keep peace in the house, but she had started to smash plates and scream out the window that she was married to a "queen," weeping loudly for hours, so that he was ashamed to even leave his apartment.

Then things calmed down. One day, he told the Mambo King, he came home from his job waiting tables downtown and found that she'd cleared out of his apartment: a few days later he was served with divorce papers, the grounds being that he was incapable of fulfilling his manly functions with her. Not only was justice not served, but she was awarded alimony payments of fifty dollars a week, which was a lot of money in those days.

"Thank God," he said, "that she finally remarried, a few years ago."

"Sounds crazy to me," said the Mambo King, shaking his head. Then he stood up and rapped Enrique on the shoulder, saying, "Well, I hope things are better for you now?"

"Yes, they are."

"Good." And he left.

And with the Guatemalan man, who'd had bad luck, he remembered the poor rich Englishman, a dapper fellow who also hung out at the Park Palace, the one who fell in love with a beautiful brunette who drove him to suicide.

So many years had passed.

He remembered the short priest from the local parish who resembled Humphrey Bogart and always seemed to be looking down women's dresses.

Now there's a man who had made a big mistake.

And, speaking of bad luck, what about his friend Giovanni,

who managed the boxer Kid Chocolate, a jaunty Cuban welter-weight. Another waiter, Giovanni had a ticket to millions, and what happened? His boxer called the champ a fairy and paid for it in the ring, getting pummeled into a coma.

What happened to his Cuba? His memories?

Having watched the match on Friday Night Fight of the Week, the Mambo King waited for his friend Giovanni, who lived in the building next door, to come home, saw him walking up the street about one in the morning with his son, carrying a canvas bag. He raced down the stairs just to say, "I saw what happened. How is he?"

"Not good."

"Look, then, come back with me to the apartment and we'll have a few drinks."

"Okay."

And as they sat finishing off a bottle, Giovanni said, "Pssssht, just like that. All his training, all those fights. Psssssht, a crying shame, you know?"

The last bar of that strange line of bad-luck music really pinched his heart, because out of nowhere he started to hear Elva and René, his old dance team, shouting at each other. René accusing his fine-looking wife of cuckolding him, and Elva denying it to tears and then, because he did not believe her, turning it all around and boasting about all her young and handsome virile lovers, so that René lost his self-control and stabbed Elva to death with a kitchen knife. Afterwards he threw himself out the window.

That was another bad-luck thing that had happened in 1963. Thank God, the Mambo King thought, that the music changed swiftly, moving on again.

Toward the end, while listening to the wistful "Beautiful María of My Soul"

IT HAD COME DOWN TO THIS: HE had turned around to find that the temporary job he'd taken to fill his idle days had lasted nearly twenty years.

Passing through the lobby, he would remember when he was a cocky and arrogant musician, and think to himself, Who would have dreamed that things would turn out this way? (And millions of people watching him on the rerun of the *I Love Lucy* show could never imagine that he had his own life, never see him as a super.) He'd gotten used to smelling like plumber's gum, his nails blackened with grease and oil. Tenants tapped the pipes (in claves time) and he answered quickly, some of those jobs being nightmares. (Trapped under a sink in a hot kitchen, the linoleum floor beneath him rotting with roaches, crinkly and gnarled witch's hair growing out the bottom of the sink, hanging down into his face, the man struggling with a seat wrench to unscrew the J-joint or sink trap for hours in the stinging heat of the day. Or going into an apartment that had been locked up for a month because the tenants had gone on vacation and entering the kitchen to find that they'd turned off the refrigerator but left the door closed so that a blue fungus had proliferated and spread across the floor and everywhere he looked in that room were roaches feasting on that blueness. Or the time he had opened a closet and a million roaches, clinging one to another, had fallen on him like an old coat. These were some of the things he did not like.) But when tenants called him he always answered quickly. Wishing to fill the emptiness of his days, those many years back, he had fixed loosened doors, leaky faucets, cracked windows, saggy walls, faulty electrical sockets. He had installed a fancy bronze-tube lamp, like those found in old post offices and in library cubicles, over the mailboxes, and even found a new mirror for the narrow lobby, taking the old speckled mirror off its mounts and leaving it out for the garbage collectors on the sidewalk. (The children of La Salle Street, loving destruction, gleefully smashed the mirror.)

Rotund and slowly putting on weight, he began to take on the shape of a cathedral bell. He had his old favorite suits let out and retailored about thirteen times in a few years, so often that his tailor put elastic in the waistbands. Amazed by his own immensity, he sometimes stomped down on the back stairway, enjoying the way the rickety structure shook. Though he was having more difficulty breathing and his walk had slowed, the Mambo King was happy there was more of him to take up room in the world.

As he sank into the bathtub, the water would rise unexpectedly to the rim.

That was around the time when the pains got so bad that his old pal Dr. López wanted to put him in the hospital.

He went on the radio that year, a nostalgia hour. The pianist Charlie Palmieri, a bandleader and arranger, was on the same program. Palmieri talked about starting out with Tito Puente and then branching off on his own in the fifties, traveling cross-country before "racial barriers" had been broken, playing dances up in the mountains, and the way he had been the one to discover Johnny Pacheco, a dishwasher who played the flute in the kitchen, jamming along with the featured band, his playing so lively that Palmieri hired him on the spot.

And then it was "Thank you, Charlie Palmieri," and over the radio an oceanic rumbling and the melody of "Twilight in Havana."

"My next guest today is someone who was very much a part of the scene in the fifties here in New York. It's my pleasure to introduce the bandleader and singer Cesar Castillo. Welcome."

As he sat there telling his and Nestor's story, what the scene was like then in the dance halls where the Mambo Kings used to play, the Imperial Ballroom, the Friendship Club, the Savoy in the Bronx, and the quirky things that happened, like the all-baldhead contests and the great battles of the bands, stuff like that —the interviewer would occasionally break off and play one of the old Mambo King records, then return for more talk.

"And how did you feel about Desi Arnaz?"

Cesar laughed. "A nice man."

"I mean, musically?"

"A tremendous talent, untrained, but really good for his musicians. You know, me and my brother once played his show."

"Yes."

"But to get back to his talent. I ran into Chico O'Farrill one day and we got into the subject of reading charts. I mean, I had never learned to read, and from what I could tell, neither could Arnaz, and that led me to asking Chico as to what he thought of Desi Arnaz as a talent, and he said the man was very good for an untrained musician."

"But no one has ever considered him very authentic or original."

"*Bueno*, I think what he did was difficult. For me, he was very Cuban, and the music he played in those days was good and Cuban enough for me. You know he sang a lot of old Cuban ballads on that show."

But mainly he talked about the different dance halls, which bands were playing where, and the crisscross of musicians and the chumminess of the songwriters—"A lost epoch," they concurred.

"And who do you like now?"

"Most of the same. My favorites have remained much the same."

"You mean el Conjunto Mambo Kings?"

"No, I've always liked Puente, Rodríguez, Fajardo, Palmieri, Machito, Beny More, Nelo Sosa. I don't know, I guess you can name them and I'll like them. And there's Celia Cruz and the singer Carlos Argentina. I could go on, there are so many great talents still working."

"And yourself?"

Cesar laughed, puffed on his cigarette.

"I'm still working here and there. Nothing spectacular, you understand, but I'm still out there exercising my vocal cords."

"To our benefit." Then: "Well, now we're going to sign off, but before we do, I'm going to leave you with this fine little *canción.*"

With that, the interviewer cued "Beautiful María of My Soul," which played out of windows, out of car radios, and at the beach, where fine young women lying out in the sun, bodies shiny with suntan lotion, and hearts and heads filled with thoughts of the future, heard the song.

Occasionally, he would get a call from an agent or a promoter talking about bringing him back into the public's eye.

Usually nothing happened.

But one day he was hauling garbage out the basement, dragging the heavy incinerator cans out to the curb, when he heard a car horn. A Mercedes-Benz had pulled up and, sitting behind its wheel, looking plush in a white sable coat, plumed hat with leopard-skin band, his old Mambo King pianist, the fabulous Miguel Montoya.

It took him a second to figure that out. "Miguel, *hombre!*"

And soon they were embracing.

"My God, but you look prosperous."

"Yes," he said. "I can't complain."

Later they drove over to one of Cesar's favorite spots on 129th Street. Miguel must have been in his late seventies, but he seemed still to be going strong and, by his own account, had done well for himself, making Muzak recordings in California—his was the creamy, velvet, dulcet-toned piano playing "Moon River," "*Quizás, Quizás, Quizás,*" and "Beautiful María of My Soul" that came out over supermarket, airport, bus-terminal loudspeakers everywhere—and writing scores for low-budget Mexican horror films with titles like *The Beautiful Vampires of the Hacienda of Terror!* (Cesar had seen that film in the Bronx in 1966. He had gone to see it with his nephew Eugenio and a few of his friends—Louie, a lanky Puerto Rican, and Víctor, a newly arrived Cuban—and they had sat in the bluish glow of the horrific light in a theater crowded with worldly children who laughed and clapped while watching the big-titted female vampires —their breasts rounded, pointy, and succulent under their black transparent gowns—bounding across verandas, where sombreroed musicians played, and crashing through high-arched windows to claim the amorous favors and blood of their male victims.)

A nice long afternoon, drinking and getting reacquainted, and Miguel finally bringing up one of the reasons, aside from friendship, for his visit. "A promoter I know, an Englishman who lives in London, has been wanting to mount a revival show at the London Palladium and he asked me to put together an orchestra and a lineup of singers. Of course, I told him about you."

"Yes?"

And the notion of traveling to Europe, to England, where he had never been, made the Mambo King happy.

"It's all being planned now, but I have some good people lined up already. And who knows, maybe we can take the show on a tour, to Madrid, Paris, Rome, all those beautiful places."

Miguel was enthusiastic enough to keep the Mambo King informed about the whole business, calling him every few months, but then he stopped hearing from him: and when he called Miguel's number in Phoenix, Arizona, where he had his home, someone who was taking care of Miguel's affairs informed the Mambo King that his old friend was dead.

"*Coño!*"

Once, he had almost seen his daughter again. He still corresponded with her, but what was she but a few fading lines of ink on paper? Then she wrote to say that her ballet company was going to be appearing in Montreal, Canada, in a production of *Giselle* with Alicia Alonso. Now in her early thirties, she had something to do with running the corps de ballet, and would he like to see her in that wintry city? Yes, he wrote. They made the arrangements and he bought a ticket, but the morning of the flight to Montreal he allowed his symptoms to blossom, and he could not move from his bed, and settled for a long, static-ridden conversation with his daughter at ten-thirty in the evening. His voice tired and trying to explain the pains in his body and the pains in his heart.

Then it was: "Well, I'm sorry we did not get the chance to see each other, Papi."

"Yes, daughter. It's the same for me. Another time?"

"Yes."

"You take care of yourself, my daughter."

"Yes, you take care of yourself, Papi."

And goodbye forever.

On another night, a singing job, and he came up out of the coolness of the basement, where it always felt like autumn, and undressed before his mirror. Off with his gray utility uniform, off with his belt with its loop of apartment keys, his shorts, his dirty white socks, and down the hallway to the bathroom.

Then the reverse, getting dressed. First, cologne behind his ears and neck; then talcum powder under his arms and on his hairy chest, with its scar over the right nipple. Clean pair of striped boxer shorts, then high silk socks with garters. On with his flamingo-pink shirt and fading white suit, tight around the middle, the front buttons straining under the threads' pull. Then on with his sky-blue tie and silver tie clip. He rubbed slick Bryl-creem into his hair, put a little Vaseline under his eyes to help disguise the wrinkles, then applied a wax pencil over his wisp of a mustache, like Cesar Romero's in the old movies. Then he put on his white golden-buckled shoes and spit-polished the soft leather with a chamois cloth. When he finished that, he looked himself over. Satisfied that he had not left a stitch out of place, he was ready to go.

Later, Cesar and his musicians were on the stage of the Club Tropical Paradise in the Bronx, a place run by Puerto Ricans who had been big Mambo King fans, finishing up their second set, a string of classics like *"El Bodeguero"* and *"Cachita,"* which had gotten even the old grandmothers and grandfathers to shake their bodies and laugh gaily as if they were young again. He had watched a wisp of a woman, thin and bent over like a branch, in a many-layered black dress from another age, turning into a twelve-year-old girl, her arthritic shoulders pulsing forward as if she'd just joined a conga line. Inspired, the Mambo King had blown his trumpet hard, winked, and shouted, *"Vaya!"* the notes of his solo sailing the rippling sea of 3/2 time, and the music had sounded so good that even his drowsy bass player Manny, tired from his day's work, began to awaken.

And with that they had gone into another song, and the Mambo King, despite a bad urge to urinate, began to dance, moving his big frame on the tiptoes of his white golden-buckled shoes. He sang and blew his trumpet hard as if he were a young man in Havana getting drunk and charging down the street with all the energy in the world, blowing until his face was red, his sides ached, and his head seemed ready to burst. Stepping back, he had turned toward his musicians, signaling the turnaround-and-out.

"Ladies and gentlemen," he said—

. . . in the Hotel Splendour, wishing he didn't have the bad pains . . .—into the microphone. "Thank you so much. We're glad you're enjoying yourselves."

And with his bladder full to aching (liver, kidney, hole-torn gut), he clicked off the microphone, stepped down off the wooden platform, and made his way across the crowded dance floor in the darkness, accidentally touching some nice female bottoms. Moving through that room, he felt surrounded, pressed, overwhelmed by youth. In this crowd of mostly young people, he felt ambassadorial, as if he were there to represent the declining older generation, closer to death, as they say, than to the light of youth.

—Running in a field, the ground rushing under him like a river—

So many pretty young women with big half-moon gold and pagoda-shaped earrings and with lightning-whipped curls and nice asses on slender, long-ankled dancers' legs. Silky blouses, thick with femininity, quivering and sheeny in the red party lights. Jostled, and lumbering, he pressed close to a woman who smelled like jasmine and sweat.

Nearly sixty now. And were the young chicks looking at him, the way they used to, up and down, and hoping that he might walk over and strike up a conversation? Now they treated him with a cheerful respect, with looks that said, "My, but he might have been a lady-killer once upon a time." In the old days he couldn't walk down the street without some pretty woman looking him sweetly, longingly in the eyes, but now? *Dios mío,* he had to work a lot harder for his seduction, and if he wanted a younger woman he'd have to pay for her, because now the women who desired him were not young chicks anymore, and that was something he couldn't accept.

But then, as he was making his way toward the toilet, he felt someone tugging at his jacket sleeve, and taking hold of his elbow, a pretty woman of thirty, thirty-five. *Coño!*

"Señor Castillo? My name is Lydia Santos. This is my cousin Alberto"—across the table from her, a thin-mustached man who resembled the 1930s film actor Leon Errol. "And I just wanted to tell you that I really like your music. You know, I have seen you before, years ago, when I was a young girl. My father would take me to the Teatro Hispano to see all the shows. I saw you there and in Brooklyn. And sometimes up in the Bronx. What was the name of that other place?"

"The Savoy," her cousin said.

"Yes. We played there a few times. With the Glorious Gloria Parker Orchestra. Many years ago. In 1954, it was."

(And now, on top of this memory, Glorious Gloria Parker and Her All-Girl Rumba Orchestra, playing a rumba version of "Moonlight Sonata," and one night Cesar and Gloria huddled at a table drinking daiquiris, and Gloria, magnificent in a flame-red dress and mantilla comb in her hair, saying to the Mambo King, "Would you guys like to work with us on second bill at this place in the Catskills?" and this fading out to a moonlit night where at three in the morning the Mambo King and Glorious Gloria are tottering along the edge of a lake, enchanted by the reflection of the moon and stars, teary with light in the water, and the pines stone-blue in the distance, and at one moment when the two bandleaders were standing close enough to feel each other's breath, she turned to him and put two of her fingers inside his shirt, her nails touching his skin and gnarly hair, and she said, in the fashion of that time, "Come on, ya big lug, why don't you kiss me?")

"I was just a kid, but I really liked your orchestra."

"Thank you, it's very much a compliment. Coming from so pretty a woman." And he bowed.

But there was suffering in his expression. The Mambo King wanted to stay and talk, but his bladder was aching. "Some more drinks here!" he called to the waiter.

Then he leaned forward and said to her, "I'll come back later so that we can talk, yes?"

Continuing toward the hallway toilets, thinking about that young girl of thirty or thirty-five. Lydia Santos. Most of the younger women he met had never heard of his orchestra, the Mambo Kings, or if they knew the name it was one out of dozens of other antique orchestras whose records their parents played when they were feeling nostalgic.

"I was just a kid, but I really liked your orchestra," he heard again as he made his way past the blaring jukebox.

At the end of a narrow foyer was a bolted-shut fire door, which disturbed him. He had once played a club in Queens where a fire had broken out in the kitchen deep fryer and they had had to smash in the fire door to the alley with an ax. (Wished that had happened at the Club Havana.) Huddled against the door, people were coughing and weeping because of the smoke and fear. That's why he always checked the fire exits.

—The fire engines sounding on the night of Nestor's death—

Along the hallway wall, a line of young men waiting to use the toilet (for urination, defecation, sprucing up, smoking *yerba,* the inhalation of cocaine), and among them the groom, *el novio,* for whom this party was being thrown. The young men were really fucked up and happy. One running joke in the line? About how the groom's sex organ was going to be sore by the following afternoon. He answered, "It's already been sore for a long time" —and they all slapped five.

In the presence of the young men, and buoyed by the attention of Lydia Santos, the Mambo King forgot his age and adopted the posture of a young wolf, with his collar and bow tie loosened. Exposed was his chest of tangled fleecy black-and-gray hair, and, on a chain, the crucifix and money amulet and the small bronze head of Changó nestling against the primeval dampness of his skin. A tallish fellow complimented the Mambo King (even though he had pushed the groom for one of those new disco groups with fancy machines, syn-drums and synthesizer pianos, but the bride's father had said, "A group is a group, and this Cesar Castillo's a real pro," which meant that Cesar charged a lot less than the others, and who cared if his music was a little old-fashioned?) and then offered the Mambo King and his bassist a drag of his marijuana cigarette.

No, thank you, he preferred rum over smoke, because smoke made him feel crazy, hear voices, and suspect that his dead brother Nestor was just around the corner.

Another young man made polite conversation and asked the Mambo King his opinion about the upcoming Panamanian, Rubén Blades, whom Cesar had heard and liked. "You must have known a lot of the greats in your time, huh?"

"Yes, you name 'em . . ." Puente, Eddie Palmieri, Ray Barretto, Pérez Prado. I knew a lot of guys going back a long time. Talented guys with style and good musical ideas who vanished into thin air. And they had to work hard. Most of them are where now? A friend of mine, a really good *conguero,* watches the dinosaur bones over at the Museum of Natural History. I have another friend, works as a steam presser downtown in the fashion district. He's too old to do anything else, but in his day he was a good trumpet player. You can feel bad for him, but he had his glory, and besides, for whatever reasons, that was his calling. He knew what he was getting into, *¿sabes?*

"Don't get me wrong, my friend," he continued. "You can make a living, but it's not easy, and forget getting rich." He peeked ahead to see if the line was moving and said to Manny, "How long is that guy going to be in there, huh?"

When he finally got into the smoky bathroom, he was startled: a green-and-blue parrot feather was floating in the toilet water. Taking out his big thing, he emptied his bladder. As he shut his eyes—curls of smoke from his cigarette rose into them —he thought about the young woman: he imagined her kneeling on the tile floor and undoing his trousers.

Come on, *hombre,* give the woman a break, he chided himself, and this brief image of desire dissolved, broken up in a wave of melancholy. He'd always thought his big *pinga* would take care of things, that he could get what he wanted by staring into a woman's eyes with his pretty-boy looks, press home his manhood by treating his ladies like shit, with arrogance, as if they were worthless, once his desire ran out. And there he was, an aging musician, with what to show for all his years in the world?

Wince of pain while remembering how he would carry his young brother on his shoulders across the yard in Cuba: his clinging, loving brother Nestor, his younger brother's thin hands gripping his neck, the kid laughing whenever Cesar bobbed up and down and neighed like a horse. Rode him to that shady part of the yard where the ladies of the household would gather to sew and wash and gossip. That big tub, filled to the brim with hot water and rose-scented soap, his mother saying to him, "First Nestor, and then you, my son."

The ladies of the household: *Mamá,* Genebria, and her friends, four jolly black women involved with magic who were always laughing at him and joking about his vanity, that one day it would get him into trouble. What were their names—he tried to remember now. Tomasa, Pereza, Nicolena, and Nisa, swirling around him in their red and yellow and mango-colored skirts, laughing. He hadn't thought of them for a long time, those cheerful women gathering around him and spoiling him to death with kisses.

Memory, repeated memory, of looking up into his mother's eyes and finding pure goodness and affection.

Pure goodness, his mother, but she could not do shit against the power of his father, who beat her, beat him, and tried to beat his free spirit into the ground. Frightened his younger brother to death so that he would go through life like . . . a little girl. That powerless goodness.

Why was he thinking about that suddenly, those years later in the Hotel Splendour?

Looking in the bathroom mirror, he laughed at himself. "Shame on you, *viejito*, for even thinking about that young woman."

How could he think about that young woman when he was wearing a *faja*, a girdle?

What had the doctors told him in the hospital?

No more pleasure in this life for you.

Now he checked himself out sideways, sucking in his stomach. With his head tilted up in a noble fashion, he bore some resemblance to the Cesar Castillo of Mambo King fame, whose face adorned the cover of that immortal album "The Mambo Kings Play Songs of Love."

Leaving the toilet, he moved briskly, chest out, huge belly in, thumped shoulders, patted the children who were running circles around the adults, waved hello and winked at the older ladies. Then he made his way back up to the stage. As he stood before the microphone and turned to click on the standby switch of an amplifier, he felt acid surging in his gut. Earlier that night, he had had two plates of *lechón asado,* which he'd seasoned with a handful of salt and the juice of a hearty lemon; then *tostones,* crisply fried and browned, French fries, *arroz moro,* some *yuca.*

The rum, however, was what cut into his gut. It went down his gullet like melting ice but started to burn in the vicinity (kissed by a thousand women) of his vibrating diaphragm. Occasionally, he chewed a Rolaids antacid. Over the years, he had guzzled bottles of milk of magnesia and ordinary milk to relieve his distress. At times, he even tried an invention of his own,

which he called a "69," milk and rum and crème de menthe or
Amaretto, as if the candy taste and limpid texture could ward off
the pain. And although the attacks in his gut and the throbbing
in his kidneys and liver sometimes woke him in the middle of the
night, and good friends like Manny the bassist, Bernardito, and
Dr. López had advised him to take better care of himself, he
continued to ignore them.

Soon enough, the Mambo King and his musicians launched
into another set of pieces like "The Cuban Mambo," the "Tre-
mendo Cumbancha," "Cua, Cua, Cua." Then it was bolero time
and "Beautiful María of My Soul."

As he had for years and years, the Mambo King sang that
bolero, his vocal cords quivering, his face radiant with sincere,
love-drenched emotion: arms spread wide before his corpulent
body, he sang to the women with all his heart. And looking at
the crowd, his eyes found Lydia: she had been staring at him, a
bent straw dangling from between her cherry-red lips. He sang
the last verse of the song to her, and only her. While navigating
the melancholic beauty of that melody, he had thought to himself:
There goes that young chick again, looking at me.

(Oh, Christ, Jesus, my Lord and Saviour, please explain on
this sad night why so many people have cried.)

They played till around three-thirty, and then the musicians
gathered around a table, waiting for their pay. There were still
a lot of people out on the dance floor, silhouettes of clinging
bodies, a room of shadows under the pink and red lights, tight
circles in the glare of the computer-controlled jukebox flashing:
MOST POPULAR SELECTION! The bride's father was reminiscing by
the bar, and taking his time. It was just as well: the musicians were
exhausted, particularly Manny, slumped in his chair and whispering, "When is that man finally going to pay us, huh?"

"I'll take care of it. Don't you worry."

"Yes, of course, how could I forget my friend!" And the
bride's father handed Cesar Castillo an envelope containing three
hundred dollars—that was fifty dollars for each of the five musicians, for seven and a half hours of live music, plus a fifty-dollar
tip to split among themselves—a good night.

While the musicians collected their instruments, cables, and
microphones, the Mambo King, tie loosened, shirt open, stopped

by Lydia's table to say goodbye. First he shook her cousin's hand, a manly handshake, but with Lydia he displayed gentlemanly aplomb, kissing the knuckles of her right hand. As he did so, he felt her hand warming. And she blushed, too.

Then he said to her, "Could this *viejito* take the pleasure of calling you sometime?"

"Yes."

On the back of a Budweiser beer coaster she wrote, "Lydia Santos, 989-8996."

"Thank you."

Was she really interested in him, or was she just being nice to an old man? Still, he couldn't help kissing her hand again and following this up with a tender smile. Then, like a king cock, he strutted out the door with Frankie.

He and Frankie got a lift with Manny. Riding west on the Cross Bronx Expressway, the Mambo King was far from tired. He did not yawn, he did not lean back in the car seat lolling, he did not even particularly feel the pains in his gut anymore. Instead, he tapped his feet and felt like partying. Manny dropped the Mambo King and Frankie off on La Salle Street and wearily made his way home, where he would lock up his bass and amplifier in his *bodega.* But Cesar?

"Frankie, you want to come upstairs and have a drink with me?"

"It's five in the morning."

"You can stay with me."

"Let me go home. My wife is waiting."

"Come on, she knows you're with me."

Up the stairs to Cesar's apartment they went, beyond the hallway and into the kitchen, where Cesar made them nice drinks. In the living room he put on one of his favorite records, "Dancemania" by Tito Puente, and then they sat on the couch drinking. *Coño,* that young woman had liked him, and now the world buzzed with well-being. He had the sensation that goodwill was flowing into him, that he was the center of a benevolent and beautiful universe. Exhausted, Frankie soon dozed. But Cesar remained awake, jubilant and happy, as if everything around him were showing him affection: the old couch, the easy chair, the Victorian-looking chairs by the window which he had brought up from the basement, the big blue-tubed Zenith color TV, his conga drums, his maracas saying "Cuba," his stereo console. The glint of old and new record spines in the cabinet, the half bottle of Bacardi rum, his black instrument case, all communicating love.

He kept a little Cuban flag on the television and in the corner of the room a little cabinet dedicated to the memory of Nestor. He and Nestor and the other Mambo Kings smiled at him now from atop an art-deco seashell bandstand circa 1950. Then the other framed pictures on the wall smiling at him: Tito, Pérez, and yes, once again, he and Nestor posed alongside Desi Arnaz.

(For one moment, as he sat by the window in the summer's heat in that room in the Hotel Splendour, Cesar Castillo had the impression of standing before the door to Desi Arnaz's apartment, his brother Nestor, alive and well and young, beside him.)

Then there were more pictures of his family. His niece and nephew as babies, then toddlers, and onward into life: Leticia in her First Communion gown, Leticia pictured with a blue-tasseled mortarboard on her head on the day of her graduation from Sacred Heart of Mary High School, Leticia on the day of her wedding to a nice Jewish fellow named Howard. Eugenio as a soldier of Christ on his confirmation, in the Chapel of Corpus Christi, black missal in hand, the spirit of Christ radiating light behind him. A shot taken of Cesar and his dead brother and Delores in front of a Chinatown restaurant a few hours after his brother and sister-in-law had gotten married. Delores in a polka-dotted dress, holding a flower; Nestor in a smart-looking blue serge suit. Pictures of his daughter, Mariela, taken in Havana when she was little.

And among these pictures, the Mambo King imagined himself with Lydia, posed as if he were a young man again, looking forward to a million nights of love and a bright, happy future, as if he would be able to relive and do certain things over again. Even the tick-tocking clock on the kitchen wall seemed to be smiling at him.

Then abruptly the sun began rising out of the east and the window burned with an orange-and-red light. And like a character in a bolero, the Mambo King happily felt young again: while Frankie the Exterminator snored away by the kitchen table, a name flew, light as a falling flower, through Cesar's world-weary soul, flew through the layers of macho and doubt, anger and contempt. "Lydia."

The next week the Mambo King nervously called Lydia Santos, inviting her out to dine with him.

"Yes, I would like that," she told him.

The first night they went out, the Mambo King found himself pacing up and down on the 96th Street Express platform, waiting for her train from the Bronx. He wore a lavender leisure suit, white wing-tipped shoes, and a black-brimmed lacquered cane hat. Big shades, so that she would not be able to check out the stage droop beneath his eyes. Lowlifes seemed to be everywhere around him. Long gone were the days when you could take a nap under a shady tree in the park without worrying that someone would go through your pockets. He'd come and gone from jobs on the subway, witnessed fleet-footed thieves stationed by the subway doors, reading the *Daily News* sports page one second and, pssst, the next moment, just before the car doors closed, yanking off a thick gold chain or a purse or a radio and running down the platform. Snap of the fingers, like that. He once saw a man walk into a car and slash open another man's shirt so he could get at the other guy's wallet: the victim did not even stir. He had seen jackets pulled off the backs of sleeping men on trains, shoes yanked off feet. And the number of beggars! Never used to be so many of them in the old days. He'd give to the old, not the young men. There was an Indian fellow whose body seemed to have been cut in half. He would wheel himself through the subway cars on a skateboard, holding out a tin cup, which Cesar always filled with change. (How did that poor suffering man take care of his business in the toilet? What love did he have in his life?)

And now things were so filthy: back in the 1950s, the subway platforms were clean. On each column there was either a one-cent gum or a five-cent candy-bar machine; no newsstands, no pizzerias, no hamburger, hot-dog joints. No shit, piss, dirty rags, piles of garbage . . .

Fare 10 cents, cane seats, and white enamel strap handles.

(He now closes his eyes and sees that he is walking down the street with Nestor again.)

He tried to mind his own business, while party-anxious squads of teenagers with loud radios crowded the platform. *Coño*, the Mambo King thought, sticking close to the edge of the platform. *Coño!*

"Hey, man, do you have a cigarette?"

"Sure."

"Chesterfields? Who smokes Chesterfields?"

To that, the Mambo King felt like responding, "That is the preferred brand of the Mambo King, Cesar Castillo." But he looked away.

"You have a quarter?"

"No."

"You mean, you have no money?"

"No, I'm sorry."

"Whatchew sorry about, you old faggot!"

She was half an hour late.

"My sister who looks out after my kids had trouble getting to my house."

He was angry about having to wait for her: fifteen years ago, she would not have found him waiting there. He would have waited an extra ten minutes and then he would have gone out without her.

"Come on, let's go." And they caught a local down to 23rd Street.

They rode in silence for much of the way, but then he told her, "You look pretty."

She was wearing a navy-blue dress with black felt buttons and white trim, dark nylons and black high heels. She had brushed her hair back and into a ponytail; a dark, nearly brown rouge and mascara, and a light pink lipstick all intended to throw the heat off her few wrinkles, and off her sadness, too. She was pretty, her skin was good save for a small scar in the shape of a star or bursting flower on her forehead.

"I figured that we would get something to eat," he told her. "And then go out dancing."

They went to Violeta's, where Cesar was always treated well, drank a few pitchers of sangria, and fumbled around for conversation. Aside from flirtatious jiving, Cesar had never really known how to talk to women. To sing romantic boleros, yes, to commence audacious seductions, to tell a woman, "You're beautiful, baby," yes. But what would he say to a woman nearly thirty years younger than himself?

When the waiter came by, Cesar Castillo grabbed him by the elbow and said to Lydia, "I want you to hear something, Lydia, a little piece of music."

And to the waiter: "Do me a favor, Julio, put on one of those tapes for me?"

From a cassette player behind the counter came a snow-blizzard version of "Twilight in Havana."

"That was my orchestra, the Mambo Kings. Do you like it?"

"Oh, yes!"

"With your parents' generation, I was a little famous. How old are you, anyway, *querida?*"

"Older than thirty."

"Yes?"

They listened to the music for a time, and he talked about Cuba. In those days it was a big subject with him.

"I haven't been back in twenty years. With Castro there now, I don't think I'll ever get back."

"And you have family there?"

"Some. I have a brother there, who doesn't seem to mind things; two others in Miami. And my father. He still lives on the farm where I was born. In Oriente."

And he told her about his daughter, Mariela, a ballet dancer with a Communist dance company headed by Alicia Alonso. His daughter, who existed in his life in the form of a few occasional letters.

Perhaps he also had bastard children, but if he did, he didn't know their names.

"See, the worst part of it is that things don't exist anymore."

"What things?"

"Cuba."

"It will change perhaps," she said. "I have friends who say that Fidel is about to fall."

"Everybody says that. But even if that were to happen, things would not be the same. Too many people want to kill each other down there . . . And for another thing, I'm not a young man anymore."

"Don't say that!"

"I wear these big glasses so that you don't see this old *viejito*'s eyes."

"Take them off! Let me make the judgment."

And he took off his sunglasses.

"You have young-looking eyes. They're green, aren't they?"

"Twilight in Havana" turned into *"Los Guajiros,"* and the upbeat tempo of this old *guaracha* piece had Lydia tapping her glass.

What else had she said to him that night—he tried to remember:

"I've two children, Rico and Alida. I live up near where you were playing. I work in a factory downtown."

"And you were married, yes?"

"My husband is in Puerto Rico."

"Puerto Rico, nice place. You know, I've spent time down there. In San Juan, and out by Mayagüez. That's really beautiful."

Later (and this was a pleasure for him to remember) the Mambo King took her to the Club 95, where they danced the *merengue* all night. (That was right next door to the senior citizens' hall, where he had once seen Machito up on a ladder, putting curtains on a window.) That old-fashioned twirl-your-partner country dance from the Dominican Republic was back in vogue, and Cesar Castillo, an old man, showed her how to do it. And it impressed her that he seemed to know just about everyone in the place. And though he drank and smoked too much, he behaved in a gentlemanly and dignified manner. Everybody who greeted the Mambo King at their table seemed to have a good word for him and showed him respect—that was just what she wanted.

And he was generous. Around two o'clock in the morning, his sides began to ache, and so he yawned and said, "It's very late, Lydia."

They left the club together. She thought they would be going to the subway, but on the street he called her a taxi.

"No, no, you get in," he said, and they got in together.

At La Salle Street, he said to her: "I live over there in that building. Now you tell him where you want to go, okay? And think about me."

From the street corner in the shadow of the 125th Street El, he watched the cab continue its way north. At first she thought of telling the driver to pull over at 125th Street and Lex, so that she could take the subway and pocket the difference, but it was very late, and she felt that, old man or not, this Cesar Castillo was kindly, the type of fellow who would help her out. Frugal with her money, a woman who nursed drinks until her ice cubes melted and her lemons were sucked dry, she sat in the back of the taxi, holding on to one of the straps, luxuriating in this sudden comfort. And when she stopped, up on 174th Street, she gave the driver a dollar tip.

He took her out at least once a week, on whatever nights they could both manage. In his gray utility uniform, feet up on the cluttered worktable, the Mambo King would call her in the late afternoon, his questions having a wonderful and reassuring effect on Lydia: "How are your children? Is there something I can get for them that you need? Or for you? Do you need extra light bulbs or fuses for your apartment? Tell me, *mi vida,* anything you want."

Invigorated by her companionship, the Mambo King became cheerful in those days. Ana María, Delores's sister, took one look at him during an evening meal and declared, "I don't believe it, your old brother-in-law is in love! Look at his gooey eyes!"

They'd go to joints like the Tropic Sunset or the New Sans Souci, places where he had sometimes worked. These were nice clubs, he'd tell her, but nothing like what used to be around: nightclubs done up like the insides of Egyptian temples, clubs with thirty-five-girl chorus lines, with glittering chandeliers, long-legged cigarette girls, shoeshine boys, and formal dress codes.

"This generation," he would say to her, as he'd say to Eugenio, "has lost its sense of elegance."

He did not tell her about the Club Havana.

Sometimes he'd take her to the Roseland Ballroom, where an older crowd hung out. When they weren't mamboing on the dance floor, they would sit at a little table in the back, holding hands and drinking rum and Coke. Now and then someone would come over and reminisce about the great ballroom era.

There were times when an angelic cast would pass over his features and she would say, "How young you look now." He never tried to kiss her and was content just to be seen around town with her. And he was always buying Lydia presents: dresses and boxes of sweets, perfume from the drugstore.

Then, on Puerto Rican Day, he met Lydia and her two kids at the 59th Street station and took them over to Fifth Avenue to watch the big parade. On one of the floats, surrounded by pom-pom-twirling, pink puff-brassiered and mink-bikinied showgirls with plumed headdresses, stood Mr. Salsa himself, Tito Puente, white-haired and imperial, waving at his fans. Then processions of dancers and Channel 47 television personalities—a float featuring the winsome Iris Chacón, a Goya foods float with conga players in black-bean costumes, then more floats with *salsa* bands, and a float in the shape of the island of Puerto Rico and on its throne the splendid Miss San Juan; country dancers and guitarists and vocalists singing mountain *pregones*.

After this great spectacle, they made their way through the park, visiting the beer stands again and again, and buying the children treats: *cuchifritos, pasteles,* and sausage sandwiches. Garbage cans overflowing with melting ice cream and soda, bees everywhere; ants teeming on the sweet garbage-can rims. They went to the zoo, into the monkey house, the monkeys bounding from rung to rung with their pink asses protruding like pompous lips into the air and their lanky arms grabbing through the cages: they stood for a long time watching the monkeys eating everything thrown at them: pieces of Snickers, popcorn, hamburger buns, peanuts, chewing gum, even shreds of a plastic Puerto Rican flag, families leaning close over the railing—"*Mira, mira el mono!"*— the Mambo King with his young *pollita,* one hand around her waist and the other holding the hand of her daughter.

He'd take them all out to eat and they could have whatever they wanted, and when their eyes flared with desire while passing a Baskin-Robbins ice-cream parlor or a toy shop, the Mambo King would lead them inside. He'd take a crumpled five-dollar bill out of his pocket and say, "Go ahead." And at the end of these days out, he would either put them in a taxi or ride the train with them up to the Bronx, protecting them with his sword-tip cane.

Slowly he got to know her. She worked downtown on 26th Street, off Sixth Avenue, in a factory that manufactured eyeglass frames. Her job consisted of grinding holes into frames with a pen-sized drill (wearing goggles), so that small rhinestones could be glued in. She was hired to take the place of a man who, having had that job for twenty years, went blind. She had no insurance, it was an eight-and-a-half-hour day, and she earned $2.50 an hour. Working there, she made just enough to pay her bills and get to work, so that she could have just enough to pay her bills and get to work. And there had been a few men who liked her, as long as her children weren't in the picture. But he liked the children and was good to her.

That's all she wanted, without going any further, she'd tell him: "That you be good to me."

They had been going together for two months and were watching television in her living room in the Bronx. The Mambo King was massaging her feet: she was tired from standing all week, and when he finished massaging her feet, he began on her ankles, and his hands moved up to her thighs, and he expected her to turn away, because who wanted an old man? But she said, *"Sigue.* Go on," and closed her eyes, and soon his hand was kneading her womb through her panties, which soaked through with moisture, and wiry pubic hairs stuck out the sides, and then he did what old men always talk about, knelt between her legs, and while some cowboy movie played on, with *vaqueros* chasing a herd of cattle, he pulled her panties low and tongue-kissed her and just could not believe it when she pulled him forward. He stood before her with his trousers still on, and it looked as if he had stuck a beer bottle down the front of his pants, because she asked, "And what is that?" and touched him there and gasped when he showed her, the way Genebria had when he was a kid, and for a moment he felt immortal.

Then he smothered her with his body: she was nicely plump, with the scars of a cesarian section above her thick black pubic hair, which was not much of a shield, and she had stretch marks all over her breasts, but looked so beautiful, and even though his bones ached and his guts twisted, he went at her for a long time, and when with his enormous stomach he finally burst, he flew headlong through a field of redness, ground his teeth, and felt her interior doubling back on itself like a warm silken glove turned inside out.

From that night on, she took to calling the Mambo King "My pretty old man," and "My *machito.* "

Though he was sixty years old, he suckled her breasts like a baby, thinking to himself, What luck I have. I was born in 1918, and here I am with this young chick."

When he'd finish in bed with her, he'd fall back like a dead man, his eyes fixed on the wall, daydreaming about youth and strength and speed, his face nestled against her breasts.

Afterwards, he said, "I love you, Lydia."

But he didn't know if it was the truth of his heart: he'd lied so often to women over the years, had mistreated and misunderstood so many women, that he had resigned himself to forgetting about love and romance, those very things he used to put in songs.

All through the night, like a young man, he whispered, half singing, "The thought of not possessing you is an agony I cannot bear."

IT WAS A SUNDAY AFTERNOON and the church had set up a block party on 121st Street. Father Vincent had asked Cesar to provide the music. He had rounded up some of his friends and had asked the Puerto Ricans with the slick black hair to play rock 'n' roll.

Lydia turned up in a pink summer suit which fit her well when she first wore it, a present, like so many others, from Cesar. But in the intervening months, the Mambo King had gone to her apartment in the Bronx with several pounds of groceries, pastries, and steaks from the plant on 125th Street, and when he learned that she had a weakness for chocolate, he had started to buy her pound bags of bitter Dutch chocolate from a fancy European-style shop near the university. And they were always going to restaurants, and when they weren't doing that, Lydia was busy proving herself as some kind of cook, taking his money and going crazy at the supermarket—cooking all the Cuban and Puerto Rican dishes, like fried plantains and roast pork and rice and beans, and Italian food, too. Cooking up big pans of lasagna and pots of spaghetti with seafood (*alle vongole,* as she called it), and served up big salads doused in olive oil. With all this, she had started to get fat.

As his prodigious manly appetites began to wane under the onslaught of the years (his penis had thickened and stretched from years of use and occupied his trousers like a dozing mutt), he became more and more interested in food. She didn't mind, though her nice butt was more pronounced. As for the kids? They had not eaten so well in all their lives, and they were happy whenever the Mambo King visited them in the Bronx.

So she had put on a few extra pounds. What did that matter when he gloried in the expansiveness of her youthful flesh? He could suck her nipple gratefully for an hour, until it turned purple and grew distended between his teeth and lips; he would revel in the kneading of her quivery flesh. And her hips got much bigger and were ready to burst the seams of her dresses. More men looked and spoke to her as she passed by. And while this made the Mambo King proud, as it used to when he'd make an entrance with the likes of Miss Vanna Vane back in the old days, he'd scowl sternly at these oglers, throw his chest out as if he was ready to fight.

After setting up, he had waited on the stage for her. As the priest was giving a speech about how the poor inherited not the earth but God's "other bounties," Cesar spotted Lydia in the crowd, and just seeing her made him happy. Up on the stage, he had thoughts like: I love you, baby, I send you my kisses; I can't wait until we are locked in a lovers' embrace.

Those were the days when he had started to tell himself that he was in love, truly in love with Lydia. The kind of love he hadn't felt since his first loves back in Oriente, like the love he had felt for his wife back in the Cuba of the 1940s.

(It was all coming back to him in his old age. Fantasies about what might have happened to him had he remained with her, hadn't left their small town for Havana and his destiny. He might have gotten himself a good job through her family, maybe work in the sugar mill as foreman. He might have had himself a little orchestra for the weekends and for festivals in Cuba, satisfying at least part of his wish for a musician's life. And his brother Nestor would have remained in Cuba with him, too. He might have fathered a brood of loving sons, instead of a single daughter, to keep him company in his sunset years. And instead of all that pussy? He might have contented himself with a mistress or two in town, the way his father, Pedro, had. Even this fantasy did not hold water, because eventually he would have had to leave Cuba.)

That day, the musicians opened their set with a jam instrumental called "Traffic Mambo." The Mambo King wore a light pinstriped summer suit, and his thick head of hair was shiny with hair tonic. His voice echoed against the buildings as he leaned into the microphone, announcing, "And now, ladies and gentlemen, it's time for a little *charrrannnnnnga!*"

Having spotted Lydia, he put on a good show to impress her. As he turned in circles, he was astounded by his love for her: even the knots in his gut and the swirling juices inside his body seemed to go away when he thought about her. Memory upon memory: Lydia's naked body, Lydia sitting before a mirror brushing out her hair, her plump buttocks, the plum-shaped darkness between them, and the Mambo King's aged member lolling on his belly and then growing stiff—just from looking at her. Then he'd fuck her from behind, inserting himself into that plum of space, and it gave him just what it seemed to be promising: heat, and moisture, curvaceous grip.

(*Dios mío, Dios mío*—toasting the busyness in his heart and

mind—I really had fallen for that woman and, *coño,* fallen hard
for her, the way my poor brother fell for that Beautiful María
piece-of-shit from Havana, the way I fell for my wife. And so he
swallowed the rum, and then had a pleasant experience: a slight
elation, the sensation that he was breaking the law of gravity and
lifting with his chair off the ground, and then the fan, turning
from atop the dresser in his room in the Hotel Splendour, hitting
his face, and then a whisk of air hitting him dead between the legs
and licking at his penis through the slot in his boxer shorts, a lick
like the morning licks of youth, and boom, he found his thing
stiffening, though not fully, because of the lick of the air, the rum,
and his thoughts of Lydia, a beautiful sensation: if he was a
younger man, the Mambo King would have masturbated, floated
off on clouds of speculation and hope of future seductions, but
now, in his current condition, masturbation seemed sad and
hopeless, and so, instead, he took another sip of his rum. On the
record player spun that great Mambo King tune "Traffic
Mambo," except that it sounded much different from the way he
remembered it: sounded as if there were a hundred musicians
playing on the version he was hearing now, with all kinds of
instruments added: glass bells and harps, church organs and Oriental chimes. Sounded as if there was a river rushing in the
distance and the chaos of a hundred automobiles honking their
horns all at once. Plus he hadn't really remembered that the
trumpet solo played by his dead brother Nestor had been so long,
it seemed to go on forever in the version he was now hearing. The
Mambo King's confusion made him get up. There was a small
mirror over a sink: then a closet-sized bathroom, just enough
room for the commode and the shower. He was drunk enough
by now that, as he looked in the mirror, all the lines of age and
sadness had more or less been smoothed out, the gray of his hair
seeming more silver, the jowlishness of his face more like the
mark of substance rather than excess. He washed his face and then
sat down again. He found himself rubbing his legs: the underside
of his legs was riddled with thick, distended varicose veins, blue
and as twisty as the thick vein that burst like a river with tributaries up the underside of his big thing. These weren't little varicose
veins like those showing through little-old-lady brown nylons,

but worm veins, all up and down the backs of his legs. He touched them for a moment and laughed: how he used to pick on his wife in Cuba the day he noticed that a few varicose veins had appeared on her legs, calling her *feita*— ugly—when she was still so young and, in her way, pretty.)

From the stage he watched Lydia like that hound who watched the basement entrance of the building down the street. An old German shepherd with matty coat and milk-cornered eyes, barking at every passerby and sniffing between the legs of every canine interloper. Lydia paid attention to the Mambo King, watching him faithfully from the street, but then she went over to get herself a sandwich from one of the tables, and men started to speak to her.

What were they saying?

"Why don't you dance with me?"

"I can't."

"But why?"

"I'm with the singer of the group over there."

"Cesar Castillo?"

"Yes."

"But you're so young! Why are you with that *viejito?*"

That's what he thought they were saying.

But the men were just being friendly. When the Mambo King saw her dancing with one of them, he was suddenly overcome with vertigo. Why was she dancing the *pachanga* with that fellow? Twenty years ago he would have smiled, telling himself, "So?" But now the heat of humiliation burned at the back of his neck and he felt like climbing down off the stage and separating them.

Then he devised a strategy to regain her attention and remind her of her loyalty. "I dedicate this song to a very special woman in my life. This song is for my woman, Lydia Santos."

But she continued to dance with the son of a bitch, and he felt depressed.

Work was work, however, and the Mambo King and his musicians played other numbers: mambos, rumbas, *merengues,* boleros, and a few cha-cha-chas. He hadn't suffered through a set like that since the days after Nestor's death. When the group finally took a break and began to pack up—there was a local rock 'n' roll group waiting to go on—he made straightaway for Lydia, who pretended that nothing was happening.

"Cesar! I've been waiting for you!" And she kissed him. "This is Richie."

The man she had been dancing with was a slender-looking fellow in a nice clean *guayabera,* handsome even with a pock-scarred face.

"Mucho gusto, " the young man said, but the Mambo King would not even shake his hand.

Then he said to Lydia, "Come on, I want to talk to you."

"Why are you doing this to me?"

"Because I am the man and I don't want you with anyone else."

"We were just dancing. The music sounded good. We were just having a little fun."

"I don't care. I told you how I feel."

They were standing just inside the lobby of 500 La Salle, Cesar's building.

"I may be an old man to you, but I'm not going to be cuckolded because of that. I was this way when I was young, and I am not going to change now."

"Okay, okay"—and she put her hands up and then gave him a kiss on the neck. He patted her nice *nalgitas,* and as the anger drained from him, said, "I'm sorry if I sound so harsh with you. There are a lot of wolves out there. Come on, let me buy you an ice cream, and then I want you and your children to meet someone."

He made a burning sound: "Pssssssssh, my, but you look good, Lydia."

And: "Look what you do to me."

They attended the block party like everyone else, Cesar treating her children as if he were their father—or grandfather. That afternoon he introduced Lydia to his friends. Frankie and Bernardito had met her before. They had all gone out with their women to restaurants together. Still, he took her by the hand and with his king-cock strut introduced her to his other friends on the street. His mood seemed calmer now. And she did not feel so bad. She did not mind that he was nearly thirty years older, though sometimes when they were in bed together she felt this terrible weight of mortality on her. His spectacular sexual nature sometimes made his whole body shake: his face would turn beet-red from his efforts to impress her, and she was afraid that he might have a heart attack or a stroke. She'd never had any man like him and so spoiled him with praise and adoration that he started to become deluded with the feeling that he had become exempt from the ravages of the years. She was overwhelmed by him. She felt, as had scores of other women before her, his bestial nature.

He would be shoving himself inside her and she would make it a point of saying things like "You're going to burst me apart." And: *"Tranquilo, hombre. Tranquilo."* And she moaned and shouted. She didn't want him to get the look of boredom that other men sometimes got with her, after a certain point. She wanted to say and do everything that he wanted her to, for the simple reason that he was good to her and her children.

So, he was a little jealous. She forgave that; after all, he was an old man, even if he was a pretty old man. That's what she had taken to calling him, he'd remember. *"Dame un besito, mi viejito lindo."* And whatever one could say about his current situation, that he worked as a superintendent and took small-time jobs here and there as a musician, he had been some kind of famous man. Even though she was thirty-five years old, she had still not lost her childhood awe for the crooners of his generation. And the man had even been on television. She knew the very episode of the *I Love Lucy* show that he and Nestor had appeared on: he'd even brought her a box of photographs to look at, and had given her one of himself with Arnaz and his poor dead brother. Proudly, she had shown it to people in her building.

He was the kind of man who had done a lot in life. He didn't just hang out, like so many others. He was wise and would be able to help her. Looking at pictures of him when he was young and a pretty boy made her sigh. Sometimes it killed her when she would think about young men. Of course she wished he was younger, but she also knew that he would never have stayed with her in the days of his glory. So she had him now in his decline. So what, she would say, if he had jowls, a huge stomach, and

testicles that reached halfway down to his knees (like his *pinga!*).
What did she care about that, as long as he promised to help her
children out?

(She had to tell herself this, yes?)

Later, he finally got the chance to introduce her to the family.

"So this is your young *pollita?*" Delores said to Cesar.
He shrugged.

On Delorita's television blared the film *Godzilla.* Pedro was
in his traditional spot, the easy chair, reading the newspaper and
having a drink. Sitting behind him on the couch, Leticia with her
baby. She'd come up from Long Island for a visit. She played
with her baby's toes, spoke baby talk, oblivious to the television
and the rest of the commotion in the apartment. Her brother,
Eugenio, shared the couch, sitting close to the window. He'd
propped it open a bit and put an ashtray there on the sill so he
could smoke and brood in peace. Cesar always liked to see him,
which was not often, but the kid always seemed pissed off: he'd
been that way for a long time. (Eugenio never understood any
of this. An innocent at heart, he had a temper that flared when,
as with the other Castillo men, melancholia abruptly came over
him and he would suffer from his own plague of memories. When
he was angry, he would find himself saying things he did not
really mean, such as "Everybody in the world can go fuck themselves" and "I don't need anyone," which had frightened many
people away from him.)

Now he would turn up at the apartment on La Salle Street,
disappointed and bitter.

When Cesar brought Lydia into the living room, Eugenio
was struck by her good looks. He liked pretty women, too, and
leapt out of his sullenness for a moment, as if jumping out of an
airplane. "Why, helllllllo." Eugenio was friendly to her, but once
the introductions were over, his mood reverted and he sat by the
window, thinking. The older he got, the more he picked up on
his long-dead father's temperament. He went through moods of
prolonged anguish and discontent: his eyes grew sad over the
smallest thing, his face drooped over the fact that life was not

perfect. Although he was not consciously aware of it, Eugenio had by now acquired the same expression he forever associated with his father, the same shattered expression of Nestor Castillo in his role as Alfonso Reyes, who would appear again and again at Desi Arnaz's door. His father's shattered expression, on entering that room, hat in hand, guitar demurely by his side, his face in some kind of agony.

(When he was a kid, his father's expression was "Cuban": melancholic, longing. Arnaz had it, his Uncle Cesar had it, Frankie, Manny, and most of the Cubans who walked into the household, jitterbugs and all, had it.)

"Eugenio, I want you to meet Lydia!"

Eugenio stood up and bowed. He was wearing a black turtleneck—in summer!—bluejeans, sneakers. He was supposed to go downtown and meet some friends who were trying to fix him up with some woman, but he didn't care. At least at the apartment Aunt Ana María was around to give him a nice big kiss now and then, and he never had to explain his moods to her, the way he had to with his girlfriends.

"So you're Lydia?" asked Delores. "The young chick with the old rooster." And she laughed, setting the tone for the afternoon.

Later they had dinner, and that was when Cesar noticed how Delores seemed to glare at Lydia. It couldn't be jealousy about her looks. Delores had held up well over the years. What was it?

Well, the Mambo King told himself as he reeled dizzily in his room in the Hotel Splendour, no one in the family had ever thought that Delores felt love for Pedro, not even when he was younger and courting her.

And she could have had me, he told himself.

Was that it?

It had more to do with the fact that, now Eugenio and Leticia had moved out, her reasons for staying with Pedro had gone out the window.

The Mambo King had once heard her say: "If he dies, I'll be better off."

But there was something else: after so many years of waiting, she had finally enrolled in college.

It hit her one day while sitting in an English literature class that she couldn't bear it when Pedro's hands searched under her robe at night: it didn't take much for her nipples to get hard, just touching them did that, but he fancied that it was the particular motion of the same thumb that he held a pencil in that did it, the ball of his thumb just touching her and her nipple getting hard. And so his thin but long fish-headed penis went inside her. And she went somewhere else, far away from that room.

(She was on a bed with Nestor, getting it from behind, raising her haunches so high because when he'd turn up he never seemed to have much time, as he was always dressed up in a white silk suit, like the one he'd worn on the night he died and when he appeared on that television show—he'd barely enough time to pull down his trousers, but she was always in bed waiting for him. And because he liked to do it from behind—he used to say he felt that it went in the deepest like that—she always let him. Sometimes she turned to cream where she was sitting, had to pull herself together. Tired of weeping at night and of losing herself in books and in the petty activities of running a household. By that time she had felt like bursting into pieces.)

And her feelings showed, because later, after Cesar had taken Lydia home, Delores exulted in deriding him: "She's very nice, Cesar. But don't you think she's a little young for you?" (Riding him, the way she used to nearly thirty years ago.)

"But why fool yourself with her? What have you got to give her, except some money?"

"Ask yourself, what would she want with an old man like you?"

(And he had to hold his tongue, because everyone knew what had happened to Delores while taking some night courses up at City College. She had fallen in love with a genteel literature student, a man younger than herself, with whom she went to bed for several months. And because of the way it ended, with the man running away from her, she had become more careless with herself and went walking on a bad street on her way home from college, and two black men pulled her into an alley and tore off the nice necklace Nestor had given her and they took her watch and a bracelet that had been a Christmas present. Then one of the men pulled down his trousers and the other threatened to kill her if she said a word, but she let out with some kind of howl, lit windows for blocks everywhere, and the men left her there, clothing torn up, lying on the ground, her books all around her.)

"Listen here, Delorita. Say whatever you want to me, but be good to her, huh? She's the last chance I've got."

So happiness came back into the Mambo King's life. Like a character in a happy habanera, he went through his days listening to sonorous violins and moved through rooms thick with the scent of flowers, as if out of a *canción* by Agustín Lara.

(Now he remembers riding along the dirt roads from Las Piñas on a borrowed mule, a cane hat pulled low over his brow and a guitar slung over his back, and, coming to a field of wild-flowers, dismounting from his mule and walking out to where the flowers were thickest: crouching and looking through the stems and blossoms, sun hot in the sky and a rattling cutting through the trees: now he picked hibiscus and violets and chrysan-themums, irises and hyacinths, tranquil among the bees and bur-rowing beetles and ants teeming around the sole of his soft leather shoes: deep inhalation of that fragrant air and the world going on forever and ever. Then he was on his mule again and making the approach to the farm. On the porch of their house, his mother and Genebria, always so happy to see him. And the Mambo King, very much a man, strode toward the house, kissed his mother, and presented her with the wildflowers, his mother whiffing them happily, saying, "*Ay, niño!*")

And he seemed happy. Whistled and shaved every day and wore a sweet cologne and a tie and shirt whenever he went out with her. Happiness, that's all he talked about, standing on the street corners or in front of the stoop with his friends. She was turning him, he boasted, into a young man. I'm getting young, he would think, and forgetting my troubles.

He only wished the pains had gone away and that he could do as he pleased, without being bothered.

And Lydia? She supposed she was falling in love with him, but she had her doubts. Just felt so desperate to get the hell out of that factory. Wanted anything better than what she had. Wished to God that she had finished high school, wished to God she had a better job. She wished to God that she had not slept with the foreman, because everybody in the factory found out, and it made no difference in the end. She did it because he, like all men, had promised something better. But once she went as far as to lie back on his desk and hike up her dress, he got all offended that she wouldn't do the rest: get on her knees and take care of him like that. "What I told you is off!" he shouted after the fifth or sixth time she'd visited him. "Forget the whole thing"—and he dismissed her as if she were a child.

Wished she was smart like Delores (though she did not want her unhappiness) or had a job like Ana María in a beauty salon (she seemed to be happy).

Wished that the Mambo King was thirty years younger.

Still, she saw the good in him: liked the respect people showed him and the fact that he seemed to work so hard. (Sometimes when they went out or when she watched him onstage it was hard to imagine that the old man would spend hours a day on his back with a wrench trying to fix a clogged sink trap, or that he climbed ladders and plastered walls, that his back had achy muscles.)

He was good to her and this affected Lydia like music, turning her bones into humming pipes and making honey drip out her valves. He was so happy with her he didn't want to play jobs anymore, because that took time away from her. After a job, and anxious to see her, he would turn up at her apartment at three-thirty in the morning, carrying a wilting bouquet of flowers and a bag of party leftovers. With keys to her apartment, he would quietly open the door and make his way to her pink bedroom. Sometimes she was up waiting for him, sometimes she was fast asleep and the Mambo King, forgetting all his troubles, would strip down to his shorts and his sleeveless T-shirt and climb into bed beside her, falling asleep with his white-haired arms wrapped around her.

When they'd go to bed, she felt vindicated in her affection for him. She liked violent lovemaking and looked forward to her physical release, these orgasms which made her scream. She liked it when he kissed her all over. The laziness of his bones and the pure volume of his experience had made him more patient about lovemaking. Languidly exploring the alluring bud of her femininity, he discovered a mole just inside her labia majora, and he kissed this mole until he tasted a vegetable sweetness seeping through his teeth. When she came, grinding herself into his face, he felt as if he was being devoured, too.

Later, he would bite every one of her spinal knobs, and when he reached her *nalgitas,* she spread her bottom wide for him, and he licked her uplifted rump, with her flowery asshole, and mounted her. Something like floating on a violent sea, his testicles and legs being pummeled by her: he floated off on her, as if on a raft, closed his eyes and faced the sea, which he thought most beautiful, a stretch of murky blue waters which he remembered from the Merchant Marine off the coast of Sardinia and which burst radiantly with golden helmets and silver-and-red dots of light with the sudden appearance of the sun. These joyful moments always made him think about marriage, but he'd restrain himself, knowing that this desire would pass and that he was old.

They had been together for almost a year when he asked her to move in with her kids, because the trips back and forth from the Bronx and Manhattan were becoming a bit tiresome. That very day he took her down into a basement storeroom and showed her two little beds and a dresser and a small black-and-white television set and a lamp that he'd bought for them. But she had to be honest: "I can't, *hombre.* The children have their school and friends and it wouldn't be right." Then: "But I can bring them down for the weekends."

She'd always wonder about that decision. She could have quit her job, stayed for a time with him, and looked for another. But there was something about him that frightened her, a look that he'd get in his eyes sometimes, a little too dreamy for her taste. She thought it might be the beginning of senility, and where would that leave her? Taking care of him, like a nursemaid. And she would have been deceiving herself to say that she didn't sometimes look at younger, more slender men, whose faces were smooth and untroubled, or that it didn't sometimes embarrass her when he took her out dancing and wore that velvet hat with the feather and the orange shirt and white linen suit, a gold chain around his neck, like a *chulo.* She preferred it when he tried to be elegant, and told him so, but he kept saying, "No, I want to be youthful, too."

Still, bringing the kids down to stay with him for the weekends was a good deal for her: it focused his generosity on her family. Cesar provided whatever the children needed, clothing, books, shoes, toys, medicine, pocket money. (And they loved him for it, covering his face with kisses—holding them, he would think about Eugenio and Leticia when they were small.) He'd take them for walks through the markets, buying clothing for her off the racks, and sometimes took her downtown to the big department stores, where he sometimes paid $60, $70 for a single dress! He made room for her in his dresser and she began to keep clothing there: a drawer filled with her lacy panties and brassieres, a rack of her clothing hung in the closet. When she was not doubting the situation, she felt happy with him, liked the spaciousness of his apartment, and considered the neighborhood swanky in comparison to where she lived, 174th Street and the Grand Concourse, in the South Bronx.

And on Saturday mornings Ana María treated her to a nice shampoo and hairstyling at the beauty salon.

"It's so nice that you're with Cesar. He seems so content," the good-natured Ana María would say.

"You don't think he's too old for me?"

"No! Look at Cary Grant with a young chick, or Xavier Cugat with that coochie-coochie girl, Charo. And look at Pablo Picasso, his last wife could have been his granddaughter. No, there's nothing wrong with a bachelor like him finally finding the woman of his dreams, even at his age."

"How old is he?"

"Almost sixty-two, I think."

Working slowly and carefully, Ana María always gave Lydia the looks of a ravishing Hollywood starlet of the forties. Actually, with her dark oval Spanish face, almond eyes, and pouty, thick lips, she bore some resemblance to the Italian actress Sophia Loren. Made up by Ana María and wearing one of those nice new dresses and high heels, she would head back to La Salle Street, her walk deliberate, one foot tiptoeing in a line after the other, as if she were walking a tightrope, so that her hips really swayed, and the men on the street made remarks as she passed. She en-

joyed that. What would her husband have said to that? Once
stretch marks had appeared on her breasts and they had gotten
a little saggy from having the kids, he had started to call her "old."
And she was only twenty-eight! In the end, he'd left her because
they were trying to draft him for the war and it was back down
to Puerto Rico and then the Dominican Republic for him. So
these remarks appealed to her vanity. And there was this one
fellow, Pacito, who worked in a florist's shop, who always handed
her a single rose when she'd go by, asked her for dates, or at least
to hang around and talk with him, but she always remained
faithful to Cesar.

It didn't help things when Delores pulled her aside and said,
"Cesar's a very good man, but you have to be careful with him.
That's all I have to say, just be careful."

Or that Mrs. Shannon always looked at her disparagingly
from her window, where she'd sit with her wild mane of silver-
gray hair, her plump arms resting on the sill.

But she did feel for him. For his suffering. On many of those
nights it seemed the Mambo King, who sometimes slept like a
lamb, had his bad dreams.

In the middle of the night, he would feel his father beating
him with a switch. He would wince like a hound on the farm, a
dog hiding in the corner. He would hear his mother calling to
him from a distance, far away, as if beyond the faintest star in the
black sky, "Cesar! Cesar!" He would writhe in bed, because when
he opened his eyes she was not there.

Then there was a dream that had started to plague him in
those days with Lydia, almost a beautiful dream, he remembered
now.

It involved a river like the river that used to run by the road
from his farm toward Las Piñas, its banks thick with trees and
prosperous with birds. He was always riding a white horse in this
dream. Dismounting, he would make his way through the dense
woods to the water, curly and cool, with bubbles of life and
thin-legged insects with Chinese eyes and transparent wings
floating on the surface. Kneeling (again), he would scoop up the
water, wet his face, and then take a drink. How delicious that

water always seemed. Then, he'd undress and jump in, floating on the water and watching the sun breaking through the star-shaped leaves and tongue-like fronds and daydreaming about something he'd once heard as a schoolboy (His school? A single large room, near one of the barracks at a nearby sugar mill): that in the days of Columbus, there was a race of Indians who lived in the treetops, and sometimes he would imagine their lives out on the branches, jumping from acacia to mahogany to breadfruit tree. But always the sky grew dark and in the water he'd smell blood, like the blood that sometimes appeared in his urine. And then he would look down the river and see that there were hundreds of naked women, bursting with youth and femininity, bodies damp and beautiful in the sun: and some would hold their arms out to him imploringly and some would lie back on the ground with their legs spread wide and he'd want them so bad, daydreaming about making love to one hundred women at a time, as if that would make him immortal. But then he'd hear click-clock, click-clock, click-clock in the trees, and when he looked up he saw hanging from the branches skeletons everywhere, like wind chimes, hanging off every branch on every tree, the sounds they'd make frightening him.

In the middle of the night she would wake to urinate and find him sitting up, short-breathed and gasping, or murmuring painfully in his sleep and flailing about the bed as if he were drowning. She would watch him shake and then couldn't imagine what he had been dreaming about, never knew what to do when he got out of bed and went into his kitchen, where he would sit at the table drinking rum or whiskey and reading some book.

They were happy for a long time, despite her doubts about his age and the pains that sometimes racked his body. But then, abruptly, things started to come apart. One night after he had taken Lydia and the children out to eat, he lay doubled over in bed with terrible pains in his gut, as he'd eaten a big pot of Dominican chicken and rice, which had been hotly spiced with sausages. With Herculean effort, he managed to get himself out of bed (everything about him quivery because he had put on so much weight) and struggled down to the bathroom, where he tried to exorcise the burning insect larvae inside his gut, retching out, with the beer and plantains and the rest, tadpole-shaped dollops of blood, tails veiny and fluttering in the toilet water. Then he just barely made it back to his bed, where he collapsed, shaking with obesity and fear. That was the night of the strange dream, when he saw seven spirits, five of whom he recognized immediately: Tomasa, Pereza, Nicolena, Nisa, and Genebria, women he had known from Cuba. Then there were two shoeless men wearing rags and straw hats, whose faces were covered with white paste like carnival corpses. Circling around the Mambo King, they were chanting:

"Cesar Castillo, we know you're very tired and soon it will be time for you to die."

Again and again and again.

"Cesar Castillo, we know you're very tired and soon it will be time for you to die"—like a nursery rhyme.

They harassed him for an hour and then slipped off into the night (they would return in the darkness of his hospital room three months later) and the Mambo King, a sweaty mess with heaving chest and bloated stomach, sank back into bed and felt his limbs swelling: when he woke in the morning, his skin was covered with blisters and sores, the kind which used to plague his father in Cuba, when things had gotten very bad. And he was ashamed to take off his clothes in front of Lydia and would make love to her wearing a shirt, turning his head away when she would look at his face.

When the pains got even worse, he looked up an old friend who worked in a pharmacy and sometimes gave him pain pills for toothaches. While his friend recommended that he go to a doctor, he gave him a small jar of painkiller pills anyway. Instead of seeing a doctor, Cesar took the pills and drank some whiskey, feeling so much better that he lumbered down the stairway and stood out in front of the stoop to enjoy the early-spring weather. The sun felt good on his face and a mood of great optimism came over him. And things were very interesting now. Looking across the street that day, he saw himself and Nestor walking up the block. Then a big checkered cab stood idling in front of the building with Desi Arnaz stepping out and removing his hat —Miguel Montoya and Lucille Ball behind him.

And across the way, he saw lines of people waiting in front of the Club Havana. He blinked and the lines were gone.

Then he saw an unbearably beautiful woman standing in front of the *bodega,* stared at her and realized that the woman was Beautiful María, who had taken his brother's soul. Someone should show her a thing or two. And so he walked over to her, grabbed her roughly by the wrists, and dragged her upstairs to his apartment. By the time they'd gotten into the bedroom, he had removed all of his clothes. "Now I'm going to show you something, woman."

And he buggered her with his huge thing, but not in a gentle way where the woman's insides get all soft; not in the way where he would finger her at the same time so that she would come. He did it violently, showing María a thing or two. Except it wasn't María, it was Lydia.

"*Hombre,* why are you trying to hurt me so?"

"Oh, no, *niña.* I don't want to hurt you, I love you."

But he kept taking those tablets. And they would put him in a bad mood.

"You know there's something I've never told you," he said one day while visiting her in the Bronx. "And that's my opinion of Puerto Ricans. Everybody knows you Puerto Ricans are jealous of us Cubans; there was a time when it was very rough for a Cuban to walk into a Puerto Rican bar. But that's not your fault, not at all. The Puerto Ricans hate us Cubans because even the lowest Cuban who came here with nothing has something now."

"Children," Lydia said. "Why don't you go into the living room and watch the television." Then: "Why are you telling me this when you know my situation?"

He shrugged.

"You know what? You're crazy. What have I done to you?"

He shrugged again. "I say what I think."

"If you think I take things from you because I have no money, you're wrong."

"I was only talking about some Puerto Ricans, not all."

"I just think you're trying to start something with me. Now, please, *hombre,* why don't you just relax and sit here, I'll make you something nice—I have some *chorizos* and potatoes I can fry up with eggs."

"Yes, that would be good."

He sat for a long time, watching her cooking. He smoked a cigarette and then he stood up and put his arms around her. She was wearing a nice soft pink Woolworth's slip, without anything else on underneath, and when he put his hand on her bottom the softness of youth made him feel sad.

"I'm just an old man and I'm probably going to get worse, do you still want me?"

"Yes, yes, *hombre*. Don't be so foolish, sit down and eat your breakfast and later we'll take a walk up to the movie house on Fordham Road."

Pacing in the halls of his house, he became more and more like that old German shepherd with matty coat and milk-cornered eyes who watched the basement entrance of a building down the street. He'd wait and wait for Lydia to return, stand by the window, wait by the door. And when she finally came home, happy with her rose, they would start to argue.

"And where were you?"

"At the florist's."

"Well, I don't want you going there anymore."

She tried hard to understand him and said, "Cesar, I think you are being a little unreasonable. Don't worry about me, *querido*. I'm yours. Worry about yourself, *hombre*. You're too old not to be going to a doctor if you're not feeling well."

But he pretended not to hear her.

"Well, I still don't want you talking to any men."

He slipped in and out of these moods. One Friday night, while toweling himself off after a bath, he daydreamed about Lydia. She was going to turn up at eight and they would go to a movie on Broadway, eat a nice dinner, and then go to bed together. He imagined her taut nipple in his mouth, kissing her quivering thigh. When she came, her whole body shuddered in waves, as if the building was shaking. That was something nice to remember, something nice to look forward to. That, and some of the *flan* Delores said she was going to make for him. Cesar really liked that *flan,* and so he decided that after having a drink he would go upstairs to visit his brother's widow.

He'd had a hard day, his body aching. Even the pills weren't working very well anymore. And he'd been bothered by *mareos,* dizzy spells. In reasonable moments he saw that he had been a little unfair to Lydia and he wanted to make things up to her. She would bring her kids down and stay with him through Sunday. Saturday night, he'd play a job, a party at the School of the Ascension.

He needed to rest, but it was past seven, and so he made himself another drink. Better to drink than to take those pills. He sat thinking about Lydia. Promised to reform. Yes, it was those pills making him act cruelly toward her. So, calmly, he went into his bathroom, took the pills, and flushed them down the toilet. Better to just drink, he told himself. Feeling tense, he went upstairs to get a piece of the *flan.* After so many years he still felt an attraction to Delores, and could not help but greet her with a fast little slap to the ass. But times were changing. When he had done that playfully with Leticia, she had chided him, saying, "A polite man doesn't do that, especially an uncle."

And now Delores said, "Cesar, are you going to be drunk when your woman arrives?"

Was that her reaction to a friendly slap on the butt?

"*Óyeme,* Cesar, I'm only telling you this because I care for you."

"I came here for *flan,* not for lectures."

She put a small plate of *flan* before him, which he ate ravenously. Afterwards he went into the living room, where he and Nestor used to write all those songs, greeted Pedro, and killed time sipping coffee and watching television with him. Now and then, when he heard the subway coming into the station, he got up to look out the window to see if Lydia was among the subway crowd. Around eight-thirty he started to get worried and went downstairs again to wait. He had another glass of whiskey at nine, then waited by the stoop for her until ten.

By then he found himself walking back and forth between the subway kiosk and his building. He felt like growling, and if anyone looked at him in the wrong way, his face would turn red, his ears would burn. Passing his friends in front of the *bodega,* he tipped his hat but did not speak to them. Merrily, he whistled a melody. His friends had brought out a milk crate and a television. They were sitting, engrossed in a boxing match.

"Come on, Cesar, what's wrong with you?" they'd call, but he just kept on his way.

By eleven he decided that something bad had happened to her: that she was robbed on the subway, or worse. Standing on the corner, smoking one cigarette after the other, he imagined Lydia standing naked in a bedroom and climbing into a bed with cool blue sheets alongside a younger man, planting kisses on his chest and then taking him into her mouth. The florist? Or one of those men who stood on the corners giving her the eye and wondering what she was doing with the old man. If he could have run up to the Bronx like a young hound, he would have. He'd tried calling her: there was no one home. He went through a period of remorse over his suspicions, prayed to God (if there is a God) that nothing had happened to her. Around midnight, he was drunk in his living room listening to mambos and watching television. By then, he'd tried calling her a dozen times without getting a response, and he fantasized that she was cuckolding him. He said to himself, I don't need anything from a woman.

Around one o'clock, Lydia called him. "I'm sorry, but Rico came down with a bad fever. I had to wait in emergency all night."

"Why didn't you call me?"

"There was only one phone and I was in and out with the child. Always people waiting to use it." Then: "Why are you being so stern with me?" And she started to cry. "You're so stern."

"How's the boy?" he asked more calmly.

"It was food poisoning."

"Well, are you coming here?"

"*Hijo,* I want to, but it's too late. I'm staying with the children."

"Then I'll say good night to you."

"What do you mean?"

"I mean that I don't take this nonsense from anyone. *Que te lleve el demonio!*"

In the Hotel Splendour the Mambo King winced as he swallowed more whiskey. Although he was starting to have trouble reading the time on his watch and he felt as if he were being propelled through a dense forest by a powerful wind, and the same mambo record, "The Mambo Kings Play Songs of Love," had been playing over and over, he ached happily for another drink, the same way he ached that night to be reunited with Lydia.

Slamming down the phone, he waited for Lydia to call him, sobbing the way the broads used to when he played around with them. He sat by the phone, and when it didn't ring, he said to himself, To hell with her. But a few hours later he felt that he had been stupid and cruel and that he was going to burst unless he could do something to get rid of the bad feelings inside him. He began slowly to understand what had plagued his younger brother those years before, this pressing melancholia. He fell asleep without having tasted more than a bit of *flan;* he felt something like a bloody rag being pulled through his body. It was a funny thing, pain. The pain was sharp enough that he somehow felt more slender, rather than so heavy. The pains multiplied and were so bad that he wanted to get up out of his bed but could not move. He wanted some of the pills he'd gotten on the sly for toothaches, but each time he moved, the pain got worse. Around six in the morning, the sun started to shine through the windows, and the sunlight gave him strength and he managed with a great shove to get up off the bed. Then, in an epic show of will, and clinging to the walls, he made it to the bathroom.

Things did not improve. He would take the train to the Bronx unannounced and turn up at her door, drunk and convinced that she had some man hidden there. He would walk down to the corner and find that old hound sitting at the foot of the basement stairway, felt happy the day he watched the old hound take on a younger mutt in a street fight, snapping at the younger dog's legs and sending it whining through the streets. That's what he would do, he told himself, to all her young men —the ones he saw taking her to bed every night, because now, in the dresses that he had given her, and smelling sweetly of his perfumes, she was the most desirable woman in the world.

As he thought about those days, some confusion set in. There was something else going on, too, wasn't there? His health was getting worse each day. Pink urine, swollen fingers, and little bouts of humiliating incontinence, when he would feel his own urine leaking down his leg and he would think, Stop, but nothing would stop. That humiliation made him want to cry, because even though he was an old man, he liked to think that he was clean, but those days, he feared, had gone forever.

And Lydia? Her face drained of color: she thought how she had almost moved her kids out of their apartment in the Bronx, and how she would do anything for that man; even forgave his age and his foul moods for the sake of love, and she felt that no matter what she did, he was bent on fucking things up. For the first time she started to think about other men. Thought that if a nice man walked up to her, she would go with him. She thought his world-weariness was spreading like a poison into her, and that even her sweetness couldn't offset it. She found herself crying herself to sleep at three every night. He would come home, strip naked, climb into bed beside her: sometimes he would make love to her though she hadn't even opened her eyes.

He would whisper, "No matter what, Lydia, this old man loves you."

But then something became unbearable. Whenever she wanted to talk to him, he never heard her voice. He bought her flowers, new dresses, toys for her children. He blew kisses into the kitchen, but he would not talk to her.

One day, when he asked her to spend the weekend with him, she told him, "Cesar, I'm taking my kids out to visit my sister in New Jersey."

And he nodded, hung up the phone, and holed up for the

three days and his health slid out of him and into the toilet for good.

Now the medicines, the tubes, the blinking machines, the pretty nurses, and the doctor again:

"You have all the signs of systemic failure. Your kidneys, your liver are all going. Keep up your drinking and you'll end up in the morgue. I'm sorry to be so blunt, but that's the truth."

"Is it that bad?"

"Yes."

"Thank you, Doctor."

IT HAD BEEN OVER FIFTY YEARS ago in Cuba when he was in school, he told himself, that his teacher, Señora Ortiz, would make him fill pages and pages of newsprint scraps with additions and subtractions, because he used to use an odd, contrary logic when it came to numbers—for example, writing $3 + 3 = 8$, simply because the numbers were round-bottomed like an 8. She'd send him out to count things and add them up, and so he'd find himself in town counting the houses (one hundred and twenty-eight) and the number of horses on a given street (seven tied up to porch railings on Tacón), and once he even tried to count the number of yellow hibiscus in a field, losing track and falling asleep on the soft ground after two hundred or so—a beautiful day.

And nearly fifty years since he'd first mounted a stage to sing.

And nearly forty years since he'd been married.

Then thirty-one years since leaving Havana.

How many thousands of cigarettes had he smoked? How many leaks had he taken? Belches? Fucks, ejaculations? How many times had he ground his hips into a bed, with an erection, thinking that the mattress was a woman and waking with the insides of his underwear damp?

Remembered trying to count the stars one night while lying on his back in a field in Cuba when he was a kid hiding from his father, and feeling as if the Milky Way was going to swallow him. He stared so long and lost count so many times that he began to feel faint-headed.

In his own way, he wanted to be someone significant.

How many drinks had he had that night?

He figured a dozen, full, hearty glasses, as they might say in one of the ads.

He did more figuring. Bottles of rum and whiskey, enough to fill a warehouse, all turned into piss. He'd consumed enough food and left the world enough shit to fill Fort Knox. (Behind this, the memory of being seized with cramps on the road outside Cleveland, so badly they had to stop the Mambo King bus so he could crouch low in the grass and relieve himself, with trucks and cars whizzing by.)

Endless numbers of cigarettes.

A million smiles, pinches on nice female bottoms, tears.

Women telling him like Vanna Vane used to, "I love you," and he'd say, "Yes, I feel it," or "And I love you, baby."

And for what?

And how many times had he knelt in church as a kid praying? Or whispered as he slept, "Oh, God," or "Jesus Christ"? Or had watched a woman's face contort with pleasure and heard her crying out, "Jesus, Jesus, Jesus"?

His life was much more beautiful when he believed that a benevolent angel walked behind him.

Twenty-three years since Nestor had left the world. He still had the funeral card, tucked among the letters and other things that he had brought with him that night.

SOMETIMES WHEN THE MUSIC got faster, he would feel like a kid running up and down the steep and beautiful stairways of Santiago de Cuba. Sometimes a fast song took him far from the Bronx to Nueva Gerona, to El Valle de Yumurí, and to the mountains of Escambray, took him strolling through the city of Matanzas, threw him into the waters off the Hanabanilla falls in Las Villas, placed him on a sorrel crossing the tranquil valley of Viñales in Pinar del Río, left him perching on the ledge of a mountain cave in Oriente, peering out over the winding Río Cauto. The music set him leaning drowsily under the shade of a bottle-palm tree in Holguín. Late in the night he returned to a street in Santiago he had not thought about for years, with its narrow, two-story houses with slanting tin roofs and high-shuttered windows, palm trees and bushes and wildflowers that went flowing over the walls. He found himself standing atop a stairway, looking down, three flights below, to a small park, flowers and bushes surrounding a fountain, and in the place of honor a heroic bust. On a bench, a pretty girl in a short-sleeved polka-dot dress, reading a newspaper. The Mambo King, sixteen years old, walking toward her, the Mambo King nodding and smiling, the Mambo King sitting beside her.

"It's a beautiful day, isn't it?"

"Yes."

"Would you like to go dancing later?"

"Yes."

And the music redrew the blue cloudless sky and the sun rolled like a ball across his room in the Hotel Splendour, red and purple streaks across the room, and he heard the heavy bronze bells of the cathedrals of Santiago and Havana ringing simultaneously, he heard the *tttling-tttling* of a bicycle and blinked and saw the Havana night, shoots of light in the sky, a thousand trumpets and drums in the distance, cars honking, and the low murmur, like an ocean, of nighttime crowds.

He was running now past La Casa Potín, the Surtida Bodega, and the good bakery smells of La Gran Vía!

A drink in the Pepe Antonio Café with some musician pals, circa 1946; a fuck with a woman he met while strolling along, window-shopping on Obispo, what an ass on that dame, my, but how she smelled nicely of sweat and Candado soap, and her nipples were taut, brown, and smooth as glass beads. What good days, catching Beny More up at that club, La Palma, at Jibacoa beach, or heading down the Paseo del Prado with his brother Nestor toward La Punta off the Malecón, the harbor drive, to catch the ferryboat over to Guanabacoa, the two of them leaning on the railing, checking out the pretty girls. In a creaseless *guayabera,* he lowers his dark glasses so that this one dish, in a sailor's blouse and a tight white skirt, slit riding high, could get a good look at his killer-green eyes. Inhalation of the sea, sun warming their faces, tour boats in the harbor, clanging buoys. And then they're climbing the stairway up to a nice little seafood restaurant, El Morito, with its pink walls, tin roof, and shaded balcony overlooking the love-enriching sea, and they devour a pot of yellow rice cooked in chicken broth and beer, thick with shrimp, scallops, oysters, mussels, clams, olives, and red peppers. The day's so tranquil, where did it go, so tranquil they're feeling lazy as seagulls.

Sometimes when he closed his eyes he saw himself as a little kid sitting in the front row of the small movie theater in their town, watching the stony-faced Eusebio Stevenson leading the musicians of his pit orchestra through tangos, rumbas, and fox-trots, which they played as background to the silent films of Tom Mix, Rudolph Valentino, Douglas Fairbanks, Jr., and so many others who galloped, danced, and swashbuckled. The future Mambo King leaning forward to watch the black man's whorl-knuckled hands, gray in the cinema light, stretching, stretching across the keyboard. Later, he remembers, he'd followed the man out into the street and to a little café on the corner, where he would sit at a table in the back, quietly eating his *chuletas* and rice and beans, the kid waiting for him and watching Eusebio bolt down one brandy after another, drinking until a certain lightness entered Eusebio's hard expression and he would make his way out into the street, Cesar Castillo following after him and pulling on his jacket, begging him, "Can you show me how you make those notes?" and keeping up with his zigzag motions (And who does this remind you of, *hombre?*) as he weaved down the cobblestone streets, muttering, "Leave me alone, kid. You don't want this life," and waving the future Mambo King away. But he kept saying, "Please, please, please," that being one of the few times in his life that the Mambo King, even as a child, began to cry.

"Please, please," he kept repeating, and so adamantly that Eusebio took a long look at him, tipping up his black-brimmed hat and saying, "Well then, suppose I do teach you, what are you going to pay me? You have any money? Your family have any money?"

Then: "Leave me alone, I must be paid." But Cesar persisted, and when Eusebio sat down exhausted on the church steps, he said, "I'll bring you food." Then: "And I can bring you rum."

"Rum? Well then. That seems fair enough."

So he started taking music lessons, bringing Eusebio a pot of stew or rice and beans, whatever his mother had cooked that day (she gave him the food), and a jar of rum, which he'd fill from a cask that his father kept in the stone house where he would slaughter his pigs at the edge of their field, and all went well, with the kid learning a little piano and trumpet, until the day that his father caught Cesar filling the jar and gave the boy the beating of his life, slapping his face and going at his legs and back with a knobby branch that he pulled down from an acacia tree. And he remembers how that really started all the bad blood between him and his father, because now his son was not only a free spirit but a thief to boot! And he would not stop taking the rum, no matter how well his father hid it, and he kept getting caught and got more beatings so that he learned to hold his arms in an arc over his head and to take his beating like a man, never crying, insolent and disrespectful, and strong because, after a while, he hardly felt the stick, the belt, the fist. He sometimes arrived at Eusebio's house with black-and-blue marks on his arms, bruises which touched Eusebio's heart. (Why did these memories keep coming back to him?)

And Eusebio Stevenson himself waiting on the porch, clapping his hands when he'd see Cesar approaching. "Come along!"

There was a mattress on the plank floor of his parlor, a few chairs, a table, a coffeepot, and by a back door that opened out to a thick bush, there was a chamber pot. But then, in the center of the room, against the wall, was an upright Móntez & Co. piano, its soundboard facing decorated with mother-of-pearl nightingales, stars, and arabesque moons.

"Do you have the rum?"

Cesar had carried it wrapped up in one of his mother's scarves. He gave him the jar, which Eusebio emptied into a beer bottle.

"Good," he said. "Now sit here and we'll begin."

The first lessons involved the demonstration of simple chords, the idea of playing the bass with the left hand, the melody and chords with the right. Eusebio seemed cruel, showing no mercy in spreading Cesar's small fingers wide across the fingerboard and stiffly pressing them down. He told the boy to memorize the scales; emphasizing this, as he couldn't teach Cesar how to read music. He impressed the boy, however, with talk about major and minor chords, chords of joy and friendliness and chords of sadness and introspection. Then he demonstrated what could be done with a single chord, playing all kinds of melodies above it. And now he was hearing Eusebio saying something else that he would always remember.

"When you play music you have to remember that just about everything composed has to do with love and courtship. Especially when you learn to play your older music, like the habaneras, *zarzuelas,* and our own Cuban *contradanzas.* It has all to do with romance, the man holding a woman around her waist, bowing to her, and then having that one moment in which he may whisper something in her ear, the ladies like that. In the case of the *contradanzas,* there's a minute's pause, hence the name, 'against the dance.' And during that pause the man would have a chance to talk to the woman." He then began to play "*La Paloma*" and then demonstrated all the different styles of piano, including a ragtime piano he'd picked up while living in New Orleans once.

"And you have to remember, boy, that what people want is to throw up their arms and say, '*Qué bueno es!* How wonderful,' when they hear the music. Understand?"

Yes, love was so beautiful, the music told him, pulling him through the fields at night when the owls hooted and the shooting stars passed overhead in the sky, all the planets and stars melting like wax.

Grief endless, and over the countryside, sad bonfires and his Papi's voice, his Papi giving him a beating, and he would form an arc over his head with his elbows for protection, never crying, taking his punishment like a man. Even on those nights when he couldn't believe what his father was doing, when he was just a little kid holding the door that his father pounded on so hard trying to get inside to hurt him.

Y coño, he would call me over and pull me hard by the arm, and hold my arm by the elbow, squeezing: he had powerful hands from his day's labors, hands covered with cuts and calluses, and he'd say, "Boy, look at me when I address you. Now tell me, *niño,* what is it exactly that I am seeing in your eyes? Why is it that you turn away from me when I walk into this house, what is it that you are hiding from me?" And if I told him that I was hiding nothing from him, his hold would get harder and no one could pull him off me, nor would he stop—I refused to cry, the Mambo King has never cried over a man—and he would hold me until my arm turned black-and-blue or until my mother had pleaded long enough with him not to start something with me, *un niño.* "If you want to start something, why don't you go back to town and start something with those men who insulted you?" And then he would start to take it out on her. And so, when he would come home in such bad moods and he asked me or one of my brothers why we had mischief or disrespect in our eyes, I stepped forward, I had the disrespectful answers. If he asked me, "Why are you looking at me in this way, boy?" I didn't keep my mouth shut like before, I answered, "Because you're drunk, Papi," and then he would beat me, but it would happen very quickly, and he would hit me until his palms were dark red and hit me until he saw how cruel he was being, and then he would call me over and ask my forgiveness, and because he was my Papi, I was happy to be back in his good graces again, and so you know that's why I took this from him, because my father is my father.

And he saw his mother again, saw his mother's loving face, indistinguishable in memory from the stars he'd watch from the porch at night in Cuba.

"Te quiero, niño" is what she used to say.

He was only a little boy then. He used to fall asleep with his head pressed against his mother's breasts, hearing her heartbeat and those little gasps. That was when the Mambo King had sweeter ideas about women, when his mother was the morning light, the light burning through the treetops. That was the time when he felt that he was part of her very breath, wishing, wishing (and here the Mambo King feels a tightness around his eyes) that he could do something to end her sadness.

Pressing his head against her belly, he'd wonder, "What's inside there?"

Years later, as a man, kissing women's privates, he'd tremble with the recollection of how he'd imagined the whole world inside his mother's womb.

"My mother, the only mother I'll ever have."

She was sewing his shirt and running a thick cord through the soles of a ratty pair of shoes to repair them. "Ay, I used to love dancing when I was a young girl."

She had one prized possession, the only thing he would remember from that household as having any value, an old mahogany music box from Spain, a family heirloom. It had a big bronze key, whose head was shaped like a butterfly, and it played a cheerful *zarzuela*. She would wind the key and say, "Come dance with me, child."

He was barely big enough to reach her waist, but she took him by his hands and led him dancing around the room.

"And when this part of the dance was over, the man bowed and the woman took hold of the hem of her dress like this, and lifted it slightly off the floor—in those days the women wore dresses that dragged on the floors and had long trains behind them. And many layers underneath."

"Many layers?"

"Yes, son, some women wore a hundred layers underneath their skirts. *Vente!*"

"One hundred layers . . ." In his happiest dreams he would seduce a woman with a hundred-layer dress, but because it was a dream, under each layer he would find a garter, a warm thigh, a silky pair of underdrawers, and underneath that, a womb opening to him. "One hundred layers . . ." He hadn't thought of that for years and years. "It's all a fading memory, you see." She lifted him off the floor and the room went spinning around him. Then he saw Genebria in the kitchen doorway. She was clapping her hands and broke into a strutting waltz, as if performing a slow dance at carnival. Three steps forward and she shook her shoulders, her head also shaking like a horse's.

Ay, poor *Mamá*, dead but calling out to him from the cheery kitchen, "How many *plátanos* do you want?" And that's where he stood now, in their kitchen in Cuba, watching his mother peel off the thick skin of plantains, and through the window he could see the plantain trees outside, and the mangoes, papayas, *guanábanas, yuca,* and avocados growing here and there. Genebria chopping up garlic and onion and tomatoes, and, cooking in another pot, *yuca.* Beautiful to see that again.

And he remembered standing in front of the Arab's shop with his younger brother, *el pobre* Nestor, and finding among the lard, rice, sugar, coffee, the endless strands of sausages, near the dresses and Communion gowns and coils of rope, wire, spades, and axes, the shelf of silk-skirted dolls, a guitar. And who taught him that? A lanky insect-looking mulatto named Pucho, who lived in a forest of crates and palm fronds. He'd find him in his yard, sitting on the hood of an abandoned car, singing with such a tremor in his voice that he made the hens run in circles under his feet. He lorded over them with his music and made them sing, "Caaaaaccccckkkaka." He'd made his own guitar out of plywood, wire, and nails, and it looked like a Dominican harp. But he knew how to play, knew magic, knew the chants to Changó.

Adiós, my friend . . . *Adiós.*

Yes, love was so beautiful, the music told him, taking him again to his friends. *Adiós,* Xavier, sitting out in front of his ice house in a steamy mist, with his pot of rice and beans and his accordion.

Adiós!

And he saw the orchestra leader Julián García on a stage before him, waving a baton, and he stood up nervously beside Julián and he began to croon, *adiós, adiós,* and he saw Ernesto Lecuona, "a helluva nice guy, dignified, a little snotty-nosed, but a true gentleman, who taught me the meaning of a good habanera." And he goes running down into the plaza, where a band is playing during carnival, lingers near the stage, trying to figure out all the fingerings on the instruments, but it's hard because they're only lit by lantern light, and it's then that he sees a hand reaching down to him and pulling him up onto the glory of the stage, performing for the people.

And suddenly he remembers all these faces, pretty young

female faces that he spent endless energies chasing, some of whom he loved, and some of whom he hardly knew.

And I loved you, Ana, don't think I ever forgot that time we went walking in Holguín, even if it was a long, long time ago. We walked so far from your parents' house that you were certain your Papi would come after both of us with a belt, and so we headed for the park, and whenever we passed through the shadows, where no one could see us, your hand tightened around mine and the air around us seemed charged and then we'd kiss. We stole only a few kisses, I never saw you after that, but don't you ever think that memory has left me, memory of youth and loveliness, how I've often wondered the way things might have been between you and me . . . And I loved you, Miriam, so what if I was a coarse kid who would stick his tongue out at you because you were such a snooty-looking rich girl, coming out of that grand house with your mother, who had a huge rump and walked holding a parasol. I know you were interested in me by the way you would steal a glance, I noticed even when I tried to pretend you weren't there. Remember how I would stand in front of the movie house singing? And you would come by, snooty as ever, until the day when you smiled, and everything changed. You and I were together for a month before they found us out, kissing in the parks and behind bushes, two happy children, and then your Papi, a judge and highly placed in the Gallego Club, found out through gossip, and they sent you away to live with your aunt. How could I have known that I was "lower"? How could I have known that your father would make such a ruckus over a few harmless kisses? . . . And I loved you, Verónica —remember how we just held hands and I nearly burst out of my trousers, and that for all your efforts you could not help looking at me, and remember the time when you couldn't resist and you touched me quickly with your palm. A spasm flushed through me as your face, blushing, turned away; milk seeped out of me and you stood in the corner with your fingers spread apart, waiting for the color to drain out of your face, and I went home with this gummy mess in my trousers, but we were never to be . . . And I loved you, Vívian—when the adults were too tired to watch us, we would go out to the veranda the better to hear the string bands, and then we would sit on the stone wall and press our foreheads together, and sometimes you would let me kiss you, but not just an ordinary kiss, but with my tongue. You parted your teeth just wide enough to let the tip slip in, but not all of me, I smelled too much of tobacco. "Always trying to be *un gran macho,* " you would say. Then there was the time when I ran into you after church and we went through the Camposanto to look for your aunt's grave, but instead found ourselves kissing against a tree, and gasping, you told me, "I hope you're the man who will be my husband and to whom I will lose my virginity," but I was stupid and became very angry, thinking "Why wait?" especially because of the state I was in. I was insatiable as a young man, Vívian, insatiable, and that's why my fingers would crawl through your defenses until you had no choice but to turn red in the face and run home to your family, but I loved you, understand? . . . And I loved you, Mimi—though you never let me fuck you in the normal way, you took me out beyond your father's shed and lifted your skirt and let me fuck you in your ass, or was it between your buttocks, I don't remember, just the cream and the smell of your body and the way your rump just kept lifting as if you really wanted me inside your vagina, but you kept your hand there over the opening instead and kept pushing me back out, do you remember? And how in the end we would go walking through town but without touching or holding hands: I thought you were feeling a little sad, but after we had done it, I somehow felt ashamed, as if everybody knew. We did it that way every week for months, and then you came to my father's house and I refused to let you inside, and when you cried, I cried, but you never believed me . . . And I loved you, Rosario, because of the way you smiled at me when we'd pass each other on the street, and I loved you, Margarita, though we never got very far in our lovemaking, just giving each other pecks on the cheek, but you'd make love to the palm of my right hand with your fingernails, digging them in deep and then giving me a look as if to say, "See, macho, what you might expect from me?" I was intrigued, enchanted, Rosario, but you know that your brothers didn't want me near you, a lot of people didn't want me near anyone. Someone should teach him a lesson, is what most people thought, and you know how many, including your brothers, tried. I was never Tarzan or Hercules, all I ever wanted was a little comfort, a few kisses. Did I ever tell you that on the night of June 11, 1935, when I was supposed to take you to a dance, I went walking along some side streets and a gang jumped me, six, seven boys, and what they wanted was to drag me through the dirt and shit, beating me down because I didn't fight back, just held my hands up, saying, "Come on, fellows, what are you doing?" They not only beat me down but rolled me in a thick pit of mud and shit, and I woke up an hour after the dance was over, with this strong stench in my nostrils and the feeling that you would never even look at me, that everybody would know that I had been rolled in the shit, and that's why I never went back to see you—I thought everybody knew, understand? . . . And I loved you, Margarita, for standing across from me in the plaza, under the yellow light of a Chinese lantern, in a white dress, with a red bow around your waist, shyly smiling at me from across the way, shy because you thought I was too handsome to talk to, but if you knew what I felt like deep inside, it would have made a difference; that's why I never gave you the up-and-down the way I did some of the others, that's why I turned away when you finally worked up the nerve to walk up to me smiling—you see, because in my household I had been made to feel like shit, so no matter how handsome I might have seemed, I looked in the mirror with disappointment. It was only because of the way some women looked at me that I knew I was worth something more, but if you left it up to me, I would have spent my life hiding like a monster; I loved you because you seemed to finally love me . . .

And now beautiful snow was falling, Bing Crosby snow, twirling-in-circles-with-your-mouth-open snow. Baltimore 1949 snow, coming down from heaven.

Then he was walking along with Nestor, going to all the different dance halls: the Palladium, the Park Palace, the Savoy, someone saying, "Benny, Myra, I want you to meet two good friends of mine, *compañeros* from Cuba, and really great players, too. They surely know their way around a *son* and a *charanga*, know what it is. Benny, this is Cesar Castillo, he's a singer and instrumentalist, and this is his brother Nestor, one of the best trumpeters you'll ever hear."

"Cesar, Nestor, I want you to meet a nice guy and, you

know, a helluva musician. Fellows, meet Frank Grillo—Machito."

"A pleasure."

"Cesar Castillo."

"Xavier Cugat."

"Cesar Castillo."

"Pérez Prado, *hombre!*"

"Cesar Castillo."

"Vanna Vane."

. . . pushing up the skirt of her sundress . . . taking off her panties, and his sex organ inflamed by sunlight and blood. Moans of pleasure in the solitude of the woods. His thick tongue jammed up high between her legs. Swig of wine, kiss of her ankle.

"Oh, Vanna, aren't we having a nice picnic today?"

"You said it."

Hearing the music, he remembered feeling the pork fat of his dinners in Cuba dripping down his chin and onto his fingers, which he'd lick with pleasure. Remembered a whore struggling with a thick rubber on his member, how he had tried to pull it down over himself, how her fingers took hold of his fingers, and then how she used both hands to get it all the way down over his thing. He remembered pressing the valves of the trumpet a thousand times, remembered the beauty of a rose, remembered his fingers slipping under a wire-frame 36C brassiere, Vanna's, his fingers sinking into the warm skin. He remembered hearing alley cats at night, the Red Skelton radio show in the alley. From the sixth floor, the Jack Benny show, and then, years later, in the courtyard, *I Love Lucy.*

Clouds of smoke from the incinerator hurting his eyes, clouds of smoke breaking up over the rooftop.

His mother holding his hands, his mother closing her hands around his.

His mother's soft heartbeat . . .

And he runs up the stairway again and finds Nestor playing that song again—Oh, brother, if you knew how I've thought of you all these years—and he sings this new song, this fucking song he had been working on for a long, long time, and when he's done, he says, "That's how I feel about María." And, love-struck, he looked out the window as if it were raining flowers instead of snowing.

"Even though I hate to admit it, brother, that's a nice little song you've written. But why don't we do this with the chorus."

"Yes, that's much better."

And with a sly smile on his lips, he nodded to the *quinto* player, who was banging down hard on the drums with his taped-up fingers for the intro, bap, bap, bap, bap! Then the piano came in with its vamp, then the bass, then the horns and all the drums. Then another nod from Cesar, and Nestor began to play his horn solo, the notes flying across the room like firebirds, and so mellow and happy that all the musicians were saying, "Yeah, that's it. He's got it."

Cesar dancing with his white golden-buckled shoes, darting in and out like agitated compass needles, and he went back running through Las Piñas as if he were a little kid again, blowing horns and banging pots and making noise in the arcades . . .

Floating on a sea of tender feelings, under a brilliant starlit night, he fell in love again: with Ana and Miriam and Verónica and Vívian and Mimi and Beatriz and Rosario and Margarita and Adriana and Graciela and Josefina and Virginia and Minerva and Marta and Alicia and Regina and Violeta and Pilar and Finas and Matilda and Jacinta and Irene and Jolanda and Carmencita and María de la Luz and Eulalia and Conchita and Esmeralda and Vívian and Adela and Irma and Amalia and Dora and Ramona and Vera and Gilda and Rita and Berta and Consuelo and Eloisa and Hilda and Juana and Perpetua and María Rosita and Delmira and Floriana and Inés and Digna and Angélica and Diana and Ascensión and Teresa and Aleida and Manuela and Celia and Emelina and Victoria and Mercedes and . . .

And he loved the family: Eugenio, Leticia, Delores, and his brothers, living and dead, loved them very much.

Now, in his room in the Hotel Splendour, the Mambo King watched the spindle come to the end of the "The Mambo Kings Play Songs of Love." Then he watched it lift up and click back into position for the first song again. The clicking of the mechanism beautiful, like the last swallow of whiskey.

When you are dying, he thought, you just know it, because you feel a heavy black rag being pulled out of you.

And he knew that he was going, because he felt his heart burning with light. And he was tired, wanting relief.

He started to raise the glass to his lips but he could raise his arm no longer. To someone seeing him there, it would look as if he were sitting still. What was he thinking in those moments?

He was happy. At first, things got very dark, but when he looked again, he saw Vanna Vane in the hotel room, kicking off her white high heels and hitching up her skirt, saying, "Would you do me a favor, honey? Undo my garters for me?"

And so he happily knelt before her, undoing the snaps of her garters, and then he slid her nylons down and planted a kiss on her thigh and then another on her buttock, where the softest skin, round and creamy, peeked out from her panties, and he pulled them down to her knees and with his majestic, ravaged visage between her legs he gave her a deep tongue-kiss. And soon they were on the bed, frolicking as they used to, and he had a big erection and no pain in his loins, so big that her pretty mouth had to struggle with the thick and cumbersome proportions of his sexual apparatus. They were entangled for a long time and he made love to her until she broke into pieces and then a certain calm came over him and for the first time that night he felt like going to sleep.

T HE NEXT MORNING, WHEN THEY found him, with a drink in his hand and a tranquil smile on his face, this slip of paper, just a song, lying on the desk by his elbow. Just one of the songs he had written out himself:

Bellísima María de mi Alma

Ami
¿Oh, tristeza de amor,
porqué tuviste que venir a mi? Dmi
Bmi
Yo estaba feliz antes que
E7
entraras en mi corazón. (repetir)

Ami
¿Cómo puedo odiarte
si te amo como te amo? Dmi
Bmi
No puedo explicar mi tormento
E7
porque no sé como vivir sin tu amor.

A
Que dolor delicioso
D
el amor me ha traído
Bmi   E7
en la forma de una mujer.
Dmi
Mi tormento y mi éxtasis.
Ami
Bella María de mi Alma,
E7
María, mi Vida...

Ami
¿Por qué me maltratabas?
Dime por qué sucede de esta manera? Dmi
Bmi
¿Por qué es siempre así? E7
Ami
María, mi Vida,
E7 Bellísima María de mi alma. Ami

WHEN I CALLED THE NUMBER
that had been listed on Desi Arnaz's letterhead, I expected to
speak with a secretary, but it was Mr. Arnaz himself who answered the phone.

"Mr. Arnaz?"

"Yes."

"I'm Eugenio Castillo."

"Ah, Eugenio Castillo, Nestor's son?"

"Yes."

"Nice to hear from you, and where are you calling from?"

"From Los Angeles."

"Los Angeles? What brings you out here?"

"Just a vacation."

"Well then, if you are so close by, you must come to visit
me."

"Yes?"

"Of course. Can you come out tomorrow?"

"Yes."

"Then come. In the late afternoon. I'll be waiting to see
you."

It had taken me a long time to finally work up the nerve to
call Desi Arnaz. About a year ago, when I had written to him
about my uncle, he was kind enough to send his condolences and
ended that letter with an invitation to his home. When I finally
decided to take him up on his offer and flew to Los Angeles,
where I stayed in a motel near the airport, I had wanted to call
him every day for two weeks. But I was afraid that his kindness
would turn into air, like so many other things in this life, or that
he would be different from what I had imagined. Or he would
be cruel or disinterested, or simply not really concerned about
visitors like me. Instead, I drank beer by the motel swimming
pool and passed my days watching jet planes crossing the sky.
Then I made the acquaintance of one of the blondes by the pool,
and she seemed to have a soft spot for guys like me, and we fell
desperately in love for a week. Then ended things badly. But one

afternoon, a few days later, while I was resting in bed and looking through my father's old book, *Forward America!,* just the contact of my thumb touching the very pages that he—and my uncle —had once turned (the spaces in all the little letters were looking at me like sad eyes) motivated me to pick up the telephone. Once I'd arranged the visit, my next problem was to get out to Belmont. On the map, it was about thirty miles north of San Diego along the coast, but I didn't drive. So I ended up on a bus that got me into Belmont around three in the afternoon. Then I took a cab and soon found myself standing before the entranceway to Desi Arnaz's estate.

A stone wall covered with bougainvillea, like the flower-covered walls of Cuba, and flowers everywhere. Inside the gate, a walkway to the large pink ranch-style house with a tin roof, a garden, a patio, and a swimming pool. Arched doorways and shuttered windows. Iron balconies on the second floor. And there was a front garden where hibiscus, chrysanthemums, and roses grew. Somehow I had expected to hear the *I Love Lucy* theme, but that place, outside of birdsong, the rustling of trees, and the sound of water running in a fountain, was utterly tranquil. Birds chirping everywhere, and a gardener in blue coveralls standing in the entranceway of the house, looking over the mail spread out on a table. He was a white-haired, slightly stooped man, thick around the middle, with a jowly face, a bundle of letters in one hand, a cigar in the other.

As I approached him, saying, "Hello?" he turned around, extended his hand, and said, "Desi Arnaz."

When I shook his hand, I could feel his callused palms. His hands were mottled with age spots, his fingers nicotine-stained, and the face that had charmed millions looked much older, but when he smiled, the young Arnaz's face revealed itself.

Immediately he said, "Ah, but you must be hungry. Would you like a sandwich? Or a steak?" Then: "Come with me."

I followed Desi Arnaz down his hallway. On the walls, framed photographs of Arnaz with just about every major movie star and musician, from John Wayne to Xavier Cugat. And then there was a nice hand-colored glamour-girl photograph of Lucille Ball from when she was a model in the 1930s. Above a cabinet filled with old books, a framed map of Cuba, circa 1952, with more photographs. Among them that photograph of Cesar, Desi, and Nestor.

Then this, in a frame: *I come here because I do not know when the Master will return. I pray because I do not know when the Master will want me to pray. I look into the light of heaven because I do not know when the Master will take the light away.*

"I'm retired these days," Mr. Arnaz said, leading me through the house. "Sometimes I'll do a little television show, like Merv Griffin, but I mainly like to spend my time with my children or in my garden."

When we had passed out of the house through another arched doorway, we reached a patio that looked out over Arnaz's trees and terraced gardens. There were pear, apricot, and orange trees everywhere, a pond in which floated water lilies. Pinks and yellows and brilliant reds coming out of the ground and clustered in bushes. And beyond all this, the Pacific Ocean.

". . . But I can't complain. I love my flowers and little plants."

He rang a bell and a Mexican woman came out of the house.

"Make some sandwiches and bring us some beer. Dos Equis, huh?"

Bowing, the maid backed out through a doorway.

"So, what can I do for you, my boy? What is it that you have there?"

"I brought something for you."

They were just some of my uncle's and father's records from back when, Mambo King recordings. There were five of them, just some old 78s and a 33, "The Mambo Kings Play Songs of Love." Looking over the first of the records, he sucked in air through his teeth fiercely. On the cover of that record my father and uncle were posed together, playing a drum and blowing a trumpet for a pretty woman in a tight dress. Putting that aside, and nodding, he looked at the others.

"Your father and uncle. They were good fellows." And: "Good songwriters."

And he started to sing "Beautiful María of My Soul," and although he couldn't remember all the words, he filled in the missing phrases with humming.

"A good song filled with emotion and affection."

Then he looked over the others. "Are you selling these?"

"No, because I want to give them to you."

"Why, thank you, my boy."

The maid brought in our sandwiches, nice thick roast beef, lettuce, and tomato, and mustard, on rye bread, and the beers. We ate quietly. Every now and then, Arnaz would look up at me through heavy-lidded eyes and smile.

"You know, *hombre*," Arnaz said, chewing. "I wish there was something I could do for you." Then: "The saddest thing in life is when someone dies, don't you think, *chico?*"

"What did you say?"

"I said, do you like California?"

"Yes."

"It's beautiful. I chose this climate here because it reminds me of Cuba. Here grow many of the same plants and flowers. You know, me and your father and uncle came from the same province, Oriente. I haven't been back there in over twenty years. Could you have imagined what Fidel would have made of Desi Arnaz going back to Cuba? Have you ever been there?"

"No."

"Well, that's a shame. It's a little like this." He stretched and yawned.

"Tell you what we'll do, boy. We'll set you up in the guest room, and then I'll show you around. Do you ride horses?"

"No."

"A shame." He winced, straightening up his back. "Do me a favor, boy, and give me a hand up."

Arnaz reached out and I pulled him to his feet.

"Come on, I'll show you my different gardens."

Beyond the patio, down a few steps, was another stairway, and that led to another patio, bounded by a wall. A thick scent of flowers in the air.

"This garden is modeled after one of my favorite little plazas in Santiago. You came across it on your way to the harbor. I used to take my girls there." And he winked. "Those days are long gone.

"And from this *placita* you could see all of Santiago Bay. At sunset the sky burned red, and that's when, if you were lucky, you might steal a kiss. Or make like Cuban Pete. That's one of the songs that made me famous."

Nostalgically, Arnaz sang, "My name is Cuban Pete, I'm the King of the Rumba Beat!"

Then we both stood for a moment looking at how the Pacific seemed to go on forever and forever.

"One day, all this will either be gone or it will last forever. Which do you think?"

"About what?"

"The afterlife. I believe in it. You?"

I shrugged.

"Maybe there's nothing. But I can remember when life felt like it would last forever. You're a young man, you wouldn't understand. You know what was beautiful, boy? When I was little and my mother would hold me in her arms."

I wanted to fall on my knees and beg him to save me. I wanted to hold him tight and hear him say, "I love you," just so I could show Arnaz that I really did appreciate love and just didn't throw it back into people's faces. Instead, I followed him back into the house.

"Now I have to take care of some telephone calls. But make yourself at home. The bar's over there."

Arnaz disappeared, and I walked over to the bar and fixed myself a drink. Through the big window, the brilliant blue California sky and the ocean.

Sitting in Desi Arnaz's living room, I remembered the episode of the *I Love Lucy* show in which my father and uncle had once appeared, except it now seemed to be playing itself out right before me. I blinked my eyes and my father and uncle were sitting on the couch opposite me. Then I heard the rattle of coffee cups and utensils and Lucille Ball walked into the living room. She then served the brothers their coffee.

When I thought, Poppy, my father looked up at me and smiled sadly.

"I'm so happy to see you again."

"And, son, I'm happy to see you."

My uncle smiled, too.

That's when Arnaz came in, but he wasn't the white-haired

gentleman with the jowlish face and kind, weary eyes who had led me around the grounds. It was the cocky, handsome Arnaz of youth.

"Gee, fellows," he said. "It's nice to see you again. How are things down in Cuba?"

And I couldn't help myself. I walked over and sat on the couch and wrapped my arms around my father. Expected to find air, but hit on solid flesh. And his neck was warm. His expression pained and timid, like a hick off the boat. He was alive!

"Poppy, but I'm glad to see you."

"It is the same for me, son. It will always be the same."

Embracing him, I started to feel myself falling through an endless space, my father's heart. Not the heart of flesh and blood that had stopped beating, but this other heart filled with light and music, and I felt myself being pulled back into a world of pure affection, before torment, before loss, before awareness.

Later, an immense satin heart dissolved and through a haze appeared the interior of the Tropicana nightclub. Facing a dance floor and stage, about twenty tables set with linen and candles at which sat ordinary but elegantly dressed people—your nightclub clientele of that day. Pleated curtains hanging down from the ceiling, potted palms here and there. A tuxedoed maître d' with an oversize black wine list in hand, a long-legged cigarette girl, and waiters going from table to table. Then the dance floor itself, and finally the stage, its apron and wings painted to resemble African drums, with birds and squiggly voodoo lines, these patterns repeated on the conga drums and on the music stands, behind which sat the members of the Ricky Ricardo Orchestra, twenty or so musicians seated in four tiered rows, each man decked out in a frilly-sleeved mambo shirt and vest decorated with sequined palms (with the exception of a female harpist in long-skirted dress and wearing rhinestone glasses), the musicians looking very human, very ordinary, wistful, indifferent, happy, poised, and ready with their instruments.

At center stage, a large ball microphone, spotlight, drumroll, and Ricky Ricardo.

"Well, folks, tonight I have a special treat for you. Ladies and gentlemen, I am pleased to present to you, direct from Havana, Cuba, Manny and Alfonso Reyes, singing a bolero of their own composition, 'Beautiful María of My Soul.' "

The brothers walked out in white suits and with a guitar and trumpet in hand, bowed to the audience, and nodded when Ricky Ricardo faced the orchestra and, holding his thin conductor's wand ready to begin, asked them, "Are you ready?"

The older brother strummed an A-minor chord, the key of the song; a harp swirled in as if from the clouds of heaven; then the bassist began to play a habanera, and then the piano and horns played a four-chord vamp. Standing side by side before the big ball microphone, brows creased in concentration, expressions sincere, the brothers began to sing that romantic bolero, "Beautiful María of My Soul." A song about love so far away it hurts; a song about lost pleasures, a song about youth, a song about love so elusive a man can never know where he stands; a song about wanting a woman so much death does not frighten you, a song about wanting that woman even when she has abandoned you.

As Cesar sang, his vocal cords trembling, he seemed to be watching something profoundly beautiful and painful happening in the distance, eyes passionate, imploring, his earnest expression asking, "Can you see who I am?" But the younger brother's eyes were closed and his head was tilted back. He looked like a man on the verge of falling through an eternal abyss of longing and solitude.

For the final verses they were joined by the bandleader, who harmonized with them and was so happy with the song that at the end he whipped his right hand up into the air, a lock of thick black hair falling over his brow. Then he shouted, *"Olé!"* The brothers were now both smiling and taking bows, and Arnaz, playing Ricky Ricardo, repeated, "Let's give them a nice hand, folks!" My uncle and my father bowed again and shook Arnaz's hand and walked offstage, waving to the audience.

> Oh, love's sadness,
> Why did you come to me?
> I was happy before you
> entered my heart.

How can I hate you
if I love you so?
I can't explain my torment,
for I don't know how to live
without your love . . .

What delicious pain
love has brought to me
in the form of a woman.
My torment and ecstasy,
María, my life. . . .
Beautiful María of my soul,

Why did she finally mistreat me so?
Tell me, why is it that way?
Why is it always so?
María, my life,
Beautiful María of my soul.

And now I'm dreaming, my uncle's heart swelling to the size of the satin heart on the *I Love Lucy* show, and floating free from his chest over the rooftops of La Salle, so enormous it can be seen for blocks and blocks. Cardinal Spellman has come to the parish to administer confirmation to the sixth-graders, and my friends and I are hanging out across the street, watching the hoopla, which has been announced in all the newspapers; limousines, reporters, clergy of every rank, from novitiates to bishops, crowded outside the church. And as they file into the church, I notice the enormous satin heart, and it makes me afraid, so I go into the church even when my friends, tough hoods in sleeveless black T-shirts, call me a little girl for doing it, and yet, when I'm inside, there's no confirmation ceremony going on, it's a funeral. A beautiful flower-covered coffin with brass curlicue handles is set out in the center aisle, and the Cardinal has just finished saying Mass and is giving his blessing. That's when the organist starts to play, except, out of each key, instead of pipe-organ music, instead of Bach, what sounds is a mambo trumpet, a piano chord, a conga, and suddenly it's as if there's a whole mambo band in the choir stall, and when I look, there is a full-blown mambo orchestra straight out of 1952 playing a languid bolero, and yet I can hear the oceanic scratching, the way you do with old records. Then the place is very sad, as they start carrying out the coffin, and once it's outside, another satin heart escapes, rising out of the wood, and goes higher and higher, expanding as it reaches toward the sky, floating away, behind the other.